LIVE BAIT

FABIO GENOVESI

TRANSLATED FROM THE ITALIAN
BY MICHAEL F. MOORE

OTHER PRESS
NEW YORK

Copyright © 2011 Arnoldo Mondadori Editore S.p.A., Milano
Originally published in Italian as *Esche vive* by Mondadori in 2011.

Translation copyright © 2014 Michael F. Moore

Lyrics to Thin Lizzy's "The Boys Are Back in Town" by Philip Parris
Lynott, 1976, copyright © Universal Music Publishing Group.

Production Editor: Yvonne E. Cárdenas
Text Designer: Julie Fry
This book was set in Scala and Nobel.

10 9 8 7 6 5 4 3 2 1

Library of Congress Cataloging-in-Publication Data

Genovesi, Fabio, 1974–
   [Esche vive. English]
   Live bait / by Fabio Genovesi ; translated from the Italian by
Michael F. Moore.
   pages cm
   "Originally published in Italian as Esche vive by Mondadori
in 2011"—Verso title page.
   ISBN 978-1-59051-681-2—ISBN 978-1-59051-682-9
   1. Youth—Italy—Fiction. 2. Self-actualization (Psychology)—
Fiction. 3. Tuscany (Italy)—Fiction. 4. Psychological fiction.
1. Moore, Michael, 1954 August 24– translator. II. Title.
   PQ4907.E563E7313 2014
   853'.92—dc23

                                        2014006779

Publisher's Note:
This is a work of fiction. Names, characters, places, and incidents
either are the product of the author's imagination or are used
fictitiously, and any resemblance to actual persons, living or dead,
events, or locales is entirely coincidental.

Boy wants a car from his dad
Dad says, "First you gotta cut that hair,"
Boy says, "Hey, Dad, Jesus had long hair"
and Dad says, "That's right, son, but Jesus walked everywhere"

David Berman
"The Frontier Index"

GALILEO WAS A MORON
(SUMMER 2005)

One... two...

We're counting. The water in the irrigation ditch is flat and dark and looks like a blurry photograph of mud. It's a July afternoon in 2005, and we're looking at the water and counting.

By we I mean Stefano, Silvia, and me, Fiorenzo: a dumbass name, I know. We have to count to ten. Easy. I like counting. It makes things feel easy, safe. Mathematical, you could say, and you feel safe because math is perfect and you never go wrong if you trust it, as Galileo himself used to say.

Except Galileo was a moron.

You heard me, Galileo Galilei, who was from Pisa so all the schools around here are named after him and last month all my classmates at middle school did Galileo for their science projects and I did nuclear energy instead, not because I like nuclear energy but because the last thing I wanted to do was suck up to a guy who made up all kinds of shit and then wrote one day that the earth rotated around the sun and the pope wanted to burn him at the stake and so he said, *Sorry, my bad, I was just kidding.*

But that's not why he was a moron. Galileo was a moron because he said nature's an open book, and the book's written in the language of math. So in his opinion everything in the world and in life—all the people and trees and shells and

1

starfish and sea horses and traffic lights and jellyfish—can be broken down into numbers and geometric figures. What a pile of bullshit. If I said it everyone would tell me to shut the fuck up and they'd be right. Except Galileo said it so it must be true, since he was a genius and lived in a time when everyone was a genius or an artist and didn't waste time at the grocery store, the post office, or the corner bar...they were busy dreaming up poems or paintings or, in this case, important scientific laws.

Bullshit. In Galileo's day they didn't have bicycles. They didn't have electricity, and when they had to go to the bathroom they'd use this nasty bucket and then dump it out the window into the street without looking to see if anyone was passing by. They didn't even know how to make ice—can you believe it— and there used to be people who came down from the mountains selling snow, and people used to buy it.

And here we are acting like once upon a time everything was fantastic and deep and nowadays we're just a bunch of morons...and it's true, we are morons, except the way I see it we always have been morons, from the caveman days up to this very afternoon, when Stefano and Silvia and me are standing here by the ditch counting.

And if we want to compete to see who's the biggest moron of all, then I'm about to become the world champion.

Three...four...

According to the Book of Nature, we can count to ten. I take it back: we *have* to count to ten. Otherwise the firecracker hits the water too soon and fizzles without going off. We've tried it a hundred times. The bottom of the ditch is covered with duds, but you can't see them because the water's so murky.

But if you light it, wait ten seconds, and then throw it, the flame's so close to the powder there's nothing the water can do about it. The firecracker lands in the ditch, starts to sink, and *pow*, off it goes, and up come bubbles and muck and any creatures with the guts to live down there. Fish, eels, frogs. Their lives come to an end and they all float to the surface, belly up, at the same time. Looking down at them from the banks, all you can see are the white stripes of their bellies breaking the water, swollen and dead.

But the stripe we saw this morning was totally different. It was big and black and bursting with life, a noisy back fin that slithered around like it had all the time in the world, splitting the water in two. It's official: no question about it, there's a monster in the irrigation ditch. So far the only one to see it is Stefano, but you can't always trust him. He's one of those kids who'll wake up his mom in the middle of the night when he has to pee since he's afraid to go to the bathroom alone.

But this morning all three of us saw it. You couldn't miss it: it was huge. We were sitting on the dried mud on the banks, fishing, when holy shit out jumped this big black thing.

Stefano screamed that it was a shark, Silvia that it was a dolphin, but they were both wrong. Come on, it's freshwater! Sure, in the Amazon jungle there might be blind dolphins that live in the river. But we're not in the Amazon here, we're near Pisa, and this isn't even a river, it's a small irrigation ditch that smells like fertilizer. So if the monster isn't a dolphin and isn't a shark, then what the hell is it? There was only one way to find out, and this time it would take more than a firecracker. No, we needed something heavy-duty.

M-80s. Six of them: professional quality, magnum size. Tied together with duct tape. Stefano said, "*Isn't that too much?*" in that whiny voice that immediately pisses people off. Me and Silvia didn't even answer. We gave him a dirty look and wrapped the tape real tight around the bottom, too, so it looked like one fat stick of dynamite, like a hand grenade. One step short of calling in the army.

Five . . . six . . .

We argued for half an hour over who got to throw it. Stefano shook his head and started kicking at the dirt. "*It's not fair! You're always pushing me around just because I'm little.*" Then we realized that what he really wanted was *not* to throw it. So we explained the situation to him and he quit whining. He walked away, looking upset, to a spot where he could still watch what was going on.

Choosing between me and Silvia was a lot harder. Sure, I was the one who came up with the idea of the mega-bomb, but she was the one who paid for it, so we were even. When push came to shove, there was only one way to decide: a game of one-two-three shoot.

Shoot!

I was odds, she was evens. I won.

It was a pretty cool moment, the last time in my life I won a game of one-two-three shoot, at least with this hand, my right. The same hand that can barely wrap itself around this big fat bomb right now. My palm feels powerful, pulsing with fire and gunpowder. I'm the king of the ditch!

Okay, Mr. Monster, you think you're so tough? Well, take this!

My arm is pulled back and my T-shirt sleeve is all bunched up. I hear the sizzle of six little flames burning as one. It sounds like a breeze but it's powerful, like a serpent's nest or a bomber jet or the geysers around Larderello. It's mind-blowingly powerful.

All three of us count together, getting louder and louder, and the numbers march by in clear and precise order and we are totally into it, resolute, sure of ourselves, and awesome...

Seven...eight...BOOM!

There's a ringing in my ears. I see Stefano running away and screaming. I can't hear him but I can tell he's crying. What's he got to cry about? Silvia's standing in front of me like a statue. But she's not looking me in the face. She's looking down.

I look down, too, and I see what she's seeing. I see an empty space.

Well, it's 2010 today and a few years have gone by, but that empty space has stayed inside me. This is how the rest of the story went, more or less. Maybe it wasn't duct tape. Maybe the monster was just a tree trunk rolling around because of the heat or the polluted water. But that feeling of emptiness got stuck in my head and is still there, just the way it was that day.

Because real emptiness is totally fucked. It's not nothingness. On the contrary.

Let me give you a couple of scenarios, just to explain.

One: You go into a hotel room and open a drawer to put away your stuff. The drawer is empty and you start to put in your underwear, T-shirts, and socks.

Two: You go back home; in your bottom drawer you keep all your money, hidden in a shoebox. You bend down, open it, and the drawer is *empty*.

So, you've got two drawers and they're both empty. But is it the same thing?

No fucking way.

Because real emptiness isn't finding nothing. It's finding nothing where there's supposed to be something. Something important that's always been there, and then one day you look and you realize it's gone.

Like that afternoon in July 2005, when my ears were ringing and I looked down at my arm that starts at the shoulder and bends at the elbow and continues all the way to the wrist. And after the wrist, nothing. A hand was supposed to be there. My hand. It's always been there. It's been there for fourteen years and now there's only air, the putrid air of the ditch.

That's what I mean by emptiness.

One two three four five six seven eight . . . Boom!

Because Galileo was a big moron.

And I'm an even bigger one.

METAL DEVASTATION

So yeah, I'm missing a hand. My right, and I'm not a lefty. That is, I am now, but I wasn't back then. Back then I used my right for everything. To eat and to scratch and to hold the remote or a ping-pong paddle. And to throw firecrackers, unfortunately.

Here in Muglione, where everyone is so friendly, they call me Handy or Hans but mostly just Lefty. Like they call bald guys Hairy or Curly. And Maurino the janitor, Pavarotti, since he's mute.

That's the way it always goes; what you don't have matters more than what you do have, and being minus one hand seems to matter more than the fact that I do have—for example—another hand that is still perfect, as well as both my legs, both feet, and all my taste buds.

But that's all right: it's been five years and today I manage to do lots of important things. Things you do every day without thinking, like putting on your shoes, washing up, eating. I had to break them down into little pieces and put them back together in a completely different way. It took a while but the time passed and I learned. In a way I think I even grew.

Not my hand, though. It didn't grow back. I swear I thought about it. Right after the accident it was my first real thought. For a couple of seconds I wondered whether my hand might grow back. Which isn't such a crazy idea, because, after all, when crabs lose a claw it grows back just like before, and if you snap off a lizard's tail the same thing happens. So it doesn't sound so crazy to me.

Come on, we're a superior animal, right? So why is it that crabs and lizards can pull off something like that and we can't? Even lobsters, for Christ's sake, *lobsters*! They've got two giant claws, and if they happen to lose one in a fight or it gets stuck in a net, the claw grows back! And since it takes a lot of energy, the lobster stops growing. I'm not kidding, that stupid animal at the bottom of the sea stops growing so all its energy can go to the claw, and after a while there it is, brand-new and whole, ready to raise hell in the water. You see, a lobster can do it, while we, who are supposed to be the masters of nature, only know how to grow back useless parts like fingernails and the hair on our heads or between our legs... big deal.

Bada-boom.

Giuliano rattles his drumsticks on the snare drum and brings my head back into the garage. He settles into place on his stool. The other two guys, instruments in hand, give me the nod. We're ready.

One, two...

And we're back at it with the numbers again, with this counting game. It's been five years already but every time I count it gives me the creeps. But it's okay, a creepy feeling is just what we need right now, it wakes me up and energizes me, because it's time to kick ass.

One, two, three, four... Come on!

The guitar starts off with a killer riff, a solo for two beats, and then in come the drums with the slippery sound of the snare and the bass breaking in; I stare at the wall in front of me and shake my head to the rhythm of the song, my hair flying all over the place.

Two more instrumental beats and then it's my turn, I do the vocals. What do you expect, it's not like I had much choice with only one hand. Yeah, I know, the Def Leppard drummer cut some records even after he lost an arm, but have you heard them? Lucky for me I've got an awesome voice.

And tonight's a historic moment because I'm singing in Italian. In a way I lost, I was totally against the idea, but on May 1 in Pontedera there's a high school battle of the bands called PontedeRock, organized by the Young Democrats, and there's this stupid rule that the songs have to be in Italian. So we put it up for a vote and decided to sell out. We translated three pieces and tonight we're rehearsing them.

Stop. Another drumroll and it's my turn to cut in.

Horror rises from the tomb
And you can't save yourself
The Undead calling to you
Is sticking in his blaaaaade.

I blast out all those *a*'s in a loud shriek, powerful and sky-high. The Italian fucks up the rhythm completely but I have to admit I thought it would be worse, a lot worse.

You can run and you can hide
But the graveyard is waiting
And the jaws of the damned
Are thirsting for your bodaaaaay.

Then the chorus. If the song is good the chorus should open it up, make it explode, like a rocket going higher and higher until it bursts in the sky.

Horror rises from the tomb
Horror rises from the tomb
He follows you like a shadow
Horror rises from the toooooomb.

On the bass Stefano looks at Giuliano, who's beating on the drums. Tonight we're on fire, we're fierce, and now the tempo changes and the guitar cuts in. Here it comes, now...now...

"Stop, stop! Antonio, what the fuck?"

"What...me? There's no guitar lick there."

"Yes there is."

"No way, the lick comes after. There's the second chorus, then the lick starts."

"Yeah, but here there's a mini-lick, you're the one who asked for it!"

Antonio looks at the others. Stefano, who hasn't changed much in the past five years, looks down to avoid contradicting him. Giuliano, instead, gives him an angry, sweaty stare.

"Okay, guys, I forgot. Peace."

"Peace my ass. We're recording!"

Okay, okay, this time I'll do it right. I promise. But first a cigarette, okay?"

They put their instruments down and all three go out. I don't smoke because it fucks with my voice, and even smoke in the room can mess up my high notes. So they put on their leather jackets and go outside and leave me in the garage.

But we've got to get a move on; by tomorrow we have to have three songs ready to give to the selection committee. I'm the one who went to speak with them, and of the five, three had dreads. Guys who like feel-good music, with one of them singing about holding hands and picking flowers and all you need is sunshine and it'll be all right. We're basically fucked, but we pretend we're not.

And we also pretend that Antonio messed up by accident and it won't happen again, even if we all know what the real problem is: Antonio is too handsome for his own good. He's almost six-six with abs and broad shoulders and a killer combination of dark hair and green eyes that makes girls go gaga when they first meet him.

In addition to Antonio's being so handsome, the problem is that the rest of us are so ugly. What I mean is if it wasn't for my hand I wouldn't be bad, but Giuliano and Stefano are butt-ugly. I like them but it's true. Little Stefano must weigh 110 pounds and has buckteeth that you see even when his mouth is closed, and Giuliano is a fat-ass with such a massive double chin that it looks like he's got a fanny pack tied around his neck.

Take the other night: we were all coming to rehearsal together, and in the town square there were these older guys that only Antonio knows and they see him with us and shout, *"Anto', what the fuck you doing, hanging with the spaz patrol?"*

For real, so then it's hard to believe in the band and play well. You start to wonder what you're trying to do, what you're going to accomplish, what you think these four fuckups are doing in this shithole of a town playing music that no one likes and...

Luckily the cigarette break ends, the guys come back in, and we look at each other with fierce and eager eyes.

Metal Devastation is ready to rock.

ALBERTINA

It's April, nine a.m., and it's freezing cold on a bike.

If I pedal fast my body warms up, but I get hit by more air so I feel cold; I don't know what's better. It was definitely better to take the scooter, but I'm out of gas and I'd rather spend the rest of my life on a bike than ask my dad for money.

This morning, however, I'm filling in for him at the shop and I take the money. I earned it, it's not a tip, so no problem. Except I'm skipping school, but since there's a double period of math today that's not a problem either. The only real problem is that between math, physics, and philosophy, there's a risk I might not even graduate, so I'd be fucked. Enough already. Starting tomorrow I'll hit the books, I'll show them I understand, that I apply myself, yes, starting tomorrow I'm turning over a new leaf, I swear.

But this morning I have to open the store. Dad's away with the boys for a race in another region and a bait-and-tackle shop is like a pharmacy: some customer might have an emergency and you always have to be there.

We used to be able to close occasionally when Magic Bait wasn't the only bait-and-tackle shop in Muglione. You used to be able to go to Albertina, which was the owner's name and everyone called it that. Since it didn't have a real name or even a sign, you'd never figure out it was a shop and not a regular house on the outskirts of town unless someone told you. Albertina lived there. It had a long, narrow room with a counter and a few fishing rods and reels and bait, but in the back behind the boxes there was a door and every now and then she'd open it to get something and you could see there was a kitchen back there.

And this was really convenient because if you needed bait at some weird hour all you had to do was ring the bell and Albertina would be there and make her way to the door, at a snail's pace, and give you what you wanted.

In fact, once me and Stefano wanted to go to the irrigation ditch at dawn and try out our own special bait, made of flour, jam, dried fruit, and Nesquik. We had tasted it and it was good, really sweet, which is perfect because when carp smell something sweet they go nuts and swim to it in droves. And if the bait we invented worked, we could sell it and become rich and famous.

True, I never heard of anyone becoming famous for carp, but that summer we kinda believed it, me and Stefano. We even came up with a name for it, the Magic Carp Special, with a recipe so secret that not even we would remember it if by some fluke it worked. But we had to test it, and to do so we needed one euro's worth of maggots to put on the hook. It was six in the morning and back then Dad still didn't have the bait-and-tackle shop so we went by Albertina's and rang the bell. What I mean is that first we stood there for ten minutes saying, *You do it. No, you. No, you. No, you ring the bell, haven't got the guts? What, like you do? Yes, I do. Really? So prove it, ring. . .*

In the end we both put our fingers on the buzzer and pushed together. At that hour, in silence, the sound passed from the finger to the arm like an electric shock, and right then and there I felt like getting on my bike and running away.

For a little while nothing happened, just the sound of the buzzer echoing in the empty room. Then a light turned on and the door went *click*. Albertina stuck out her head with its frizzy black-and-white curls and asked what we wanted without saying hello. She wasn't angry, just half asleep.

"Maggots, please, ma'am."

"How many?"

"One euro's worth, please."

She disappeared inside and then came back with the maggots in a clear plastic bag. She gave them to us, took the coins, and said, "Anything else?"

"No."

She nodded and went back inside. The light turned off again.

For the whole trip through the empty fields and the sticks and stones I was quiet and confused, wondering if it was normal for grown-ups to be awoken at dawn for one euro's worth of maggots. I didn't think so. In her place I would have been royally pissed off.

Then we got to the irrigation ditch and I thought about it some more.

The special bait didn't work. As soon as it hit the water it dissolved. But we still had the maggots, so we stuck them on the hook and then along came the carp, the catfish, the forkbeard, and even some doctorfish, and we immediately forgot about the bait.

Strange: in the morning we thought we'd become millionaires and half an hour later we knew we wouldn't, but we didn't care because the fish were biting. Something strange and beautiful, very beautiful, if you ask me.

But not if you ask Dad. This is the type of thing that would piss him off royally. It's what he calls "making do," and making do is for losers.

"Fiorenzo, the only thing that matters at the end of a race is the finishing order, first, second, and third. And the next day, no one remembers who came in second or third."

This is what he'd tell me right after the competitions, because for him that's all there was in life. The surrounding world is only the hard, mixed foundation for designing the trails needed for cycling races.

Normal dads bring their children to the amusement park, the zoo, the movies, to buy action figures, or, in this case, to fish. Mine only took me to cycling practice. I learned so fast that at first I was better at cycling than at walking. For me it was normal. Just like it was normal to pedal behind the team car alongside professional champions who explained to me the right gear ratio for every leg of the race.

Sometimes I even let myself do whatever I felt like, and if we came to a hill and they said, "Now downshift or you'll hit the wall," I could easily shake my head and insist on the same tough ratio they used. Then I would feel my legs turning to wood and that pain in the upper thigh, right in the middle, so I would start to push with my whole body and my shoulders and in the end I'd be panting like an asthmatic dog.

And so it went year after year, with Mom getting mad and Dad ignoring her, and me pedaling and timing myself and thinking about the day I'd become world champion. I had already written my acceptance speech.

Then, on the very day that I beat my own record for climbing Monte Serra, I put together the mega-bomb with six firecrackers and it was *sayonara*, right hand. *Sayonara*, biking.

Dad didn't come to see me in the hospital. What I mean is, he came but he couldn't handle looking at me without crying, so he went away and I saw him again when they released me. I went home in my pajamas, and when you get out of the car in pajamas it means you're not doing so great. Dad was there at the door and for a second I couldn't look him in the eyes and he couldn't look at me either. Me because I was ashamed, him I don't know.

But then he gave me a poster that he'd had a photographer make, a photo of Fiorenzo Magni—you see I'm called Fiorenzo because of him. Magni was the Lion of Flanders and he finished the Giro in 1956 with only one hand: he had fallen and cracked a collarbone and wasn't able to grip the handlebars with the hand on that side. But rather than give up, the Lion of Flanders tied one end of a rubber inner tube to the handlebars and held on to the other end with his teeth. That way he was able to somehow hold on during the toughest ascents. In that strange position he rode through half of Italy and climbed the fiercest mountains, and on the poster you could see him with legs that looked like wooden beams wrapped in thick ropes, people shouting everywhere, and him in the middle with a serious, resolute expression— gritting his teeth, crouching down, and continuing to climb— with his eyes staring straight ahead.

I looked at the poster and then at my dad. And he said to me, "Here, Fiorenzo. Take a good look at this picture. For you this is how it's going to be from now on."

Then and there I was shocked. Was he really thinking about taking me back to Monte Serra to climb it with an inner tube between my teeth? He was crazy, it could kill me. At the very least I'd lose a few teeth.

But I'd misunderstood. He said that for me that was how it was going to be from that day on, but he didn't mean cycling. He meant life.

In fact, he never took me cycling again. And he never again told me that if I worked hard and fought I could win anything.

That's the kind of stuff he told Mirko Colonna, the friggin' Little Champ, who he discovered one day by accident in some godforsaken town in the Molise region. A freak of nature who gets on his bike and wins with his eyes shut, no sweat, leaving everyone else in the dust.

And I'm trailing far behind, the last in the race, a tiny dot in the distance. For Dad it's more like I've disappeared completely, withdrawn from every race till the end of time.

Them's the breaks, no sense in my lying about it. Right or wrong, them's the breaks. But I'm not the kind who gives up.

Bite down on the inner tube, Fiorenzo, bite down on the tube and grit your teeth.

THE HOUNDS OF FATE
(RIPABOTTONI, MOLISE REGION,
ALMOST CHRISTMAS)

There're two of them, half dog and half wolf, and they're lurking behind the Colle di Sasso to guard the shepherd's icebox. It's not a real icebox, but on this side of the hill the snow never melts so it's the spot where the shepherd keeps his food supplies.

They're scrawny with spiky fur and no names or chains, so they could run off whenever they feel like it. But the shepherd would find them before morning was out, and spend the rest of the morning beating them silly. They're dirty, they're hungry, but they're not stupid.

That's why they don't dare to touch the food under the snow. They might be dying of starvation but they wait for the shepherd, who comes by every so often and tosses them something. But sometimes fate steps in to lend them a helping hand. With a rabbit or a pheasant or even a pet dog who's made it this far for some terrifying reason. And then they eat.

Like now, when from the top of the hill they hear the crunchy sound of footsteps trampling the snow. The two dogs raise their heads and start to drool.

They don't know that what they're hearing is an eighth-grader with a black garbage bag that he wants to use as a sled to slide down the only place where there's a patch of snow. They don't know that his name is Mirko Colonna and that this morning he ran away from school because the other kids wanted to beat him up. They only know that he'll make a much richer meal than a rabbit, and he's not nearly as fast. They crouch behind a thornbush at the bottom of the hill and wait for lunch to slide straight into their mouths.

But the boy is taking forever. He sits down on the bag, then he gets up again, dries his hands, studies the descent... In the meantime the dogs glare at him from behind the thorns, their paws trembling from the wish to jump him.

Then finally the piece of meat up there makes up his mind, gives himself a push, and slides down. He picks up speed and lets out a shout, *Weeeeee!* as long as the time it takes him to crash halfway down, right against a root poking out of the snow. Then one of the two dogs can't take it anymore and dashes out; the other follows him and in a heartbeat they're running up the hill with a ravenous growl in their throats.

And the idiot doesn't run. No, he sees them coming and he just sits there, motionless, with his arms to his side, the better to be torn to pieces. It takes him a couple of seconds before he can stand up, leave the bag on the ground, run toward the top of the hill, and jump to the other side. The dogs instead lunge rabidly at the bag and fight over it, ripping it to pieces, then they freeze with the shredded plastic in their mouths and realize they're acting like animals. They howl and start to chase the human all over again.

Who in the meantime has reached the bottom of the hill and leapt onto a yellow thing with two circles underneath, started to spin the air with his legs, and is fleeing toward the edge of the woods and the road.

The dogs don't know that it's a bicycle, a busted-up girl's bike that gets busted up even more every day at school. Because his classmates hate Mirko Colonna, him, the Little Genius whose steady stream of A-pluses has devastated the average for the rest of the class.

The other morning, before the essay test in Italian, Damiano Cozzi came to him in person. A guy so big that darkness fell over Mirko's desk.

"Listen here, you little prick, you know what's going to happen to me if I don't pass today's test? They're going to make me get a job. And do you know where? At my uncle's, and my uncle's job is to dress the dead. Did you know the dead get dressed? They get dressed and before that they get washed, too. I don't know how you wash a dead man and I don't want to know. But if you write another A-plus composition today and the teacher comes out with his usual bullshit about how compared with you the rest of us are pathetic, then I'm fucked. So you can bet that the first dead man I wash will be you. Get it?"

And to make himself dead clear, he took Mirko's pen and broke it with two fingers. But he didn't need to. Mirko had understood perfectly, and in fact he wrote the most ridiculous composition in the world. Except this morning when the teacher came back with the essay tests, he was completely freaked out.

"Children, the essay topic I gave you was Christmas and consumerism because it's that time of year and I wanted to know your opinions. But your classmate Mirko Colonna completely ignored the title and wrote a page explaining why teaching is a pathetic and embarrassing job. I read it and reread it, and I've come here to say goodbye because I quit."

The principal came in and everyone stood up, everyone except Damiano Cozzi, who remained sprawled on his chair, which was tiny for his ass. By now he knew where he was going to end up, and his only thought was whether you had to wash the dead down there, too, beneath their underwear.

"Mr. Giannaccini, please take a minute to think this over. Now that you're tenured..."

"Madam Principal, that will be sufficient; what does it matter whether I'm tenured or not...read this, please, read this and then tell me." He handed her the composition, but the principal raised her arms and took a step back as if he had handed her a scorpion, then made a quick run for the door.

Mirko Colonna made a run for the door, too. He asked if he could go to the bathroom but in reality he ran away from school. He was going to get in trouble, maybe even get suspended, but it was still better than getting killed by Damiano Cozzi. Except on his way back home he came up with the idea of the sled, and now maybe he was going to die, devoured by the shepherd's dogs. So there really is no escaping fate.

The dogs follow him and snarl and know nothing about bikes, tenured teachers, or essay tests, but they might know something about fate. And they definitely know how to run.

The woods come to an end and the asphalt road begins. Mirko aims to go downhill but the dogs pop out from that direction so he is forced to turn around and launch his bike in the opposite direction, toward the ascent of Monte Muletto. He jumps up so he is standing on the pedals and pumping with his legs as fast as he can. The dogs aren't used to this hard and slippery thing called asphalt and they have to figure out how to move on it.

But it takes them only a few moments; the road gets really steep and that piece of meat bouncing ahead of them must be worn out by now. They can feel it in their four paws, born to run. Imagine how he must feel. And in fact right now he is struggling, folded in two. The smell of his sweat is reaching the nose of the beasts, who pick up steam and get ready to fight over the most tender bits.

But unbelievably the boy doesn't quit. Maybe it's the ravenous growling coming from behind, or the final burst of the survival instinct, but he finds the energy to stand up on the pedals again and push. But the curves get tighter and the next one feels like a wall; the boy turns around, redfaced and out of breath, and the dogs are getting closer, closer...

Then from behind it all, behind the boy and the dogs and the struggle of each of them to survive, comes the roaring of an engine.

It's a car, someone's coming, the boy turns and waves an arm, calls out for help. Right away the car lets loose a metallic sound that covers his voice and the trees around him.

"Keep pedaling! If you put one foot on the ground I'll run you over. Keep pedaling!"

The car accelerates and passes the dogs, honking the horn. They move to the side of the road and keep running; the car suddenly swerves in their direction, pushes them to the shoulder, and screeches to a halt. The door opens. The two dogs freeze. They don't understand anything, but the guy approaching them looks like an even bigger meal.

Only he seems less defenseless, and in his hand he has an iron rod like the one the shepherd uses. One dog goes to one side and one to the other; they lean forward and get ready for the attack. But the human being is faster. He runs at one and hits him on the back with the stick. A deep blow, a sharp pain, and from the mouth of the beast comes the sound of a candle being snuffed out.

The dog staggers for a second, sees the other one escaping down the hill, and as soon as it remembers how to use its paws it dashes after him. Toward the trees and as far as the snow on the other side of Colle di Sasso, where the shepherd might already be back and hasn't found them standing guard.

And, facing the prospect of more beatings, the two nameless dogs get lost in the woods and disappear from this story forever.

In the meantime Roberto Marelli has gotten back in his car, set down the iron rod, and started to drive uphill in first with an engine that is wheezing.

He was a competitive cyclist for twenty years, and for another ten he trained boys. He knows a lot of champions and he invites them to a lot of official ceremonies, like this one in the province of Campobasso to celebrate the arrival of the Giro d'Italia next year.

But he had no idea of how godforsaken this place was, and he was late leaving Muglione and now he doesn't even know where the place is, and he wanted to run over the two dogs in the middle of the road who were blocking his way. But then he saw that kid up ahead on that shitty bike, and everything else ceased to exist. Because the little squirt was going and going without turning around, at an incredible pace, flying through the curves in perfect style with a propulsion that seemed never-ending.

"Keep going, push! If you touch the ground I'll break your legs! All the way to the top, come on, you can do it, one-two, one-two, one-two!"

The kid wobbles for a second but he sees the hood of the car approaching from behind and starts pounding on the pedals again, powerful and desperate. You can tell he is exhausted, he is spreading his thighs and rocking his upper body, yet he keeps climbing. The energy you manage to find inside when your batteries are dead, that's the secret of the great champions. We've all got a tank, and we're all good for emptying it. The difference that makes a champion is what he does when the tank is empty. And this little bastard up ahead is a champion.

"One-two, one-two, one-two! Release and push, release and push, come on, we're almost there, come on, we're theeeeeere!"

The kid nails the last curve and, up where the top of the hill opens out, he presses on with his head held low, shifting the bike from side to side like the serious climbers, who climb in a kind of ballet. *En danseuse* is the technical term; Charly Gaul did it, José Manuel Fuente did it, and now this little runt on a godforsaken road in Molise is doing it, too.

The climb ends, the kid stops, and his bike falls to the ground. He bends down, raises his arms in surrender, and says, "Mister, I don't know you, I didn't do anything..." He bends down even lower and throws up.

Roberto stops the car in the middle of the road, jumps out, and bangs his knee against the door. He curses, pulls himself together, and runs toward the kid with his eyes popping out. The kid sees him and covers his face with his hands, closes his eyes, and gets ready for the first blow. Which doesn't arrive. In its place he feels a light and warm thing on his back, a blanket that the man puts over his shoulders.

"Who the hell are you, kid? Get in the car! Who the hell are you?

KITTENS

Mee-oooow.

Mee-oooow.

The newborn kittens make this tiny little noise that sounds like crying and fills me with incredible distress. Not to mention that it's dark and the roads are quiet, and in this silence the lament from inside the box sounds like something from beyond the grave, like the voice of a ghost calling me.

But tonight is a great night and nothing can bring me down. The news is clamorous: PontedeRock is letting us play. Next week Metal Devastation is going to devastate Pontedera!

I had misjudged them, those Rasta guys on the selection committee. Yeah, okay, we have to sing in Italian, which sucks for heavy metal, but for now it's a start. We come, we win over the audience, and once we've made a name for ourselves we can play on our own terms and do whatever the hell we want. As AC/DC says, it's a long way to the top if you wanna rock 'n' roll. And we wanna rock, yeah!

Mee-oooow.

Mee-oooow.

Damn kittens. Dad had said right away that having the two dumpsters placed near the store, one next to the other, would be a disaster. One dumpster, okay; we didn't need two.

Mee-oooow.

Mee-oooow.

Dad says a lot of stuff, always in that tone of voice that spits in the face of any doubts. He explained to me that you had to be firm at a bait-and-tackle shop. The customer comes in and buys, but first he asks you questions. Important, picky questions, maybe he wants to know whether it's the right time for a certain kind of fish, whether it's better to lure it with worms or corn kernels or cornmeal, and you can't answer that it's all the same and shrug your shoulders. If you do, give or take a month and the Chinese will take over the shop and start selling plastic T-shirts and colored lights. No, in a bait-and-tackle shop you have to give confident, clear answers, black-and-white, even if fishing is really unpredictable and shrugging your shoulders would be the most honest reaction.

But I still have to admit that Dad hits the nail on the head most of the time. In fact, even when the municipality put the two dumpsters next to the shop, I ran to ask him if he was happy, and he, all serious, went, "Oh, Fiorenzo, I had asked for one, only one for Christ's sake. Instead they had to outdo themselves and put in two, now it's our problem."

Because in Italy a dumpster's a dumpster, people throw in a bag of trash and that's the end of it. But if you put two dumpsters next to each other, then the area becomes a public dump and you have to get ready for the apocalypse. That's what Dad said, and to me it sounded like bullshit. But then the junk started piling up.

TV tubes, broken sinks, refrigerator doors, bed frames and mattresses, broken toilets, mudguards, etcetera. They pass by at night and throw them in. Sometimes there's so much stuff that it stops traffic, or it stinks so bad that we have to pick it up ourselves and take it to the dump.

But the biggest mess is on days like today, when they throw away newborn kittens.

Mee-oooow.

Mee-oooow.

I didn't go home. I ate at the store, lasagna from the deli, and then I ran out because at nine I have rehearsal with Metal Devastation.

I'm dressed just right, leather jacket with studs and combat boots, because heavy metal is serious stuff and you can't go playing in a sweat suit. But first I have to cut through the back roads like a thief with this box under my arm.

Dad never takes them. He says that I'm a kid and if they catch me they'll let me go, but if they catch him it'd be a mess. Because he's a grown man and there're no more freebies when you're a grown man. Not to mention that he's a public figure, a former professional and the sports director of the Muglione Cycling Union, and the newspapers are looking for any pretext to massacre him. I pretend to believe him and hug the cardboard box with the cats inside, and I go where I have to go.

Mee-oooow.

Mee-oooow.

But everyone's got problems of their own. Me, for example, I'm late for rehearsal. And I should also be studying history for tomorrow, since maybe the teacher is going to quiz me and I know squat. I've been out of the house since this morning, haven't cracked a book, and would maybe be better off skipping school tomorrow, too. Yeah, good idea, tomorrow morning I'll go fishing and bring the book with me, that way I can study by the ditch. At home it would be more comfortable, but since Mom's been gone I'm almost never there. The less I see of Dad the better, and I'm sure he feels the same. I mean, not exactly the same: I can't stand my dad, while he, on the other hand, couldn't care less about me. Right now I could be in my room or in hell, it would make no difference to him. For him it's almost as if I were dead, too, like Mom. Except I died when I was fourteen, the day I blew my hand off. And now that he's found this friggin' Super Champ, I'm a little more dead.

There's a little wall that comes up to my chest and separates the courtyard of the Youth Center from the street. I lift up the box, lean against the wall, and try to reach as far over the other side as I can to shorten the drop.

At two feet from the ground I could stop, but the kittens in the box are meowing with fear and it makes me feel bad, so I try to stretch a little bit more. But I'm a jerk, I overdo it, my feet slip, and goddamnit my good arm gets stuck, and I'm left with my legs in the air, the box in the courtyard, hanging half on one side, half on the other, with the wall sawing my stomach in two.

At times like this it would be helpful to have another hand.

In the meantime, since I'm always so lucky, I hear noises from the other side of the Youth Center, a door opening and some voices. Foreign voices. What are foreigners doing at night at the Muglione Youth Center? Not to mention, what will they make of me being stuck up here like this?

My arm won't hold up for long, I can feel it, it's hurting too much. But what's worse is the pain in my ribs on top of the wall. With my legs in the air on the street side, my upper body on the other, the blood is rushing to my head and I don't want to even think about the leather on the jacket that is definitely getting ruined.

"Ja, ich erinnere mich! Das war lustig!"

The voices are closer and closer. By now they're in the street. *Mee-oooow.*

Mee-oooow.

Okay, I try to put an end to this. I have to give myself a push backward with my arm, as strong as I can, and hope to end up on the asphalt. If it's not enough, I'll fall headfirst into the courtyard, and I'm fucked, me and the kittens down below, but I don't see any alternatives.

Then I breathe deep and I count, one, two, three...now! And for once in my life this counting business doesn't bring me bad luck: I tear my T-shirt, and maybe a shoulder muscle, too, and I fall, ass first, and a spasm of pain goes through me, from my sacrum to my hair. But at least I'm in the middle of the road, on the right side of the universe.

"Ah, Tiziana, komm, zeige uns dein Haus, komm..."

Here they are. They arrive on the sidewalk like black ninepins in the dark. I stand up, stagger, they see me and stop talking. I start running.

ALL TIGERS ARE LESBIANS

Here we are, Tiziana, you knew this might happen. You hoped it wouldn't, you begged them not to come, and instead ... Your friends from the master's program in Berlin have come to Italy from Germany France Spain Holland Sweden. A symposium at the University of Florence, two days of meetings. You found out about it at the last minute but you still managed to pull it off. You showed them around Florence, Siena, and even the Tower of Pisa, which they'd seen already but it's always nice to be there on the lawn looking at Japanese tourists taking pictures of each other pretending to hold up the tower. All the Japanese do it, from the little girls carrying Hello Kitty bags to the business-men wearing ties, every last one of them. And you said maybe it's a required photo, their government demands it, and when they go back to Japan they have to show it at the border to reen-ter the country.

It came to you spontaneously; you just said it and everyone laughed their heads off. Petra and Cheryl and Pascal and even Andreas. How long had it been since you'd said anything that intelligent? At least seven months — not since your last evening with them in Berlin, in other words.

Seven months is a long time, almost a year. Now you're thirty-two, and seven months without stimulation are a waste, a mortal sin against yourself and your intelligence. Because intelligent ideas come from intelligent environments, like coconuts from palm trees. You never see a coconut popping out of a plane tree, or a clever idea arising from a day in Muglione. So then, Tiziana, what made you come back?

A master's degree in human resources management. Top tier. Only one student for every European nation, and out of all of Italy they chose you, Tiziana Cosci. Your dad had them do an article in the local paper, and your departure from the train station became a community event. There was even the band, *the town band*, for Christ's sake. Then luckily the train pulled out and the town remained back there, vanishing with the notes of the national anthem, and ahead of you were the five most splendid years of your life.

In an apartment paid for by the university, to share with Cheryl and Akiko, an American girl and a Japanese girl. The start of months and months of adventures, fascinating classes, incredible characters, and bars and restaurants and parties where the next day you don't remember what you did but at the same time you'll never forget.

Two years in a master's program, a splendid summer in between, and another two years on a short-term project for Deutsche Telekom. After that it was time to file applications with various international corporations and organizations. Your classmates applied to the most prestigious firms and they all got jobs. Everyone except Akiko and you. That is to say, they would have hired you in a heartbeat, but the two of you made a different choice. You chose to return home, to your small towns that were struggling to survive because of a lack of organization.

These little towns had lots of potential, but they needed someone who knew how to mobilize their resources and talents and give them a direction. In a miraculous act of survival they produced the two of you and sent you out into the world to learn and to hone your skills. Now it was your duty to return home and help your people to hold their heads high once again.

Give back splendidly the splendor that was given. Akiko had said it in Japanese and it sounded amazing, but it wasn't bad in Italian either. That's what the two of you decided one night, and in September you were back in Muglione.

No band this time around, but the mayor decided to keep at least one of his campaign promises and open a youth center. He took an old warehouse far from the town center and asked you to become the starting point for the rebirth of Muglione.

Okay, fine, just enough time to renew old contacts, study the social context, and inform the newspapers so they'll know about this new reality. Then the most down-and-out little town on the whole Pisan plain will no longer be a byway on the road to Florence. It'll be like Peccioli, but even better. Peccioli made a name for itself by recycling trash. Muglione was going to make it, instead, thanks to the enthusiasm and energy of its young people. Yes, that's it, let's get started right away. Come on, Tiziana, quick, quick, don't waste a minute, come on come on come on.

Except it took a long time—three months—to make the office fit for occupation. It took you much, much less time to realize that you'd completely fucked up your life.

And now, in late April, your friends from Berlin are in Tuscany. You found out they were coming and immediately you were terrified. Terrified they would see your town, your job, your life. So far you've been saved by the busy schedule of their symposium and the beauty of Florence. At five o'clock you close the office and rush off to see them. Maybe a tour of the Ponte Vecchio, Piazza della Signoria, underground restaurants with brick walls, and everything is going to be all right.

In the meantime they talk to you about what they do, the lives they live from airplanes to advisory meetings for governments. Governments, for crying out loud! You nod and you feel something eating you up inside. You're not jealous, you never have been. It's not that you want to be in their place. You want to be *together* with them, the way it was supposed to be. But you manage to keep these thoughts bottled up inside without letting them slip. You keep smiling, nodding your head, so everything's under control.

At least until they start up with this *Komm, Tiziana, zeige uns dein Haus*—Come on, Tiziana, show us your place.

They ask you when you're there in Pisa, at the tower. In Germany you always used to say you were born *near Pisa*, so you must be close to home, your friends are thinking. Come on, Tiziana, make us happy, show us where you live.

All right, fine, let's try to minimize the damage. It's almost dinnertime and you take them to the Youth Center, you show them around and make up some stuff about work being under way to rationalize the space. That's why it looks so empty: all the equipment is in storage.

You don't like lying to your friends, and you're really bad at it. You get agitated and jumpy and you laugh with a weird face; someone standing right in front of you wouldn't know whether you were a liar or just plain crazy.

But you have no alternative. You already tried keeping quiet the whole way to Muglione, passing one dreary little town after another, and the silence was deadly. Stretches of wasted, neglected fields, hardscrabble land on which nothing grows except scattered patches of dried-out vegetation. And Cheryl, who is really an angel, tried to say how *wunderbar* the Tuscan countryside was, but she knew and so did everyone else that there was nothing *wunderbar* about it. For crying out loud, it's not even countryside. It's flat empty fields—just dirt and mud and putrid irrigation ditches down the middle—every now and then a forlorn tree, an abandoned barn, or a hooker by the side of the road, sitting on the ground in glittering sequins against a pitch-black background. Even you can't believe that such a decrepit and anonymous place exists in the universe. So obviously a few lies could come in handy.

But in the end, when for better or worse you show them your office and propose a quick return to Florence for a nice dinner at a trattoria, Andreas says, *Nein, Tiziana, ich habe genug von Florenz, können wir nicht Spaghetti oder so was bei dir essen?*

Forget about Florence, they want to see your house and have a spaghetti dinner together. Like old times. Something simple, warm, among friends. The horror.

But you can't say no. You want to, with all your heart. Or maybe it would be better to drug them, like they do in spy movies, bring them back to Florence, leave them senseless at the hotel, and run away, change your phone number, and die in their eyes forever in this godforsaken place. But Andreas is the one who asks, and you never could say no to Andreas.

Even though he asks to see your apartment, two rooms plus kitchen–dining room in the middle of nowhere, and inside it'll smell like the irrigation ditch that flows under the building, and even worse Raffaella will be there, your roommate and former high school mate, who is unfortunately your best friend in Italy.

You go in; the swampy smell is even stronger than usual. Maybe it's just your imagination. But the underwear and socks placed on the radiator to dry are not your imagination. Raffaella comes out of her room listening to Milli Vanilli; she's wearing exercise pants and a red fleece top that makes her look even fatter than she already does when she's naked. And her hair, oh my God her hair. Has your hair gotten like that, too, in the past eight months? Does it have the same disheartening effect on every-one who sees it? You can't think about that, not now, maybe not ever.

But your friends are smart, cosmopolitan people. They know how to behave. They say hello to her, give her a hug as if they've known her all their lives.

Raffaella speaks very little German, and with an awful accent, but your friends insist on everyone dining together. She has already had a tub of cream cheese with tomatoes, but she'll keep you company. Oh joy. Everyone is happy and enjoy-ing every little thing, so at this point you hope it will all go okay. In a second everyone's sitting at the table and there's wine and a conversation begins in rudimentary German, but it does the trick.

This is how the conversation goes, more or less:

"I can't believe it, with Lars? Give me a break, she's nice and all, but he could do a whole lot better, no?" says Petra.

You nod in agreement. You've drained the spaghetti and now you're distributing it on the plates. Thank God there's a jar of pesto in the house. Thank God and thank Raffaella. Who isn't doing half bad. She doesn't talk a lot but she doesn't lose her cool. She only understands snatches of what's being said but she smiles when she's supposed to and everything is going fine.

You manage to smile, too. While you're handing the pasta over to Andreas a drop of oil falls on his pants but he laughs, touches it with a finger, and puts it in his mouth. He says, "Excellent, Italian olive oil," and the stain already seems to have disappeared. The same way his blond hair always looks perfect, with that perfect bed-head look.

This is what your homes in Germany were like, a hundred times messier than this one, but in a more chic and sophisticated way. Stacks of CDs thrown in the corners, piles of books holding up the telephone and the stereo... It wasn't confusion, it was life in the fast lane. Here instead if you look at the curtains over the window, the ceiling light above the table, the potholders hanging from the stove, you start to feel asphyxiated.

"You're so mean," says Andreas, "they're good together, so what if she's a little homely and he's handsome? If it were the other way around you wouldn't even notice."

You nod to him, too, and on the spur of the moment, without a second thought, you come out with an offhand remark. Which at the moment you don't realize is going to be your downfall.

You say, "Of course, women in general are better-looking than men. They're more showy, they care more about beauty. It's nature. I mean, it's human nature, because in animals it's the exact opposite."

"In what sense the opposite?"

"I mean, in the animal kingdom the males are more beautiful, more showy."

"You're right, damn it, you're right," says Pascal. He looks at you all excited. "Like, take peacocks, for example..."

Pfau is the German word for peacock. Raffaella doesn't know it, and taps you on the shoulder to ask you. You say *Peacock* in a low voice and everything is back to normal.

"Like, the male peacock is amazing, with that fantastic tail and all the rest. But the female is gray, with almost no tail: a wallflower."

"Roosters are beautiful, too, with that crest and those long colored feathers..."

"Yes, and the hens, instead, are homely."

"Fantastic!" Andreas laughs and claps his hands. "*The Hens Are Homely*. It sounds like the title of a film. Like, fantastic!"

Everyone laughs, repeats the title of the imaginary film, and you all start inventing the plot. The only one who doesn't jump into the conversation is Raffaella, but she looks around and smiles and says, *Ja, ja*, and everything's all right.

"Yes, and deer, too!" says Petra. "The male deer has enormous antlers, all branched out, and that splendid coat. The female, instead, is smaller and has no antlers..."

Everyone nods, Pascal tosses back a glass of wine, looks at you, and says, "You know it's true, it's *so true*, Tiziana, you said something brilliant. For crying out loud, why aren't you with us all the time? We miss you so much."

You laugh, you drink, you're so happy. And your fear about bringing your friends home, that maybe the place was too provincial...well, maybe the only thing provincial about it was your fear. Bringing them here was a great idea, and your remark about the animals was brilliant, and the spaghetti came out really...

"Like, you know, but, it's not always true," says Raffaella in her broken German.

"Come again?"

It takes her a while to put together the sentence. "You see, well...the peacock, okay, the deer, okay, but the tiger?"

"In what sense?"

"In the sense that the tiger is different. The tiger is a lot more beautiful than the lion."

"Than the lion?"

"Yes, it's a lot more beautiful, isn't it?" Raffaella stops, sees that everyone is staring at her, especially you, with a look in your eyes that's terrifying. She could stop now, say she was mistaken, that when she was little she hit her head hard and has never fully recovered. Instead she digs herself in deeper.

"Yes, well, I know, you all think the lion is beautiful, and I agree. Yes, the lion has the . . . help me out here, Tiziana, how do you say . . . the hair of the lion, how do you say it in German . . . Oh, okay, *die Mähne*, thank you. The mane is beautiful, yes, okay. But the body is only one color, and the tiger instead is a hundred times more beautiful."

"And?"

"And the female in this case is more beautiful than the male, the tiger is more beautiful than the lion. No?"

No one answers. Silence and more silence. Out of desperation you ask whether anyone wants more spaghetti, but no one answers you either.

Then Pascal leans over the table and speaks. "In other words, Raffaella, you are saying that the tiger is more beautiful than the lion, but . . . like, in the sense that the tiger is the female lion?"

"Yes, exactly. And she's a hundred times nicer than the lion."

A chill comes over you. You press the fork against your wrist to take your mind off the present. You look at the window and the darkness outside. Maybe if a meteorite were to come out of the sky and flatten Muglione you could survive this, a quick and resolute way to end the story. Dream on, nothing can take you away from here. From this squalid dinner in this squalid place with this nitwit who thinks the lion is the male and the tiger is the female. Not even at elementary school...

You press the fork against your wrist even harder. You want to see blood.

In the meantime Raffaella keeps babbling on and on. "Yes, the lion is nice, but the tiger..."

The others look at her, exchange winks, and can't hold back their laughter, and the most awful thing is that they don't let you in on the joke, they don't look at you and on the contrary they try to hide from you the fact that they're laughing. Because for them Raffaella is a part of you, of what you are today. You belong to the group of those they make fun of, in their eyes you and she are one, and you also believe that lions mate with tigers.

"Shut up, what the fuck are you talking about?" You jump to your feet and point your fork at her. "Lions don't mate with tigers, they're two different animals! Lions go with lionesses, for Christ's sake, any retard knows that!"

Then you run into your room and lock the door, forever.

And even if you can't see what's happening in the dining room and can't hear anything, you can imagine that idiot Raffaella with her eyes staring into space, as if this were the first baffling discovery she'd ever made in the thirty years of her life. And in fact after a while you can hear her, but she hasn't backed down, and with her excruciating German she asks quietly, "Excuse me, okay, the lioness...yes, I hadn't...but so I've gotta ask, then who does the tiger do it with?"

The answer comes from Cheryl, who, as always, is the kindest. "The tiger does it with other tigers," she says. "Tigers stick together."

And Raffaella's such a moron that now she thinks all tigers are lesbians.

HAPPY BIRTHDAY, CHAMP

So, yesterday's rehearsal didn't just go well, it went *great*. We were one, we were compact, we were fierce, a war machine that advances straight and crushes everything in its path.

Maybe it's because we're psyched for the festival, maybe it's because we finally get to play on a real stage with a real audience that can't wait to see us, but now that we're headliners we have to deliver.

This morning my ears were still ringing from the volume, a wall of sound. Luckily I don't need my ears so much in fishing. I need my eyes, one to keep on the float, the other to keep on the pages of the history book. I bring the book with me, I really do. I didn't go to school today because if the teacher quizzed me she'd mop the floor with me, but I said that this morning I'd study and I swear I'm studying. So in the next few days she'll quiz me and I'll get a good grade, and I'll start the final dash toward graduation. Yes, everything's perfect, yes everything. I mean, apart from the fact that I don't have enough bait. All I need to do is stop by the shop and I'll be all set.

I lean my scooter against one of the dumpsters, I go in, the door goes *driing*. I say hi to Mazinger between the shelves. His real name is Donato and he's a regular customer. But as soon as

Dad sees me he jumps to his feet, comes out from behind the counter, and heads for the door.

"Just in time. I've gotta run. See ya."

"Where are you going? I just dropped by for a second to grab some worms."

"No, you've gotta stay here, it's a busy day. In a little while we've got a delivery, put it over there, it's important."

"But, Dad, I'm busy."

"So am I. I've got people arriving at the station and I have to pick them up. I was almost going to leave Mazinger in the store but I'm afraid he'll steal something."

"WHAT?" Mr. Donato speaks through a little device attached to his throat that makes him sound like a robot. That's why we call him Mazinger, like the Japanese robot. "I—HOPE—YOU'RE—KIDDING—ROBERTO."

"Just kidding... but, Fiorenzo, heads up, keep an eye on him."

"DON'T—BOTHER—I'M—GOING—AND—NEVER—COMING—BACK—YOU'VE—LOST—A—CUSTOMER."

Dad nods, waves his hand, and disappears into the street. The door closes by itself, slowly but surely. Mazinger stares at the closed door for a second and then turns around suddenly. "YOUR—DAD—IS—A—SHIT."

Go to the head of the class, Mazinger. I say yes and look at him for a second, just long enough to lose it. The sight of Mazinger is enough to blow your mind. He's almost eighty years old and dresses like a meathead my age. I mean, you can't believe the way they dress him.

His nephew used to go to middle school with me. His name's Silverio but he wants everyone to call him Silver and he studies at a kind of fashion and performing arts school in

Florence because he wants to become a model or a designer or a singer. He always wears the latest fashions but as soon as they're out of style he wouldn't be caught dead in them. But they're practically brand-new so rather than throw them away he gives them all to Mazinger, and since he's skinny they fit him to a T, and since he's old he doesn't give a crap how he looks. Today, in fact, he's wearing silver shoes, skintight satin trousers, and a neon-blue shirt with the word PLAYBOY written on it. To see him you'd think he was a Travolta wannabe who got lost on his way to the disco and has been stuck wandering through the fields for the past forty years.

But I can't let myself get distracted by Mazinger and his look right now. I have to study and not listen to bullshit.

I go behind the counter and put away my fishing jacket, rod, and tackle box, everything except my history book. I wanted to go fishing and I can't, but I said that this morning I was studying and I'm going to study. For stuff like this, the shop is better than the irrigation ditch.

Chapter 14, "Europe before the Second World War," good, good, good...

There are black-and-white photos of poor people wearing big, stiff overcoats; dusty, almost empty roads. It looks a little like Muglione, apart from the overcoats, but I have to focus. The only thing I have to do is read and underline the most important passages and get into place for the final dash to graduation. Good, good, good...

"HE'S — A — WISEASS — CUZ — HE — RACED — BUT — HE — WAS — A — DOMESTIQUE — IF — HE'D — BEEN — A — CHAMP — WOULD — HE — SPIT — IN — MY — FACE?"

I tried to keep my head lowered over my book. Maybe if I ignore him Mazinger will shut up and leave. I can't lose my focus. I have to keep my eyes glued to the history book and repeat everything I read...

So, the nation that was worst off was Germany. There was this ridiculous crisis and the money wasn't worth shit and people would go to buy bread with a wheelbarrow filled with reichsmarks, and a postcard stamp would cost seven figures but that wasn't a big deal, since maybe in that situation people didn't have many occasions to send postcards. The overwhelming feeling was that they'd lost their shirts, that they'd been ripped off, and this feeling grew bigger every day and the people got really pissed off, and...

Driiing.

The door opens. I look up and there are three giant boxes, one on top of the other, coming into the store. Underneath there's a pair of legs that come to an end in flip-flops, so it must be Sirio. Sirio works at the town hall but he's also secretary of the Muglione Cycling Union, and he wears flip-flops in the winter, too. He says his big toe is too big to wear shoes. He applied for disability but so far they haven't given it to him.

"Oh, Roberto, give me a hand, please, I can't take it anymore," he says from the other side of the boxes.

I go toward him and my eye falls on his big toes sticking out of the flip-flops. They really are big.

"Sirio, it's me, Fiorenzo, my dad's gone to the station. Give it here, I can manage it."

"Oh, hi, Fiorenzo. Careful, you'll hurt yourself, let me take care of it. Just tell me where..."

He staggers and sweats like an animal. He doesn't know, but I can manage just fine with one hand. I take the first box and place it in the corner under the picture window, he does the same and pushes the boxes forward with his belly, then he straightens himself up, all sweaty.

"Jeez, this weight's killing me. I've got a hernia, let me show you, it's like having a third ball." He sticks his hand in his underwear, widens his legs, and starts working on it with his eyes on the ceiling and the tip of his tongue sticking out. "Uh, I gotta run, they're doing attendance checks at the town hall lately; if they don't find me I'm fucked."

He says goodbye to me and Mazinger, and I'm already opening the first box.

Inside are reels and reels of red, white, and green ribbon.

"What the hell is this?"

"THE—DECORATIONS—FOR—TODAY—I—THINK."

"For today? Why, what's today?"

"THE—BIRTHDAY—OF—THE—LITTLE—CHAMP—OF—COURSE—DON'T—YOU—READ—THE—PAPER?"

No I don't read the paper. All it's got is a bunch of bullshit about town fairs and the squabbling between the suck-ass towns of this godforsaken plain. Why would I want to read it?

But Dad does, for the articles about junior cycling. I pick it up from the counter and find out the friggin' kid's birthday is being celebrated in the town square at five. There's even a band and an official delegation from Molise and the roads are closed.

So that's why Dad had to run. So that's why rather than fishing I'm stuck here with Mazinger. He wants his little champ's party to be awesome, and doesn't give a rat's ass whether I'm left carrying the bag.

I grit my teeth, I grit them hard, I feel my nerves screeching in my head.

"THERE—IS—ALSO—A—GIANT—CAKE—SHAPED—LIKE—A—BIKE."

Yeah, I know. There's even a group playing in the town square till late.

Once me and my posse went down to the town hall and asked if we could play and the town's youth counselor (an old geezer, of course) told us, *Great idea, kids, go through that door over there and explain your proposal.* He pointed to the door and the four of us headed toward it, ready to rock, except the door was a side exit from the town hall and we found ourselves back out on the sidewalk, down and out and pissed as all hell.

But I have never, and I mean never, been as pissed as I am now. Why the hell didn't Dad ask me to play? Okay, I know, it's not the right kind of music, but still, he doesn't know, he's never heard us play and never wants to, so he could've easily asked. I would've said no anyway. No way was Metal Devastation ever going to play at a town party and shout *Long live the champ!* Fuck that!

Calm down, now. Don't lose it. I've got to study. Yes, I go back to the counter and dig into my book. It's the best way to change my luck. Tomorrow I'll volunteer for the history quiz and the teacher will question me and I'll know everything and I'll get an A-minus or even better. Yes, go for it, Fiorenzo, that's the spirit. Fight fire with fire.

In the meantime I get a text message. It's from Stefano.

History quiz today. Teacher got mad and gave you an F. Big party downtown. Giuliano says let's go goose some girls. You in? (10:03)

SENIOR CENTER

From the BitterSweet Girl blog.

Post published today at 11:45 a.m.

Hi everyone,

Hope you're having a great day.

And I hope it'll be a great day for me, too.

I'm writing from the office, and don't tell me I shouldn't because at this hour there's no one and I don't have anything to do. If I weren't writing these lines, I'd be staring at the wall opposite my desk. Is that what you want me to do? Please say no.

Guess what I found outside the door today? Exactly, more kittens. It's become an invasion. I wonder how people can be so cruel as to abandon little kitties like that. And why here? A woman told me it's because I treated them so well the first time and people have started taking advantage. What am I supposed to do, drown them? Hang one from the gate as a warning?

I've got to run. Let me close by saying the weekend is near and I hope it comes quickly, but then I'd feel like such an ordinary person, the kind who works all week thinking only of Saturday and Sunday, then spends all day Saturday and Sunday resting because they're worn out. Oh God, am I that ordinary? Please tell me I'm not.

XXOO to everyone.

BitterSweet Girl

You reread the post because you detest typos. There aren't any. You posted it a few minutes ago and you've already got three comments. Not bad, except for the fact that it's always the same three people, and that'll be the extent of it. WTF? The blog's on the web, it can be read all over the world, and out of six billion possible readers a grand total of three is pathetic.

The comments are from Raffaella, your cousin Lidia, and Carmelo, a paraplegic kid you met at a party for volunteers.

1) Sweetie, you're not ordinary, you're awesome! ☺
2) My little cousin, cheer up! It's spring. XXOO! P.S. Hugs to the kitties, too!
3) BitterSweet, you're always so profound and unique. I'm so lucky to have you as a friend. Suffering is part of life, don't give up. Giant kiss, Carmelo.

That's the long and short of it. It'll have to last till tomorrow, when you write something else and they write their comments again, always the same stuff, more or less, and always the same people.

Carmelo even told you about this awesome software that shows you how many visitors come and see what you write, and at what time, and where they live.

You installed and tested it right away. And your momentary enthusiasm crashed as soon as the program confirmed that the three people who wrote comments were indeed the only ones who read you. It came as no surprise, but somehow this made it worse. To know something awful and to see it are not the same thing. It's like the difference between knowing that snakes are poisonous and getting bitten for real.

And on the subject of messages: the other day Luca texted you out of the blue.

During your last month in Berlin he had written you all the time, after a one-year silence. He wrote that he was thinking of you, that he missed you, that he was just back from a weekend on the island of Elba with his girlfriend and had been bored to death and knew that with you it would have been different.

Luca is three years older than you. Luca, who on the first day that you met him in the department told you what he wanted to do in life and now he was doing it. He got accepted into the Ph.D. program he wanted and is studying with the professor he had as an undergraduate and he always seems sure of himself, as if the world were his oyster and he didn't need anyone.

And you still couldn't figure out, deep down, whether you wanted him or wanted to be him. At any rate, you did have him, at least whenever his girlfriend would go to Milan to see her parents. And every time, he would tell you that it was all over with her, that as soon as she came back they would talk, and every time you pretended to believe him.

Then you left Germany and you swore that you would erase him from your life. And distance helped you to see how truly sleazy he was: a worthless guy who thought only about himself and had a million excuses for doing whatever he felt like.

What an idiot you were to fall for it. Luckily the passage of time changed you, experience changed you.

In your last days in Berlin, however, all it took were three or four texts in the middle of the night and Luca was back in your head. He said that you seemed so far away, that he would probably never see you again, that the two of you were made for each other, that he knew it and you knew it. That's what he said.

So maybe Luca had a little something to do with your decision to return home. And it was no accident that you sent him a text from the train on your way back. He answered that he couldn't wait to see you, you told him you would be home the next day, and then he wrote a text to you at two in the morning that you had to read three times to be sure of what he was saying.

Tish, the wife is fat as a whale. She's due in two weeks and unbearable. I need a night with you to unwind. What time can I come by? (02:12)

You deleted it almost immediately, but it was too late. Because you can't get him out of your head.

So it's better to think that Luca had nothing to do with your decision to return to Muglione. No, you came back only because you truly thought you could help your hometown. That's the reason you're here today. The only reason.

Chief and sole employee of the Muglione Youth Center, in which the handful of teenagers left in the town have never set foot.

But luckily—well, because of a mix of luck and the fact that the owner of the neighborhood bar just dropped dead—the seniors are now coming to the Youth Center.

Eugenio's corner bar, where you could also get coffee, cigarettes, and lotto tickets, shut down from one day to the next after poor Eugenio got stopped in his tracks by friendly fire during a wild boar hunt, the leading cause of death among the men of Muglione. So the seniors, dazed and confused, started coming to the Youth Center, walking in off the street. At least it was heated, the local papers arrived every morning, and the tables used for checking scholarship opportunities and business brochures were also perfect for playing cards.

And if they do ask for information every so often, it never has anything to do with young people. It's always the phone numbers of medical specialists or application procedures for free hearing tests. All stuff that you knew nothing about, but you got busy and read up on the laws that apply. You've got a six-month contract and after that God knows what's going to happen, and you won't look good if someone from the town hall drops by and sees that the Youth Center is always deserted. So you need to at least keep the seniors happy.

Also because if you lose your job you just might have to move in with your parents, and that is one thing you couldn't handle. Your mother would immediately remind you that your sister is five years younger and living in Genoa with her husband, an engineer, and a wonderful baby who looks like Little Lord Fauntleroy. And you would have to repeat to her that you don't want a life like that, so dull, so cautious, and always the same. *Well what do you want, then? You always know what you don't like, well, what is it that you do like, Tiziana?*

There are women who give up their careers for love, others who give up love for their careers. You don't have either. You just plain give up. It's enough to make you want to kill yourself.

And the thoughts you write on your blog are your only safety valve. You decided to stop, it's true, and that friggin' software that shows you how many hits you get told you loud and clear what a total loser you are.

But then, a couple of days after you installed it, the program showed a new visitor. From America. The United States. Every night at more or less the same time an American connects to your blog and reads you. He never leaves a comment; maybe it's a language issue. Maybe he can read Italian but doesn't want to try writing it. He's afraid to look like a jerk because he cares about you, about your opinion. He's a sensitive guy who landed on your blog by accident and couldn't tear himself away. Maybe he's waiting for the right moment to contact you and . . .

You keep updating your blog, and every day you write a few lines with this hope. Maybe you could dedicate a couple of thoughts to America, just to encourage him to go for it, to write his opinion, his name, anything.

Tomorrow maybe you can write about Obama! Of course, if you talk about Obama you're sure that he'll write a comment (for some reason you exclude the possibility that he is a she). Yes, Obama, great idea.

Yes, Tiziana. *Yes we can.*

Muglione Celebrates the Little King

Big Turnout for the Young Champ from Molise

MUGLIONE. Yesterday there was a giant birthday party downtown for Mirko Colonna, the young champion who in a few short months has led the Muglione-Berardi Furniture Cycling Union to the top of the regional leagues. Attended by Mayor Barracci, a delegation from the town of Ripabottoni (Campobasso), and the regional secretary of the Italian Cycling Federation, Castagnini, the party was even bigger than the annual Feast of San Pino, patron saint of the town. Proof of the enthusiasm for this champion, who has just turned thirteen and has so far participated in twelve races for rookies, winning all of them. A fierce and energetic competitor, Colonna confirms his shyness when he gets off his bike. While he doesn't break a sweat in a climb, his real struggle is to break a smile, even when the mayor awards him the keys to the city, and even when the time comes to cut the giant bike-shaped cake. We asked him where he got his passion for the pedal, what it feels like to be a champion, and how he saw his future in cycling. He answered simply and politely, "I'm sorry, I don't know." He couldn't be more different from his discoverer and trainer, Roberto Marelli, an institution in local cycling, who was glowing, understandably. "Mirko is a natural talent," he tells us, "we're working hard on training and preparation, but everything comes to him spontaneously. This party is a way of thanking him for all the happiness he gives us. And he is happy, even if he's shy by nature and can't show it." Future plans? "I don't want to talk too much, one step at a time, all his times are outstanding and we have every reason to aim very high." We ask him whether the rumors are true that professional teams want to option him. Marelli replies, "I can't talk about it. Some people have come calling, big names, but Mirko is still too young and it doesn't make sense to get too far ahead of ourselves. But it's clear that in his legs he's got the ability to win the Giro and the Tour and even the Classics one day." Everyone listens to the speeches of the mayor and the various public officials, but the champion is gone. He's already in bed, resting up for the all-important Bertolaccini di Montelupo Trophy, scheduled to take place next Sunday. By the way, we think we already know the winner's name. (*Gianni Parenti*)

THE THIRD RING

This morning I don't know why I came fishing. Maybe because I wanted to come yesterday or because when I fish my mind goes underwater and I stop thinking about what happens on land. And now my grade in history is a lost cause. The teacher gave me an F in absentia; what's the point of going to school anymore?

Yes, but starting Monday I have to shift gears. Saturday is the day of the Pontedera festival, and until then I can't let myself get distracted by school, but starting next week I'm going to hit the books, yes, perfect, excellent. And today, just for the sake of change, I started fishing at a spot I've never tried.

The whole plain is crisscrossed by irrigation ditches connected to each other. It's practically the same body of water moving through various straight and narrow canals, coated with lime slicks and bordered by reeds in the middle of barren fields. In fact, some people call them "the ditches" and others "the ditch," because if you treat each little piece as independent then there's a lot of them, but if you see them from above they're a single dark network like a black cage over the town.

And while I'm thinking I keep an eye on the floater, which is sitting motionless in the still water, barely leaning to one side. That's the way it's supposed to sit, because it means the bait is lying on the bottom, and carp and tench live close to the bottom. They have two tiny whiskers on either side of their mouths and they use them to move around in the mud and find something to eat. And if they pass by here, they'll find two kernels of corn with a nice worm on top, hiding a golden hook that'll pop out when it's too late.

No two ways about it, there's a lot I know about fishing. One day I've got to make up my mind to shoot a documentary. The series will be called *Great Emotions a Short Walk from Home, with Fiorenzo Marelli*. It'll teach people how to plan exciting fishing trips without having to travel halfway around the world.

Yes, because there are these ridiculous videos, like *Angling for Big Fish in Canada* or *Gigantic Adventures in the Antilles* or *Record Catch in the Rivers of Mali*. But give me a break, how much does it cost to fish in style in places like that? Just tell me where I'm going to find the money to go there, to those faraway places jumping with salmon and sturgeon and marlin.

My series will teach, instead, how to have fun at places closer to home, so close that maybe you walk by every day and wouldn't even think of casting a line in them. Drainage canals that run alongside country roads, stormwater basins, irrigation ditches in the middle of fields that collect rainwater and fertilizer — in other words, all of our local landscape.

I can already see myself... *Hi, I'm Fiorenzo Marelli. Today we're going to learn how to choose the corn kernels and how to stick a worm onto a hook, how to bait an earthworm, how to tie a perfect fisherman's knot...*

While all these acts are impossible with just one hand in the beginning, with time you discover the thousands of possibilities offered by your feet and your mouth and then your problems are gone. Why ignore it? The fact that I'm a "young one-handed fisherman" gives me an edge and everyone will want to see my documentaries.

It makes me feel good all over; I can already imagine exactly how I'm going to feel when it all comes true. But then another, darker thought creeps into my mind and ruins everything. The thought of my mother.

I mean the fact that my mother won't be around to congratulate me. For my fishing documentaries but also for my performance at the Pontedera festival this coming Saturday night. It's not that I would have wanted her there. I mean, a heavy metal band that brings along its mothers? Seriously lame! I would have had to tell her *No, Mom, you can't come, I'll tell you all about it later but the place isn't for you, it's for kids.* And she would have acted like her feelings were hurt, but the next day she would have asked me to tell her all about it, and I would.

But instead.

Instead she died, last year, out of the blue. She was waiting in line at the bank and they say she said something but it didn't make any sense, then she went down and it was all over. It was March 14, but for me she died on the 18th, because in your head it always takes a little longer for the people you love to die.

Right then and there you struggle to take it in, to make sense of it, and you don't even have time to think because you find yourself talking to some well-dressed guy with a serious face who asks you whether *the lady preferred soft pastel colors or a nice classic wood that never goes out of style,* and he shows you the models in a catalog of coffins, I'm not kidding, and I'm the one who has to do it because Dad doesn't want to talk to anyone and just stands there staring at Mom. And then there are the relatives and friends and strangers who come to show you how sorry they are, and they say profound, important-sounding things like *Poor dear* or *We have to learn to accept* or *Everyone's time comes, there's nothing we can do.*

Then there are the other people you have to tell. The people who only see your mom on the holidays and have no way of knowing she's dead. But they are people you absolutely *must* tell. Not for their sake but for yours. Because if you say who cares and don't call them, you'll be the one in the wrong and you'll pay for it dearly on Christmas or Easter when the doorbell rings and at the door you find a woman you haven't seen in an eternity, she says hello with a Christmas cake in her hands, looks up at you with a smile and asks, *Where's Antonia*, and then the sinking feeling sets in when you have to tell her that Mom is dead, and telling her stirs up all the pain as if it were happening again, and the woman doesn't know what hit her and then she hugs you and starts crying and you have to console her, *you* have to console *her*. And while you're standing there at the door for an hour hugging a crying stranger, you wonder why you didn't make a couple more phone calls that awful day. All it would have taken is a couple of phone calls.

All this just to say that when someone dies it's a mess, and it takes a while to realize it. For me my mother died four days later, the afternoon of March 18, when I decided to escape from everything and everyone and I took a ride on my motor scooter to the irrigation ditch to check whether the carp were running.

But I took a curve a little too sharply on the dirt road, my rear wheel went out from under me, and I fell. I didn't get hurt but there was a piece of rusty metal that scraped the skin on my leg. Rusty metal can give you tetanus and I've always been afraid of tetanus, because when I was little I didn't want to get the vaccination and the lady who gave the shots told me that without the vaccination I would get tetanus, and if you get tetanus you start to bleed from your ears and your eyes and get lockjaw and a river of blood fills your throat and you choke.

I got up from the ground and studied my leg and I didn't know if the tetanus shot was still good, if I had to go to the emergency room or if instead I could relax. But there was a very easy way to relax: all I had to do was tell Mom and hear her say the usual thing, *What are you worried about, Fiorenzo, it's nothing.*

So it was on that day, March 18 of last year, I swear that despite the doctors and the undertakers and the coffin catalogs and the funeral, I swear to God that I picked up my cell phone and dialed my mom. I stood there, with the cell phone to my ear and my eyes scanning the empty plain, *brrrr-upp* (since for some reason it was ringing), *brrrr-upp*, then at the third *brrrr-upp* I realized.

Something gigantic and hard entered my throat from my stomach, climbed up to my brain and switched my head off. Darkness. Total darkness.

And in that moment I realized that my mom's phone would ring this way forever, that she couldn't hear me anymore, and she couldn't know anything about anything that happened to me. My mother was dead. On the eighteenth of March last year. Right around here, in the fields crisscrossed by the irrigation ditch, at the third ring of my cell phone.

POLE CLIMBING

Stefanino didn't go to school either.

He hasn't slept in three days and now and then he gets dizzy. If he went to school he'd risk falling asleep and maybe the teacher would realize it and lower his grade, ruining the B average he's erected like an invincible wall through a year of hard work. Now of all times, with only fifty-eight days to go until finals.

But it's not finals that keep him awake at night. Right now his number-one anxiety is much nearer; it's called the Pontede-Rock festival. Tomorrow night Metal Devastation is playing live for the first time in front of a real audience.

Madness. Stefano was sure the organizers would say no. That's the way it always goes, Fiorenzo and Giuliano ask the whole world if they can play and everyone answers *No thank you* or more often a simple *No*.

Instead the Pontedera guys said yes. Just a few days before the festival. Another band must have pulled out at the last minute because they didn't feel like playing to a crowd of unruly kids who can't wait to make fun of you.

A little like school, during gym, when Coach Venturi (may he rot in hell) has the monthly pole-climbing competition and all of Stefano's schoolmates wrap themselves around the pole, shinny up, and touch the metal on top, so the teacher can mark their times and update their positions on the chart. When they're done they all sit around in a circle and get ready for the funniest moment, when it's Stefano's turn.

And Stefano remains glued to the friggin' pole with his arms twisted around it and looking upward, at the highest point he's supposed to reach, he looks at it and strains but he can't even make it five inches off the ground, his feet planted scandalously on the floor. And in the meantime Coach Venturi (that bastard) times him, every thirty seconds he updates the crowd and pretends to sleep or he yawns and everyone laughs. While Stefanino is gazing up and struggling with his arms and legs and has an expression on his face as if he were on the toilet and is waiting only for the teacher to say *Enough, Berardi, that'll be enough, for pity's sake.*

But the coach always keeps him there a little longer, for at least five minutes, with the excuse that he wants to give him another chance. Then when everyone is tired of laughing he lets him go with the same wisecrack every time, *Come on, Berardi, let go of the pole and head for the locker room, I've got other things to do between now and Christmas.*

Then the final gust of laughter, everyone roars and slaps each other on the back repeating *Christmas, Christmas, ha ha ha.* Stefano lets go of the pole, all sweaty and red with his eyes lowered, and the only positive thing that comes to mind is that this awful moment is still at the furthest point possible from next month's pole-climbing contest.

But last week, on his way to the locker room after the umpteenth humiliation, Fiorenzo's voice thundered through the gym, freezing everyone in his tracks, especially Stefano.

"Coach, I don't know who the bigger idiot is, you always telling the same lame joke or the kids who laugh at it every time."

Dead silence. Everyone turns around. Venturi just stands there with the stopwatch in his hand.

"Marelli, you're exempted, what more do you want?"

Fiorenzo didn't answer right away. Stefano looked at him, frozen in his tracks halfway from the pole to the locker room. He had been about to disappear, with his gym suit off and his jeans back on, ready to go back to normal life, without sweating, without huffing and puffing, without competing. *Fiorenzo, I mean it, you're exempted, what more do you want?*

"Some people win the Nobel Prize, some help people in the third world, and what do you guys have to boast about? That you know how to climb a pole. Why, that's fucking awesome, the only ones who can do it are you guys and the monkeys, congratulations."

"No one here is boasting about anything, Marelli, this is a test."

In the meantime Fiorenzo ties his hair back, approaches the pole, and grabs it with the only hand he has. He bends his other arm and hooks it around the pole, puts his legs in the right position, stares Venturi in the eyes, and climbs.

He makes it to the top in a time that isn't the best or the worst of the group, he's just as good as everyone else, everyone, that is, except Stefanino. He stops at the top and stays there, looking down with a smile somewhat crooked from the effort. He shouts, "So a guy with only one hand can do it. So what's the big deal about pole climbing?"

"No one said it's a big deal," says Venturi, looking up.

"So why do you have to be such wiseasses?"

"No one's being a wiseass, Marelli."

"Yeah, you are, and you're making fun of Stefano."

"No one's making fun of him. We're just joking because he can't do it."

"What do you make of it now?"

"Well, actually now it's worse," says Venturi, and he casts a glance at Stefanino. "In other words, Berardi, even your friend Marelli can do it with only one hand, how is it that you can't get off the ground between now and Christmas?"

And everyone laughs, even louder than before. And they shout *Christmas, Christmas.* And the laughter covers up the squeaking of Fiorenzo's thighs as he slides slowly down the pole. He touches the floor with his eyes staring at a point where there is nothing, then he straightens his T-shirt, loosens his hair, and walks away nervously toward the locker room.

As he walks past Stefanino, who is still motionless, he says, "Don't worry, I made my point even if they're pretending I didn't. Head high, soldier, head high and we'll triumph."

This happened a week ago, but Stefano and Fiorenzo haven't said a word about it, not then and not during their rehearsals at night. Not a word.

Just as they've never said a word about how anxious Stefano is about tomorrow night at Pontedera. It's worse than having to do a hundred pole climbs in a row. And in this case Fiorenzo wouldn't defend him for a second. On the contrary, he'd be as mad as a hornet, or as mad as Coach Venturi.

What if they skip a beat or are out of sync, or a string breaks during the performance? Jesus Christ, what anxiety. And Stefano never wanted to play an instrument anyway. It was Fiorenzo and Giuliano who came up with the idea of forming a band. *Come on, Sté, I can sing, I can play drums, we need a bass player.* Come on, come on, come on... and in the end Stefano said yes, because saying yes was the easiest thing in the world. But then you find yourself like you are now, with this performance to face, and then nothing is easy anymore.

In fact, tonight was going to be another sleepless night, Stefanino knows it and maybe he won't even try lying down. The only upside of these all-nighters is that he's finally catching up on his schoolwork.

Because Stefano Berardi still hasn't turned nineteen, he goes to school in addition to playing in a band, but he also has a part-time job that helps to make ends meet. It's convenient because he can do it at home, on the computer, while he's surfing the net or watching TV. And he manages to bring in three thousand euros a week, more or less.

It all started a year ago, and it involves Britney Spears cleaning bathrooms at a roadside diner, and husbands who want to see their wives surrounded by a gang of Senegalese men. But Stefano can't talk about it right now because the door bangs against the wall and in comes his brother, all pissed off.

His name is Cristiano and he's in eighth grade, when kids usually see their older brothers and sisters as role models. Usually, but not always.

"Listen up, butt breath, tell Mom I'm not eating today, okay?"

"..."

"Did you hear what I said? Are you alive? You tell her I'm not talking to her anymore."

"To who?"

"To Mom! She's the one who let him into our house, and I don't want him here."

"You don't want who?"

"The friggin' Little Champ."

"Oh. So why don't you tell her?"

"Didn't you hear anything I just said? I'm-not-talking-to-her! And I've already told her a billion and one times. But she always says *Poor Mirko, he's so far away from home and he doesn't know*

*anyone, and we've got so much room here and we have to be good
and share what we—*"

"Yeah, and you know, she's not all wrong."

"Gimme a break, Sté. You think she's right 'cause your
head's in the clouds and you don't know shit about life. But in
the real world no one shares anything with anyone. The Little
Champ, for instance, what does he share? He's always winning
and couldn't give a shit about anyone else. I don't like the races
anymore. They used to be a lot more fun."

"Because you were winning."

"Not all the time! I would win, then I would lose, then I'd
win again. With that kid instead it's no fun anymore. They even
made a special jersey for him, can you believe it? All gold, really
nice, with the words 'Little Champion' written on the back. Get
it?"

"All right, I get it, but if he's the best what do you expect?"

"Okay, so if this is my house what do I expect? I expect to be
left alone, all right? And until he leaves, I'm not talking to Mom
and I'm not even going to sit down at the table."

"Suit yourself. Who cares?"

"About what?"

"Let's say Mom doesn't care whether or not you eat with us."

"Oh yeah? Then I'll kill myself."

"How?"

"I don't know. I mean I'll go on a hunger strike. If I stop eating I'll die of starvation, right?"

"Yes, but it takes forever to die of starvation. It's quicker if
you die of thirst."

"I can't, the summer is almost here and Mr. Roberto says we
have to drink a lot."

"You don't sound like someone getting ready to die."

"No, in fact I have no intention of dying. I only want that ass-hole out of my house."

"Okay. So it doesn't matter whether you stop eating. All you have to do is tell Mom the magic word."

"What magic word?"

"Come on, you know it. Ano..."

"Ano? What are you talking about, Sté?"

"Anorexia! Mom will go out of her mind, you know."

Cristiano thinks about it for a second, then practices. "Mom, I've stopped eating because I've got anorexia..."

Hearing his own words gives him the chills. He nods and opens his eyes wide with joy at having found the perfect plan.

"Awesome! But you have to tell her for me, Stefano, tell her right away!" He disappears down the hall but then comes back and pops his head in again. "Awesome!" he says, and this time he really does disappear.

Stefano sits there at his desk for a second, facing the blank computer screen, and maybe...

Maybe he could make up an excuse for tomorrow evening. Not anorexia, but maybe if he stops drinking... but he would have had to stop a few days ago, damn it, why do great ideas always come too late? But what about sleep instead, he's way ahead of the game with sleep deprivation. Can you die of it? In the sense that at some point the struggle to stay awake could kill you? No, maybe it would be easier to go crazy. That would be perfect, too. If you go crazy they put you in the hospital, so they could forget about him playing in the concert.

With this hope in his heart, Stefano goes downstairs to lunch.

VIBRODREAM

You draw a curly black line on a sheet of paper, then three parallel lines, then another, less straight line that ends with another curl, then you write your name with a bunch of curlicues. *Tiziana Cosci.* That's what you do when you're nervous.

When you should be explaining to young people all the red tape required to open a small business, or identifying the challenges for a fresh college graduate in creating a professional profile, and instead everything veers inevitably toward another round of briscola or rummy.

When you organize an intermediate course on business English and only one kid shows up, an eighth-grader from Molise who needs tutoring.

When one afternoon a week you open the "job opportunities workshop" so the local companies can come and explain the types of young professionals they need, and instead every time you get stuck having to listen to salesmen pitching vibrating armchairs or super-convenient Depends or funeral parlors that promise to give you a "nice gift" if you let them know whenever one of the Youth Center's denizens kicks the bucket.

When you are sitting and listening and you realize that none of this makes any sense and the right thing to do would be to stand up, knock over the desk, and escape through the window, across the yard, down the county road, and run, run as fast as you can until your heart bursts.

At moments like this, Tiziana, you draw curlicues and scribbles all over a piece of paper, and sometimes, like now, you feel like drawing waves, one on top of the other, all in harmony, in agreement, soft and light...

"I know what you're going to say, Miss, that Vibrodream is just another vibrating armchair, but it's not, and do you know why not?"

"No," you answer. This is the worst kind of salesman, the type who tries to string you along with questions. Do you know why? Did you ever wonder why? Did you ever happen to? The best are the ones who don't get too enthusiastic. They come, say a couple of things about the weather, a couple of free compliments, and then a quick description of their product, fast and automatic.

But this is the type who asks questions.

"No, Miss, Vibrodream is not the usual vibrating armchair. And do you know why? Because normal armchairs vibrate, or they lift up to help seniors stand, or they massage your feet. So you might wonder what's different about Vibrodream."

"What's different about Vibrodream?"

"Vibrodream does *all* of these things at the same time. It's very convenient, both money-wise and space-wise. With your permission, our company is ready to provide you with a trial model for no money down so your clients can experience for themselves its benefits and effectiveness. We're sure that many of the people who come to your center will be excited by Vibrodream, which is why we're going to leave you the contact information you need for your clients to order one for themselves. And obviously, for every order we get...well, I'm sure you wouldn't mind if we were to express our gratitude in the form of..."

"But I really don't..."

"Not another word, come now, it's only fair. What's more, it would make us very happy. Not to mention that Vibrodream has another key feature that might make you say *What's the use of that*, but, between us, Miss, it's the most important aspect, maybe Vibrodream's strongest selling point. Do you know what it is?"

"..."

"It's that the armchair is upholstered from top to bottom with a special completely waterproof and stainproof velour fabric. And please forgive my frankness, Miss, but you need to understand that these massages are extremely relaxing, and at a certain age the bladder gets a little unpredictable, shall we say. During the trial month, accidents will happen. But while this might be a real problem with other, cheaper brands of arm-chairs, with the Vibrodream all you need to do is wipe a wet washcloth over the offending area—and maybe over the floor, as the case may be—and presto, everything will be like new."

You stop nodding your head, increase the size of the curli-cues on the page, and dig your pencil into the paper. The tip breaks, the little black pieces scatter, the paper tears. You have to get rid of the vibrating-armchair salesman immediately. Immediately.

Because in thirty seconds tops you're going to have a meltdown.

And you can't have a meltdown now. In five minutes the business English class is starting, which means you're going to be seeing Mirko, who's in eighth grade and doesn't understand the difference between *what* and *who* and so you practically have to tutor him in the basics. Like when you were twenty and used to do tutoring for makeup money and movie tickets. So if this armchair is really as relaxing as he says, you have to try it out right away. Before some senior with a leaky bladder sits on it and puts its stain-proofing to the test.

"Do you have it in navy blue?" you ask. Blue is your favorite color. Like the waves on the sea.

"Yes, of course, cobalt blue. I just picked it up from an old folks' home in Florence. It was there for a month and then they ordered ten. You're in luck, Miss, I'll go get it for you."

The salesman closes his datebook and disappears. You smile. Which is the most absurd thing in the world right now, but it comes naturally. You don't know whether it's a good sign. And all of a sudden you see yourself from the outside, sitting there, not moving, with a pencil in your hand and that smile on your face, and you feel like an idiot. It's the fifteenth time today you've felt like an idiot. You write the number 15 on the page.

The smile is frozen on your face. Maybe it's asleep. Maybe it's palsy. You touch your mouth with two fingers, there's still feeling, no palsy.

You write the number 16 on the page.

IZHEVSK

"No, no, no. No way. I said no and I mean no."

"Fiorenzo, listen, do you understand that..."

No, I won't listen, so don't ask me to understand. It's nine o'clock, and at nine o'clock we're supposed to eat, I come home with some rotisserie chicken because on Fridays we eat chicken, and then we sit down at the table to eat and while we're eating we're quiet because we're watching TV. That's how we like it.

But tonight I came home and Dad had this weird look on his face and I looked down at the table and rather than two plates there were three. At the time it seemed strange but I still hadn't figured it out, I ran off to my room, I don't know why, I wasn't thinking anything in particular but I could feel a kind of fear, like animals who when something bad happens can immediately feel it in their bones, instinctively. And in fact I opened the door and I couldn't believe my eyes.

The friggin' Little Champ of Molise was sitting there, relaxed, on my bed watching my TV and holding in his hands a back issue of *Metal Maniac* from my collection. He turned around and looked at me, all peaceful, and I tore the magazine out of his hands, put it back on the shelf where it had been in chronological order, pointed straight at him for at least ten seconds, and then went back into the kitchen with an irresistible desire to kick the shit out of something. And I started to utter a string of *no*s.

"No, no, no. No way."

"Fiorenzo, don't make such a big deal. It's just for tonight. Tomorrow I'll find a place for him to stay."

"Find one tonight, why don't you?"

"Really? Where? It's nine o'clock at night. Tonight he's staying here."

"What's wrong with a hotel?"

"A hotel? Stop talking nonsense. Tomorrow I'll find him a place."

"You already found him a place, what was the problem? Villa Berardi wasn't luxurious enough for the young master?"

Dad looked at the door that faces the hall and lowered his voice. "They don't want him anymore."

"So if they don't want him does that mean that I'm stuck with him?"

"Lower your voice. He can hear you."

"Who cares if he can hear me? In fact, I want him to hear me. I want him to hear that he's busted my balls!" I turn toward the door and I shout, "Kid, you've busted my balls!" Because he should know, the friggin' Little Champ, that he might have fooled everyone else but not me. He's the town hero, when he walks down the street everyone comes out of the stores to greet him, every Easter they have a contest at the elementary school for the best poem and this year the winning poem was about him. And Dad expects me to believe that he can't find him a place to sleep? No, I won't fall for it, it's all part of his sneaky, slimy plan. First he takes over my town, then my house, now he wants to steal my room? If I'm not careful, he's going to take everything I own.

"Why don't the Berardis want him anymore?"

"I don't know, the mother says that Cristiano doesn't get along with him."

"You see? Even his teammates can't stand him."

"Without Mirko there would be no team, don't you get it? The sponsors, including the Berardis, pay because he is on it. Yes, their son competes, but the only reason he gets his picture in the paper is because Mirko wins. You should hear how pissed off they get when he passes the finish line and doesn't straighten out his jersey and you can't read the logo and—"

"I don't care, Dad, it's none of my business. The only thing I know is that I need my room, I have to print some stuff for the band. Tomorrow's a big day because we're playing at..."

I get to this point and then I stop. What does Dad care anyway?

He opens the hot pack with the chicken inside. I had them add some roasted potatoes; I got them because tonight I wanted to feel right. He doesn't say anything about the potatoes, the same way he doesn't ask about the band or about what's happening tomorrow that's so important, he doesn't ask anything about anything. He just serves the potatoes and pieces of chicken on the plates. Three plates.

"Listen, Fiorenzo, it's just for tonight, Mirko's going to sleep here tonight and that's all there is to it, okay?"

"Oh yeah? Oh yeah? Oh yeah?" In my head a million possible sentences and strategies spin around, like the pictures in a slot machine spinning faster and faster and you can't even recognize them and in the end I say the only thing I didn't want to say. "Oh yeah? That's all there is to it? Let me put it to you this way, Dad. It's either him or me."

Dad lifts up his head and looks at me, but he doesn't say a word. He squints his eyes as if he didn't understand what I just said. Truth is I didn't understand it either. But now it's out there and all I can do is keep this serious look on my face as if to say *Yes, exactly, that's just what I wanted to say*, something along those lines.

"It's either him or me," I repeat. And I fold my arms over my chest. They're skinny and white and still untattooed, to my embarrassment. That's why this pose doesn't give me an air of power. So I put them back down along my sides.

"Wait, I didn't realize," he says, "you have someone who will put you up?"

I can't believe it. I can't believe it. I mean, I thought I had just thrown down the gauntlet. It's dark and if I leave the house who knows where I'm going to spend the night, the month, my life. And instead Dad thinks it's a great idea. Because my room is actually too small to fit two, and maybe I'll stay up late and there's a risk that the super champion from Molise won't get enough rest. So if I left everything would be perfect.

"'Bye, Dad, goodnight. Sweet dreams to you and your little champ," I say. And after words like that I should leave immediately. But instead I look all around, standing stock still under the fluorescent light of the kitchen.

Because, give me a break, if I go I should take something with me. I don't mean a suitcase, but at least a few things. For a second I think of the hoboes in comic strips, who are always wearing sandals and have a pole over their shoulder with a little bundle of stuff tied together on one end. I don't have sandals but I am wearing clogs, which are more or less the same. So all right then, this is how I'll go. Like someone from the comics in the Sunday paper.

I head toward the door, with my pajamas and clogs, that's all I need.

"Fiorenzo, don't be an idiot, where the hell are you going?" Dad says. It's too obvious that he doesn't believe me one bit. He says it because he has to. Like the vodka commercials that tell you to drink in moderation.

"Look, Dad, it's none of your business where I'm going. I'm an adult now and I'm leaving, so I won't bother you anymore."

Yes, now is the time. Now I can leave with my head held high. It's none of his business where I'm going, I'm not scared and I'm walking straight down my path. Because in reality I do have a place to go. I'm going to the bait-and-tackle shop.

I leave just the way I am, and I'm outside in the night.

Full speed ahead and straight down the road
Where I'm bound who the hell knows
Don't you see, it's just who I am
Indestructible
Danger, danger, save your soul
Read the writing on the wall
Where you live, the angels are blind
Midnight, and I'm speeding down the road
Midnight, and I'm doing fine on the road
I'm doing fine
On a road that never ends.

I sing as loud as I can. I shouldn't because in half an hour we're rehearsing and I risk burning out my voice, but the scooter is really loud and if I don't shout my voice gets drowned out by the firing pistons. And these lyrics are fantastic, every time I hear them I feel like I'm living inside them, tonight more than ever.

Even if it's not midnight, it's nine o'clock and rather than the highway I take the county road, the only serious road in this area, and this cow town hugs it like all the others on the plain, like nasty little ticks attached to a giant snake passing through.

I mean, I don't know if ticks can stick to snakes. I figure they're too hard and the snakes will get the better of them. That's the secret, being hard. And I'm hard, hard as a rock. Where I go the angels are blind, but fuck, I'm indestructible.

But damn it's cold. These pajamas really are light, the scooter's going at top speed and I lean forward to try not to feel the ice-cold air entering through the blue fabric to my skin and down to the bone. And if I wake up with a sore throat tomorrow I'm fucked. We're fucked. I don't even want to think about it.

I pass a bunch of cars. I'm cold. I'm hungry.

That nice chicken with potatoes that I picked up at the deli is being eaten by Dad and the Little Champ, while here I am on the county road with my ass frozen and my stomach empty. I'm so mad I take the roundabout too fast and almost skid into a wipeout.

For a couple of years now there have been roundabouts everywhere, and before each one is a sign. But for the right and left exits there're never any indications while for straight ahead there's a sign that says ALL DIRECTIONS. So I think to myself, if that one goes in all directions what good are the other two? I dunno. I could ask a cop, but better if I don't mess with cops right now. First, I haven't got a permit. I had my scooter modified, switching the gas pedal to the left, and I can drive it just fine, but the thing is I don't have a permit to drive it. And right now I don't even have a helmet, or clothes. So I'd better not go looking for trouble.

Besides, even if the exits off the roundabout really do take you somewhere, I'm the last person a cop's going to tell. Because maybe they lead to secret places with religious cults hidden in the fields, private bathhouses reserved for mayors and town commissioners, or military bases where they work on top-secret projects. That's why there's nothing written on the signs.

In the Soviet Union there was this town called Izhevsk, and since it was where they used to manufacture Kalashnikovs the Russians didn't even mark it on the map: the town wasn't supposed to exist. I know because when I was in elementary school I always used to watch the Giro d'Italia on TV with Dad, and every time they did a close-up of a racer he would say *I know that guy, he's a buddy of mine, I used to race with him in the junior leagues.* But my hero was Pavel Tonkov, who was a phenomenal Russian cyclist as well as the only racer my dad didn't know personally. How could he know him, he came from Izhevsk, that mysterious little town you can't find on the map and the only thing we know is that it's at the foot of the Urals.

So maybe if I take a right or a left at one of these roundabouts I'll end up on a strange journey and end up right there, in Izhevsk. I'll move there and my whole life will get back on track. I'll find a job at the Kalashnikov factory and in my free time go fishing on the Izh River, which gives the town its name, and maybe while I'm fishing I'll meet Pavel Tonkov and we'll become friends.

Here's another roundabout, slow down. And maybe I really will take a right or a left, yes, I just might be... but on second thought, the climate in Izhevsk must be worse than here, and they don't make Kalashnikovs anymore, and I read somewhere that Tonkov never went back to Russia and nowadays is managing a hotel in Spain.

Midnight, and I'm speeding down the highway
Midnight, and I'm doing fine on the highway
I'm doing fine
On a road that never ends.

It's not midnight, it's not the highway.
And if I'm doing fine, well, it sure doesn't look like that to me.

BRITNEY AT THE REST STOP

Villa Berardi is supposed to be called Villa Isola, which was the name of old man Berardi's first wife. Except she was a strange lady who never talked and when he found someone better he had Isola locked up in a kind of asylum, and from then on everyone called it Villa Berardi. But the old-timers still called it the Crazy Lady's place.

I ring the video intercom and Stefano says *Come on in I'll be right down*. Right down? I don't think so. He always takes forever to leave his room, what with closing the programs and turning off the computer and walking all the way to the garage. Me, instead, I'm half an hour early, because at the shop there's no TV and nothing to read except for rod and reel catalogs, not even a sofa to sit on. I figure that whether you live in a McMansion or in the storeroom of a bait-and-tackle shop makes all the difference in how much time you like to spend at home.

The friggin' Little Champ lived here for four months, not half bad. And it makes me laugh out loud to think that now he's living in my tiny room, with my dad next door snoring up a storm and the irrigation-ditch stench coming in through the window, the narrow walls surrounding the bed and the piles of records, CDs, and DVDs and magazines and posters that look like they're going to fall all over you when you're lying down on

the bed looking up...my records, my magazines, my posters...
there, the urge to laugh is gone. I keep walking, staring at the
globe lights illuminating the lawn and listening to the exagger-
ated sound of my footsteps crunching the gravel.

I'm wearing whatever I could find in the shop. Over my
pajamas a camouflage fishing vest and rubber boots instead of
clogs. With each step my boots make the sound of a duck hitting the ground after it's been hit by gunshot.

At the end of the driveway is a wrought-iron parapet that
covers the cars and Stefano's scooter and his brother Cristiano's
bike. Bordering the driveway is neatly cut grass along with a
marble ping-pong table and the few nice plants you can try to
grow in these parts. Because between the dampness and the
black reclaimed swampland, nature is pretty severe in the land-
scaping possibilities it offers around here. Brambles, nettles,
and invasive ivy do okay, but fruit trees have a hard time of it
and for flowers it's really tough.

The Berardis spent a fortune on this garden. They drained
the land with giant pumps and brought in good topsoil from
somewhere, truckload after truckload. They can afford it.
They're the richest family in Muglione and if it were still the
Middle Ages they'd be our lords and masters and every now and
then they'd come into town to beat us up for fun.

There are four Berardis but when they go on a road trip they
take two cars, the dad with Stefano and the mom with Cristiano, and they leave half an hour apart. That way, in the event
of a fatal accident, there will still be two Berardis in the world
to carry on the family legacy. Like the Coca-Cola bosses — Sirio
once told me that Coca-Cola has a top-secret recipe that only the
two bosses know, Mr. Coca and Mr. Cola, who in fact live sepa-
rately and never meet, because let's say they meet in a building

and the building collapses on top of them, Coca-Cola would basically die with them.

At the time I believed him, but I should add that I must have been twelve, thirteen max, definitely younger than fourteen because he told me while he was taking us to a race. And then, while I was racing, since as you pedal your mind goes off on a tangent, the thought crossed my mind that maybe Mr. Cola was also the owner of half of Pepsi-Cola, and then he could never meet Mr. Pepsi either. And I started to think that the poor guy might have a ton of money but he sure led a lonely life. I wanted to tell Sirio as soon as I finished the race, but then we did badly and Dad chewed us out, calling us a bunch of wusses, and I didn't say anything to anyone.

In the meantime it starts to rain. All day long we've had typical Muglione weather, meaning nothing: no clouds, no wind, and no sun, an empty palette where God says I'll deal with it later, I'll deal with it later, I'll deal with it, and then he never does.

The garage door is open, I go in, and every time I do I find myself surrounded by all this fantastic equipment and I tell myself that we're a band that really rocks.

Old Berardi, Stefanino's grandfather, made his money owning one of the first furniture stores in the area. Then his daughter came up with the idea of specializing in furniture for boats, and even though I don't know what difference there is between furniture for a boat and for dry land, the Berardis got even bigger. They do ads on the local TV channels and are the top sponsor for Dad's team, whose full name is supposed to be the Muglione-Berardi Furniture Cycling Union.

But it's no thanks to furniture that Metal Devastation has this awesome equipment. A 32-input mixer with a professional voice setup, two Marshall valve amps with headboards, a Tama drum set with double bass and a ton of tom-toms and hi-hats, modified B.C. Rich guitar and bass for a more powerful sound, and I sing into a microphone that they only make by special order. When we went to Siena to buy everything, the clerk called the boss and the boss asked us if we were going on tour. We said we were, and sooner rather than later.

But this over-the-top sonic power, like I said, doesn't come to us via Berardi Furniture. No, we owe it all to Stefanino himself, and the money he makes from a little job he does on the side. It started about a year ago, and I remember it well because one day Stefano was really worried and he told me everything and swore me to secrecy.

Basically, Stefanino enjoyed surfing websites that had jokes and other dumb stuff. That's how he is, laughing his ass off at wordplay that doesn't make anyone else laugh, like *I'm hungry, let's go to Turkey.* Or *What's the smelliest city? Pittsburgh.* Shit like that.

And he really enjoyed funny mashups. He made his own and sent them to those sites, using a nickname, SteMetal. Photoshopping ridiculous situations, like a goat in a bikini, Britney Spears cleaning the toilets at a rest stop, a decrepit old man feeling up Monica Bellucci from behind. It didn't take long for SteMetal's mashups to build a cult following. Because the quality was phenomenal: you'd see the scene and know it was fake, but at the same time you couldn't help but say *Oh my God, it's so real,* because right in front of your eyes there she was, Britney with a toilet brush in her hand, and the shadow on the bathroom wall was perfect, and she smiled at you from within the lighting and atmosphere typical of pay toilets at rest stops. So was the old guy tormenting Monica Bellucci and in the meantime leering at the viewer... like I was saying, you know it can't be true, but you look at it and can feel hope building for all of us.

And it was through this last creation that Stefano moved on to adult material. A guy sent him a picture of a half-naked woman and asked him to show her in bed with a porn star. It took Stefano only twenty minutes. He took a shot from a hard-core scene, stuck the woman in the porn actress's place, adjusted the light and shadows, and sent it back to the guy. Perfect. The guy thanked him with words like *You're a genius, you're a god* and posted it on a sex forum. And that opened a floodgate of requests.

Hundreds, from all over the world. He couldn't keep up with them. Stefano goes to school and plays in a really serious band; it's not like he can spend his whole life in front of the computer cutting and pasting pictures of naked people. He explains it in an e-mail he sends all these guys. And almost all of them reply in the same way in Italian or in English or in some other language but all of them bursting with hormones. *I realize you don't have time for everyone but if you can find some for me I'll pay you, and generously.*

They started sending him money in envelopes, then he opened up a PayPal account and now they pay him online, to the tune of three thousand euros a week. He could make a lot more but he doesn't have time to respond to all the requests. Which at first he thought would mostly be from men surrendering to the reality that they would never be able to fuck a certain woman — actress model wife's sister much hotter than the wife — so they would pay him a ton of money to at least *see* themselves getting it on, in an image that made it look as if it really did happen.

But this was a minority of his work. It happened, sure, but most of the time a husband sent him pictures of his wife, or a guy sent pictures of his girlfriend. Basically, of women they could have whenever they wanted, and so Stefano didn't understand the need for a fake picture. These guys asked him to create a scene in which the wife or girlfriend cheated on them with another guy. Take your pick: often a super-hung black guy or even another woman, or maybe a specific individual like a friend a colleague a relative, and in these cases they would also send him the picture of the guy Stefano had to cut and paste into their company.

And this is the point where it started to bother Stefano. He was afraid the mashups would be used as false proof of cheating, to ask for a divorce or something along those lines, and then maybe his perfect work would end up in a courtroom and his name would pop up and he'd spend the rest of his life in jail. That's why he called me that night and told me everything.

He had even come up with a plan. He would cancel his Internet service and e-mail address, wait till dark and take his computer out into a field, set fire to it, bury it, and then return home; before going to bed he would say a prayer and hope that from that day on the whole business would be over and done with.

To me it sounded perfect, but then he told me how much money he was making through this stuff and then I said *Let's think about it for a few days.*

And in fact everything became clear as the days passed. The people who didn't receive their photos wrote again, begging to be satisfied. And often the ones doing the begging were the two together, husband and wife, him and her: they weren't on their way to a courtroom; they wanted to use the mashup to get off. Because people from all over the world like this kind of an idea, the wife goes to bed with an unknown black guy or a colleague or a friend of the family. They look at the picture and they get hot.

We tried to understand the phenomenon, but it's not easy. Also because we're not exactly experts in sexual matters.

I know, I know, heavy-metal imagery is all about wild sex, every night a different woman, females grabbed by the hair and spun around till they crumble in your hands. Yeah, yeah, but heavy-metal imagery also includes fights against dragons and sea monsters and world domination by the law of metal, so let's forget about imagery, okay? That's why it's called imagery, it's stuff we imagine, but reality is something completely different.

The reality is that once Stefanino kissed his cousin in middle school. She was worried about kissing some guy she liked, so she wanted to be prepared when she got there. And since his cousin was very outgoing, she tried the same test with me one month later. This is the sum of our sexual experience so far.

The rest we only know indirectly, thanks to the stories of Antonio, who many nights after rehearsal tells us about the stuff he does with his girlfriends. And we in the band every so often tell him that the next time he should try to do this or that, if it's feasible he does and then the next time he tells us what her reaction was, maybe she said *Oh, I like that*, and we listen, holding our breath, and feel as if we, too, were there with that girl, and we get as excited as animals.

So maybe we can understand the people who get excited by Stefano's mashups. It's something we can understand, yes, and we can especially accept the three thousand euros a week deposited into Stefano's account and the mind-blowing equipment that fills up the garage and turns us into a band that really rocks. And...

Vrooom.

The garage door opens with a screech that makes the blood rush to my hair. Maybe a tree fell on the garage, maybe a floor of the villa collapsed, or else Giuliano has arrived. I turn around and see him. He waves to me.

He must weigh two-hundred-and-twenty pounds, but he's always bare-chested. Summer and winter, Giuliano is always bare-chested; he says that T-shirts are one of the cages of the system. The only thing he's wearing is a pair of overalls with the logo of his dad's garage, where he works even though he doesn't like fixing cars. He's really good at taking them apart piece by piece, but putting them back together again is a pain. He says that the day his dad quits, he's going to change everything and open up a giant car crushing business. But in the meantime there he is learning the trade and at night he takes his frustration out on the drums. He's got the drumsticks in his hands and he squeezes his eyes shut, opens his mouth, and lets out a belch from the bottom of his stomach that even I can hear.

"What's wrong?" he says.

"Me? Nothing. Why?"

"No reason." He goes to the drums and sits down. He lights a cigarette.

"Giuliano, listen up, if you want to smoke go outside, it messes up my voice."

"Don't be a pain, come on."

"No, don't you be a pain. Tomorrow we've got the concert."

"Exactly, and we're going to kick some ass, just you wait," he says. He sits on the stool, adjusts himself, gets close to the cymbals. And he keeps staring at me.

"Oh," he finally says. "Listen up, tomorrow night are you coming dressed like that?"

I take a good look at myself. In blue pajamas, a camouflage vest on top, and rubber boots below. I look like someone who's trying to fish for carp from his bed.

"Are you nuts? You think I would go like this?"

"I don't know. I'm just asking." He burps again, raises his drumsticks, and says, "I've come up with a new tempo, listen."

He lowers his head and starts off with a furious drumroll, the double bass below and a crash to the platters here and there. He plays like a chainsaw that opens to become a machine gun that shoots at the blades of a helicopter while someone next to it is cutting the grass.

I've got a feeling that tomorrow we really are going to kick some ass.

DAMN MOTHERBOARDS

Divo Nocentini is seventy-three and his job used to be fixing TV sets. As well as radios and the first VCRs, but mainly television sets. He had a shop downtown that was called Nocentini Electronics and inside there were piles of broken TVs with the symptoms written on a piece of tape attached to the screen. DOESN'T WORK, NO VOLUME, PICTURE YELLOW.

Each with its own ailment, each with its little problem inside that might be a loose connection, a burnt-out fuse, or stuff like that. He took them one at a time, they were big heavy TVs and he carried them outside to a bench, because Divo liked to work outdoors. People would come by and stop to talk about the mayor's office doing fuck all, the Giro d'Italia, the best time to plant zucchini, and in the meantime they'd admire the thousands of strange pieces inside a TV that, when connected, created the magic of showing a man in Milan saying hello while you're sitting in your living room watching TV.

Then the motherboards arrived and it was all over.

Divo Nocentini twists his mouth and spits on the ground. It's dark anyway, no one is around and the street is so full of broken glass and shredded tires that some spit on the asphalt can only beautify the panorama.

The motherboards ruined everything; specialized centers sprung up for every brand and now when your TV set breaks you have to take it to these effete gentlemen in white shirts who open it and change the motherboard and ask you for a shitload of money. Change an entire motherboard: it makes no sense. It's as if you had a callus on your foot and you went to the doctor and he said *No problem, we'll amputate your leg.*

The effete gentlemen in white shirts specialized in a single brand, the others they wouldn't even touch. And for serious professionals like Divo, who made no distinction between the various TVs, and not even between a TV and a toaster, there was suddenly no place.

Just as there is no place here in Muglione to spend time after dinner. Ever since Eugenio died they all get together at the Youth Center, which is right across the street, but it closes at five and if you want anything to drink it's strictly BYOB. The only bar left open at night is the one at the gas station on the county road, and before you go in you'd better say your prayers. It's always full of Romanians. Or Albanians. Or Moroccans. Especially tonight. At some point they started yelling at each other and banging their chairs, he was in the corner playing cards with Mazinger and Baldato, they told them to knock it off and one of the guys got right in his face and asked him if he had a problem. And Divo and Mazinger and Baldato grumbled, but quietly and only to each other, and only long after the guy had walked away and couldn't hear them anymore.

The more Divo thought about it the madder he got. Those Chinese manufacturers that open TV service centers and send motherboards from China and steal work from you. Those Romanians and Albanians who come into town and steal the peace. Why can't everyone stay in their own country? Divo went on his honeymoon to San Remo and did his military service in Civitavecchia, but that was enough, then he stayed in his place. If everyone did the same the world would be better, or good enough, at least. Instead nowadays the people born in this town can't find a job and can't even enjoy their retirement, and have to rush home because these streets aren't safe for anything after sundown.

Once upon a time you didn't have to lock the door before going to bed. Once upon a time a handshake was all the contract you needed. Once upon a time...

And he freezes. For a while he's been hearing a sound, but now it's inside his head without having ever entered it. And now that he recognizes it, it's too late to turn around and take another route. It's the sound of metal striking something, and that something is the side of a scooter, and the person hitting it is a thug who looks Slavic. But now he's not striking it anymore. Now he's looking at Divo. He has giant bolt cutters in his hands and a pair of eyes that are worse than the knives he definitely has in his pockets, unless they're syringes or pistols, or syringes and pistols together.

"What you looking? What you want?"

Divo doesn't reply. He doesn't want anything, what could he want? He was passing by. If he had noticed the sound he would have passed by someplace else, but he was thinking of those damned motherboards and didn't notice. But how can he explain this to the Slav?

"What you want? Get lost!"

Divo nods yes but he doesn't move. He's trying to remember how to turn around and disappear. His heart is beating fast, every now and then it skips a beat.

The Slav pulls himself up, fixes his T-shirt, and is maybe getting ready to jump him. His heart beats even faster. They look each other in the eye. Slavic eye to cataract eye.

Then, from around the corner, on the other side of the road, something all white appears. White skin, white hair, covered with blank newspaper pages to shield itself from the rain. It's Mazinger and Baldato, and Repetti is there, too.

They see him, say hello, then they see the Slav there in the middle.

"Hey, Divo, what's going on here?" they say, and stop in their tracks.

Divo doesn't reply. Come on, it's clear what's going on, isn't it? Does he really have to say?

"Old men," says the Slav, "mind you business, okay? Go home."

He says it, but his tone is different from before. He's not as scary to Divo. In fact, now Divo can talk. What's more, now he can't keep quiet.

"No, buster, this *is* our business. This is our home."

Divo's heart beats faster when he says this. He starts to tremble. But not in a bad way. No, it's strange but it's not bad. On the contrary. It's a little like when he used to make love to his wife, once upon a time, six thousand years ago.

The Slav looks at him, turns and studies the others, and stoops down to the ground. Maybe he's collecting a knife or a syringe. Instead he picks up the bolt cutters, gives a kick to the scooter, and suddenly rushes toward Divo.

What can he do? He covers his face with his hands, stops breathing, and gets ready to die.

The guy is getting closer and closer, the cutters in his hands and his eyes staring straight at Divo. But when he's right on top of him, the Slav jumps to the other side of the street and keeps running until he disappears into the perfidious darkness of the town.

And here, by the light of the streetlamp, four old men meeting in the rain are still standing. They don't know what to say or do. Their hearts are in their throats and they give each other serious looks.

The thrill inside, they all had it. It's clear, palpable. They thought they'd never feel it again, had almost forgotten it, but here it is, good as new, it's come back in without knocking. And they'll do everything to make sure it never goes away.

BEEP, BEEP, BEE-BEE-BEEP

From the BitterSweet Girl blog.

Post published today at 11:07 p.m.

Dear Friends,

Here we are at the end of a sunless Friday. And tonight the weather decided to liven things up with a little rain. Well, the best thing you can say about some days is that they finally come to an end.

Today in the office a boy felt sick and fainted. The ambulance arrived fifteen minutes later, even though the clinic is only a couple of blocks away. In the meantime he revived, but they still took him away because there wasn't a doctor on board and they couldn't take the responsibility of saying that he was all right.

To fall ill while you're waiting in line to find out whether there's a job for you: that tells you everything you need to know about our country. The situation is grim, with no sign of better things to come. An outrageous government and an opposition party that doesn't know where to throw its hat. Any change, even in the next few centuries, seems impossible.

But it wouldn't be that difficult. In America it didn't take long. The Americans decided to change and they chose Obama. I have a lot of confidence in him. He has brave new ideas, a vision of the world and specific projects, he illustrated them to the American people and the people decided to vote for him. Kudos for them this time.

And kudos for us, too, for making it to Friday. I didn't think I could. Now I'm going to have a cup of milk with cereal. After a day like today I deserve some cookies, too. I was about to say "little cookies," but combinations like that make me sad: little cookie, little snack, little stroll.

Kisses (not little kisses),
BitterSweet Girl

Five minutes and the first two comments have already arrived. The usual suspects, obviously.

From your cousin:

Enjoy your milk and many, many cookies, love! ;) Obama yes we can!

And from Raffaella:

I feel so sorry for that boy, poor kid! Is he doing better now?
Was he cute? Lol!

At least your cousin lives in Milan, but Raffaella lives in the next room, and the two of you are about to have milk and cereal together. Does it make any sense?

And the only comment you wanted was from the American, your foreign admirer who visits your blog every day. He lives in Mountain View, California, those words about Obama were put in there for him. Even if he still hasn't come by to read you today, as the magic little program tells you. Maybe he's away for a job, an interesting job that takes him all over America. He's an active person who doesn't spend his whole life in front of the computer.

Even the story about the boy fainting in line was put in there for him. You needed it to draw a parallel between the Italian and American situations, but it didn't really happen. I mean it did, someone really did feel sick at the Youth Center, but it was an old man. He was sitting at a table playing cards but it wasn't that he felt sick. He'd just drunk too much. But that wasn't a story worth repeating.

You're always very clear, no alcohol and no cigarettes at the Youth Center. But old people are set in their ways, half the time they don't understand and the other half they pretend not to. Often, in the middle of a particularly intense card game, someone might get confused and beckon you with a finger to order a Cinzano or a glass of white wine: this is the most depressing thing in the universe if you think of the projects you had in mind when you came back from Germany. That's why you put so much venom in your voice when you answer *I'm not a waitress and this is not a bar, and let me remind you that in here it's strictly forbidden to drink alcohol.* So the old people, who nod their heads but in reality couldn't care less, bring their own bottles from home. And maybe it's because of the prohibitionist atmosphere you've created, but now at the Youth Center they're all drinking like there's no tomorrow and it was clear that sooner or later someone was going to get sick.

Yes, this would be a great story to tell, a true story that shows everything you need to know about this country. A thirty-two-year-old young professional who graduated at the top of her class, with a drawerful of master's degrees and international diplomas, who finds herself playing babysitter to a gang of alcoholic seniors and has to do all she can not to lose a useless super-temporary job with almost symbolic pay.

But for the moment the less said about this story the better. You have to be patient and take good notes, then when your contract expires look for someone who will publish a no-holds-barred account of your experience. Perfect, yes, you've got no shortage of material and writing skills, all you need is time to type it up on the computer. And if there is a positive side to this town without nightspots, movie theaters, art shows, or friends, it's that you've got loads of free time for projects like this. Except that you're wasting it, Tiziana, you're wasting your time. With this blog, for example. And also with the English lessons you're giving to that middle school kid who doesn't understand anything. It was supposed to be an intermediate course for business English and instead you're tutoring a child. How much more depressing can it get? And what will be your next step? Washing your uncle's car for ten euros? Are you waiting for a tooth to fall out so the tooth fairy can bring you some money?

Enough, you have to cut this stuff to the bone, eliminate any waste of time. In fact, today you told Mirko that you can help him only with his English, for anything more he'd have to look for someone else. Maybe he is a champion on a bike, but at school he's at the rock bottom of the class. It's not that he has bad study habits or doesn't understand: it's that the information doesn't penetrate. You talk and explain and one second later it's as if you said nothing. Poor kid.

Stop right there. Stop thinking so much. Otherwise you'll feel bad and end up doing his homework for him and writing his compositions and practically taking his middle school exam for him, the umpteenth time you do nothing for yourself and waste time on someone who doesn't even appreciate it.

Enough. Now you have to write that report, not a second to lose. You take the computer, create a new file and start typing, and not...

BEEP, BEEP, BEE-BEE-BEEP.

Someone's honking his horn on the street. To the rhythm of a stadium cheer.

It's Pavel. Raffaella's boyfriend. Speaking of wasted time.

From dawn to five he's a construction worker and at night he restocks the shelves at the supermarket, but he's still got half an hour left to spend with Raffa. He's Romanian, but you don't know from which city. He never says anything about where he's from or his family, you only know that he's Romanian and he's convinced that he's a born comedian.

BEEP, BEEP, BEE-BEE-BEEP.

Oh, and he ignores the existence of doorbells.

Raffaella always waits until the last minute to get ready. She dresses and puts on her makeup, even if he spends only half an hour and they never go anywhere.

And while you really do like Raffa, you can hardly say she's the prettiest girl in the world. She's not tall, or thin, or even the type where you could say *Well, maybe if she were a little taller, or thinner*...no, Raffaella is ugly no matter how you slice it. You're sorry to think that way, but you do. Actually, it's not that you think that way, it's just the way it is.

But Raffaella has the great virtue of not creating problems for herself. She knows how to handle men—even this getting ready at the last minute, while Pavel is honking his horn, is deliberate. She says that to hold on to a man you have to make him wait.

Her advice sounds like words from a distant past, lessons for young ladies from a 1950s manual dedicated to aspiring housewives. Maybe that's what your mother did to snare your father, who at the time was a construction worker like Pavel and still hadn't become the Porchetta King. And maybe it'll work with Pavel, whose mentality is also very 1950s.

But in all honesty, the only thing you care about is that Raffaella and Pavel not make too much noise.

"Come on, open up!" Pavel shouts from behind the door. Forget using the doorbell. "Open up, I'm a Romanian burglar and I want to rob you!"

Raffa is still in her room getting ready, so you have to open up before the neighbors get angry or scared, depending on individual intelligence.

You open the door and Pavel is standing there, as always, with his index finger and thumb in a gesture as if his hand were a pistol. He smiles at you and says "Bang bang," then he gives you three kisses on your cheeks and enters. Always the same joke. Like your father and your uncle and all the men in your family, each with his own silly joke that he repeats all his life in the same way, as inevitable as a conviction, and they don't even think about the possibility that after decades it stops being funny. Maybe you're partly to blame, since every time you force yourself to smile you encourage them to continue.

Pavel comes in. His dirty-blond hair full of gel and slicked back, a shiny white Adidas tracksuit with gold stripes, identical Adidas shoes, and that mustache that looks like a long thin caterpillar crawling across his lip.

He plops down on the sofa, but first he hands you a plastic bag from the supermarket. Every night he finds a way to sneak something out, little things that he thinks make girls happy. A box of cookies, a pint of ice cream, a shower cap, this time a basil plant.

What's worse is that he often gets it right. This basil plant is so cute.

"So, Miss, how we doing? What you women doing home alone?"

"Nothing. The usual."

"Of course. But are we going to find you man?" He winks an eye. "You know, Tiziana, I got friends who are perfect. Like Nick, you know Nick?"

"..."

"Come on, my tall friend, the one who work at construction site with me. You know he like you."

"Does he even know me?"

"No, but he like you. I told him you a schoolteacher."

"I'm not a schoolteacher."

"And that you've got nice tits. Not big like Raffaella's, but better face and ass. And he like you."

"..."

"So tomorrow I bring him, okay?"

"No, thanks anyway, you're so kind, but no."

"I bring him, I bring him. I was bringing him tonight but he run away."

"Is he shy?"

"No, but there was problem. We stop on way. Paolino's scooter was outside. Strange because he always bring it in; instead it was out on the street."

"Paolino is another friend of yours?"

"He work with me at construction site. But he too little for you, eighteen; don't try to outsmart me, Miss, you for Nickie, okay?"

"How could I forget."

"Good. Paolino has super-hopped-up scooter, and he really love it. We talk about big cars, Nickie and me. Nickie is saving up to buy rally car, because he love rallies, he live for rallies."

"I'm already in love..."

"But Paolino is always talking about scooter, which he say takes off like missile and almost flies; he even had F14 logo designed on top. You know what F14 is?" Pavel opens his arms like two wings and makes a sound with his mouth like a jet engine, and then at intervals a sputtering, like bombs being dropped on third-world countries.

"Yes, the airplane, I know."

"So you see, we were coming to you tonight, me and Nick. So me and Raffa here on sofa and you and Nick in you bed, right?"

"If you bring him here I'll call the cops ... I'm joking. Go on ..."

"But in street we see Paolino's scooter, chained to pole. And we come up with idea. He say his scooter flies? So we tie it with rope to limb of tree in front of his house. That way the next morning we wait for him outside and say *Oh my God, Paolino, look up in sky! It's your scooter. It really does fly!*" Pavel laughs so hard he falls back on the sofa.

"..."

"But first we had to break chain, and Nick always has these giant bolt-cutters in car, because he used to steal scooters and bikes sometimes, in early days. Not anymore, now he just work. But the bolt-cutters are still in his car, so we're getting ready to break chain, but while we there old man comes down street. And he stand there looking. I stand up from scooter and look at him but Nick runs away ..."

Pavel stops talking and turns toward the bedrooms. "RAF-FAELLA, WHERE ARE YOU? I'VE GOT TO GET UP EARLY TOMORROW!"

"All right, excuse me, but how did things end up with the old guy?"

"With old guy? Oh, nothing, then some other old guys come and I run away, too. I'm not going to get in trouble over a joke."

You nod yes blankly, you smile, lean your back against the window, above the radiator that for some reason stays on until June. The window makes a noise that only you can hear, a slight but sinister *crick* that stings your bones.

"Pavel, I'm here, are you coming?" Raffaella is at the door with her arms outstretched, wearing a tight white miniskirt and striped top. Her compressed flesh pops out from above and below.

Pavel sees her and jumps to his feet, takes two steps and gives her a bear hug. He kisses her, she kisses him, and their hands rub all over each other.

You adjust yourself a tiny bit with your back against the window. Another *crick* from the glass. Glass is made from sand, even if it seems impossible. They heat it up a lot and it becomes a luminous paste, then they work it and in the end it becomes glass. But how do they do it? How do they do it?

The kiss continues against the wall right across from her, with tongues writhing and every now and then a burst of laughter or a gurgling sound.

But how do they do it. How do they do it.

THE PEASANT AND THE LORD

All right, maybe a coma is the closest thing to death, but sleeping in the back room with the live bait comes pretty close. Believe me, after last night I know what I'm talking about.

It wasn't a great idea, I admit it, but I had no choice. In fact, I have to sleep here tonight and for who knows how many nights, with the hope that maybe I'll get used to it. And it's not good to get used to something like this.

To the smell of worms, and especially to the sound. And people may think they know worms, but there are a thousand kinds: earthworms, night crawlers, Korean lugworms, rock worms, white worms, sandworms, bloodworms, peanut worms, bobbit worms, honey worms, rag worms... but the king of live bait is always *him*, the flesh fly larva, otherwise known as the maggot, and he's the one that makes you feel as if you were locked up in a tomb.

Last night, after finding a cot, I made a nice bed with chum sacks, covered myself with a tarp, and said goodnight to all my enemies; I don't need anyone, I'm fine the way I am. But I wasn't fine the way I was. The smell of the worms was the first problem. It's not even stinky, it's just strange, maybe a little salty. But I forgot it as soon as I heard the noise. I was in the dark with my eyes open and it got louder and louder.

Luckily the sound of the refrigerator kicking in or a car passing by drowned it out every once in a while. But then it came back, a kind of steady, constant rustling, a rustling mixed with something quietly scratching. Millions of worms and billions of little legs twisting and turning all night in the dark inside little boxes trying to find a way out that wasn't there.

And there I was, lying down on sacks of amaretto-and-cherry-flavored chum, thinking that this was the sound you heard in the coffin. In fact, there it must be even louder because you're completely isolated in a narrow wooden box, and the worms are on top of and even inside you doing whatever they want.

I could write some nice lyrics about it for the band. It's a theme that different groups have sung about but people never get tired of, I think. So last night I started coming up with the first verses of the song.

But another thought filled my head: my mother really is underground, and she's been hearing this sound for a long time. Maybe things are better now, a year has gone by and the worms have finished their job, I think. But it's still really awful. It's a hundred times better to have yourself cremated. A nice strong flame and it's adios amigo. It's a little like the ending of a song. I hate the ones that fade away...you're listening and you really like it and suddenly for no reason the volume goes down, the band keeps playing but the sound gets muffled and in the end nothing is left.

Much, much better are the pieces that go out with a bang, a crescendo of instruments revving toward a solid ending, building up and then striking two or three final notes all together, *bam, bam, baaam*. A real ending, blunt, without any tapering off. Out in a blaze, lights out.

With these thoughts in my head, for better or worse, I fell asleep. Four or five hours of a very uncomfortable sleep, but this morning I was up at eight, the sun was shining, and I had a huge desire to do something. To move myself, shake myself, even for no reason or purpose, anything but stand there and do nothing. Just like all those worms in their boxes.

I opened the store and cleaned the window and started redoing the bulletin board with pictures of fish caught by our customers.

"What's going on, fresh catches?" I hear behind me, together with the *driing* of the door opening. I'm startled but I manage not to turn around. It's Dad, I don't want to give him any satisfaction.

"Sell anything?"

"I just opened."

"Of course, it's Saturday, business won't start for a little while," he says, all cheerful, and he stands there at the entrance without doing anything. Truth is, he wasn't even supposed to come this morning, we agreed that he's working this afternoon, so what's he doing here? Maybe he wants to know how I'm doing, maybe he's worried about me. I mean, it wouldn't be strange for a normal dad.

"Any deliveries?"

"I told you, I just opened."

"Right, right. Are you hungry? Did you have breakfast?"

"No."

"Did you have anything to eat last night?"

"No," I say, but it's not true. After rehearsal I hung out at Stefanino's and we demolished a couple of frozen pizzas.

"Fiorenzo, if you want to go to the café, go ahead, I can stay here."

"Uh-uh. You have to be here this afternoon." I keep my back to him while moving around the pictures on the bulletin board. "Look, Dad, I'm not coming this afternoon. Don't go telling me you won't be here because I'm going to Pontedera. Tonight we're playing and—"

"Of course, no problem. We're doing two hours of training to loosen the legs and at four I'll be here."

"Uh, the afternoon hours of the shop start at three-thirty."

"Okay, so I'll be here at three-thirty, all right? Get going to the café now, have something to eat. Do you have money? Or do you want to go for a spin? Go wherever you want, I'll hold down the fort."

I stop messing around with the pictures and turn around with a jerk. Dad has a kind of smile on his lips, but not on the rest of his face. He's got his hands in his pockets and the team windbreaker and on his head the cap with the writing MUGLIONE-BERARDI FURNITURE CU. Saturdays he's always like this: in a prerace state of mind. But this morning there's something more, I can feel it, I know.

Or maybe I'm wrong and there's nothing strange behind it. Maybe Dad got up and suddenly turned into a decent person. The stupid shit that happens in fairy tales.

"Uh, Fiorenzo, I was thinking... in a little while you've got your final exams, right?" he says. I swear, just like that, he asks me about school.

I don't answer. He turns the rods in the window so you can see the brand names from outside, and continues. "Well, that's a pretty big challenge. When are they?"

"A month and a half, almost two."

"Are you worried?"

"Not too much."

"Good boy, you have to worry just the right amount. Not too much, otherwise you'll panic, and not too little, otherwise you won't have the drive. Just the right amount. Good boy."

"Dad, listen, I'm not coming back to the shop today. Don't even ask. Today I'm going to Pontedera. Tonight is the most important night of my life. If you're not here I don't care, the shop will stay closed."

"But I..."

"I know it's Saturday but it'll still be closed, I'm not staying."

"But I'll be here, I told you! What makes you think I won't be?"

"I don't think anything, just make sure you're here."

"Well, here I am."

"Good."

"Good."

And we say nothing more. He walks around the shop with his hands behind his back, like a customer who doesn't know what he wants. I go back to moving around at random the pictures of the catches. There's one with a little boy next to a giant beluga. It's a fisherman's trick, take a picture of the catch next to something small, to make it look bigger. Children, Chihuahuas, midgets.

Maybe Dad really is here because he feels guilty. Last night he couldn't sleep, he realized how awful he'd been in the evening, nothing strange about that.

"You know what I was thinking, Fiorenzo, when you're at the shop you could bring your books, so during the dead hours you could study."

"I always bring my books. But last night I left the house in kind of a rush, you know how it is."

Dad says yeah, looks in another direction, and starts to wander among the shelves again like an idiot.

"Anyway, I still study a lot," I say, "and at school I'm doing really well." I don't know why I said it. It's not like he asked, and it's not even true.

"Good to hear. How many subjects you flunking?"

"Zero."

"Good. What subjects are you doing best in?"

"The usual. English, history, Italian."

"Right, right. You always did do well in Italian. I think you could even tutor. Did you ever think about it?"

"No. I mean, uh, maybe later on, when I'm in college."

Because after high school I want to major in languages. English is too important. There are singers who have nice voices but their pronunciation is laughable, so they end up singing the song from *Titanic* at weddings. But I want to become great at it. I want to give interviews in English and for the people who hear me to ask if it's true that I'm not American.

The first time I said that I wanted to major in languages we were at the dinner table and Mom said, *Good idea, then you can take me on trips and be my interpreter.* But Dad said, *So what's the point of my keeping the shop, then?*

Because for him the university would be too much. Come on, who am I fooling? One hand, the only son of a father with a bait-and-tackle shop, the writing is on the wall.

That's how Dad thinks. Or how he thought. Because on this weird morning instead he goes, "Yes, of course, at college you'll have to do tutoring, it's so expensive. But I think you could already start now."

"Maybe, but I don't have time."

"I don't know, maybe for little kids. Elementary school, middle school."

"Well, sure, it doesn't take much for them."

"Yeah, you know, just saying . . . I might even have a little kid who needs tutoring. And wouldn't you know it, in Italian." He says it with a distorted voice because he's bent down to pick up a pair of padded rubber boots. He can't reach so he has to go almost flat on his belly, grab them, and pull himself up all red in the face. "This time of year we can put these guys in storage, okay? I don't think anyone's going to be needing them in the sum . . ." And he stops talking.

He stops because he's turned toward me and I don't know what look I've got on my face but it's definitely one of those looks where when you see it you freeze with a pair of padded boots in your arms.

"Dad, leave."

"Wha . . . ?"

"Leave, now."

"What is it, the boots? You want to keep them here? No problem, no—"

"Take those damn boots and do whatever the fuck you want, but please leave and don't come back, understand?"

" . . . "

"Dad, you've got some nerve coming here to ask me something like that, to even *think of it!*"

"Besides the fact I didn't ask you anything, I—"

"That little shit kicks me out of my room and I'm supposed to help him with school? You come here and act all nice, so I, the idiot, will tell you I'll help him, because I'm so moved that for once in my life you asked me how I'm doing at school, and . . ." I continue to spit things out rapid-fire and the whole time I'm hoping that Dad will stop me and tell me it's not true, that I've dreamed up a crazy scenario, that I've misunderstood and the kid he wants me to tutor is someone who has nothing to do with the Little Champ. Anything would please me. Anything except what he really says:

"Fiorenzo, it would only be a couple of hours a week. Oh, and of course you'd get paid."

He takes off his cap and his hair sticks straight up on top. It would make me laugh if I could manage to laugh. He keeps his cap between his hands, which are clasped in front of him. He looks at me sheepishly, like a peasant from the Middle Ages who stops working because his lord and master is passing and he has a huge favor to ask him, like being spared a flogging.

I look at him and wish I did have a whip. Or at least something nasty to say. In fact, right then and there I can feel a giant rage building inside me, getting bigger and bigger, but at some point it bursts into a thousand bitter, puny little pieces, and I stand there. Looking at my father the peasant with cap in hand saying *Master, please don't be too harsh with me.* The typical peasant who, as the lord continues on his way, will stab him in the back.

"Dad, leave. If you need tutoring call a teacher."

"Wait, but you'd be perfect."

"Why me? What's in it for me?"

"Because you're good, you're so patient. Mirko is a bright little boy, but at school he's no rocket scientist...he was already held back one year."

"When?"

"Sixth grade, I think."

"He flunked sixth grade? He must be retarded!" I say with a big laugh. I didn't know and it sounds unbelievable. He flunked sixth grade, what an idiot.

"He came down with meningitis, he almost died."

"Yeah, I'm sure...well, if he's retarded you have to find him the right tutor, a special ed assistant."

"But he doesn't need a teacher. All he needs is a little smattering of Italian, history, geography..."

"Don't even think about it."

"Please, Fiorenzo, you'd be perfect. You're so good at school and in Italian you have such high grades. You're so patient and—"

"I am not!" I holler. "It's all bullshit!" I crumple up the picture of the boy with the beluga and I keep hollering: "You don't know what my grades are, you don't know shit! It's not true that they're high. Once upon a time they were. Once upon a time lots of things were different. Lots. Not a fucking thing is the same anymore. And I hate that little twerp, do you get it? I hate his guts! So why the fuck are you asking me? Do you want to humiliate me? Do you want me to move out of the shop, too? Do you want me to leave town? Do you hate me? That's what it is, isn't it? You hate me. What did I ever do to you, tell me, Dad, what did I ever do to you? Is it because of Mom? Because of my hand? Why do you hate me so much?"

"Fiorenzo, calm down, are you out of your mind? What do you mean, do I hate you, are you joking?"

"No, I'm not joking, Dad, I'm leaving. I'm going to live in Pontedera. Watch me. Now you can be happy. I'll move and you'll never see me again. That way you'll be happy..."

"Fiorenzo, what are you saying, calm down, where are you going? I...I...you see, I didn't want to ask, I swear. But..."

"But?"

"But he says it's either you or no one."

"He, who?"

"He, Mirko. Either you or no one."

Either me or no one? What's that supposed to mean? What does that little bastard son of a bitch want from me? He steals my town, my dad, my room, and now he tries to pull this on me? He wants to humiliate me all the way, I get it. I get it but at the same time I can't believe—"

"Fiorenzo, I don't know why. That kid's hard to understand, he never speaks. Usually he's no trouble, you tell him to do something and he does it. But this time he's digging in his heels. He says it's you or no one. And without help he's done for, they might not even let him take the finals."

I don't say anything. I think of the fact that my first-term report card was bad, but Dad didn't even look at it. If you ask him what high school I go to, I'm not even sure he knows.

"Fiorenzo, I'm not joking, if he flunks all hell will break loose. His family entrusted him to me, but if he flunks there's a good chance he'll have to go back home to Molise, don't you see? In a year and a half he can enter the junior leagues and he'll mop the floor with all of them. You know how many heart-beats he has at rest? Thirty-five a minute, if you listen you'll be shocked. It's not a heart, it's a submarine. This kid is going to become my Eddy Merckx, guaranteed. But if he flunks it's all over, Fiorenzo, all of it. And I...I don't know, you're so good and intelligent and I know you could save him. Only you can do it, I'm begging you, with my heart in my hands, and..."

"Dad, listen, is he free tomorrow?"

Dad freezes. At first he doesn't understand, just stares at me with that peasant-like look. "Tomorrow is the race..."

"So tell him to come on Monday, here to the shop."

"Oh my goodness, Fiorenzo, I don't know how to...I... thank you, Fiorenzino, thank you so much, I—"

"But now you've got to go, okay? And be here today at three-thirty, on time."

"Of course, of course, even at three if you want, at three I'll be here! Thank you, Fiorenzo, thank you! I..." And he keeps saying thank you again and again with my name in the middle, while I shoo him away with my hand. He leaves the shop walking backward, so he can keep looking at me and thanking me from the doorway and from the other side of the window, then the door closes and I don't hear him anymore.

I said okay, I'll help him, and I'm not kidding. Starting on Monday I'm going to help the Little Champ of Molise prepare for his finals. If someone had told me that an hour ago, I would have called him an idiot and spent the rest of the day laughing. And instead it happened. My father's words convinced me.

But I'm not such an idiot, I hope this much is clear. It wasn't that bullshit about *Fiorenzo, you're so good and intelligent, only you can save him...*

Give me a break. Like I was saying, maybe I am a moron but I still have my limits. I liked the other thing that Dad said much more, what was it? Ah, yes...

If he flunks all hell will break loose. If he flunks he might even have to go home, to Molise.

If he flunks it's all over, Fiorenzo, all of it.

A KIND OF ANNIVERSARY

"I'm Tuscan."

"You can tell," she says, smiling. As if to say it's nice that you can tell. "From Florence?"

"No, from Muglione."

"Never heard of it, sorry."

"It's small but it's nice, kind of. In some ways maybe not, but maybe yes, too."

"In Muglione do you have the Tuscan hills?"

"No, not really . . . it's strange. Everything's flat, then over in a corner there are four hills that come out of nowhere. Perfect for training. If there's a god of cycling, he must have put them there."

"In your opinion, is there a god of cycling?"

"In my opinion, yes."

"So you're polytheistic?"

". . ."

Roberto Marelli freezes. He had already started to say yes, but that word sent him into a panic and he is stuck looking like an idiot, hang-jawed with a quivering smile.

Bologna, September 30, 1989. The Giro dell'Emilia race has just ended. A group of twelve racers were competing, Roberto was one of them but in the end he came in twelfth and a Soviet guy won. And now he's talking to a dark-haired girl with a nice tan and a light-green dress, who instead of shoes is wearing a pair of gym socks.

Roberto had a fast spurt, in a tight sprint like this he might even have won. For that matter, in the past few months he'd started to receive the doctor's "special treatment," train more than ever, and take everything he was supposed to take, except that Monte San Luca was in the final and he lost his legs. Roberto can't handle the tough climbs, and the long climbs, and the wind, and the sudden variations in rhythm. In other words, there's always a good reason for the fact that he never wins.

But he's a good lieutenant, he helps the others to win. Once the TV zeroed in on him and on the news they talked a lot about him, because he'd taken twenty water bottles from the team car in a single snatch and climbed back up to the head of the group to bring them to his teammates. Stuck in his rear pockets, under his jersey, between the suspenders of his shorts. Twenty water bottles all at once. And now everyone calls him the Bartender. It's not a fantastic nickname but it's still better than nothing. Without a nickname in the group you're nobody. But right now Roberto is hoping this girl in gym socks doesn't know that he's the Bartender. Just as he doesn't know what *polytheist* means.

One night he asks the team physician, who explains that a polytheist is someone who believes there are a lot of gods rather than just one. Roberto is happy it wasn't an insult and starts phoning the girl in the gym socks; they get married and go to live in the town built by the god of cycling. If this god exists.

But twenty years have passed and today Roberto, rather than many gods, is thinking there's not even one. Not even one, damn it. Because a woman who at the age of forty-three is waiting in line at the bank and out of nowhere falls to the floor and dies...come on, how could something like that happen if so many gods were on duty? Obviously it couldn't. Even if there were only one it wouldn't happen. Instead...

Today Roberto is driving the team car and thinking a lot about that day twenty years ago. Today is their wedding anniversary. If you can call it an anniversary when one of the two is no longer around.

Yes, damn it, of course you can call it an anniversary. You know, a date is still a date, even if the person you could congratulate, give a gift to, or get mad at for forgetting again this year is no longer around.

After all, it's only normal that today, which *would have been* their anniversary, Roberto is thinking about it. About things like how in twenty years of conjugal life he never asked his wife why she was wearing gym socks that day instead of shoes. The kind of things you stop thinking about over time but that cross your mind every now and then, but you shrug your shoulders and say, *Well, who cares, maybe one day I'll ask her.* And then one day she isn't around to ask.

"Easy ratio, kids, loosen your legs!"

He's shouting at the kids in front of him. He makes a face and adjusts himself on the car seat. Damn hemorrhoids. Having to sit behind the wheel to sculpt the physique of others has devastated his own body. For someone who's almost fifty years old he's pretty lean and toned, but every now and then his ass is on fire and he's grown a hard, protruding gut that has nothing to do with the rest of his body. It seems fake, and a good look at it almost makes you laugh. But it's not fake and it doesn't make you laugh one bit. They call it trucker belly and his dad had one, his dad who drove a truck. When he was little Roberto used to look at it and hope that it was all because of his father's job. And he would think, *Anything but that — two hundred kilometers a day, not a drop of beer as long as I live.* But that's stuff you think when you're twenty, and you don't realize that the day will come when things will have a mind of their own and you say *All right already, nothing I can do about it*, and at best you try to salvage the salvageable.

Roberto adjusts himself on the car seat again, a sharp pang in his ass shoots to his head, he hits the horn by mistake and the kids look back, accelerating.

"No, relax, false alarm, I said slow!"

The kids obey. The kids give him a lot of satisfaction. They start racing when they're eight years old, in the early youth category, boys and girls together. The first time you put them on a bike it seems like a bad fit, like two pieces of a puzzle that aren't meant for each other, who you want to hammer together whether they like it or not. They're chubby or skinny, too short or too tall, awkward and unsteady.

But then you teach them how to stay on the seat, to pedal properly, hands low on the handlebars and torso parallel to the road, and now look at the six kids in front of the windshield, what a sight. They're fifteen or sixteen years old, junior league, and they're already at one with their bikes. What a huge satisfaction.

But Mirko, hanging in the back of the group, is in a league of his own. Roberto first put him on a racing bike not even five months ago, and it was as if cycling were all he had ever done in life. Long legs, thin arms, short torso but a wide rib cage. And a lethal motor in his body.

Basically he has that thing they call greatness, and true greatness you can recognize in a heartbeat. Here before the windshield are six kids all pedaling with the same ratio and the same safe last-few-minutes-of-training speed. But one of the six is another story entirely. It doesn't take biomechanical tests or special tracking to understand it. All it takes is the naked eye.

"Kids, say goodbye to Massimiliano. 'Bye, Massi, see you tomorrow at one in front of the office."

Massimiliano gives a nod with his head and his helmet, then he removes a foot from the pedal and stops at the gate to his house. The group continues on its way.

The training sessions used to end at the clubhouse, now instead Mr. Roberto's team car goes from house to house, like a cycling school bus, to make it easier for the kids and their parents.

You have to meet the families halfway. Because nowadays with the murderous traffic on the roads, the stories of doped-up kids and the idiot faces of soccer players in newspapers and on TV as if they were heroes or something, parents prefer to take the jeep and accompany their children to the soccer field. So for the crazy few who still decide to put their kid on a bike, you have to try to meet them halfway.

"Slow down, kids. Cristiano, move to the left, it's your turn."

Because they're about to arrive at his house, Villa Berardi. They take a detour that leads away from the country road and for two minutes everything around them becomes peaceful and greener and less dusty, in the shade of the tall, neat hedges that line the road. And if it's rare nowadays for families to let their children do cycling races, it's unheard of for a rich family.

The first Giro d'Italia was won by a brick mason, the first Tour de France by a chimney sweep. They were followed by a long, sweaty line of smiths, bakers, carpenters, and farmers. The main ingredient of a great cyclist is hunger.

Cristianino is a good kid, not to mention the son of an important sponsor. But soon he's going to discover sex and discos and then it'll be *sayonara* to cycling.

"Say goodbye to Cristiano. And don't forget. Be on time tomorrow, not late like you were last time."

And they continue on. Mirko is always last, butting up against the hood of the team car, head down. He waves goodbye to Cristiano and then starts pedaling again. For four months he would dismount from his bike at Villa Berardi, too, but then Cristiano didn't want him anymore. At that point Mirko could have crowned him with his bike or at least told him to go fuck himself or spit in his face. Instead nothing, he even waves goodbye to him as they leave. Whatever.

But right past the gate, behind the curve that leads to the main road, a car is blocking the way. A black Buick Terraza with a giant skull painted on the door, which is open. The kids can pass on their bikes, but not the team car. Roberto honks the horn and gets his mouth ready to blurt out a couple of *fuck-yous*. From behind the Terraza out pops a bare-chested tub of lard. He must be about eighteen and six foot six. Then another boy, Berardi's oldest son. And then his own son, Fiorenzo. They're carrying big boxes, cases, yards of black cable. And suddenly Roberto remembers what he promised his son this morning: *Not at three-thirty: today I'll open at three!* He looks down at the clock on the dashboard: 4:10. Shit.

The fat-ass comes back to close the door of the Terraza. Roberto shifts into gear and meets his son's stare. He honks the horn, Fiorenzo nods and goes back to loading the van. Roberto looks into the rearview mirror for a second and then doesn't look back.

Since they're turning onto the country road, it's a very tricky moment. Trucks have riddled the asphalt with potholes, which pass by as thick and fast as a hailstorm. The edge of the road is lined with crosses and flowers and ribbons. The amount of cats who die there every year has to be calculated by the ton. They don't even have to cross the street to die: the trucks pass by so fast they suck them directly off the windowsills.

"Kids, say goodbye to Mikhail."

And then it's Emanuele's turn, then Martin's.

Until the only one left in front of the team car is Mirko, the Little Champion from Molise.

There's a curve to the right, the road is squeezed between abandoned houses, stores that change their names once a month, and loads of empty lots. Even a real estate agency has FOR RENT on the window. Further ahead is the former warehouse that is now the Youth Center. Outside there are a bunch of seniors seeking out the sun.

"Come on, Mirko, crank it up, give us one for the fans!"

Mirko automatically stands up on the pedals, lowers his head, and in a fluid progression goes from twenty to forty an hour without breaking a sweat. Roberto never ceases to be amazed.

The team car starts honking, the seniors turn around and see the Little Champion arriving, line up on the sidewalk, and raise their arms: "Go, Champ! Go go go go go, burn up the field, leave 'em in the dust! *Alé*, go go go!"

The Champion passes and so does Mr. Roberto's team car. The seniors look at them from behind until they disappear beyond the gas station.

Then they sit back down at the tables, which they've moved outside today because of the sun. They make some small talk about the Champ and tomorrow's race but return almost immediately to the subject they had been discussing before the interruption. Because today there's some really big news, and Divo has come to the best part.

"And what did that piece of shit have to say?"

"He told us to mind our own business and go home."

"I can't believe it, it's disgusting. They think they can boss us around?"

"Yeah, but I told him, 'Listen up, buster, this is our business, this is our home.'"

"Good for you! What did he say?"

"He acted like a tough guy. He got out giant bolt cutters and showed them to us, like he wanted to split our heads open. But then he realized there were too many of us..."

"YES—WE—WERE—ME—TOO—AND—BALDATO—AND—REPETTI," says Mazinger, all puffed up. Today he's wearing an orange hoodie with a cappuccino and skateboard logo on the front.

"We were four against one, so I told him, 'Remember one thing, buster, maybe you can take one of us, but there'll still be three more of us, and after that your ass is grass. We'll take you out and throw you in a ditch. A guy like you has no documents, to say the least, and no one would recognize you. You'd end up like the unknown soldier!'"

"Good man!"

"Yes, but why did you have to go bringing up the unknown soldier?" asks Baldato, a veteran who moved north from Caltanissetta thirty years ago.

"What did he ever do?"

"Then he came running at me. With those bolt cutters in his hand. But I got into position, planted square on my legs. When I was a kid I did some boxing, I'm not completely unprepared. I was on my guard. In the meantime these three were advancing from behind. And the Slavic guy was no idiot. He realized acting tough wasn't going to get him anywhere with us. He leapt to the other side of the street and ran off like a rabbit."

"Good! Like a rabbit!"

"SHAME—THE—POLICE—WEREN'T—PASSING."

"Please, what do you expect the police to do? Wish you a good night and continue on their way."

"True, they don't even stop them. They stop us because we're harmless. They gave me a fifty-euro fine because the headlight of my three-wheeler was out. It was daytime, can you believe it! Meanwhile there are these foreigners transporting drugs and disease and bossing everyone around."

"YEAH—AND—NOBODY—EVER—THINKS—ABOUT—US."

"Yeah," says Baldato, "they ignore us completely."

"But listen up, guys, we're not alone," says Divo. "There are many of us."

Baldato gives him a serious look and nods. "And we're pissed off."

"And we're right."

"AND—WE—HAVE—LOTS—OF—FREE—TIME."

The old men stare at each other, silent, the thrill growing in their bodies, shining behind their cataracts and the dark lenses of their eyeglasses. The ones wearing a cap remove it, shake hands, and hug each other with a round of pats on the back. Then Baldato puffs out his chest, takes a deeper breath than he has in years, and starts to chant "I-ta-lia, I-ta-lia." In a moment everyone is united, the song becomes a single shout, raucous and emotional. Louder and louder. "I-ta-lia! I-ta-lia! I-ta-lia!"

"Gentlemen, gentlemen! What's going on?" Tiziana rushes out of the office. She was in the middle of a sentence of the report she's writing on the exploitation of young Italian workers. In reality it was the first sentence of the report and she had been stuck on it for an hour, but everyone knows the opening is the most important part and once you get it right the rest is downhill.

"Gentlemen, I'm telling you for the thousandth time. This is supposed to be a Youth Center, and I have no problem with your coming here, but actually you shouldn't be. So I'm begging you, can you at least avoid drawing too much attention to yourselves? Okay?"

The old men look at her, put their caps back on, and wink at each other. They don't even need words: they're mentally connected.

"We were just singing 'Italia Italia,' Miss."

"I know, but if you start shouting out on the street sooner or later someone is going to—"

"It's our town, Miss."

"I know, it's my town, too, but what's that got to do with anything?"

"YES—BUT—WE—ARE—ITALIANS—AND—SENIORS..."

"Exactly," says Divo. "It means that we're here, and that we were here before anyone else."

"All right, gentlemen, but I still don't understand what that's got to do with..."

But the old men have stopped listening to her. As one they turn their backs on her and face the road.

Their road, their houses, their town. Their business.

PONTEDEROCK

We're here. Holy shit we're here. The festival has started and there are tons of people and in a little while it's our turn. Holy shit we're here.

They told us to wait behind the stage and not to go too far, well, who's going to move? There's no other place in the universe I'd rather be.

I mean, okay, we arrived a little early. We were afraid of unforeseen circumstances during the trip, like a flat tire or a tsunami that would wash away everything from the Marina of Pisa to Pontedera or giant rats born in the toxic water of the ditches that would lay waste to the province. But nothing of the kind happened and so we've been here behind the stage for four hours now. As a matter of fact, when we arrived there wasn't even a stage, they were still putting it up.

But now it's eight o'clock and the first band has almost finished. Ten groups, one after the other, four songs each, and we're next. We have to play while it's still light out. I would have preferred pitch black, it's more scenic, but this is okay, too, no problem. We're a war machine, a hand grenade tossed into the middle of the crowd, and when a bomb explodes it always does damage, dark or no dark.

To see that we're not kidding just take a look at us. All four of us in leather pants, chains crossing our chests, different types of studs on our belts, on our armbands, and even around our necks. As well as combat boots, windblown hair, and T-shirts of the historic groups who have influenced us the most (except for Giuliano, who is obviously bare-chested).

We're outrageous, omnipotent, and ready to demolish Pontedera.

All of us except Antonio.

He can't keep up. The best he could do was a studded belt around his waist, as thin as the ones girls wear, no chains, and hair that is neither long nor short that he slicks back with gel. *With gel!* If you were to take a picture right now, we would look like the fiercest band in the world together with a passerby asking us for directions to a discotheque.

Meanwhile the group onstage is starting its last song. They're doing reggae (what else) but none of them have dreads, and from the looks of them they don't even smoke ganja. I bet that four out of the five of them learned music at the parish and on Sunday mornings they play acoustic guitar at Mass. They end with a cover (why am I not surprised?) of Bob Marley, "No Woman No Cry." Except since the rule is to sing in Italian, it becomes "*No donna non piange,*" though, in my opinion, there's a lot to cry about. But the crowd applauds, someone shouts out "*bravi*" and someone "*bravo,*" maybe for one member of the band, or maybe for Bob Marley.

What do we care, we're here to burn down the house, Bob Marley, Sundays at church, and the ears of these people who came here by chance and don't realize how lucky they are. Like the people who one night in 1969 went out for a beer and saw Black Sabbath at the pub, or the ones who lived next door to Ron

McGovney's garage and from their backyard could hear Metallica getting ready to change the world. These guys in Pontedera don't realize it, but one day they'll be able to say *I was at the first concert of Metal Devastation.*

"Uh yeah, yeah, *uomo, rilassati. Tutto andrà bene pace gente, tutti amici,* uh yeah..."

The last song of these Jamaican altar boys rolls out flat and monotonous, as useless as all music with upbeat rhythms.

I hope they finish as soon as possible, but maybe it's better if they go on for a while. Because right now I feel something strange in my stomach, like a million ants that are circling and circling, then climbing out of my stomach and crowding into my throat, exiting through my mouth and covering my face with a kind of effervescent burning.

But it's gonna be all right, it's a trick of tension, and the moment you start playing the tension is transformed into adrenaline. At least that's what they say in interviews.

"Guys," says Stefanino, "I'm going to the bathroom for a second," with the voice of a little bird dying a slow death in a freezing-cold winter.

"Again? Move your ass, we're up next."

He nods his head up and down just once, slowly, then he waddles off on his journey to the portable toilets.

The song ends, the crowd applauds. They don't go wild with clapping but there's still a smattering of applause, the group says goodbye, thanks everyone, and gets off the stage. We cross paths on the iron stairs. They're red in the face and a little confused, and they stand there staring at us with stupid smiles. They look at our leather and our studs and our patches and our T-shirts. Go ahead, take a good look. Maybe you'll finally realize that this is how a serious band should dress.

"Guys, your turn, are you ready?" the technician asks from behind the mixer. I answer yes with a twitch, he gives me the "OK" sign. "Everything's set up, just climb up onstage, attach the jack to the instruments, and you're ready to rock."

He's pushing forty and I like him immediately. Not much hair but it's long and tied back with a rubber band. The belly, the goatee on his double chin, a Blackmore's Rainbow T-shirt, and definitely a high school experience identical to our own, with the dream of making it big in music and classmates giving you a hard time. He didn't quite make it but things could have been worse. He's the sound technician for the municipality of Pontedera, so in a certain sense you could say he's making his living off music. He doesn't earn much, but maybe he's the type who saves, and he definitely isn't the type with a woman around adding to his expenses.

The mixer is behind a plywood panel that hides it from the crowd. Once you pass it there's the stage with the colored lights and the sea of people waiting to see you play. All the high schools of Pontedera, all the young people from the plain, but above all the members of my class and especially Ludovica Betti, the title holder: the prettiest girl in school and the biggest bitch in the world.

And now in front of all these eyes our moment is about to explode. At school we have to hide behind the desks, and spend recess in the hall corner near the restrooms. But now that's over, today is our day, it's time to get onstage and leave all these people with their jaws hanging. It's time to climb the stairway to heaven like total rock stars.

In the meantime Stefanino is on his way back from the toilet. He's reached the iron stairs and is climbing them with his head down. It takes him a while; he holds on to the railing and keeps his other hand on his leg. He lifts his eyes toward us. He's pale as a sheet, staring into space and sweating. He looks like one of those guys who tries to climb Mount Everest but dies.

"Sté, what's up?" No answer. "Are you high?"

He nods, an exhausting movement. Giuliano tries to put the bass into his arms: for the moment he's holding it, so we're ready.

The crowd beyond the panel is calling us. A ton of voices that tangle, every now and then someone shouting *where's the music*, others shouting out the name of a schoolmate along with the word *slut*. Fantastic.

I cast a glance at my technician friend at the console. "We're here."

Giuliano opens his eyes wide and raises his drumsticks in the air as if they were clubs.

"Perfect. Ah, you kids are..." The technician looks down at a sheet of paper taped to the mixer. "You guys are Metal Devastation, right?"

I puff up my chest, we all say yes. He makes a check mark on the paper and looks up. "Nice, a real ballsy name. Now go out there and kick some ass!"

Yes, my friend, you can bet on it.

"*Come on!*" I shout, and we step out onto the stage.

The people, the lights, the rows of eyes looking at us from below. This is what I've dreamed about so many times that I feel like checking to make sure I'm not in my pajamas and lying down with a streak of dry drool on my cheek. But I'm awake and psyched and ready to make the crowd go wild. A round of applause begins, polite. The real applause we're going to have to earn.

Giuliano sits down at the drums, Antonio and Stefanino connect the pedals, I take the microphone. For the moment I keep my right hand in my pocket. In a little while I'll take it out, I'm not at all ashamed if I'm missing a hand, I'm made of metal and nothing can harm me. But for now I feel more secure this way.

And I start to breathe again. One, two, the crowd stares at me and someone whistles and someone shouts, but mainly they're waiting. They're waiting for us. I think about it, and suddenly a burst of energy swells my throat and shoots through my body like a whip. I grab the microphone and shout, "Hello, Pontedera!"

The voice echoes among the housing projects and the warehouses around the square. But no one answers. There are scattered *yeah*s, but from two or three of our friends, metalheads like us, so they don't count.

"People, enough with the Muzak, are you ready for a jolt of metal?"

Silence.

"Are you ready to tear down the city?"

"..."

"We're Metal Devastation and we're here to burn down the house. Are you ready for an attack of heavy metal?"

"..."

"I said" — I inhale, wink an eye, and shout out in a single breath — "are you ready for an attack of heavy metaaaaaaaaal?!"

Finally the silence breaks. A voice calls out, then two, five, six, and then they become a single universal chorus raised to the heavens by everyone there.

They shout, "*NO.*"

What do they mean, *no?* I swallow but there's not even a drop of saliva. I turn toward my bandmates. Giuliano is still sitting there with his arms raised and the drumsticks in midair, like a guy holding his hands up before the police. Stefanino is a shivering ghost and the bass looks bigger than him. Antonio fixes his hair and looks to one side, expressionless, like someone who was just passing by.

I turn back toward the crowd, which has stopped shouting "*NO.*" Now it's shouting something more direct: "*OFF-THE-STAGE.*"

"*OFF-THE-STAGE, OFF-THE-STAGE, OFF-THE-STAGE.*"

And they punctuate it with a sea of fists in the air pumping with the rhythm. Again and again.

"*OFF-THE-STAGE, OFF-THE-STAGE, OFF-THE-STAGE.*"
"*OFF-THE-STAGE, OFF-THE-STAGE, OFF-THE-STAGE.*"

Antonio unplugs the jack from his guitar and leaves. Giuliano's arms flop to his sides.

"*OFF-THE-STAGE, OFF-THE-STAGE, OFF-THE-STAGE.*"

I slip the microphone back into the stand and take a step back. I dig my right wrist even deeper into my pocket. I can't believe it. You don't understand shit, you're not worth shit, you don't deserve shit.

I walk away from the microphone but I see Giuliano stepping out from behind the drums; he grabs the mic and goes toward the crowd.

"Motherfuckers!" he says into it. But calmly, without anger, as if to say they should move their cars. A service announcement.

The shouting of the crowd doesn't grow because it's impossible for it to be any louder. But mixed in with it now are the sounds of coins being thrown, clods of dirt, cigarette lighters, plastic bottles, other stuff I don't understand.

I don't understand any of this.

SYLVESTER THE CAT

The ceiling is white, with a damp spot in a corner that doesn't resemble anything. It doesn't look like an animal or the Madonna or another famous figure. It's just a shapeless damp spot that I've seen every morning since I was born, so you could say that for me it has the typical shape of a damp spot.

Yes, exactly, I've gone back to my room. I had a desperate need for a real bed and a real house, at least for today. It's Sunday anyway and there's a race in Montelupo and the house will be empty until tonight.

Outside, the summer has rushed in, very early and very angry. The streets are scalding and so are the fields, the ditches are simmering and reeking of rotten mushrooms. And Muglione is empty.

Anyone who could has escaped for a day at the beach. In other words, three hours of traffic going, a little over an hour crowded onto the public beach, and then a three-hour trip back. The only people left in town are the seniors, who are sitting in the shade waiting, and me.

And I haven't got the energy to do anything. I stare at the ceiling, lying on the bed with the blinds down and the silence outside competing with the silence inside, because I didn't even turn the music on. Today is a black day, pitch black, the sun and the summer don't belong here.

Last night the return from Pontedera was a nightmare. Usually return trips are shorter, but this one never ended. We didn't know what to say so we sat there in silence. We didn't turn on the stereo. We didn't even look at each other.

And today we didn't call each other. I don't know what the others are up to but I imagine they're at home like me. At a moment like this it makes no sense to go anywhere. It doesn't even make sense to get up. It only makes sense to stay in bed with the windows closed and your eyes staring upward, in the hope that the ceiling will tell you what to do.

Last night something went wrong, okay, but what? Maybe it was a mistake for me to start with that question: *Are you ready for a jolt of metal?* I mean, a serious band doesn't say anything, it doesn't introduce itself, a serious band arrives and starts playing and that's what we should have done. We should have arrived and started pounding away, the crowd would have been electrified by our surge of power and after a couple of songs we would have had them in the palms of our hands.

Instead, no. Instead I had to ask whether they were ready, I gave them the opportunity to choose. And what do you expect from folks who listen to Milli Vanilli in the car? They don't know what they want. They haven't got any idea, so we should have given them one without asking. And in the end they would have told us, *Thank you, thank you, you've changed my life.* If they still had any breath left in them.

Yes, that's the mistake we made, the problem lies there and only there. At least I hope so. But today I'm not sure of anything. I don't even know when we're playing next. *If* we are playing. Maybe it would be better to let a few days go by and think on it. Or maybe it would be better to go straight back to the garage and play something fierce to blast everything to smithereens and realize that the festival was just a bump in the road.

I don't know, I don't know. When there's a complicated situation like this in the movies, the hero turns to someone for advice. But in reality there is never a single person who gives you decent advice or who cares about your problems, so everyone has to squeak by as best they can.

Me, for example, I invented the superadvice method and I swear it works. It's a technique that came to me by accident the first time, but it was so useful that ever since that day I have always trusted it.

But today I can't use it because there's no one around and for the superadvice to work you need people on the street. And it's a lousy day and I don't feel like doing anything.

The only positive thing: I made sure my room is practically intact. The friggin' Little Champ might have stolen it from me but at least he didn't start moving stuff around. The posters are in their places, the CDs are in alphabetical order by the bands' names. Even the sheets of paper with the notes for last night are on the computer keyboard.

I stand up and grab them with a kind of disgust, I want to tear them up and burn them, just to look at them makes me as ashamed as a thief, I don't want to read a single word. I take the first sheet and I see written on the bottom "WE'RE GONNA KICK SOME ASS!" in giant red letters. I wrote it because I really believed it. What an idiot! What an idiot!

I take all these notes from a catastrophe and start to crumple them in my hand. But underneath, next to the keyboard and a few magazines, I find him. Sylvester the Cat.

And for a second I sit there, like a stone, with a ball of paper in my hand.

Sylvester the Cat is a glass, with, of course, the cartoon character etched on the outside.

A bubble of air stagnates in my lungs, my eyes fixed on that glass half full of orange soda. I drop the paper, pick up the glass, and sniff it. No, it's not orange soda, it's orange juice. How could I think the Little Champ would drink anything fizzy.

But what matters isn't the juice, it's the glass. *That* glass. I break into a sweat. My heart beats faster. I had put it in the cabinet, way in the back, because we never open that cabinet so it's like losing it forever.

And here it is next to the computer.

The friggin' Little Champ took it, I can't believe it, he did it deliberately. How could he know about the glass? Except for me no one knows about it, and even I try to forget it as much as possible. And instead it's as if the Little Champ were saying to me, *No, my dear Fiorenzo, you can't block it out, here it is, your nice little glass . . .*

The Sylvester the Cat glass is related to Mom. Not in an affectionate sense, like she gave it to me as a gift or it was her favorite glass or anything. No, it's related to when Mom died. And in a certain sense, maybe . . . no, I mean the opposite, it's bullshit, it can hardly have, it can't . . . what I mean to say is maybe, that's what it is, in a certain sense maybe this glass has to do with the fact that Mom isn't here anymore.

But just a little. Really, just a tiny bit. I mean not at all, less than zero, I'm talking bullshit, but what the hell's gotten into me today, delete, delete everything . . .

What a shitty day.

MONDAY IN THE LOCAL NEWS

It's Monday morning, 8:45, you pay the newspaper man and wish him a nice week. He nods, that's all. He's usually really talkative and tells jokes and sometimes even starts doing imitations of TV hosts and Berlusconi. But he doesn't even say hi to you. Another mystery of this impossible town, where the best-selling magazines at the newsstand are *Wild Boar International, All Rally Plus, Oystermen's Passion, Popular Carp, Guns and Shots, Hunting with Bullets,* and *Knives.*

But today is Monday morning, a new week begins, and you've decided to shift gears. No more negativity, no more pessimism. May has begun but it feels like summer, and all you want to do is smile, feel good, and give another chance to this weird period of your life. Starting right now when you've picked up the newspapers and are on your way to the office and it's going to be a nice day. Better than yesterday, at least.

When you finally said okay and went to the beach with Raffaella, Pavel, and his friend Nick (Nikolaj). You didn't know that he was coming, too, otherwise you wouldn't have gone. Or maybe you would have, if only not to be stuck in an empty town with all that time on your hands to sit down at the computer and try to write that report/exposé, or a new blog post with the expectation that your man in California would finally find the courage to speak with you.

No, much better to go to the beach. Versilia. A Sunday outing like in films of the 1950s. Even if the public beach was filled with dirt and cigarette butts, even if there wasn't one free inch and there was so little space between you and the hirsute mini-muscleman on the next blanket that you were ready to file a sexual harassment suit every time he turned.

And on your other side was Nikolaj, who every now and then asked, *Is everything all right, Tissiana?* in a tone of voice that said, *If that guy is bothering you, I'll beat the shit out of him.*

But you continued to read with your head lowered, in the hope that Nikolaj would give up and join Raffaella and Pavel, who were busy playing paddleball in the middle of the crowd.

Raffaella, you have to admit, is amazing in her way. First day on the beach, as big and white as a mozzarella, yet she had on a teeny red bikini that you wouldn't wear with a bag over your head even after six thousand hours in the gym. But there she was, jumping up and down, running, playing by the water, and laughing like mad the few times that Pavel let her score.

You'd gone back to your book with your eyes but then you realized that you had Nikolaj on the left, the hairy man on the right, and in front of you a couple of young muscle boys covered with tattoos. One of them was spreading lotion on his abs. They turned and gave you the once-over, looking at you everywhere except your face.

And every time it happened you felt strange. Okay, yes, you took a look at yourself in the mirror before going out and thought you weren't half bad in a swimsuit. *Not half bad* is a huge compliment when it's coming from you. And on the beach as soon as you took off your dress Raffaella put her hands in her hair and said, *Oh my God, Tiziana, you look like a model, how do you do it, I hate you ... No, I was joking, but I do hate you just a little.*

And Pavel was thinking the same thing. In his own words: *What a body! Oh, Nick, after you sleep with her you owe me big favor.*

Nikolaj trained his eyes on the sand and said nothing, apart from indicating agreement with his head.

But Pavel had better not be counting on this favor too much, since it's out of the question. Nikolaj's not bad-looking, you might even call him handsome. *Hunky* is what Raffaella would say. He's the same age as you, but unlike most Italians you look at him and see a man. A man, handsome or ugly, with a man's face and a man's hands and a man's skin. Who knows why Italians the same age as you, the ones who went to school with you, for example, if you see them today they're not men. They were kids and then they aged, but without ever becoming men. And you don't say it in the sense that's figurative or moral or any of that stuff. You mean it physically. No profile, no features, no nerves. They're still kids except they've lost their hair, put on some weight, gotten a few wrinkles. They look like sixteen-year-olds left out in the field for a year and a half to wither in the wind, sun, and rain.

Nikolaj's not like that, one point in his favor, but he still hasn't got a chance. Not out of meanness or something like that, but because you really don't understand your girlfriends who hook up with some guy because there's no one better.

In the end there's nothing wrong with being alone. That is, you might suffer from being alone, but in the wrong relationship you'd suffer twice as much, and resigning yourself to that seems like one of the saddest things in the world.

While you're walking, the newspapers are emitting the smell of paper and ink that you like so much. Yes, today could be the start of a good week. Even walking with four newspapers under your arm makes you feel good. For the office you got *The Tyrrhenian* and *La Nazione*, for yourself *Corriere della Sera* and *La Repubblica*.

The local papers are supposed to be for job ads, but in reality they're read by seniors who are avid for local news. Crime, town council controversies, obituaries. Monday is the day they like best, because there's a full report of the Saturday-night massacres with pictures of car accidents and descriptions of the disgusting things these kids did before they ultimately crashed into a wall.

Today's walk in the sunshine already feels like fresh air, you smile, the nice thing about a small town is that you can get from one place to another on foot without major impediments. All you have to do is survive the county road, but once you're across it the rest is easy.

You arrive on time, as always; the office opens at nine and every day the seniors have already been outside for a while by then. But this morning there's something strange. They're all huddled together and they've already got the newspaper. They bought it themselves, they spent money. A miracle.

Mr. Divo has *La Nazione* open and he's reading. All the others have their mouths wide open the way seniors do when they listen very attentively, as if opening their mouths will improve their hearing.

"...Moments of excision...no, excuse me, of excitement... in which they proved their character and...and their mettle..."

You take advantage of the distraction to enter quickly, your head lowered. No one says hello, no one looks at you. You have to turn on the light even if outside the sunlight is glaring, because this place used to be a warehouse and there are no windows. You sit down at your desk and start flipping through the papers.

Except you hear the agitation outside, the comments, and you're curious. What could be so interesting in *La Nazione?*

You take it and turn to the provincial news. Nothing special. Controversies about stores owned by the Chinese driving Italian-owned stores out of business. A woman who won a prize for recycling. A short article about a high school festival in Pontedera.

You had also thought about organizing a concert here in Muglione where the local groups could play and get to know the Youth Center. But at the town hall they told you that the high volume would disturb the citizens.

PONTEDERA. The first ever Pontede-Rock festival was held on Saturday night. The event brought together the best musical groups formed by high school students from the Pisa area for an evening of rock and entertainment. Nine groups played one after the other on the stage. It is our hope that they might one day perform on more and more prestigious stages, maybe even the San Remo festival. This is a hope that...

You flip through a few more pages. Ads for sales, discounts, promotions. Then the local sports pages, page after page filled with absurd rankings and the names of people and places you've never heard of. There's even a picture of Mirko, your English pupil who never learns anything.

A whole page dedicated to him.

Colonna Dominates the Bertolaccini Trophy

The Little Champ from UC Muglione crosses the finish line alone

MONTELUPO. Another epic feat for the talented young Mirko Colonna, who yesterday won the thirteenth seasonal cup with disarming ease. At the three-quarter mark, when the best were facing the San Vito hill and the first sprint had begun, Colonna took the lead, setting a diabolical pace. Only seven athletes attempted to stay in his wake, and that was their mistake. The rhythm set by the Molise champion set them off their pace and by the top of the hill he had a two-minute lead. The short descent and head wind should have favored the pursuers, but the pack failed to find the right collaboration and the champion showed no signs of letting up, crossing the finish line with a three-and-a-half-minute lead over the athlete who came in second, the likewise talented Cenceschi of the Sigmaflex team, ranked number one among the men, and winner of the twenty-second Ettore Bertolaccini Trophy, the seventh Franco Beschi Memorial, and the fifth Montelupo Veteran's Cup. The event was a huge success thanks to the impeccable organization by the spons...

You stop reading. What draws your attention, more than the text, is the picture of Mirko. Surrounded by throngs of people, all of them fifty- or sixty-year-old men with their arms raised, he's wearing a crooked helmet over his curly hair and has his head leaning to one side, with the tired gaze of a little boy who stares at you with pursed lips and says, *Will you please take me home?*

And you kind of regret telling him you couldn't help him with other subjects. What else do you have to do, after all? Write that exposé about your experience as a temporary worker? Wait for your American to make up his mind and write to you? Call the ambulance for the next senior who collapses?

You fold the newspaper, go over to the tables, and place it there for the seniors who might want to have a look at it. Maybe it was Mirko's race they were so interested in, who knows. You're about to return to your desk when you see it, right there on the front page.

Brave Seniors
Drive Out Romanian Gang

MUGLIONE. When small towns lose their peace of mind, when it becomes dangerous to take a walk down the street and the government cannot guarantee security, the time has come for upright citizens to take matters into their own hands and say enough! That's what happened a few nights ago in Muglione, where a few "seasoned" inhabitants on their way home from a pleasant evening together didn't miss the opportunity to show their courage by foiling a robbery organized by a group of criminals from Eastern Europe. (*Story continues on page 8.*)

You flip through the paper, get to that point, where half a page is dedicated to this story. There's even a picture, with Divo, Baldato, and the other two, their faces serious and fingers pointed down. The caption explains: THE GUARDIAN ANGELS OF MUGLIONE POINT TO THE SPOT WHERE THEY FOUGHT OFF THE CRIMINALS.

SUPERADVICE

Monday morning. I wake up after a series of weird dreams, but I can say that by now I'm used to sleeping in the midst of a million frantic worms. It might not be a rock star's life, but it is what it is.

And this morning I have to go back to school, but it doesn't seem like a good idea. All of our classmates were at the concert. Already they give us a lot of grief automatically, can you imagine how they'll act now with the new material we just handed them?

No, today is not the right day to return to high school, but it's perfect for going out and testing the superadvice. And now I can explain to you what it is.

Superadvice is a perfect method in situations like this, when I'm filled with thoughts and I really need the advice of a person I respect. But since I don't know anybody like that, I place my trust in the casual words of passersby.

Sentences I overhear, not that are said to me, snatches of a conversation, snippets of phone calls, anything will work. The important thing is to grab them without stopping, it's not fair to listen to an entire conversation and then select the most suitable passages. It has to be like a net cast blindly into the water, you pull it up at the end to see what's left.

Then you take everything and wash off the useless parts, splice the pieces together one next to the other, and I swear that if it's done right all the phrases connect in the end and out comes a piece of advice that can work.

So this morning I walk around Muglione, and as soon as I see someone I pass by them rapidly, like a man who has somewhere to go and something to do. But I don't know where to go or even what to do. That's why I pass close to these people, hoping they can somehow help me.

And these are the snatches of conversation that I collected.

1. *Cups are better than mugs* (sentence spoken by an approximately five-year-old child, at the café with his mother, which he repeats endlessly: *cups are better than mugs — cups are better than mugs — cups are better than mugs . . .*).
2. *If you say that one more time I'm gonna beat you black and blue* (mother to five-year-old son).
3. *I like it more moist, more juicy. The bread is already dry, so it's a tragedy if the porchetta is dry, too* (Mario from the newsstand speaking with a cop).
4. *Let's go, please, it's late* (Philippine woman somewhere between the ages of twenty and fifty, pulling a little dog on a leash).
5. *No good deed goes unpunished, we sat there and watched like morons and they stuck it to us, well, enough already* (the man who used to fix television sets to a group of seniors in front of the Youth Center).

So this is this morning's catch, I'll have to work on it . . .

I find myself in a shitty situation: I'm living in a closet full of bait, I have my final exams in a month and a half and maybe they won't even let me take them, my pride and joy is a band that, the only time it went onstage, wasn't even allowed to begin by the crowd, I've got a dad who kicks me out of the house to let a friggin' kid from Molise stay there, and my furious reaction is to help the kid with his homework.

How can I turn these snatches of conversation into a good piece of advice?

Let's see... *cups are better than mugs*, okay, what does that mean? Maybe cups are the little everyday satisfactions, which are better than a clamorous success that is bogus and will ruin your life. Or maybe the cup is the friggin' Little Champ, who's better than me, and I'm a big useless mug that should be thrown away?

So how am I supposed to behave, should I be dry, hard, and ruthless? But the world around me is already dry and hard, like the bread for porchetta, so should I be like the porchetta, moist and juicy? Or should I just go, like the Philippine woman's dog, because it's late and around these parts there's nothing left for me, and...

No, the superadvice doesn't seem to be working today. It's my fault, I'm too agitated and I must be doing something wrong. The way I'm putting things together it could advise me to do anything, it's telling me everything and nothing, like real people when you ask their opinion, who, since they couldn't care less, will tell you the first thing that pops into their heads.

No, today it's not working, I can feel it. So I'll do this: I won't put shit together, I won't interpret, absolutely nothing. I'll take only the last sentence I heard and go with it: *No good deed goes unpunished, we sat there and watched like morons and they stuck it to us, well, enough already!*

Exactly, enough already. Those seniors at the Youth Center know a thing or two, I could tell immediately from the way they looked at each other. They get right to the point, and so do I. Enough already. Otherwise they'll take advantage, shit! But from now on it's straight to the point, and my condolences to anyone who gets in my way.

Starting with the Little Champ from Molise, who's coming into the shop at two.

But for him I couldn't give two shits.

RAIN IN THE FOREST

It's two o'clock. Actually, it's 2:03, and the Little Champ is late. It's true that for the moment it might be a question of different clocks, maybe his says two o'clock while the one in the shop is three minutes ahead, but I'm here and I go on what I see, and in this tutoring business I'm the lord and master, so my clock gives the official time. The Little Champ is giving me another reason to be heartless.

I have to admit that I'm agitated, a little. Actually, more than a little. I'm agitated, period. It's been five months now that I've been hearing about this pain in the ass from Molise: everyone says hello to him and thanks him and hugs him and I'm the only one who has never said a word. Dad talks about almost nothing else. Like the customers here in the shop, the newspapers, the people on the street. Everyone talking about the Little Champ and the great opportunity for our town.

Because in Muglione important figures have never been born, never lived, and never even passed through accidentally. We have no thermal baths or miraculous shrines, no historic treasure and no great unexploited resource. In Muglione there's nothing, apart from the irrigation ditches, the county road, and the flat fields cultivated to stubble. And us, of course, us. So the Little Champ is a gift from heaven after many years of bitter pills and humiliation before the other towns on the plain.

Perignano, the furniture capital; Casciano and its baths; Palaia, where archeological ruins keep popping out from underground. And Peccioli, Peccioli is enemy number one. Once it was a hole in the wall, even worse than us. Then they built that gigantic super-modern incinerator and it became Hollywood on the Arno. Theaters, festivals, VIPs, no taxes, no utility bills. And Muglione was left in the dust.

That's why the story of the Little Cycling Champion is making them dream so much, the idiots. Now the name Muglione can be read in the local sports pages, and the more the Little Champ grows the more Muglione's fame will grow. You have to hold on tight to him, build the appropriate sports association as he climbs the ladder, all the way up to the pros, the Giro, the Tour de France, the World Championship.

Muglione world champion! Once I heard Mr. Bindi saying it while he was opening up the window gates of the butcher shop. And the bad thing is that he wasn't talking to anyone, he was there by himself pulling up the gates. *Muglione world champi —*

Well, here he is, the future world champion.

He's outside the door. It says closed, so he doesn't open it. He brings his hands to his eyes and looks inside. I signal him to come in but he doesn't know how.

"Just push the door!"

He studies it, looks inside again, nothing.

"Push!"

Finally he extends a hand and the door opens. The bell goes *driing* and startles him. Then he enters. The door closes behind him and we're alone, me and him.

Silence.

I say: "Five minutes late. We begin well." I prepare my right arm for the handshake, and I can't suppress a diabolical giggle. Because the handshake is the most embarrassing moment in the world when one of the two guys is missing a hand. The other one smiles calmly and extends his arm, he doesn't feel the squeeze so he lowers his eyes to see what's going on and discovers you don't have a hand to shake. He doesn't know what to do, what can he do? At that point his hand is out there, ready. He can't pull it away, it would be too embarrassing: all he can do is stand there with his hand outstretched into the void and hope to die a speedy death.

In short, a serious conundrum, but to avoid this all you have to do is quickly extend your left hand like I do and grab the right hand of the guy presenting it. At that moment he doesn't understand but he shakes it anyway and everything is settled.

But this time, with the Little Champ, I don't want to settle anything. On the contrary. I can already see him taking a step forward and extending his arm and then standing there before me, mortified.

"Pleased to meet you," I say, and I lean over from behind the counter. "Pleased to meet you."

And him, nothing. He takes a couple of steps forward but keeps his arm behind his back.

"Pleased to meet you, my name is Fiorenzo," and I move my arm while still keeping it hidden. Not much more I can do. The problem is that he does nothing. He intimates a kind of half bow with his eyes lowered and remains like that. Son of a bitch.

"Come on, have a seat." I sit back down behind the counter. There's a stool in the corner by the bags for the fishing rod cases. After a while he sees it, goes over, and sits down.

"Not there, bring it over here! Come on, move it, I haven't got all day."

He moves the stool, dragging it along the ground, the squeaking hurts my teeth.

"So, I hear that at school you're failing every subject, right?"

He nods, paying close attention, but he doesn't open his mouth.

"Oh, you got a tongue? I asked you if I'm right."

"Yes, Mister," he says. He called me Mister. With the voice of a little bird fallen from the nest, with cats and dogs and lawn-mowers all around.

"But I'm not going to explain math and science, okay? I can't stand them."

"I don't have a problem with them, Mister."

"In what sense?"

"The teachers are cycling fans, I turn in a blank sheet and they give me passing grades anyway."

"Ah. Okay. Good for you, kid. Good for you."

I can't believe it. What a fucked-up town. A teacher throws away his integrity because a kid is fast on a bicycle. Like the traffic cops, who ever since the friggin' Little Champ arrived haven't given Dad a single ticket. First he was always speeding, passing a red light, parking in a no-standing zone. Now he just says he's on his way to pick up something for Mirko and the road holds no rules for him.

"What about the Italian teacher?"

"She's a lady, Mister. Not her."

"She doesn't like cycling?"

"She says that sports are the opiate of the masses."

While the Little Champ is talking he crosses his fingers and breathes badly. He can't sit still. I've always avoided him like the plague so I've never seen him up close. He has white skin with pale red blemishes, an enormous head covered with dark curls that look like a worn-out carpet, small eyes, a long, pointed nose, and a tiny mouth located a little bit too far to the right of his face. Basically, besides the fact that I hate him and I'm talking about my number-one enemy...Holy Mother of God what a mess.

I keep staring at him and he casts his eyes toward the floor. He shifts his ass on the stool again. He has a plastic bag hanging from one arm that is digging into his flesh. I feel uncomfortable for him.

"What have you got in there?"

"Where?"

"In the bag."

"Oh, my book."

"Didn't you bring a pen and a notebook?"

"Yes. Book and pen and notebook."

"So get them out, what are you waiting for? Move it!"

It takes him a minute to remove the bag from his arm, then he drops the pen, tries to pick it up and almost falls off the stool. He's a devil all right: most people would look at him and fall for it immediately. But not me, I know it's all an act, a good act but still an act. This is the same bastard who stole my dad and kicked me out of my house, the same bastard who dug up my Sylvester the Cat glass and shoved it in my face on one of the darkest days in my life. I don't care, the dry sack of shit, everyone else might fall for him but not me.

"So, kiddo, what's your weakest point?"

"..."

"Come on, what are you doing worst in, poetry, grammar, research..."

"Compositions."

"Aha, compositions are important. I'm really good at them but I can't explain much. It's all a question of talent, either you're born with it or nothing. And the lesson plan?"

"Excuse me?"

"The lesson plan, for tomorrow, for the next few days, do you have any?"

"Yes, *The Rain in the Pinewood.*"

"Oh, now we're talking. Snap out of it, kid, do I have to ask you everything? So that's what we'll do today. *The Rain in the Pinewood.* By D'Annunzio," I say. "What a bunch of bullshit."

The Little Champ's eyes dart over to mine, then all around. He's alarmed. As if D'Annunzio himself were in the shop, choosing chum for catfish maybe, and could hear us.

"Oh, what's wrong? Come on, open up to that page, can you find it or not? Hurry up, it's a really disgusting poem. Why they make you study this crap I don't know."

Piece of cake. *The Rain in the Pinewood.* My plan was to teach the Little Champ a series of absurd and offensive things to make the other kids laugh and the teacher get mad and he could forget about passing eighth grade. But given the subject I don't have to invent a thing. Just say what I think.

"Let's start by hearing what you know about this poem. Do you know anything or is it a total eclipse?"

The Little Champ for the first time twists his mouth into a kind of smile.

"What's so funny?"

"Nothing, I'm sorry."

"So why are you laughing?"

"You made me laugh."

"Are you laughing at me?"

"No, at that thing, *total eclipse.* I like the way it sounds."

"We say *expression. I like the way that expression sounds*," I say, and in my head I repeat, *Don't let him fool you, don't let him fool you*... "Can we get on with it? Tell me what you know about *The Rain in the Pinewood*."

"That it's a poem."

"No shit. And? What does it talk about?"

"About a man in the woods, with a woman."

"And what happens?"

"It rains."

"Yes, it rains. And the rain makes a kind of music in the woods, right?"

"Yes, a little."

"*A little?* What is it you don't get?"

"Well, if it's raining what are they going to the woods for?"

"Apart from the fact that it's not the woods, it's a pine grove, maybe they went there before the weather changed. D'Annunzio was a guy who went for long walks in the woods, completely naked."

"Naked?"

"Yes, and she was naked, too, what do you think?"

"But... what if somebody saw them?"

"Go figure, D'Annunzio was a pig, he used to have orgies all the time. Do you know what an orgy is?"

"Not really."

"It's a lot of people having sex together."

The idiot says nothing. He sits there all serious with his eyes popping out, open so wide you can see his brain. And right now his brain is crammed with sweaty people clinging to each other all aroused and doing God knows what. Talking about sex with someone who knows even less about it than me doesn't happen that often, it makes me feel good.

"But this stuff about orgies, can I tell it to the teacher?"

"Are you kidding? You *have to* tell her."

"Because I get a little embarrassed."

"What's there to be embarrassed about, it's the truth! And you have to say it, I mean, that's the whole story of *The Rain in the Pinewood*. He and she go into the pine grove to have sex, but it starts to rain and she wants to go home, so he starts to go on and on about the music of the rain and the happy animals and that she's a sacred nymph, in that way he hopes she'll give it up to him anyway."

"A nymph?"

"Yes, the nymphs were these goddesses who lived in the woods. You don't know shit! You see, he's not just accidentally saying that she's a nymph. What he's really saying is that she's a nymphomaniac, get it?"

"Not really."

"It doesn't matter. The important thing is that you tell your teacher these things. That's all you have to do."

The Little Champ nods, then he takes his pen and writes "NYMPHOMANIAC" on the blank page. He rereads it; from his expression you'd think it wasn't even his writing.

"The teacher never told us this stuff."

"What does she know! Middle school teachers are a bunch of assholes. They wanted to teach high school and they weren't good enough. And the high school teachers are the same, because they wanted to teach college. It's a whole chain of losers, and who do you think they take it out on?"

The Little Champ looks at me, then raises a finger from the book and points to his chest.

"Good boy, you do get it. But if you say these things during the quiz, make sure and show her that you studied them yourself and you'll get a high grade, okay? And if you don't believe me just try reading the poem, anywhere you want. Here."

"Should I read?"

"Yes."

"Here?"

"Same difference."

"Is it ok if I start here?"

"Yes, for Christ's sake, read!"

" 'Rain falls on the myrtles divine, on the broom-shrubs gleaming with flowers ... clustered, on the junipers thick with ... berries? With fragrant berries, rain falls on our sylvan faces, rain falls on our naked hands ... on our clothi ... on our light clothing, on the fresh thoughts that our soul dis ...' "

"Okay, enough. Do you get it?"

"A little."

"How much is a little?"

"Um, a little nothing, Mister."

"I knew it. Now, does he sound like a guy saying normal things to you? No, this is a guy who's trying to sweet-talk a woman, do you get it?"

"Yes, but ..."

"*But* what?"

"Nothing, sorry."

"No, tell me, I'm curious."

"I mean, here it says they have clothing."

"What of it?"

"But weren't they naked?"

"Whatever, light clothing, like a veil, a pareo. If you see a naked woman walking down the street, but wearing a veil, doesn't she look naked anyway?"

"Yes."

"And don't you turn around to look at her?"

"Maybe."

"You see? So you've got to think before you speak."

"Yes..."

"Exactly. *Yes.*"

And both of us stop talking. He draws an arrow next to the verses he read, writes "SWEET-TALK," and then looks at me. And I don't know what more to say. Everything's quiet except for a car passing by every now and then. I made him come at two because at three-thirty the shop opens. Now it's two-fifteen and for me we're done.

"All right, I'd say we've done enough for today."

He looks at me, says nothing, but that face is not a yes. In effect he just arrived, but I don't know what else to say. I've already accomplished my purpose: after the quiz he's dead meat. For me that's enough.

"Like I said, now you can go. See you." I cross my arms and give him a serious look.

He closes his book and places the notebook on top of it. "But, Mister..."

"*But* what?"

"You see, I...my problem is with the compositions, Mister."

"And?"

"I have to hand in a composition the day after tomorrow."

"And you want to do it now? Don't push your luck. Today we did poetry. Save the composition for next time..."

"But I already did it."

"So what the hell do you want?"

"Maybe if you could read it you could correct any..."

"I don't have time right now. You know what, leave it with me, I'll read it when I feel like it, okay?"

The dope takes two sheets from inside his Italian book and gives them to me. He even says, "Thank you."

And he says goodbye with a frown on his face and turns around, it takes him a while to figure out where the exit is, even though it's right in front of him. And I have to say that as an actor you can't beat him, because looking at him this way, you'd think this kid was the biggest dumbass on the planet.

But rather than go he turns around again. "Mister..."

"What else do you want?"

"I...I brought my other compositions from this year."

"Ah, and what are you doing with them?"

"They're for you, to read."

"What do you want me to read them for?"

"Like, if you want to help me, you know, maybe it would be easier this way."

"Easy, my ass. What makes you think I can spend my days reading your little thoughts? I've got tons of shit to do. Where do you get these ideas?"

"I don't know, I...the thing is, I thought you could help me."

"Listen, it's one thing to give you a lesson every now and then, but to expect me to read your bullshit, you can forget about it."

"..."

"Okay, get lost, come on, go, walk, pedal."

The Little Champ nods and gets all sad, much more than before. He even looks smaller, almost hunchbacked, and the raw material is hardly prime beef to start with. And maybe just a little bit, but barely a little, I feel sorry.

"All right, leave them there on the shelf."

"Leave what, Mister?"

"Your compositions, no? What do you think, asshole? Hurry up. Leave them there and get the hell out of here."

This time he moves fast. He takes them and puts them there. When I say fast I mean normal, human, but by now I'm getting used to his slowness.

It's a stack of papers this high, all messy and crinkled.

He opens the door and is about to go out.

"Listen up," I say. "What's this about the Sylvester the Cat glass?"

Since I don't give two shits about this jerk, I ask him like that, point-blank, and I watch his reaction carefully: every small movement of his face can help me understand what he knows about this story. Because I don't give a shit.

But the bastard doesn't move a muscle. "I'm sorry, excuse me?"

"You, in my room. You're using a glass."

"Yes."

"A Sylvester the Cat glass."

"I think so."

"Well, why?"

"Why what, Mister?"

"Why are you using it?"

"I don't know, sometimes I'm thirsty."

"No shit, Sherlock, but why are you using that glass?"

"I took it from the kitchen."

"Yes, but it was in the cupboard, in the way back, and there are thousands of glasses in there. Why did you take that one?"

"Why..."

"Yes?"

"Because I like Sylvester the Cat, Mister."

And he gives me a look that seems fake. Without the least bit of expression. Like a drawing of a face that didn't come out right. I try to sit still, reboot, motionless. A staring contest.

"Anyway, kid, you don't fool me. Get it?"

"..."

"Get it?"

"I don't...like, I don't understand in what sens—"

"Did you get it? Just tell me that you got it."

"But I didn't get—"

"Just tell me that you got it and fuck off."

He looks at me, looks at the chrome-plated fishing reels in the display case, and looks back at me. "I got it."

"Good, now get the fuck out of here."

WEAD YOU

Today is one of those days that you're happy and depressed at the same time. Both, shaken together and poured on top of an afternoon.

But it's not your fault, it's events that when they happen seem to like happening all at the same time. Maybe a week passes by with nothing, then all of a sudden everything gets all worked up for a few hours, and before you know it immobility returns. Your life is a little like that, days of nothing and moments of fire, nothing and fire, nothing and fire. A trench war.

Today you worked on English with the Little Champion of Molise, and at the end of the lesson you told him that if he wanted tutoring in any other subjects you were available.

But he said *No thank you*. He'd found an Italian master. That's what he said, *a master*. He wanted to go to the master today, too, but he wasn't home, so you convinced the Little Champ to go over his D'Annunzio lesson with you, since there's going to be a quiz tomorrow.

And he started speaking with the tone of memorization, the bored look of someone repeating the most obvious things in the world:

"D'Annunzio was a sex maniac who walked around naked all the time and had orgies with women and with men, he wrote a lot of poems but the most famous is *Rain in the Pinewood*, where he goes to the woods together with a woman to have sex but when it starts to rain and she wants to go away he makes her stay and starts to sweet-talk her with stuff about the rain and the amazing music it makes and how she's a nymphomaniac and they remove the light veil she's wearing and have sex."

All in a string and attached, just like when you were in first grade and the teacher made every pupil learn a mini-presentation for the mayor's visit to the school. *My name is Tiziana Cosci I was born on November 6, 1977, and I live in Muglione.* Or rather, *Mynameistizianacosciiwasbornonnovember6,1977,andiliveinmuglione.*

Mirko had the same tone you had that time, except that if the mayor heard him he would immediately call in social services and the police. And if by chance his Italian teacher hears him, he can forget about passing.

"Mirko, these things...how in the world can you be thinking them?"

"What things?"

"The things you just told me."

"It's D'Annunzio, didn't you know?"

"What are you talking about? Who taught you that?"

"My Italian master."

"But it's absurd, it's not..."

"I know, they're things they don't teach you at school, because they don't want to."

"Did your master tell you that, too?"

Mirko nodded, then looked at you blankly, closed his English book, and stood up.

You asked him the phone number of his master, but he didn't know. You asked him were he lives and he told you he's at the Magic Bait shop, so you called there.

An answering machine picked up. But who in the world still uses answering machines? And you couldn't understand a word, the message was impossible to hear, drowning in waves of really heavy heavy metal: *"Hello, we are...not available...leave a..."* These are the only words you can make out, what with the raging guitar and someone who's howling as if he were being skinned alive: *"See-you-in-helllll...Beep."*

"Hello, this is Tiziana Cosci and I'm calling from the Youth Center. I'm looking for Fiorenzo Marelli on a matter of a certain urgency. My office number is..."

Then she said goodbye to Mirko, that nitwit Mirko, who before leaving banged a hip against the vibrating armchair, broke his plastic bag, and dropped his books. You gave him another bag and said 'bye.

And in the office there was a wave of silence, real silence. Now that the seniors have started gathering outside, the place bears an uncanny resemblance to the warehouse that it used to be. Which it's going to go back to being if things keep up this way.

You move the mouse and the computer reawakens, the screen lights up. But the only thing in your head is the image of D'Annunzio naked in a pine grove calling a woman a nymphomaniac.

You go to your blog page. A new comment has arrived. You didn't write anything today, and nothing yesterday either. And your three regular commenters had already made their contributions to the last post.

In fact, this new comment is from anonymous, since whoever wrote it didn't leave a name. It arrived at ten o'clock this morning. An innocuous hour, when things aren't very busy, but if you calculate the time zone in California it becomes one o'clock in the morning. At one o'clock in the morning he was reading you and thinking about you. And this time he wrote.

You click on it and read, breathlessly.

Tiziana, how nice to wead you. xxxooo

Just like that, short and sincere, with that *w* that must be a typo but that makes your heart go pitter-patter.

Usually you can't stand mistakes or even abbreviations. Once you met the friend of a friend and while you might have initially been tempted the first message he wrote said, *I think ur kinda special*. Kinda. Not even in middle school, for crying out loud. Not to mention this guy was pushing forty, what was he thinking? That by writing *kinda* he'd sound younger? No way, it only made him sound dumber. You and your girlfriend renamed him Special Kinda, like Special K, the cereal with no flavor, and you never gave him another thought.

But this *wead* is another matter, a cute mistake, by a foreigner writing to you who was probably trying weally weally hard.

You reread it and smile. You say it softly, in the void of the warehouse.

"Wead."

You smile.

TONGUES UNTIED

In four years with an answering machine, this is the first time anyone's left a message. And it coincides with the first time a woman has called.

The news is clamorous. The Muglione Youth Center is looking for me, *the* Fiorenzo Marelli, and asking for a meeting. Fantastic. You can tell that someone must have been at the Pontedera festival and witnessed the shamelessness of that idiotic crowd and realized instead that Metal Devastation was serious shit. Are they putting together a festival here in town? Or are they planning a concert just for us? Maybe they realize that if they hope to raise high the name of Muglione, they're going to have to invest in us, a solid band that by a quirk of fate was born here rather than in Los Angeles.

Of course, if you want to be pessimistic, maybe they were looking for me because of the stuff with the cats. Maybe the last time I brought them to the Youth Center they recognized me and now they want to bust my ass. But I really don't think so. First, it was dark. Second, everyone leaves cats in that yard. Third, Metal Devastation kicks ass: someone had to realize it sooner or later.

It doesn't take long to reach the Center, three blocks and I'm there. At every intersection there's an old man by himself at the corner, except for the last one, where there are two. The usual old folks I've been seeing ever since I was born but I don't know what their names are or what they used to do for a living. And above all I don't know what they're doing on the street corners, standing there with their hands in their pockets watching me pass by.

Each of them has a memo pad and a pen and around his waist a green fanny pack with an elk or a deer or something similar on it. And when I reach the Youth Center there are three more in front of the door, all with fanny packs. One of the three is the guy who fixed TVs, and Mazinger is another. But he pretends he doesn't know me, so no way am I going to say hi to him. I walk by them and offer a nice tight smile as if to say *I couldn't give two shits about you, go to hell.* And then I go in.

And I'm like a blind man for a second. Damn it's dark in here. Outside the sun is beating down and in here it's like night. Not even one window and a damp smell that makes me want to cough. It's different from the bait room but gives the same impression of being in a tomb.

"Hello," I hear. A woman's voice. Nice voice.

Three round tables, a couple of newspapers and posters of Tuscany, a giant blue armchair, and off to one side a desk, a seated figure.

"Can I help you with something?"

"I think so, you were looking for me? I'm the singer from Metal Devastation."

"I beg your pardon?"

Ouch. It's not about the band. Shit, it's not about the band. It's about the cats. I can still run away, maybe. But there's no proof against me, not a shred of evidence, you can't pin it on me.

"I got a phone call from you," I say. "From a Tiziana."

"Yes, I'm Tiziana. And you are..."

"Fiorenzo Marelli. I sing in a band, we already have one festival under our belt and—"

"Ah, you're Mirko's Italian tutor," she says. And if she had hit me over the head with a bat it would have hurt less. Even the cats would have been better than this. I've got nothing to do with that little shit, what does she want from me?

In the meantime my eyes get used to the dark. The woman at the desk has longish black hair and a plain navy-blue T-shirt. She's pretty. Beauty is something I notice but tend to forget immediately, what difference does it make to me if a girl is pretty or not? My odds of going to bed with her are less than zero, so all I can do is get a good look at her and then think about her tonight when I'm alone. But for that there's porn, which is a lot more convenient. So, Miss Youth Center, you're pretty and we all know it, but I'm not one of those idiots ready to do anything for a piece of ass, okay?

"So," she says, "I called you because of a serious matter."

"Serious?"

"Yes. You might not realize it, but we're talking about a minor with obvious learning difficulties."

"Actually, I do realize it. In my opinion he's not normal."

"Let's not get carried away. One thing for certain, however, is that he's not very quick."

I sit down. I keep my right wrist stuffed in my pocket.

From up close this woman is even hotter. But not the type who thinks she's the hottest thing on two legs so she gets all dolled up. This one's just plain pretty, and maybe she doesn't even know it. But I sure do.

Under her T-shirt are two firm pointy tits. If I concentrate I can even make out the shape of her nipples...yes, I think tonight I'm going to be conjuring her up, maybe even here at her desk, she's asked me to come by for a talk and then in the end she's going to tell me I've been a bad boy and she has to punish me, and she stands up and is wearing a kind of see-through negligee and under it a pair of thigh-high nylons and high heels and she says to me, *But first you have to punish me, go ahead, hurt me...*

"Yes, you're right," I say, using the small piece of my brain that's still working. "The situation is serious because the kid is demented. He needs a special ed teacher, a school for the retarded."

"No he doesn't. What are you talking about? The situation is serious, but it's your fault."

Mine? I knew it, I can't let my mind wander for a second. What's the problem?

"Listen, I was looking for you because today Mirko repeated to me what he knows about D'Annunzio. He told me a series of outrageous things and he said that he learned them from you."

Son of a bitch. Can you see what a bastard son of a bitch he is? He acts like such a moron, all tongue-tied, he listens to things and he repeats them and even takes notes, and you tell yourself, *Mother of God, this guy's buying it hook, line, and sinker.* But he was taking the notes to fuck me up but good and get me in trouble. Son of a bitch.

"There's nothing wrong with what I told him."

"You told him that D'Annunzio was a pig."

"So. And?"

"And that he used to go around naked and have orgies and his companion was a nympho—"

The door behind me opens with a bang. I turn around and it's the three old geezers from before, all lined up.

"Is everything all right in here, Miss?"

She jumps to her feet and says, "Yes, yes, but would it be too much to ask you to knock?"

"It was just to check whether you needed anything," says the guy who used to fix TVs, and he looks at me all serious for a second. I give a big, fake smile, and the old guys shake their heads and go back outside, marking down something on their memo pads.

The beauty and I are once again alone in the tomb of the Youth Center, and for the moment we say nothing. I take advantage to get a good look at her, now that she's standing. Hips, thighs, ass. The mapping for tonight is complete.

You stood up instinctively, but now that you're on your feet you don't know what to do. You adjust one of your sandals just for show and then sit back down. The surprise incursion of the old men made your heart slip into your throat. You hope they didn't hear anything. You here alone in the dark with a boy half your age while you're saying the words *pig, orgies, nymphomaniac.*

You settle into the chair and try to pick up where you left off.

"As I was saying, were you the one who told him that *Rain in the Pinewood* is the story of a guy who wants to make love to a girl?"

"Yes, I think so. And, by the way, it's true."

"Not to my knowledge, and at any rate that's not the point. The point is that you told it to a minor who doesn't know anything about these things."

"Is it my fault if he's half asleep? He's fifteen years old, there are people who at his age are already dealing heroin."

"That's not our problem here..."

"Oh, of course, let's set aside the serious problems, society is falling to pieces but it's not our problem, our problem is to defend a pig who's going into a pinewood to fuck a girl!"

"Lower your voice, please. My problem, if you must put it that way, is how to help a somewhat simpleminded boy and a barely legal teenager who is telling him a lot of nonsense about sex."

"It's not nonsense, it's true! And listen... I beg your pardon, what I meant to say, if you'll let me explain, is that the kid is not at all simpleminded, you've gotta admit... I mean, if you don't mind my saying... I can't stand these damn formalities! Can't we just use first names and get on with it?"

You're tempted to say no. No, damn it, what does this guy want from you, he's just an idiotic kid who thinks he's smart. No, you will not drop the formalities. Who is he to teach anyone a lesson? He couldn't teach a monkey, much less a boy with problems.

But you don't answer him, and he takes it for a yes.

"Thank God for that, I can't stand being formal. Did you know that in English they don't even have the formal *you*, and everyone's on a first-name basis?"

"Of course I know."

"Great language, English, eh?"

"On this much we can agree."

"Do you speak it?"

"I lived abroad for a long time, so yes, I speak it well."

"Abroad? Where?"

"London, Zurich, but mainly Berlin."

"Far out! But where are you from?"

"Our problem at the moment is something else and—"

"All right, all right, but where are you from?"

"I was born here."

"No way! Here in Muglione? Like, you're from Muglione and you've traveled so much? Wow, this is really great to know, you see, it gives me hope."

"Hope?"

"Yeah, lots. Every day I look around and I think that I was born in a trap. You know, the things I like, here they don't even know what they are, and when I look at the people I get pissed off because they're real downers with no interests. Not just the old folks. The old folks I can understand, but the kids my age, how can they be so laid-back in such a miserable place? I don't know if you understand me, but—"

"I understand you all too well," you say. On the desk there are photocopies. You lower your eyes and pick them up to keep your hands busy.

"So you must speak English really well. Do you know any other languages?"

"Well, yes."

"Which ones?"

"Mainly German, then French, and a little bit of Japanese."

"No, I can't believe it. Fantastic. You know, I swear, you really give me hope. Can I tell you? You give me hope. Pleased to meet you, I'm Fiorenzo."

"A pleasure, Tiziana." You drop the photocopies and extend your hand. But he takes it with his left, shakes it, and then leans back against the chair. Strange. It must be a handshake that's popular among teenagers.

"Yes, a pleasure," you say. "But let's not get off track now. Listen, Fiorenzo, if you want to help Mirko you have to understand that it's a serious and delicate matter and..."

"Hey, do you know how to write in all those languages?"

"Yes...apart from Japanese, of course."

"That's perfect. Because we've got this plan to cut a CD demo. Me and my band, we're called Metal Devastation. We're already pretty well-known around here but we want to send the demo to different labels all over the world."

"Okay, but let's not get off track."

"So we need a letter, in English and German, something to explain to them who we are and what we want. Do you think you could translate it?"

"Me...well, of course, but that's got nothing to do with the problem I was talking about."

"Are you kidding? You've solved my biggest problem, you don't know how lucky I was to come here, and all because of those bullshit lessons."

"Well, that actually is the problem. You have to realize that it's not bullshit, it's a very serious and sensitive matter. From the moment you teach something to a child, you have a very specific role, and you have to perform that role—"

"Come on, give me a break, I understand, who cares. Do you care? In my opinion, not even you care. You've traveled the world, seen lots of things, what does someone like you care about a middle school quiz? Get real! Because I, like you, want to get out of this dump as soon as I finish high school. Can I ask you what advice you have for me?"

"Of course you can. The purpose of this office is to provide certain kinds of information."

"In fact, it's super useful. I feel almost stupid for not coming here before."

"You're not the only one, unfortunately."

"What do you mean?"

"I mean that no one ever comes." You look back down at the photocopies. Without realizing it you have continued to torture them and they're all crumpled up. They have information about courses for stylists, tango schools...in other words, it's no big deal if they're ruined. "Please don't tell people, but no one ever comes."

"Why don't they?"

"I don't know."

"But that's crazy."

"I know, but that's the way it is."

"But why?"

"I don't know. I mean, maybe there is a reason, but you can figure it out for yourself."

"Really?"

"Yes, really."

The boy looks at you, you look at him, you nod yes, twisting your mouth.

"Because this town is so fucked up, right?"

"You said it, not me."

"I said it and I'll say it again! This town is totally fucked up!"

You nod and smile a little.

"But listen, Tiziana, you've got to explain one thing to me... what I mean is, it's like, one day you up and left and you said *fuck you* once and for all to this dump, right?"

"Well, yes, more or less."

"Good, and you were absolutely right. Fantastic. But I'm wondering, why did you come back?"

You don't answer right away. You don't have an answer. "It's a long story."

"Tell me."

"It's a really long story."

"Come on, tell me."

"The main thing is that I don't even know why. So there's not much I can tell you."

"I get it. And do you think you'll be leaving again?"

"What do you mean?"

"I mean, if you were wrong to come back, you can always leave again, can't you?"

"I didn't say I was wrong."

"Really? So let me break the news to you. You were wrong."

And he laughs. You smile, too, even if you'd rather not. Then you look at the computer screen. One-twenty. At one o'clock you were supposed to meet up with Raffaella, since they're delivering the new sofa.

"Damn, it's late, I have to run. But, look, I really need you to get the gist of this conversation. In a situation like this you can't be getting too creative. I hope you understand."

"I don't understand shit. But I really enjoyed speaking with you."

"Okay, I guess that's a start," you say. You wanted to get pissed off but you can't do anything, you can't even withhold another smile. "And if you don't want to give lessons to Mirko, don't worry, I can go over Italian with him, too, understood?"

"Yes, that would be perfect, because I don't have any time. And I really hate that little brat."

"How can you hate him? He can't even find his way out of a paper bag."

"Don't fall for it." Fiorenzo stands up. He's as tall as you. "Don't let him fool you. He's evil, it's all an act."

"Maybe so, but I can still tutor him."

"Okay, great, you'd be taking a load off my back. And all those compositions to read, he expected me to—"

"What compositions?"

"His."

"He gave you his compositions?"

"Yes, why?"

"He doesn't let anybody read them. Sometimes he doesn't even turn them in to the teacher. He always gets an F as if he hadn't even written them. I asked to see them a few times, but he always shakes his head and refuses to speak, nothing doing."

"But I didn't even want them. He's the one who insisted, he gave me a whole stack of them. This morning he even slid another one under the shop door. Who knows what's going through that moron's head? At any rate, if you want I can bring them to you."

"No, thanks anyway, but it wouldn't be right."

"What do you care? I'll bring them to you. Oh, before I forget, can you give me your e-mail? So I can send you the letter to translate into German?"

"Okay, I'll write it down on a piece of paper. You know, I also have a blog if you're interested."

You told him. Just like that, without thinking. Why? It doesn't make any sense. Maybe you want a fourth regular commenter? And what does this juvenile metalhead care about your daily rants? You're ridiculous, Tiziana, you're an idiot. The tension and embarrassment make you almost spit out a big guffaw. You haven't acted like this since you wore braces.

"You've got a blog? Awesome, what's it about?"

"Oh, nothing, just stuff."

"Music? Movies?"

"No, nothing like that. I'm sorry I mentioned it. Don't look at it."

"But I want to, I'm interested. What's it about?"

"About my life, like a diary. I even talk about this crummy town."

"Really? I want to read it. Give me your e-mail and your web address."

You nod, pick up a pen, and turn over one of the photocopies to write on the back. "You know, by the way, one of my readers is an American," you say. Now why did you have to go and say that? You're ridiculous, you're pathetic. This kid's fucking with you and he'll show it to his friends, who will all start fucking with you and they'd be right.

But in the meantime it seems to really matter to him. "Awesome!" he says. "From America? How did he find you?"

"I don't know, but he comes by every day. I have a program that tells me who visits my blog, and he comes by every day."

"Cool. Where is he from? New York? Washington?"

"No, he lives in California."

"Fantastic. Los Angeles, San Francisco, there are fierce bands around there."

"Yes, but he likes to live a little more peacefully, he's from Mountain View."

"From where?"

"Mountain View." Saying the name of the town has a strange effect on you. Maybe you blush a little. But the expression on the boy's face changes and he starts shaking his head.

"Ah. Okay. No, Tiziana, he's not a person, then. That's the central server of Google, their headquarters is in Mountain View. It automatically connects to every site every day for updates. It's not a person visiting your blog, it's a computer."

He says it clearly and smiles serenely. And he doesn't realize, doesn't have the least idea, but before his eyes your world is screeching, shaking, crumbling to the ground piece by piece.

Like those buildings that have been in ruins for years. There are cracks and ramblers grow on top of them, yet there they are and no one knows what keeps them standing. But all it takes is a freak gust of wind and down goes the house. And you are falling to pieces, Tiziana. And so is America, your foreign admirer, and this bullshit about getting through the day with such a stupid idea at the bottom of your heart.

You have the office keys in your hand, you squeeze them so tight they start to dig into your flesh. You stare right into the boy's eyes and take a step toward him. He smiles a little less. He keeps his right hand in his pocket, his left along his side, next to a T-shirt with the words buried alive.

You take another step. You squeeze the keys in your palm, they're made of iron. They're sharp.

You're an inch away from him, a half inch. He's not smiling anymore. You're not smiling.

And you kiss him.

With your tongue. With all the tongue you've got, stuck all the way to the back of his mouth. Teeth bump against teeth like in the awkward kisses of middle school, you let the keys fall and you squeeze his hips with your hands and push against him as close as you can, your tongue goes back and forth and twists and turns and he doesn't do anything back but it doesn't matter, all that matters is that he takes everything without stopping you.

You can tell that he's not breathing, but you're not breathing either, air doesn't exist in this kind of tomb, and time doesn't exist, and not even the old folks outside and the town all around you and the sad people who don't see the sadness because they were born there and they mistake it for normal life and carry on without thinking about anything.

And now you're not thinking about anything either, Tiziana. You close your eyes and kiss him, you rub against him and kiss him, you think of nothing and you kiss him.

And where there's nothing there's nothing that is right or wrong.

NOW WHAT?

How I got back to the shop, I swear I don't know. Walking, swimming, through mysterious catacombs dug into the subsoil of Muglione, anything is possible.

I close the gate. My head is spinning, I lean against the display case for the fishing reels, I try to breathe.

The shop was closed, Dad went home to eat and left the keys in the secret place, under the flower basin here in front. But it took me a quarter of an hour to remember. I didn't even know what I was looking for, what I wanted to do...

Holy shit, what a kiss. If I breathe deep I can still smell the scent. Of what I don't know. It wasn't perfume, maybe saliva, maybe something that the woman at the Youth Center puts on her lips. Those lips. On me. Now that's what I call a kiss. A real kiss. It's something strong, but I wouldn't know if it's also nice, I still don't know, I figure tomorrow I'll be able to see it a little better. There's no risk I'm going to forget it anyway. It's practically the only thing going through my head.

I even phoned Stefanino. I had to tell someone.

"But who was it?"

"A girl."

"Yeah, but what girl?"

"You don't know her. I don't know her either."

"How much did she ask for?"

"I didn't pay her, she wasn't a prostitute!"

"Far out! What did it feel like?"

"Uh, I don't know. Like another person's tongue. She moved it around a lot."

"And you?"

"Me what?"

"What did you do?"

"Me? Nothing."

"Oh, I see. But did you touch?"

"Yeah, she was pressed right up against me."

"What did it feel like?"

"I don't know. Everything."

"What about her tits?"

Stefanino asked, and it was only then that I realized that yes, I really did, I really did feel her tits. They were crushed against my chest.

"What were they like?"

"Nice."

"But what did they feel like, what are tits like? Are they hard or soft?"

I think for a second. For two seconds. "It's like they're hard and soft at the same time."

"Damn!"

"Yeah."

"Damn, way to go! And now?"

"Now what?"

"Like, is she from around here?"

"Yeah."

"Well, so like, what's going to happen now?"

"I don't know, what do you mean?"

"I mean, okay, a French kiss, very nice. But what I meant to say is, like, you didn't stop there, did you?"

Silence. I nod even though I'm on the phone. Anyway I know that Stefanino can still see me, somehow, from over there. We don't say anything for a minute, then say *See you later, Okay, 'Bye, 'Bye.*

Stefanino's right: Now what? I don't know. I didn't think about it and I can't. Because I'm not here, not at all. The tongue of that woman from the Youth Center is still churning in my mouth and in my head, and it's going to stay that way for a while, I think.

Tiziana. Her name is Tiziana. The woman I kissed. Well, the woman who kissed me, to be accurate, but you get my drift. And not a normal kiss, but a kiss that was over the top. Okay, it was my first French kiss so I don't have too much to compare it with, but you don't always need experience to understand certain things, in my opinion. I mean, in Hiroshima they'd never seen atomic bombs but underneath the mushroom cloud they still understood that it was a really big deal.

A phenomenal kiss, with her tongue twisting and poking around, and her hands rubbing my sides and my back. And I took that kiss full on without doing squat. What could I do? What do I know how to do? Nothing, I don't know how to do any of these things, and in fact I didn't even touch her, didn't even rest my hand on her hip.

I kept my left arm frozen against my leg, and my right stuffed into my pants pocket. Sure, I could have removed it, but I didn't think it was the right moment. Usually people get embarrassed as soon as they find out that I have only one hand, and if they find out while they've got their tongue snaking down my throat it would probably be even worse. So I kept my wrist in my pocket the whole time, for that minute or that hour that she was digging her tongue into my mouth, and even afterward, when she pushed me away and took two deep breaths with a throaty sound and her eyes wide open staring at me chest-high and no higher.

She took a step back and said, *I'm so sorry,* and I said, *For what?* She said, *Go away, please, go away.* And her eyes were so wide open that at that point I pulled my arm out of my pocket, there was the risk they'd open even wider and then they'd definitely explode.

I said get out of here, go! And this time she raised her voice, and after that I don't remember anything, but somehow I found my way out the door.

Because here I am now. In the locked shop. Lunchtime. But who wants to eat? In my mouth I can still feel her tongue moving around.

And only one thought in my head.

Now what?

STUPID, STUPID, *STUPID*

Stupid. How could you be so stupid? There's no other word for it, as if you needed it, because that one captures perfectly what you are: stupid. You can sit down at the computer, open a new document, choose the biggest font, type out the word *STUPID*, and then save the file under the name "Tiziana." That's how stupid you are.

You left the Youth Center and found the sidewalk, the road, and the old folks looking at you like a jury with the verdict already written on their faces.

"Are you all right, Miss? Was that guy giving you any trouble?" And they wrote everything down on their memo pads.

You didn't answer, maybe didn't even close the office door, and walked away with your head down, unable to believe the incredibly weird thing that had just happened.

Actually, it's not something that happened, it's something that you did. That *you* did. And you are *stupid*.

Parked outside your house is a white truck with a picture of an insect dressed up as a superhero with the euro symbol on its chest. The insect is winking an eye and giving a thumbs-up.

You race up the stairs. You want to slip into your room, close the door behind you, push the dresser against it so it's locked tight, and stay there for a long long time. Let's say a week. The time it takes to die in little spurts.

You put the key in the door but it's already open, from inside you can hear a din of voices that suddenly stop. Raffaella and two men in white uniforms. They were talking, now they say hi and stand there looking at you.

The new sofa. Who the hell remembered? That's why there was a truck downstairs with the superhero insect. So it wasn't just any insect, it was a woodworm. So...oh, who gives a shit.

"Tiziana, thank goodness you're here." Raffaella is nervous, she takes you by the arm and points to the still disassembled sofa leaning against the wall. "Okay, shut up, everyone. Let's see what she says. Tiziana, I want you to look at this sofa and tell me the first word that comes to mind..."

Stupid. The first word that comes to your mind is *stupid*. And the second word, and so on, for each of the top ten spots in the hit parade. But since you have to say something, you find another, more suitable word: "Brown?"

"What do mean, 'brown'? Okay, you're right, in the catalog it was a completely different color. This one here is *brown* brown."

"Miss, we just deliver, it doesn't make any sense to complain to us."

"I realize that, but what's the sense of a little sofa like that? And besides, Tiziana, the word isn't *brown*, the word is *LITTLE*. Can't you see, it's tiny! How are we supposed to watch TV at night, by taking turns?"

You nod. Taking turns is okay, who gives a shit? In a little while Raffaella is going to have the whole sofa to herself anyway. You'll stay in your room until you die of thirst or shame. Or the police will come first and take you away for taking advantage of a minor.

But wait, get off it, he wasn't a minor. He was at least eighteen, maybe. And after all, it was only a kiss, right? But what a kiss, your tongue and your neck are killing you, you were rubbing against that kid so hard that by the end your bra was twisted.

You'd never done anything like that. Drunken parties in Germany, rock festivals in Switzerland, nights at the dance club with a posse of horny girlfriends, and somehow you'd never done anything like that. Why did you have to go and do it now, at the age of thirty-two, in the office where you work, and with a kid?

So ridiculous that he, in fact, didn't even move. It's clear, you terrorized him. And if he goes to the police to report you? They're going to arrest you, Tiziana, and take you down to the police station. As a minimum they'll fire you and they'll be right.

"Miss, if you sign here we can go," says one of the two guys.

"What? I'm not signing anything," says Raffaella. "And what do you expect me to sign? If you have a piece of paper that says *Miss Raffaella Ametrano thinks this sofa sucks*, I'll sign it immediately. You can forget about anything else."

"So we have to carry it back downstairs?"

"Yes, guys, I'm sorry."

"On our backs..."

"Unfortunately, yes. I'm really sorry, but yes. Before going, if you like, I'd be happy to offer you a glass of something, but after..."

"No, thanks." They hoist the sofa on their backs and mutter a few choice words.

And you can't take your eyes off this miniature brown sofa, which really does look like a giant turd with armrests.

You look at it and it seems to say goodbye to you on its way out of your life forever. Yes, it says goodbye and calls you by the name that is most suitable for you.

Goodbye, STUPID.

AND NOW
THE SCREAMING STARTS

Fishing rod case on my back, tackle kit between my legs, and off I go on the scooter at full speed. Today is one of those classic days when the only thing you can do is go fishing.

Hot and humid and smelly, no wind, no trees around, and above is the serene sky typical of the plain: take two or three clouds, mix them in with a clean sky, and spread the off-white result over the whole horizon. That's the sky of the Muglione plain.

I come to a spot I like because water plants grow there, a few reeds and a kind of water lily without flowers. With a little imagination you can pretend it's a lake or a pond, as long as you don't sniff at the water or take a look around.

I put two kernels of corn and a maggot on the hook, like I always do. But now I look at the maggots with different eyes. Maybe our lives are joined in this moment, so before tossing the maggot in the water I hold it in my hand for a second and make a little speech.

"Sorry, friend, but if I hadn't come fishing today I would have gone nuts. I might have done something ridiculous. I don't know. The only other possibility was setting the shop on fire, and then instead of dying in the water you'd be dying in the flames. Isn't it better this way?"

It doesn't answer. But it squirms up and down and I take that as a yes. I toss it. It touches bottom in a second because the water is shallow, the floater straightens out at the right spot, and all I have to do is wait for it to move.

But it shouldn't go down right away, because if it does it means the fish is small. Better if it starts to move over the water. A little over here, a little over there, like someone who wants to leave but can't make up his mind. Then it decides on a direction, takes off and sinks, and only at that moment should you pull on the rod and give it a yank. Then the fish'll know you've got him.

I'm scared of myself. Boy, do I know everything about fishing.

The problem is that I don't know squat about sex. And if by chance there is a follow-up with that woman at the Youth Center, I don't think my fishing skills will help me at all. Like if she's lying there waiting for me to do something, and I say, *Listen, I don't know how to put it inside, but I can recognize a carp bite from a mile away.*

I stick my hand into the maggot bag, take out a few, say hi to them, and toss them right close to the floater. I wipe my hands off on the reeds and pick up the rod, which I had leaned against my right arm for a second.

At first it seemed impossible to fish with only one hand. Besides the rod and reel, there are knots that are so complicated that lots of people get them messed up even with two hands. But at fourteen I sat down at the kitchen table and decided that I had to do it. I started with the knot for attaching the hook, and after three days I hadn't tied a single one.

Every now and then my mom would pass by to get lunch ready and then dinner, look at me, but never ask, *How many did you tie?* Because Mom was wise.

The only thing Dad could come up with was *The kitchen doesn't seem like the right place. I'm worried I'm going to end up with a hook down my throat.* And Mom would answer, *Don't worry, Roberto, if we catch you we'll throw you back in, who wants you anyway?*

But a lot of time has gone by since then. A lot. And now I can tie a hook knot in thirty seconds flat. I hold the line still with my foot. With my fingers I make the loop and I pinch it between my thumb and index finger, I slip in the hook, which I have between my lips, then I twist my fingers and pull with my foot and with my mouth and the knot is done. Fantastic.

But with sex, I figure, it's going to be harder.

First of all, I can't ask Tiziana to sit on a shelf for weeks until I learn. Actually, when she sees my right arm it'll already be asking a lot if she stays with me for ten seconds. Because a missing hand is tough; people see it and they freak.

Like in a movie they were showing the other night on the local TV station, a horror flick I'd seen a hundred times and I guess is one of my favorites. The title is *And Now the Screaming Starts*, and in it there's a ghost with only one hand.

There's this baron named Fengriffen and he marries a lady and they go to live in the family castle deep in the woods. There are lots of mysterious things around, strange people laughing at nothing, and a curse hanging over the child about to be born because the baroness is pregnant.

The curse began one night many years earlier when the nobleman's grandfather demanded the right of *ius primae noctis.* You see, one of his peasants had just gotten married and the grandfather wanted to screw the wife; the peasant rebelled, so his hand was placed on a block of wood and chopped off with an ax. And many years later the ghost of that peasant comes back to kill people and while he's at it he rapes the baroness on her wedding night.

During the movie the ghost mows people down, gouges out one guy's eyes, beats a doctor to death, and feeds a woman to the dogs. But the most horrifying moment, toward the end when the music swells and the people say *Not that, anything but that!,* is when the baroness picks up the newborn baby in her arms for the first time, looks at him, and realizes that the child HAS ONLY ONE HAND!

Screams, pounding music, horror.

I mean, come on, people are dead left, right, and center, you've seen heads chopped off and corpses with blood dripping from their mouths, but the thing that's supposed to make people really scream is a missing hand?

It seems ridiculous, crazy. Except that in the place of the newborn I see myself, and in the place of the baroness screaming it's Tiziana from the Youth Center.

And I have to admit that the scene fills me with fear. Fear mixed with dread.

But then I see a faint circle on the water. And at its center is the floater. Another circle, then two more. My mind steps away from these thoughts and focuses completely on the water. I squeeze my hand tight around the rod.

The floater turns a little, tilts, stays still. Come on, get moving, come on . . .

A small jerk forward, little by little the floater starts, accelerates, the fish is there but it wants all my attention.

Thank you, friend, I mean it. You know I'm going to let you go anyway.

EXCALIBUR

Tonight I went out with the guys, and when we go out it means we're going to the Excalibur, a pub that ended up in the middle of the famous industrial zone that was supposed to launch Muglione into the world of workstream manufacturing but instead didn't launch a thing.

It's the only place where we feel good, the music doesn't suck, and the people don't laugh when they see us come in. Maybe because there's almost no one there, or because the few who do come are worse off than us.

We were supposed to discuss the band and figure out what to do after Pontedera, but Antonio was late so I talked about the amazing thing that had happened to me at the Youth Center. But it was a mistake. Giuliano started saying that women are all sluts, and then the owner, Scaloppina, came by and added his two cents. And my apologies if we left out any of the usual complaints about women, because we said them all but there was always room for more.

Not to mention that talking about women at the Excalibur is the most ridiculous thing in the world. No woman has ever set foot there. There are two pool tables, a pinball machine, and a foosball table, and on the walls a poster of Bruce Springsteen, one of a Lancia Integrale splashing mud at a rally, one of the 1982 national soccer team, and one of Sabrina Salerno in denim hot pants with her tits hanging out, on which someone has drawn a dick near her mouth.

No, it's not a place for women. Once, when the men's room was occupied, I went to take a piss in the ladies' room, and it looked *brand-new*.

The evening ended quickly. Now it's one o'clock and we're all home. I mean, Giuliano and Stefano are at their houses, and I'm here surrounded by my worms in the storeroom.

Antonio didn't show up. At some point he sent a text that he was running late, then another saying he was running even later, then nothing.

And now I want to sleep. Tomorrow I may just go back to school, it's been a while now since they've seen me and in a month and a half I've got my finals: I'm flirting with flunking out, I can hardly believe it.

Until last year I did good at school, great even. But that was another time. I would sit down and study all afternoon and Mom had to listen to me repeat everything, because if I don't repeat things they don't get through to me. I also repeated them to my friend Rosanna, who's thick as a brick, and if she understood what I was saying then it meant I had explained it really well.

But now Mom is gone and every time Rosanna sees me she hugs me and cries, and it's no fun going over a lesson with someone who's crying. It's not that I'm trying to blame my not going to school on this. I'm not. Or, well, maybe I am.

Or maybe it's just that I woke up one morning and I became stupid. Sometimes these things can happen, like a shot in the dark, out of nowhere and all of a sudden.

Like that French kiss, and the rubbing, and her warm breath that smelled nice, like breath is supposed to smell, which is the only thing, when I think about it, that convinces me it really happened. Otherwise it could easily be a sex story told by friends who heard it from someone else who made it up.

And in the meantime I can't sleep. I turn on my other side, the cot squeaks. Right now I can hardly believe that anything will happen after that kiss. I was stupid to think so, and I'm stupid because if I look really carefully I'll discover that in a slightly addled corner of my brain I'm still hanging on to some hope.

I turn again. And again. Then I decide it makes no sense. I sit up, switch on the fluorescent light, and look for something to read.

I get up and go into the store, there are a few equipment catalogs and a lot of magazines, but I've read them all. *Fishing, Fishing in . . . , Popular Carp . . .*

And then on the counter I see the Little Champ's papers. The friggin' kid's essays.

I just might read a page. That way I'll either fall asleep or have a laugh. I pick them up and take them to bed. The rustling of the worms is really loud. They sound more like rattlesnakes than bait worms.

There must be about twenty letter-size sheets. Each one is a different composition, arranged in chronological order starting in January, when he arrived here from Molise. The handwriting is legible, but there are words in cursive and block print mixed up willy-nilly.

I take the first essay. The assignment is to write about a class trip to the dinosaur park in Peccioli. If this doesn't put me to sleep I don't know what will.

I start to read.

And I don't stop until dawn.

D'ANNUNZIO DREAMING

It is warm, very warm, but here there is shade, the tips of the pine trees above cover the sky and rustle lightly in the budding breeze. And the sun that shone through the branches in spots has disappeared, the sky is cloudy and the air has a new smell.

"I fear it's about to rain," she whispers. She is wearing a snow-white veil fluttering sinuously with her naked footsteps.

"No, my sweet, you must not fear. It's just a cloud and soon it will pass from sight. Linger not and let us go."

The rustling of the pines grows loud, constant and vast, like a wall of sound soon pierced by the sharp, moist notes of the rain.

"Behold, oh Bard...I dare not contradict thee, but I felt a drop."

"Oh, it is but a shower of gems sent from the heavens to refresh you, oh Hermione."

"It may well be as thou sayest. Yet I beseech thee, let us not go further, the naked feet were not a great idea, twice have I already been wounded."

"Fear not, my lovely, all of nature rejoices to celebrate your passage. Do you not hear it? The greetings of the bayberry, the myrtle, the juniper, the broom..."

"Ouch!"

"What hath befallen thee, oh divine one?"

"I stepped on another thorn."

"Allow me to remove it, I beg thee."

"No, no, the best thing would be to leave." The woman stops, the soft locks caress her shoulders while the dense raindrops moisten her cheek. Her heart beats impetuously in her breast.

"Leave? But that would be madness. Do you not hear how the cicadas sing?"

"No."

"They sing their delight in seeing thee, their goddess, goddess of the woods, thou art a nymph."

"Me?"

"Oh, yes, believe me, thou art indeed a nymph. Ever since the moment a generous Fate allowed me to first lay eyes on thee, it was immediately clear."

"I thank thee, but now I really have to get back. Even the ground is all wet."

"It is the humors of the world that melt by thy grace, and thou art displeased? Let us go deeper into the forest, I know a lovely corner down there in the bushes, there we will find shelter and can celebrate the harmony of nature as it pleases the gods."

"You flatter me, but those noises ... I fear we shall come across snakes, spiders, mushrooms ..."

"But no, hear thou not the song from the mud? The frogs lend their voices to express all the ..."

"Frogs? Gross me out! We would have been better off staying at the farmhouse."

"Gladly, oh nymph, but at the farmhouse there was thy husband."

"I beseech thee, oh bard, allow me to go, maybe it's nature warning us not to do anything stupid."

"But no, nature is telling us to stay, to love, what do you know about it? Do you think you know more than me? I am the Bard, come..."

The nymph suddenly turns and her pace is swift, she takes flight. She stumbles but does not fall, she gathers herself and flees. The Bard chases her, brokenhearted over the amorous harmony that had now been irremediably disrupted.

"Flee not, flee not, light nymph, your heart is a peach."

The nymph ignores him and runs.

"Your teeth are like almonds."

That one doesn't work either.

So the desperate Bard makes a leap and grabs her by her ethereal dress, but it rips so she is sent naked down the path, out of the pinewood, and toward the loutish world of indiscreet lights and eyes. The poet remains where he is, nothing more in his hands but the now lifeless cloth, evanescent souvenir of the beauty that enlivened it. He looks at his beloved from afar, his heart storming with sentiments, and he intones his lament:

"Go ahead, run, you ugly slut! First you play the tease, say that the pinewood makes you feel all hot, and then once you're there you're afraid...fucking cocktease!"

The Bard, exhausted, lets the snow-white veil fall into the mud and leans against a rough, brackish pine, then he turns his gaze in this direction.

He turns toward you.

And he looks at you with those beady eyes, that mustache with its tips pointed up, looking for some space between his big nose and his lips, pursed like a hen's ass. The lips open, he speaks.

"Ah, what a fool I was, that girl was frigid. I should have tried with you."

You look at him, he's pointing at you: "With me?"

"Certainly, with you. Tiziana, the name of a goddess, hair as black as night and as turbulent as storms of impetuous barbs that—"

"But I—"

"Listen, girlie, don't you go getting precious on me, too, because I've had just about enough for one day. Besides, everyone knows you're a slut."

"How dare you! You sound like a horse kicked you in the head."

"Oh yeah? So what do you call that French kiss with the kid?"

"What do you know about it?"

"I have my sources."

"Whatever, it was just one of those things, an impulse, even I couldn't tell you how it happened. I never did anything like that in my life, and after a second I said no, stop, I got a hold of myself. And what right do you have to judge a woman on the basis of a single moment that's completely disconnected from the rest of her life?"

"Okay, girlie, okay, now explain one thing to me…if it was just an impulse, why do you want to call him again?"

You look at him. He's smiling with that disgusting mouth of his. The mustache above it points upward, oily, with that smile. He's the slimiest man you've ever seen.

"How dare you presume to—"

"Come on, relax. So why do you want to call him again, eh?"

"But I…none of what you're saying is true, you're just guessing, I don't have the least intention of calling him."

"Oh yeah? Are you sure?"

"How dare you, what do you know about my personal business?"

"Listen, girlie, now you're really pissing me off. Not to mention that it's raining and I want to get out of here. You're dreaming, get it? Do you really think that D'Annunzio would come by to see you at night? Do you have any idea how busy I am? What makes you think I'd want to wander around this lousy town filled with ditches?"

"But... I don't know, I don't..."

"You're dreaming me, so if you ask me how I know, the answer is easy. I know what you know. Nothing more, nothing less."

"But you're saying things that aren't true, I don't want to call him again and I don't—"

"Nothing more, nothing less." A dramatic hand gesture, then he turns his nose in the opposite direction and returns to the pines, resolute beneath the rain, toward the shade of the woods.

You look at him, open your mouth, try to call him, but nothing comes out. You struggle, you twist, but nothing.

And you wake up.

It's still night, you can't breathe. From the window the smell of the ditch wafts in, baked by the heat, but that's not what it is. At least not by itself.

Call the boy again, how stupid can you get?

Where in the world do our heads wander when we sleep? Who knows? Dreams are so weird that you can read everything and its opposite into them.

Why should you call him? To tell him what? And with what nerve, after jumping his bones like that. So you can have a good laugh about this dream. You could really use one.

Well, right now you can't, but in a little while you'll get up, go to the bathroom, rinse your face, and then you will definitely...yes, you'll have a good laugh in the mirror and tomorrow everything will be all right.

You never could stand D'Annunzio anyway.

THE MYSTERIOUS EXTINCTION OF DINOSAURS

Mirko Colonna
Section 3-B (Ms. Tecla Pudda)
March 10, 2010

Assignment: *After our class trip to the Peccioli dinosaur park,*
describe your impressions of dinosaurs and explain the various
theories about the causes of their extinction.

It's not fair. I didn't go on the class trip, it was on a Saturday or a Sunday, there was a race so I couldn't go.

But it's not fair. I would have really liked to see the dinosaurs, I even told everyone that I was going, it's a kind of big park with lots of trees and bushes and you can see the whole history of prehistory from beginning to end. The ones who went told me that it starts with a kind of volcano that erupts real lava and ends with the cavemen lighting a fire and killing a bear with clubs. And in the middle are a lot of giant dinosaurs and even a tyrannosaurus and a brontosaurus and other kinds that my classmates don't know because they didn't even look at them, and I really wanted to see them but on Saturdays I can't.

But I can't really blame it on Saturday. It would have been the same if you had gone on Monday, for example, because I have to train every day. Even on Wednesdays, when the rest of the team has the day off, Mr. Marelli takes me to do an hour of motor pacing because he says it's easy for me anyway and it's sort of like taking a break.

In fact, the hard part about cycling is opening up the air, which creates resistance and slows you down. It's like, we don't see the air, it's transparent, so we think that it's nothing. Instead air is really powerful and after a little bit of pedaling with your head down you understand: even if you don't see the air it slows you down a lot.

But I'm not saying it's a bad thing, it's not an enemy or anything like that. Actually, it's like a friend who says *Slow down, guys, what's the rush, why are you in such a hurry?* In motor pacing, instead, the air doesn't speak to you because Mr. Marelli's car is in front, splitting the air in two, and I pass through without hearing anything. All I hear is Mr. Marelli yelling *Faster, faster!* and I look at the speedometer that's showing 45 an hour. I told my teammates, but it was a mistake because Mr. Marelli doesn't let them try motor pacing, so they gave me dirty looks and went away to talk somewhere else.

I asked Mr. Marelli why I do it alone and he told me that I'm the captain. But I never wanted that, I don't like being captain. I don't even like it in games, I'd rather not have any trouble and think only for myself.

If we were maybe playing war, and everyone was always fighting over who got to be the general or the commander, I always wanted to be a normal soldier who does his job and at battle's end has no more worries and can go on about his business, like smoking a cigarette or keeping a diary or writing to his girlfriend.

But on the bicycle I'm too strong, and I have to be captain and always come in first and always alone. I tried to pretend that I was slow, but on a bike you can only pretend so much. In the toughest moments the other kids sweat and pant but I'm all fresh and peaceful, and Mr. Marelli yells at me, *Mirko, what are you doing, sleeping? Move your ass and go go go!* And the others also say to me, *Go*, then when I pass them they say, *Go, you little shit* or *Up yours* or *Shithead bastard.* So I go.

But apart from biking I don't go anywhere. In the morning to school and in the afternoon to training, which takes up at least three hours, and then afterward I always have to do my homework, like for example this composition about the school trip to the dinosaur park.

I want to do the normal stuff like everyone. I want to go for a normal walk, but instead if I go out there are all these people saying hi to me and applauding and telling me to win, but no one hangs out with me.

If for example I go to the newsstand to get *Bicisport* (Mr. Marelli says I have to read it, so it's basically more homework), I pass by Mr. Bindi's butcher shop and he yells out my name, forces me to come in, and cuts me a thick slice of meat from a piece of a whole cow that he has there on the counter and he gives it to me all bloody on the paper and he doesn't want money but he wants me to eat the whole thing so I'll get the energy for the surge at the right point and win. I don't even like meat but I have to take it and I have to eat it and that giant piece of cow and blood wrapped in butcher paper is soft and wet and dripping everywhere, and I have to go home quickly to put it in the refrigerator. But I wanted to stay out for a while and talk to someone and even have an ice cream, which is my favorite food.

But even there, the ice cream man won't give me any because he has orders to let me have some only on Monday afternoon and he only gives me fruit flavors, but I think that fruit-flavored ice creams are bullshit, real ice cream is chocolate, vanilla, whipped cream, and crunch. And hazelnut.

On the road there are always a lot of old men making sure my neck is covered so I don't catch cold. In the town square boys and girls are talking to each other and I have to hang out with the old folks, who close my jacket and feel my thighs and tell me to go home or else I'll get tired.

And maybe this is why the dinosaurs became extinct. I didn't go to the Peccioli park, but in my opinion they became extinct because everyone wanted to be in charge, and tell the others what they had to do. So they fought and they got mad at each other and hated each other, so when the thing arrived that made them extinct, a volcano or a comet or the ice or a flood, they weren't able to get organized and they all died.

But with this final stab at the subject of the composition, I hope you will not get too excited, Ms. Pudda, and give me a high grade, because then my classmates will hate me. I almost want to delete this last part. Or maybe I should keep it, because in the end it's just the last four lines of an essay that has nothing to do with the topic and so I hope I'm not at risk of getting an A-plus.

I trust in your good sense, Ms. Pudda.

'Bye.

Grade:
You are right to trust me, dear Colonna.
Off-topic and rambling.
Don't use profanity.
F

THE KILLER BEAR

Mirko Colonna
Section 3-B (Ms. Tecla Pudda)
April 12, 2010

Assignment: *Episodes of violence and youthful criminality have become an everyday occurrence: it's a warning sign that shows the shiftlessness of the younger generation, deprived of the values and moral examples provided by the postwar period. How can today's young people be taught these values?*

Many of my classmates mistreat me and I don't understand why. In my home town, Ripabottoni, I knew it was unfair but at least there was a reason: they hated me because I got really high grades and the teachers compared us and gave really low grades to the rest of the class. Teachers are not very smart people and they don't understand that they create problems when they say *Look at how good Mirko is*, or *The test wasn't that hard, Mirko did it in half an hour.*

But here in Muglione I made an effort not to be hated, damn it, and I'm doing bad in every subject. If I get a passing grade sometimes it's because the teacher loves cycling and gives me a C even if I do nothing. In Italian and English, instead, I manage to do really bad because they're subjects taught by women and women don't care for cycling, or at least not the women who are teaching me.

And women are the subject that interests me the most right now.

Sunday before the race we were at the check-in area and Cristiano was saying he was tired because before coming to the race a girl had given him a hand job that sapped him of his energy. Even though they kept me away I could still hear and I wanted to ask him who she was, but like I said they kept me away so I couldn't ask. But Mikhail did, and Cristiano said he didn't want to say but that she was really pretty, and her father was a cycling fan and she knew his name because she had read it in the papers.

And ever since I've been thinking about women a lot. Because if a girl does something like that to Cristiano Berardi, what would she do to me? In the newspapers Cristiano's name might appear at the end of an article every now and then, but they talk about me all the time and say things like "thus snatching yet another prize for UC Muglione, along with his teammates Schmidt, Loriani, Berardi..." And so if a girl gave a hand job to Cristiano, what's she going to give me?

I don't know, I'm no expert on this stuff. But who can I ask? Not Mr. Marelli, I'm too embarrassed, and the team, like I said, doesn't like me, and at school only a few of my classmates are friends, and they know even less than me.

But the other day I overheard some important information when we were changing classes from science to homeroom. Saverio Mignani was saying that his back hurt and he was rubbing it. Saverio Mignani is practically a man, he already has a beard and hair on his chest and when he says something he always gives me the impression that he knows what he's talking about. And he said his back hurt because of too much fucking.

Then he stuck a cigarette in his mouth. It wasn't lit, because smoking is prohibited at school, but they can't say anything about an unlit cigarette, I think. At least they don't say anything to Saverio Mignani. He says he fucked this girl for five hours straight. And all of our jaws dropped and we said that we would really like that, too.

But he said it's not easy, that before trying you have to really know what you're doing.

Michelangelo Tazzari said, *Women have a hole and you put your willy inside, what's so difficult about that?*

Saverio slapped his head so hard that afterward Tazzari felt like he was going to throw up. And then he said that it's not so easy, that you really have to know how to put your willy in the hole because if you put it in wrong you can DIE.

You get scratched, then you bleed to death. Because inside their hole women have a kind of long, sharp needle. It's a bone, but very thin and pointed. If you're not careful how you insert your willy you can get pierced, you start to bleed, and you die.

Holy cow.

And Tazzari, again, asked what sense it made physically to have a needle inside there. And Saverio Mignani said to him, *What sense does it make for us to have that little hole at the tip of our willies? You have to aim accurately, and the bone has to fit into our little hole. Otherwise . . .*

Jesus. I've never heard of people dying from this. I mean, they do say that the first time there's blood, but I had understood that it came from her. But maybe it comes from her only because he bleeds inside her when the bone pierces him.

Oh my God, it hurts me just to think about it. These are things I'd like to ask a person who's older and more experienced and more talented. Except that I don't know anyone like that.

And my essay is done.

MY DREAM IS TO REALLY SUCK

Mirko Colonna
Section 3-B (Ms. Tecla Pudda)
May 4, 2010

Assignment: Mastro-Don Gesualdo *is a timeless masterpiece,*
a novel that succeeds in being educational and entertaining
at the same time. Write an outline of the work, then explain what
you have learned from your reading of it.

I'm really angry, and rather than write with my pen I want to
snap it in two. I pick it up and I force it and it squeaks, but it
seems to speak to me, saying *What's it got to do with me, Mirko,*
it's not my fault people are mean. I'm here to help you, I write every-
thing you want, and in my opinion you don't deserve that kind of
treatment.

It's true, I stop immediately and leave my pen alone.

But I'm still really angry. It was a beautiful day, the sun was
out and I had done a short makeup practice because on Thursday and Friday we're having longer practices for Sunday, when
there's the really really important race in Piacenza. Today Mr.
Roberto had to stay at the clubhouse to talk with the mechanic
and get the new tires ready and the inner tubes and other stuff,

and I acted like I was going home but I went downtown instead. I wanted to go for a walk like all the other kids and see people to hang out with or at least look at.

In front of the ice cream shop and all over the sidewalk there were lots of boys and girls the same age as me and I stopped and looked around and I felt good, even if I didn't know what to do because I didn't know anyone.

Look who's here, the fucking Little Champion! You like having that bicycle seat up your ass, eh? You dope fiend!

Every now and then I'd hear this kind of stuff, because next to the ice cream shop is a video arcade and the kids in the video arcade are always talking like this when someone walks by.

I pretended I didn't hear, because if you hear and you turn around then they start to say, *What's the problem, looking for trouble?* So it's better not to hear.

But at a certain point I heard loud and clear another voice calling me, it came from the ice cream shop, which is something else completely.

Mirko, Mirko Colonna!

It was the voice of Martina Volterrani, Section 3-A, the class that we do phys ed with; even if the girls and the boys are separated I can always look at her at the beginning and end of class, and I think she's the prettiest girl in the world. She's blonde with long long hair and blue blue eyes and she already looks like a grown-up and under her clothes she looks like she already has the stuff that bigger girls have. And when she talks she moves her mouth in a strange and beautiful way and if she talked to me I swear I would die. Luckily she never does talk to me.

But today she did. She was there at a table with a group of her girlfriends, all very pretty, she said my first name and last and signaled to me to come over to where they were having ice cream, I mean no, to where they were having frozen yogurt, which is lighter. Martina explained to me that they had read stuff about me in the newspaper, especially an article that had my picture, and said that in the future I would be an international sports star.

They were all very impressed and asked me how to go fast on a bike and where in Italy Molise is and if it's true that in Molise there's no electricity. I answered as best I could, then I said something that made them laugh, that one of the top problems with bikes is that the seat hurts, but after a while you don't feel anything. Then one of them said, *Oh my God, so under there you don't feel anything?* They looked at each other and giggled and I did, too, but I said, *No no, I mean yes yes, I still feel,* and after that laugh Martina put her hand on my arm. HER HAND ON MY ARM. It was warm and I tensed up and I looked at her for a second but she also looked at me and then I immediately looked the other way.

And I saw two old guys dressed in identical military jackets coming toward us and yelling.

"And I say he's all right the way he is!"

"BUT—CAN'T—YOU—SEE—HOW—SHORT—HIS—TORSO—IS—LIKE—A—HUNCHBACK." (One of the two was speaking with a device held to his throat and had a voice like a robot.)

"What do you mean, hunchback? He's gawky but he's not a hunchback."

"TO—ME—HE—LOOKS—DEFORMED."

"Yes, I agree with you there. But do you remember what Coppi looked like? When he pedaled he was like poetry, perfect, then when he got off his bike he looked crippled, with those long legs and that stunted torso. Some bodies are born to ride a bike, and he's got one, look at him. On a bike he's perfect, but on the street he looks like a retard."

"LET'S — HOPE — HE'S — NOT — A — FAKE — DIVO."

"I tell you he's the real thing, relax. Feel his legs, feel his muscles, come on."

The two old men started squeezing my legs, in back, in front, as if I were an animal at the fair or a cucumber.

Meanwhile, Martina was keeping her distance. Her girlfriends looked at each other and couldn't hold back their laughter, and I felt like I was dying. I tried to break away from the two men and they told me to be good and they squeezed my legs and one of them said, *Feel here, it's a rock*, and the other nodded and touched me and said, *Yes, but I want to see him in a serious race*, and the other one said, *Don't worry, you'll see him on Sunday in Piacenza, on Sunday he's going to leave the rest of the field in the dust, get it?*

By this time Martina and her girlfriends had disappeared without even saying goodbye. The two men carried on, fighting with each other and mentioning the names of old cyclists, then before going, one of them straightened out the collar of my T-shirt because otherwise I'd catch a sore throat, then they left, still arguing.

And now I've had enough. I'm angry. And you know what I'm going to do on Sunday? I want to not win. On Sunday I want to really suck. How is it that everyone else around me can suck and I have to always win and put on a show?

My dream would be to suck as bad as everyone else. Like my walk downtown sucked, and like those mean old men suck.

And like *Mastro-Don Gesualdo* sucks. I tried to read the first few pages and God, it is so boring.

TELL ME SOMETHING
EMBARRASSING

They say that in the morning your thoughts are clearer. Whatever. They say a lot of bullshit. Like that advice to "sleep on it." All you have to do is go to sleep and the next morning your thoughts are less complicated. Yes, but what if your thoughts are so complicated that you can't sleep a wink?

I walk down the main road and every now and then I feel dizzy. Maybe I'm tired or maybe it's the heat, mixed with the dampness and the smell of exhaust fumes. With each step I don't know whether I'm going to faint or fall asleep on the sidewalk. Lucky thing these trucks keep driving by. They almost sideswipe me and the shifting of the air keeps me standing.

Where I'm going I don't know. Definitely not to school.

This morning I can't, my head was already messed up by that stuff with Tiziana at the Youth Center, and now the Little Champ's essays have made it worse.

I stayed up all night reading them. I mean, it took me about half an hour, but then I reread them a few times and I browsed through them and put them back in order. The first thing that struck me was the handwriting. Identical to mine. Not my handwriting of today, but it's exactly like when I used to write with my right hand. And so is his way of expressing himself, the spitting image, it's shocking.

Even the personal situations are the same. This thing about being alone, those assholes at school and at the video arcade that tease you. And the problems with sex, and not having anyone you can go to for advice.

I dunno. Maybe it's a coincidence. Or somehow the friggin' kid is copying me. Or maybe it's just that everyone in the world feels so special and misunderstood, but instead in the end we are all the same and we go through the same issues and need the same things.

And the Italian teacher, she's the same one I had in middle school. Ms. Tecla Isola Pudda, that friggin' midget. We used to call her Puddin' Head or Tree Top, since her hair looked as if she had a ball of moss on her head. Even back when I had her, Puddin' Head was a thousand years old and spent the whole lesson leaning against the radiator because she was cold. She even took attendance by the radiator, and when she called you up for an oral quiz you'd sweat like a pig. And Ms. Tecla Pudda hated everyone: she used to say that we were uncouth and insensitive, maybe because her son died when he was sixteen and we were uncouth and insensitive since we were still alive.

And if the Little Champ needs a C from Pudda to be promoted, I'll book him a ticket back to Molise right away. By airplane, train, or kicks in the ass, the choice is up to him.

In a certain sense I've also made a choice. Without meaning to, perhaps. To escape from these thoughts I lift my head up and realize where my two feet have taken me.

To the Youth Center.

And since I don't have any cats to get rid of, I figure there must be only one reason for it.

What do I do, go in? Knock? It's an office, do you knock before going into an office?

Stupid questions that make no sense, also because I'm already in. And once again the darkness of an Etruscan tomb, with Tiziana back there at the desk. She has a book in her hands and she's reading. I mean, she was reading. Now she just has the book in her hands, and she stares at me. And I stare at her.

"Hi, Tiziana."

"Yes...oh, yes, of course, hi," and she suddenly jumps to her feet.

I take my hair and pull it together in the back. I try to smile, even if all the muscles in my face are pulling in the opposite direction. But I'm the boss, no beating around the bush, we're going to do what I say. And little by little my smile comes out.

"Hi," I repeat.

"Hi...listen, Fiorenzo, I'm glad you came. I should have come to you. I wanted to apologize."

"For what?"

"For everything, I'm sorry."

"But for what?"

"For everything. For...you know, for everything. I hope I didn't offend you. I swear, I don't know what came...It's not like me, I'm not like that. And I know that's the typical thing a slut says every time she's acted like a slut, but I swear I'm not like that. And if you feel offended, I understand and I apologize."

"Offended? What are you talking about? I don't feel offended at all."

"Oh, thank goodness," and Tiziana smiles, more or less. I smile, too. And now?

Silence.

To stand there, on my feet in the middle of nowhere, seems like the most ridiculous thing in the world. The last time, we rubbed against each other and had our tongues down each other's throats. Can that possibly be all over and now she's apologizing and showing me the door? Of course, what was I thinking? I'm an idiot, what did I come here for anyway, I'm such a sorry ass. And in the meantime I've still got my right wrist in my pants pocket, I dig it in deep so it won't hurt. I have to say something right away because this silence is killing me.

"You know, I read Mirko's compositions," I say.

"The compositions? Oh, right, of course. And how are they, any good?"

"I don't know. Not really. They're strange."

"Really?"

"Really."

"..."

"...And you blog? Are you still writing..."

"Oh, God no, I deleted it. It was a stupid idea."

"Ah. Okay. Yeah, there are an awful lot of blogs around."

"Yeah."

"And most of them suck."

"Yes, I know."

"I mean, no, not yours. I never saw it. Actually, sorry, I'm going to look at it later."

"I deleted it."

"Oh, right, you just told me."

"Yeah."

And this line of conversation runs out, too. More silence.

Then I remember this thing, this trick that Mom used to try when there was an embarrassing moment. Once she came into my room without knocking, but I wouldn't have heard her anyway because the volume of the stereo was mind-numbing, there was this CD by Megadeth and I was pretending I was in front of a million people at this gigantic festival, I was standing on the bed and acting like I had a microphone, lip-synching to the song, urging the crowd on and shaking my bed, and she caught me in the act. I saw her and I shot off the bed, turned the volume to the minimum, and sat there in a sweat looking at her. And Mom was even more embarrassed than me. Then out of the blue she said: "So, each of us has to say something really embarrassing, okay?"

"Huh?"

"Something embarrassing that happened to you. You tell me one, and I'll tell you one."

"No, come on, Mom, please, get out of here."

"Don't be a jerk, now you go first."

"No, Ma, forget about it, don't you be a jerk."

"Out with it, come on!"

"Okay, all right, but then you have to leave. I'm scared of wasps. Are you happy now?"

"You call that embarrassing?"

"Duh, imagine what it's like in front of other people. A wasp comes by and I have to run."

"Okay, I get it, a little."

"Good. Now can you please leave me alone, Mom?"

"Don't you want to know what my most embarrassing thing is?"

"No, I don't."

"Mine is that last night I wet my pants."

"..."

"At the team dinner with Dad. Teresa started telling me something that happened to a friend of hers and we started laughing because it was too funny, and I finally told her, *Stop, please, or I'm going to wet myself, stop or I'll wet myself,* she didn't stop and I wet myself."

"There at the restaurant? Then what happened?"

"Then I sat there for a while and hoped that no one would notice and I didn't know what to do. But then I could feel that my chair was wet so I had your father give me his sweater, that asshole, and he said, *What do you need it for, you're not even wearing it.* I tied it around my waist and I said I was going to the bathroom, but instead I ran home."

"So that's why you came back early."

"Yeah, I had to, I wet my pants."

It really was embarrassing, in fact. And I have to admit that the embarrassment of a couple of seconds earlier, over that fake concert in my bedroom, had almost passed.

So now, with all this embarrassment between Tiziana and me, Mom's trick might just work. And it's the best I've got.

"Tiziana, tell me something embarrassing."

"What?"

"Tell me something that embarrassed you. Then I'll tell you mine."

"But what, how..."

"Come on, let's do it. Right now we're embarrassed, agreed?"

"You could sure say that."

"So tell me something you found embarrassing and then I'll tell you one; you'll see that then we'll both feel better."

"I hardly think it's the—"

"Come on, quick."

"But right now I can't think of anything."

"You're so annoying! Come on, something embarrassing that you did."

"The thing that we both know doesn't count, right?"

"It's not that it doesn't count, it's that I already know it. Come on."

"All right. So I'll tell you another one. I spat."

"Whaaa...?"

"This morning. I was on my way to the office and something entered my mouth while I was yawning. I don't know if it was dust or an insect. But it went down my throat and I needed to cough. And at a certain point I spat on the ground. But one of those really gross loogies like an old person, you know, who hacks up a big hunk of mucus and then spits it out on the ground. And there wasn't anyone on the street, but at that very moment, with my usual luck, a man came out of nowhere and saw the whole thing. I lifted my eyes and for a second we looked at each other, I thought I would die."

Tiziana smiles, then she covers her face with a hand. It's a beautiful face.

She smiles and I really laugh, and I stretch out the laugh because I don't want to feel the earlier silence again.

"You're laughing? I tell you something so dramatic and you laugh?"

"You call that dramatic?"

"Are you kidding? All pressed and dressed, ready for work with a briefcase under my arm and my bag and my eyeglasses, and then I hawk a big fat loogie like a construction worker right there in the middle of the sidewalk? Nice impression I left!"

I laugh again. This time she does, too.

"I said stop laughing, it's a drama, get it? A tragedy. And you?"

"Me what?"

"Your embarrassing thing?"

Slowly but surely I stop laughing. I take a deep breath.

"Oh, of course," I say, and finally I pull my arm out from my jeans pocket. I show it to her. "You see, Tiziana, I'm missing a hand."

I'D PUT IN A HOOK

Well, I will never forget those eyes and that face.

I thought I would never forget that kiss with the tongue and her hands on my skin and all the rest, but now I don't even know where she is. Maybe in the bathroom of memory, bent over behind a door throwing up. Now the only thing I see is the look in Tiziana's eyes when I showed her my right arm without a hand at the end.

I thought she was about to scream right then and there, like in horror movies when you realize that the prettiest girl is in reality a demon, lightning strikes outside her window (because in horror movies the weather is always bad) and you see her face become monstrous. That's more or less how it went. And, like in a horror movie, at that point I ran away. But the difference is that Tiziana didn't follow me.

Because this is reality, and in reality Tiziana saw my arm without a hand and the last thing she wants is to see me again. That's what I mean when I say that horror movies are less horrifying deep down than reality. But everyone tells me I'm a moron.

And I don't get offended when they tell me, because they're right, I am a moron. As demonstrated by the brilliant idea of suddenly pulling my arm out.

Oh, how embarrassing, Tiziana, you spat on the street and someone saw you? Oh my God, how awful, I'm so sorry. I'm so lucky by comparison: go figure, all I've got is a wrist with nothing attached, take a look, funny, isn't it? Now can we make love?

Yes, I guess that was the plan. Ingenious. So I deserve to have Tiziana looking at me like that. With those eyes that I can't get out of my head, not even now that I'm walking so quickly toward the shop, toward the live bait storeroom. That's the right place for me, together with the worms, and instead I insist on hanging out with people.

Handy, Hans, Lefty are the names they called me when I was fourteen. I can hear them all right now as I'm walking quickly down the street. It's not that I remember them in my head, they're not phantom voices from the past. No, they really are calling me. I look around and realize I'm passing by the video arcade. It's something I never do because it would only be looking for trouble. The denizens of the video arcade see me walk by and almost can't believe it. They amass between the door and the sidewalk and shout, "Handy, Hans, Lefty!" "Do you need help? Can I lend you a hand?" and "Do you want to play another hand of cards?" And more of the same trash that only they and a few other monocellular organisms think is funny.

So enough already, everything I do today is clearly going to be wrong. I'm better off going back to the shop and locking myself inside. It's noon but I've already had my fill of the day.

I open the door. Dad is inside with a customer who is choosing floaters. The guy picks them up and holds them against the light, as if they were transparent and he could see through them. Dad says hi, and I signal to him that I'm going to the storeroom, to my room. I have to be alone, and there are no windows and no light back there. There is only the sound of worms swarming and wriggling and rubbing up against each other and for now that's all I need. It is what it is.

He says to me, "Wait, there's..."

But I don't wait for anything. I wag a finger no and point straight at the back. I open the folding door and I go in. And the Little Champ is seated on my cot.

It startles him and he jumps to his feet. He's dressed in his cycling clothes: shorts, the team jersey, and even the helmet on his head and the shoes with cleats.

"What the fuck are you doing?"

"Nothing, I ... nothing, Mister."

"Do you want to steal the storeroom, too?"

"No, I didn't—"

"You're always up my ass! Why aren't you at school?"

"I got out an hour early because there's a long practice."

"How convenient, the young master has to ride his bike so now he skips class."

"I really would have rather stayed at school, I don't like getting out early to—"

"Will you stop your whining, please! Always carrying on about *Biking really sucks, winning really sucks, and I can't talk to girls and I can't get an ice cream*...if it sucks so bad, why don't you quit already?"

The Little Champ looks up from beneath his helmet and gazes at me strangely, all happy. "So you read my essays, Mister!"

"No! What a pain, I said no, I won't read your lame-ass essays! Get lost, go practice and stop whining! Because if you don't like this stuff it's easy enough to stop. Do you want to know how? Easy. Sunday there's another race, right? So go ahead and lose. Lose today, lose tomorrow, and you can bet that Dad will send you back home in a heartbeat! Lose, goddamnit, how hard can it be? Losing is the easiest thing in the world!"

"But I don't... I don't know if I can."

"You don't know if you can? What kind of bullshit is that? You're really pissing me off!" I can feel something getting ready to explode inside, but it doesn't feel like anger. It's simmering in a different way. "You've got the good luck to be able to do anything you like, you idiot, but all you do is complain. Enough already! So tell me one thing..." I stop for a minute, then I decide to keep going, since the day is ruined anyway. I raise my right arm and put it in front of his eyes. "Tell me something, Champ, you with all your complaints. What would you do if you were fucked up like this?"

"Me?"

"Yeah, tell me what you would do!"

"Me? I would put in a hook, Mister."

I swear that's what he said, in all seriousness. And I can't even punch him in the nose. Maybe because he's a kid. Or maybe because I had the same idea myself. The first time I mentioned it, after the accident, I asked, *Can I at least put in a hook?* And the doctors laughed, a little.

I lower my arm and break away. "Get lost, kid, I'm pissed off today, the last thing I needed was you."

"I'm sorry if you're having a bad day, Mister."

"Get lost. And win or lose or do whatever you feel like, what do I care?"

The kid leaves the compositions on the cot, takes his bag, and gets ready to leave.

"Mister, the ones on top are two new compositions."

"I won't read your compositions, how many times do I have to tell you, *I won't reeeeeead them!*"

I'm still yelling as he runs out, closes the folding door, and *sayonara.*

And I'm left alone. In the dark surrounded by live bait.

I want to spend the rest of the day in here. With the worms, the boxes, and the Little Champ's essays.

And the look in Tiziana's eyes, which I'll never forget for the rest of my life.

THE ULTRA
FISHING CABINET CHAIR

Mr. Mariani has been choosing floaters for at least twenty minutes. He holds them up against the light as if he can see inside whether or not they are lucky. Roberto reads the newspaper and waits.

Meanwhile Fiorenzo has arrived and gone straight to the storeroom, where he found Mirko, and there was some shouting. Then Mirko came out all wobbly in his cycling shoes.

It's the first time Mariani's come to the shop, and he's probably never gone fishing. And if Roberto's intuition is still working, he has no intention of starting now.

In the end he says, "All right, these ones here," and he chooses two floaters that couldn't be more different in bulk and form. He pays. Then he throws a little conversation on the table, as if to fill the time it takes to get his change.

"Yeah, there's nothing like it, fishing is a great passion. Right, Roberto?"

"Right as rain."

"Of course, I'm no expert, but I like it. But you know what my top passion is, right?"

"Cycling."

"Exactly, cycling. Of course, I'm just an amateur, but I don't do half bad, eh? Last spring I even placed in the Monte Balbano Gran Fondo, did you know?"

"No, I didn't. Good job."

"Yeah, but then I follow all the professional races. I know all the races you rode in, can you believe it? And when you came in fourth in the Bernocchi Cup...I can even tell you who came in first, second, and third."

"What a memory, Mariani, what a memory."

"It's all about passion. And you know who's just as passionate as me? My Massimiliano. God love him, he lives for cycling. And he follows the professional races, never misses one. He practically already knows the professional world."

"Which is a good thing. Racing without watching the pro races is like swim—"

"Like swimming without water! I know, you said that to the kids at the beginning of the year. It was so great I wrote it down. And I've got a lot of faith in Massimiliano. He's got passion and the right energy. He's sixteen but he's already mature. And he wants to be a pro. And I'm with him one hundred percent of the way."

"Good. And we're trying to make him a professional." Roberto replies in half sentences. Strange, especially when you're talking about cycling. But he's already understood what Mariani is getting at.

"Well, this year he's not winning me anything. Among the preteens it was another matter, but the categories change, not much you can do about it. And now with this Little Champ that you've found...man, can he fly, where in the world did you find him?"

"Yeah, Mirko is strong. But Massimiliano is strong, too, we've got to let him grow."

"True, true, he's still got some growing to do. It's just that, to get to the point, I want to help him with this growth...Like I was saying, we know the score, Roberto, we're not improvisers, and we're ready to do whatever it takes. And I was wondering, between the two of us, what will it take?"

Roberto arranges the boxes of floaters, doesn't answer, and doesn't look up from the counter.

"Look, Roberto, I'm talking man to man: What will it take?"

"It will take legs, Mariani."

"Yes, of course, and?"

"And lungs, and brains."

"Come on, Roberto, stop pulling my leg, you know what I'm getting at."

"No, I don't."

"Let's stop talking fairy tales here. That Little Champ is strong, he's phenomenal, but you can't tell me he's operating on bread and water. You give him something extra, and you're right, it makes sense. I told you, I know the score, no problem. But look, couldn't you give something extra to Massimiliano, too? Like I said, I won't make any trouble, if I've got to sign I'll sign, if you tell me the name of a doctor who'll give him something extra, I'll be there in a flash."

Roberto closes the boxes, which go *click*, puts them back in the container under the counter, and slowly closes it.

"Mariani, listen up. If I tell you to stick it up your ass, will you be there in a flash, too?"

Mr. Mariani stands there with two floaters in his hand, struggling not to lose the smile on his face.

"Wait, Roberto, you misunderstood. I'm just asking if you can pay a little more attention to my boy. You know who the doctors are, all I'm asking is that you put me in touch with a good one, I'll bring him to the races and —"

"Mariani, get your ass out of here, please."

Mariani has stopped smiling. He places the floaters down on the counter.

"You know what I've got to say to you, Roberto? You've just lost a fan."

"Boo-hoo."

"And a racer. I'm going to take my son to Mabi-Tech. They'll know how to appreciate him. Then I want to see how you're going to feel when he becomes champion."

Mr. Mariani heads for the door, opens it, and starts to leave. But he turns around because he still has too much venom in his mouth and he has to spit it all out. "Besides, they're going to catch your Little Champ one day, you know? Sooner or later they're going to catch him using and afterward it'll be too late to say that you knew nothing, that you're falling from the clouds. No one believes you, Roberto, you were a lousy racer and now you're a lousy sports director!"

A fully accessorized Ultra Fishing Cabinet Chair, the dream of every fisherman who loves total convenience and organization. The very name provokes orgasmic reactions inside any pair of fishing pants. It's a chair stuffed and covered with leather, with four steel feet adaptable to every kind of surface and a steel structure, too, in which is lodged an infinite series of little drawers and compartments allowing you to subdivide all your equipment by type.

It's so expensive that Roberto doesn't want to display it in the shop, he prefers to keep it behind the counter. It's so heavy that it took two guys to carry it there.

But now it's light as a feather, it flies through the air and whizzes straight and steady toward the shop door. Mr. Mariani sees this half-leather half-steel thing spinning toward him, and with each turn the drawers spray around the shop like bombs from a bombardier and demolish a shelf, a reel display case, a pile of chum, and all the while the flight of the Cabinet Chair continues straight with the aim of knocking him to the ground, teeth first. But Mariani manages to get out just in time and close the door behind him. A second later and the door is gone. It explodes, a blunt impact, and shatters into a thousand pieces.

From the storeroom Fiorenzo comes running and sees there on the sidewalk this bald guy hopping around, brushing off tons of shards as if they were killer bees, and shouting, "I'm reporting you to the police! You're nuts, Marelli, you son of a bitch! You're a doper! You were a doper when you raced and you're a doper now! I'm reporting you!"

He shakes his hands in the air, thrashes about, and disappears into thin air. And in the frame of the door, or rather the former door, Mirko's head appears, still wearing a helmet, and he takes a cautious look inside.

"Mr. Roberto," he says softly. "Excuse me, but it looks like the door exploded."

No one thanks him for the news flash.

Behind him cars keep moving down the road. Without the door all the noise and stench come in.

Fiorenzo turns toward his father at the counter. He responds with a peaceful expression, leaning his head on one hand.

"But...what..."

"Fiorenzo, aren't you supposed to be in school?"

"Yes...no...what happened?"

"The Ultra Fishing Cabinet Chair."

"How did it end up in..."

"It slipped out of my hands."

"It slipped out of your hands and ended up on the..."

"Yes."

"And the door?"

"And the door got broken."

"And now we have to change it."

"You're right."

"That costs a lot of money, Dad."

"Right. But the important thing is that no one got hurt."

THE SIBLINGS TRICK

"No, you're crazy, Tiziana, let me be the first to tell you, you're out of your mind."

"She had a strange look, there was something weird about her."

"What look? She was a poor old lady all alone who wanted a kitten to keep her company." Raffaella is talking while driving and texting. Her eyes on the road, on you, and on her phone.

"No, she was strange, she had a mean look."

From the backseat the wailing of the cats in the box never stops. *Mee-owwww.*

"Now what are we supposed to do with them? Tiziana, we don't know where to put them anymore. An old lady does us the favor of accepting a kitten and you take it right out of her hands?"

"I told you, she had weird ideas."

"What ideas are you talking about?"

"Don't laugh, but in my opinion she wanted to eat it."

Raffaella turns with a start and looks at you. For a second she just sits there, then she bursts out laughing.

The car in front has been at the intersection without moving for a while. Raffaella pounds on the horn but then realizes the light is red. She indicates she's sorry with her hand and goes back to treating you like you're crazy. "What would she want to eat a cat for?"

"The crisis is tough for everyone, Raffaella."

"Get over it, who's going to eat a cat?"

"Lots of people. Like, maybe not us, but seniors...they already ate them during the war, it's not so weird to them. My grandmother told me that in wartime she used to eat cats and hedgehogs, and once she found a dead German and..."

"And she ate him, too?"

"No, you idiot, he had a leather belt, they boiled it, and then when it was softer they ate it."

"Gross! *Bleh!*"

"So what's going to stop someone from eating a little kitty, tender and sweet?"

"But she wanted it for company."

"Of course. And when you played the little siblings trick, didn't it make you suspicious?"

The little siblings trick is a classic for those practiced in the art of getting rid of cats: when you find a person who wants one, as soon as they pick it out you show them another one, identical if possible, and you tell them that they're siblings who are very attached to each other because their mother was crushed by a car driven by a drunk and you found them next to the dead mother, calling her and calling her. That way maybe the person will feel sorry and adopt both.

Raffaella told the story of the siblings to the old lady and she immediately said she'd take both, and if there was a third she would take that one, too. If you'd proposed it she might have even taken the whole box.

"And in your opinion she would've eaten them all?"

"I think so. Maybe she would have invited people over for dinner. Or she would have put them in the freezer."

"You're sick, Tiziana, you'd better see a shrink because you're really sick."

"I'm not sick at all. You're the one who didn't get a good look at her eyes, and—"

"Tiziana, let me tell you one more time, you have to learn to trust people. At least a little."

"But I do trust people."

"Of course you do. You're open-minded and you trust everyone."

"That's exactly what I'm like. Why, how do you see me? You don't see me like that?"

"Not one bit."

"So how do you see me? Go ahead, I'm all ears."

"I don't know. Actually, as I said, like a crazy lady. Come on, let's give her the kittens, the poor thing. She saw them and she immediately felt better, who knows how long she's been alone, and she was imagining having these cats at home, surrounded by joy…"

"Whatever."

"Let's give them to her, come on, let's give them up to the old lady."

"I don't know, Raffa."

"But I do. And also that metalhead kid…let's give it up to him, too."

Raffaella says it and looks at you. You look at her, then you both burst out laughing.

"Stupid!"

"No, you're stupid."

"You're stupid!"

"No, you're the one who's stupid, Tiziana. I'd give it up to him in a heartbeat, seeing how much you like him."

"What are you talking about, I don't like him!"

"I'm telling you, you like him. Or at least you don't dislike him."

"But he's nineteen years old!"

"How do you know? Maybe he's twenty-one and doesn't look it."

"No, he's nineteen."

"Is that what he told you?"

"No. I mean, I did an Internet search and...he's in his senior year of high school. Can you believe it, he's in high school!"

"And can you believe that you did an Internet search for him? And you say you're not interested in him?"

"I was just killing time, and I was curious, there's nothing to do in the office."

The cats continue to wail, *mee-owwww, mee-owwww.* It's an endless, pointed lament that plants itself deeper and deeper inside the brain.

"And so what if he's nineteen? If a guy our age goes out with a nineteen-year-old girl, then he's a stud. So who's to say we girls can't do the same? What is this, the Middle Ages?"

"Whatever, but I've always liked older men, there's something so..."

"Older, huh? You know what Pavel told me last night? *Oh, Raffi, tonight I can't make love cuz I had chicken with peppers. If I move around too much I feel sick.* Can you believe it? That's an older man for you. And Pavel is a hale and hearty country boy, the average male is worse. Much, much worse."

"Yes, but it's not just a problem of age."

"Tiziana, don't tell me you're still thinking about Luca, please? Don't tell me because I'll get really, really pissed off. How can I get it through your thick skull that the guy's a complete idiot?"

"Thinking about Luca? Not on your life…"

"So what is it, his hand? Look, if you tell me it's because of his hand, okay, I get it. But how do you know? Did you get a good look at it? Maybe it's not so awful. Get a better look, okay? You go out, spend an evening with him, and see. If you go out once you're hardly obligated to bang him…"

"No, but I don't…"

"And then if you are obligated, whatever, you give it up, never say no to a quickie."

And you both laugh again. For a while. Then slowly but surely the laughter dies and becomes a smile. You're almost home. "I don't know, Raffa, I don't think that…"

From the backseat the kittens are keeping up their lament. *Mee-owwww, mee-owwww, mee-owwww.*

"Tiziana, listen, I can't take it anymore. Let's turn around and make the old lady happy."

"But she's not—"

"She's not going to eat them, Tiziana. It never even crossed her mind. She only wants them to keep her company, she doesn't like being alone. She's normal, you know?"

No, you don't know. What does normal mean anyway? Are you normal?

"Come on, Tiziana, let's turn the car around."

You don't answer, you bite your lip and lower your eyes to the dashboard, where there's a Ricky Martin sticker that was stuck there sometime in the previous century. The car stops,

Raffaella looks at you, then looks at the road, then looks at you again.

And while you talk you grumble, "Whatever, I still know how this story is going to end..."

"Good girl!" she says.

The gears grind when you put the car into reverse.

THE *ITALIAN CHRONICLE*

Pier Francesco Lamantino writes for the *Italian Chronicle*.

He decided he wanted to be a journalist when he was sixteen, one November morning when a guy came to speak at his high school who had been a correspondent in the most forgotten parts of the world: Burma, Laos, Cambodia...Pier Francesco drank in those fantastic names and meanwhile was thinking *Me, too, me, too*...and after high school, he majored in political science and started writing himself, but about local politics and local cuisine and local food fests, all unpaid for local newspapers. Then, thanks to a stroke of good luck, he got a job with the *Italian Chronicle*. And his mother is proud of him.

Today he's around the area because he has to interview Teresa Murolo, the woman from Navacchio who for fifteen years has had a relationship with an alien. A cover story. The two would meet only in the dead of night, they even got married with an outer-space ritual, and every night they mate, either at her house in Navacchio or in Montecatini, at the psychiatric facility where she checks in periodically.

Except that half an hour before the interview Miss Teresa called in a state of agitation, saying a bunch of things with no logical connection about the end of the world and aliens coming to take her away, then she turned off her cell phone and now he doesn't know where she is.

So he can forget about the cover, forget about the story, forget about everything.

But on his way back home, while he was thinking up a ton of insults for that idiot Miss Murolo, Pier Francesco spotted a group of road signs pointing in a direction that sounded familiar without his knowing why. Muglione, Muglione...never heard of it, but...that's it! Yes, he had heard of it, a few days earlier in *La Nazione*. Something about a seniors patrol. He had thought it might be an idea for a rainy day, and none will be rainier than this morning...so he called the office and they answered *Whatever you feel like, as long as you send it in by the end of the day. And it has some substance.*

Pier Francesco called the photographer and told him to rush to Muglione; the photographer said, *Where the hell is Muglione,* but he had a GPS and managed to arrive. And they interviewed the Guardians. And saved the day.

One hour later, the Guardians are waving at the departing cars. The photographer leans his head out the window and snaps a final shot. Divo gives the camera a serious, wise-guy look. Then the old men are left alone, and they can finally have it out with each other.

"Ripetti, what the fuck did you tell him!" says Baldato.

"Uh, he kept asking, you guys said nothing, so I..."

"SO — YOU — SPOUTED — SOME — ABSOLUTE — BULL-SHIT."

"But he was insisting, *Are you sure you don't have any real problems here? Something really big, what scares you when you walk around at night?* ... How could I keep quiet? When I used to work at the cemetery that guy from *The Tyrrhenian*, Monciatti, always came by to see if there was anything strange to do a story on. Scenes of desperate parents, stuff like that. And he used to say that the news was like a chickpea pancake: without a little pepper it has no taste."

"WHAT'S — A — CHICKPEA — PANCAKE — GOT — TO — DO — WITH — IT?"

"It's got everything to do with it," says Divo. "Ripetti did the right thing. No pepper, no article. Don't you guys want an article in the *Italian Chronicle*? I do. Maybe we could've made up something besides a gang of kids who beat up on retirees, but it's better than nothing..."

He says it and everyone shuts up for a second. Then Baldato starts up, more calmly this time.

"Yes, and to be honest today's young people really are scary. We're on the skids. The other day in the square there was the commemoration of the fallen of 1915 to 1918. The anthem was about to start and these kids came by and razzed us."

"YEAH — BUT — THAT'S — NOT — THE — SAME — AS — BEATING — UP — OLD — PEOPLE..."

"Mazinger, if a person's got the nerve to insult the national anthem, they're capable of anything."

"True. In fact, when I go out I'm worried all the time," says Repetti.

"Me, too... what a life. Back in the day things were different."

"YEAH — TRUE — VERY — DIFFERENT — BACK — IN — THE — DAY."

The Guardians say nothing more. They study each other and start to nod, some with more conviction, some with less.

But two days later, the latest issue of *Italian Chronicle* sweeps away any doubts. The Guardians are four magnificent giants who dominate the cover. Upright, arms crossed, standing tall; proud, true guardians who are never afraid of anything.

Terror Strikes Seniors
Four brave grandpas vs. the anti-retirees gang

MUGLIONE (PISA). A cozy little town in the heart of Tuscany, far from the beaten path of the Grand Tour but quite delightful all the same. A little town square, a little church, a little municipality. But the problems that torment Muglione, like all the other small towns on our splendid peninsula, can hardly be described as little.

This is why four valorous "grandpas," average age seventy-plus, decided to form the Muglione Guardians, a group of volunteers who want to make life difficult for delinquents. "They think we're in the Wild West," says Divo Nocentini, heatedly, "well, now the sheriffs are taking back the town."

Another Guardian, Salvatore Baldato, a retired policeman of Sicilian origin, explains that "the most dangerous time is at night, so that's when we patrol the town, from seven p.m. to almost eleven."

"There used to be a lot of drug addicts," Nazareno Repetti tells us, "and that really was a problem. Except now they're all dead." His comments are echoed by Donato Mazzanti, who speaks through a laryngophone: "In the square there was a tree covered with syringes stuck into it, it was awful." But it is clear that the courageous watchmen are not telling us everything. Not many crimes are reported in the town, maybe a few burglaries and a couple of drunk-driving accidents. So what is the real problem in Muglione? Who are the Guardians fighting with such alacrity?

Finally the wall comes down and they reveal the sinister truth in low voices: "In Muglione we seniors are afraid. There are bad people who hate us, bad and young."

A heart-stopping reality: in this little town in warm and welcoming Tuscany, there is a gang, a dirty dozen shiftless youths who take out their frustrations by harassing retirees. "Insults and threats every day. When we cross the street or wait in line at the post office or do the grocery shopping. Young people used to be in decline in Muglione: we seniors used to be able to look forward to the future. Except lately the foreigners have arrived. There are lots of them, almost all young, and the situation has gotten worse. A few nights ago a young foreigner wanted to beat us up with a big steel bolt cutter. Nowadays we're being persecuted."

A scenario that might sound absurd, but history teaches us that it is painfully possible: the persecution of Jews in Germany began in the same way. A troubled socioeconomic period like today's, lots of shiftless people who couldn't make a living, and in the end they took it out on the weak and defenseless. Back then it was the Jews' turn, today it's seniors'. Who knows why seniors are being blamed by these amoral youths? Maybe because they live too long. Or because they occupy public housing. Who knows what other madness issues from brains addled by drugs and a lack of values?

One thing is sure: the national situation is no different from that of this small town in the province of Pisa, and this wave of intolerance could spread to the whole boot in the time it takes to write this sentence. No hoary-haired Italian should feel safe in his bed.

This is why we should all follow the example of these four seasoned gladiators, who decided to take action before it was too late. And in our hearts we should all become like the Muglione Guardians. (*Pier Francesco Lamantino*)

AN AIR MATTRESS FOR CARP

My stomach hurts. For one week I've been getting by on sandwiches from the vending machine at the gas station. Every day I keep saying, *When it starts to hurt I'll quit, when it starts to hurt I'll quit,* and now I really do have to quit.

I need a portable stove, the kind you use at camp or when the chips are down. And my chips are definitely down, if indeed I have any chips left; at any rate a portable stove would really come in handy.

I could put it in the middle of the back room, that way I could cook whatever I want. I'm a decent cook, Mom taught me how when I was little. She said that a man has to know how to prepare dinner, otherwise he'll end up marrying the first idiot who walks by so he won't die of starvation.

This is what I'm thinking because it's three-thirty, and when I bent down to raise the gates of the shop, my throat filled with the acrid taste of mushrooms and pink sauce. And that's when I said, *No more vending machines, I have to find a camp stove.*

In the meantime, tonight I'll eat at the deli.

But the first thing I have to do is sweep in front of the entrance. Instead of a door there is only a sheet of cardboard with duct tape, and you can still feel the shards of glass under your shoes. I go to the back room, get the broom, and when I come back I find Giuliano and Stefanino.

I was expecting them. They told me they had a fantastic idea for the band and they wanted to explain it to me in person. But Antonio's not there. We haven't heard from him since that night at Pontedera. A bad sign.

"Holy mackerel, it's hot in here!" says Giuliano. "How the two of you can stand to wear so many clothes I don't know." Because he is wearing blue jean overalls and is bare-chested, of course.

Stefano is holding an envelope, and he hands it over without looking at me, as if it were a summons. His not looking at me means that it was sent by Booger.

Booger is the Italian teacher. He's pretty young and wants us to call him by his first name, for the sake of equality. We explained to him that however he wants to slice it, he's still at the desk in front and gives us quizzes and grades, so we could care less about first names and prefer to be more formal, but Booger started making a big speech about institutional distances and oppressive figures and so to make him shut up we started calling him by his first name.

I open the envelope and inside is a letter.

Fiorenzo,

You've accumulated a lot of absences, that's not good: finals are around the corner, you need to come back to school.

You need to stop feeling sorry for yourself. So you've only got one hand, big deal! Think about it, if you didn't see other people, would you feel the need to have two hands? No, it would be normal to have one, just as it is normal for those of us with two to want three, do you follow me?

So I'm telling you: go back to school and don't make such a big deal about things. What more could you want? You're as normal as the rest of us.

    See you soon,

    Mr. Augusto

I take the letter and crumple it up with the only hand I have, and throw it toward the wastebasket where we keep stale bread for the chum and I shoot baskets.

Yes, of course, what more could I want, I'm as normal as the rest... so normal that he can't name a normal reason for my staying away from school. A fight with my dad, an ass-kicking band, sex with a woman? No, my problem had to be my hand. What happened? Am I losing my other hand? Do I want to enroll at a special school for the handicapped? Or did I lower my eyes for the first time in five years and suddenly realize that everyone else has an extra hand?

Poor Booger, always going on about *Kids, I know what it's like, I feel your pain*... and instead he never understands shit.

"What does the letter say?" asks Giuliano.

"The usual bullshit. But you guys have already read it anyway."

Stefanino's eyes pop out and he looks away. Giuliano makes a noise in his throat that could be either a laugh or a burp. "Yes, you're right," he says, then rubs his hands over his naked stomach and starts to wander around the shop.

A giant tattoo darkens his back. He got it after a dream one night when he had a high fever, and it could be either a burnt chicken or a fluke with a head of hair, but Giuliano says that it's a fire-breathing dragon.

While he's walking around the shop, the dragon bounces up and down, jiggling in sync with the jelly rolls around his waist, and it really does create the impression of a living thing. Dying, but living.

"Excuse me," I say to him, "weren't you the one who was so busy trying to get a girl? Good luck if you're walking around with your shirt off."

"Are you stupid? Women go crazy for this shit. It shows you're a real man. Women have had it up to here with those metrosexuals who spend all day in front of the mirror, using moisturizers and getting manicures. Those guys are useless in bed. They just lie there talking about horoscopes and skin creams and the women can't stand it anymore."

"So they fling themselves at slobs?"

"That's it, Fiorenzo, you hit the nail on the head. Take that old lady who jumped your bones. How do you explain it?"

"She's not old."

"Okay, I'll explain. For years she's been going out with metrosexuals who are middle-aged, like her, who talk a lot and boast about their jobs and take her to expensive restaurants. But at the moment of truth, in bed, nothing happens. So out of desperation, she says to herself, *Well, let's try a kid for a change, and see what happens.*"

"So, if she'd seen you first, bare-chested..."

"She jumps my bones, obviously. She realizes immediately that with yours truly there's no talk. I'm raring to go, I grab her by the hips, I get her head down and I start to bang out the rhythm like a hammer... *bang bang bang.*"

Giuliano puts one hand behind his back and the other in front, in the air, to hold an imaginary woman still. Every *bang* is accompanied by a grinding of the hips that sets the fat jiggling around his waist.

"*Bang bang bang…,*" faster and faster, with a face that's dead serious, he's sweating, I get the impression he really believes he's doing it. "*Bang bang,* oh yes you slut, yes, *bang bang ba—*"

He stops all of a sudden, halfway into a thrust, in a straddling position with his eyes on the door. I turn around, too, but with one part of my brain I already know who I'm going to find in the doorway witnessing the scene.

Who else: Tiziana.

I'd thought she would never come looking for me, but for some crazy reason she decided to come—how could it be at anything other than the worst moment? And it doesn't get much worse than this.

"Hi," says Giuliano, dead serious. He straightens up with his hands by his sides and lowers his eyes to the floor.

"Hi," says Tiziana, "am I interrupting anything?"

I don't know how long she's been here, but not too long, I think. Because otherwise she would have run away.

Instead she comes in. She's wearing a summer dress, sleeveless, and under her arm you can see a little bit of skin that is either the lower part of her breast or the upper part of her side. And it looks phenomenal, because it's dark and smooth and is definitely perfumed. But at the same time it's a little irritating, because Stefanino and that pig Giuliano can see it, too, and in fact he's got his eyes trained on that very spot. So it makes me a little angry and it gets on my nerves and I even end up feeling a little jealous. That's what I said, jealous: of a girl who one day gave me a kiss by mistake and has now come to tell me that I'm a disgusting leper and she doesn't want to see me anymore.

To feel a little less stupid I try to say something.

"Hi." Not much but it's a start.

"Hi," she says. "I'm sorry, I get the impression I interrupted something."

"No, no, not at all. They were just getting ready to leave."

Stefanino nods and starts to go toward the door, but Giuliano doesn't move. "But...it's not like we were going away or anything. We wanted to tell you about this great idea..."

"You see, I did interrupt something, I'm sorry, I can come back another time."

"No, I mean it, Tiziana, don't worry, they're leaving to go for a walk and they'll be back later."

But Giuliano doesn't even hear me. He keeps staring at Tiziana, and then at me, then Tiziana, then me...and finally he understands. He opens his eyes wide, places a hand over his mouth, points at her, points at me. He's practically turned into a mime, he even has that same idiotic expression that mimes wear in their sorry-ass performances.

"Giuliano, come on, let's go," says Stefanino, and he takes him by the arm. Giuliano moves but without looking away. He trips over the doorstep, turns around again, and they both disappear without saying goodbye.

Then the two of us are alone in the shop. Us and silence, a lot of silence.

"Hi," I say again. It worked before, I don't know why it shouldn't work again.

"Hi. I'm really sorry if I came at a time that..."

"Don't worry about it, the usual bullshit, you know."

"I didn't know if I was doing the right thing coming here— maybe you're working and it's a bad idea."

"Who cares about work? You did the right thing, you...yes."

More silence.

Tiziana looks at me and doesn't speak. I have my right arm leaning against the counter; an automatic reflex makes me feel like hiding it underneath, but in the end I leave it up there.

"I'm sorry," I say.

"Sorry about what?"

"I don't know. About last time. And also about this place. It's no great shakes, I know."

"You're wrong. It's really interesting. And there are a lot of things that I've never seen in my life."

"For example?"

"For example, that thing there, what is it?"

"What, this?"

"No, the thing above it. It looks like a mini sleeping bag."

"Oh, it's an air mattress for carp."

"A what?"

"An air mattress for carp."

"You're kidding."

"I swear, I'm not. Look, this is how it works. You open it up and fill it with air. Then when you catch a carp you lay it on top. You feel how soft and smooth it is? That way the fish doesn't get bruised by stones and twigs on the ground."

"Come on, you've got to be kidding."

"No, I'm not, I swear."

"But what sense does it make if you're going to kill it anyway?"

"Who said anything about killing it? First you remove the hook from its mouth, keeping the fish wet the whole time so it doesn't suffer from thermal shock, then you take the air mattress with the carp on top and lower it into the water, so the carp can breathe. But you can't let go because it's still tired from the struggle. You have to hold on to it with your hands and move it forward, like this, with little pushes. And as soon as it's got enough oxygen, it'll take off on its own."

With my arm I make the undulating motion of the fish escaping. With my good arm.

"How do I know you're not pulling my leg?"

"I told you I swear I'm not."

"I thought that fishermen always eat the fish."

"Who's going to eat a carp? I mean, we're talking about an animal that lives in the muck in a putrid, stinky irrigation ditch, filled with fertilizer from the fields and toads and mice. Do you feel like cooking one in the oven and eating it? Then you may as well accompany it with a nice glass of ditch water and everything will be perfect."

Tiziana laughs and I also let out a snort.

"Gross," she says. She sticks her tongue out and says, "*Bleehhh.*"

I do the same. "*Bleehhh.*"

Everything's going really great.

I've made a lot of progress since our initial *Hi*. I feel light. Tiziana didn't come to tell me that I'm a bastard for pretending to have two hands, she's not even mad at me, I think, and we laugh and say intelligent things and joke and everything is going well.

Then Mazinger arrives.

"OH—FIORENZO!" he yells at the top of his lungs.

He's wearing a silver jacket that looks like plastic and white pants with a really low crotch. He comes to the counter and gives me a pat on the back, since now his mates aren't around and he's back to being the usual Mazinger. I prefer the cold and distant version: *Good afternoon, I'll have this, here's the money, thank you and goodbye.*

243

"AM—I—INTERRUPTING?" And he looks at me, then Tiziana. With a stupid smile on his face.

"No, no," she says. "Good afternoon, Mister..."

"MAZZANTI—DONATO—PLEASED—TO...OHMYGOD —MISS—BUT—IT'S—YOU—OUTSIDE—THE—BAR—I— DIDN'T—RECOGNIZE—YOU."

"It's not a bar, it's an office, but it's all right anyway. Good afternoon."

"DID—YOU—SEE—WE'RE—IN—THE—PAPER?"

"What? No, I...who's in the paper?"

"US!—IN—*ITALIAN—CHRONICLE*—ON—THE— COVER...THEN—I'LL—BRING—IT—TO—THE—BAR— SO—YOU—CAN—SEE—IT..."

"Donato, come on, what do you need today?" I say. "Quick or the mullets will be gone."

"YES—YOU'RE—RIGHT—I—NEED—A—LITTLE— GROUNDBAIT."

He says this word and I tremble. Chum. I was hoping for something less nasty, but I can forget about it. Older fishermen have seen a ruthless and bloody world, they don't go fishing to relax. They relax on normal days; when they go fishing they want violence.

I ask him what kind of groundbait he prefers. It's a question I have to ask.

"CHEESE—OR—CORN—IT'S—THE—SAME—AS— LONG—AS—THERE'S—LOTS—OF—BLOOD—SARDINE— BLOOD—AND—SARDINE—PIECES—AND—OX—BLOOD— IF—YOU—HAVE—IT."

I look at Tiziana for just a second, but it's enough for me to realize that the carp-saving air mattress is a distant memory, lost in a tender and delicate past that no longer exists.

"There's also a new chum," I say, "made from fruit. Strawberry, raspberry juice."

"I — WASH — MY — BALLS — WITH — RASPBERRY — JUICE — OH — EXCUSE — ME — MISS — SORRY..."

Tiziana smiles, and Mr. Donato goes on: "COME — ON — FIORENZO — I'M — IN — A — HURRY — IF — YOU — WANT — TO — ATTRACT — FISH — THERE'S — NOTHING — LIKE — ROTTEN — BLOOD." He stops a second and looks at Tiziana. "YOU — KNOW — MISS — MODESTLY — SPEAKING — I'M — GOOD — AT — IT — THE — LAST — TIME — I — CAUGHT — SO — MANY — MULLET — THAT — I — NEEDED — A — WHEELBARROW — TO — TAKE — THEM — AWAY ... I — DIDN'T — KNOW — WHO — TO — GIVE — THEM — TO — THEN — I — FOUND — GINO — WHO — RAISES — PIGS — AND — THEY — EAT — EVERYTHING ... BUT — IF — NEXT — TIME — YOU — WANT — THEM..."

I remind him again that it's getting late.

"YOU'RE — RIGHT — IT'S — REALLY — LATE ... IN — FACT — CAN — I — MIX — THE — GROUNDBAIT — HERE? — COME — ON — FIORENZO — IT'LL — SAVE — TIME — FIRST — I'LL — GO — GET — THE — BUCKET — YOU — GET — THE — BLOOD."

Mr. Donato looks at Tiziana, makes a sort of bow, and rushes off.

She turns and looks at me, I look at her. I'm waiting for her to throw up on the floor, report me to the police, anything. Instead she starts laughing.

"Fiorenzo, I'm going, I don't want to be here when the slaughter begins."

"Not a bad idea."

"And I have to open the office. Or rather the bar, I don't remember what to call it anymore."

"Well, what difference does it make, you open it and whatever happens, happens."

"Yes, true ... 'bye."

"'Bye," I say. But Tiziana doesn't leave. She looks at me, looks outside. Maybe if I lean over the counter she'll give me another kiss, I don't know, through my doubts I barely stick my neck out toward...

"HERE—I—AM!" shouts Mazinger from the door. He's picked up the bucket as well as a plastic bag filled with stuff that's dripping onto the floor.

Tiziana looks at me and with one foot starts to escape. "We'll talk later, if you feel like it."

"I do. I close at seven-thirty. You?"

"Oh, you mean tonight?"

"If it works for you, yeah."

"Okay, I... okay, all right, can we meet at eight?"

"Great," I say. "At eight at... let's say in front of the diner, Il Fagiano, do you know where it is? It's just past the gas station, there's a round sign with a pheasant on it."

"Sure, why not... so in front at eight ... 'bye."

"'Bye!" I say, and wave my hand like an idiot child. I don't need a mirror to see that I've got an expression like a true moron, I can feel it right on my face.

Tiziana goes and I look at her leaving softly in the light, filled with curves in the air, a light feather on the breeze. While the blunt blows against the bottom of the bucket are telling me that Mr. Donato has already started breaking up the sardine pieces.

And I stay there with him and the ox blood and the smelly cheese and the stories about tons and tons of mullets as strong as Christians who if you don't kill them with a hard blow to the head will keep jumping until the next day.

Meanwhile I ask myself, well, what are Tiziana and I going to do tonight? Are we just going to meet up, without a plan, so she can tell me something, and then we each go our separate ways, or is it a kind of date? And what does she want to tell me, what am I supposed to do, and if the night goes on where should I take her?

But above all, did I really tell her that we'd meet in front of Il Fagiano?

THE SHOP THAT WAS
DRIPPING BLOOD

"What an amazing piece of ass! You have to see her to believe it. I didn't...I've never..."

They've been back for half an hour, and for half an hour Giuliano's been going on like this. Stefanino says that he started when they left and he hasn't stopped since.

"She looks like a porn star. No, like a refined actress from normal movies who's just decided to do some porn. Don't you get it, Fiorenzo? No, you don't, you're acting like it's all normal. So listen up, you idiot, it's not normal for shit, not—"

"All right already. I get it."

"Will you listen to him. He *gets* it. You'd think you were talking about school, damn it. You don't deserve a girl like that, you don't deserve shit!"

"Okay, okay, but are you finally going to tell me this brilliant idea that you've got?" I look at Stefanino. "Will you tell me?"

Stefano hesitates a second, takes a good look at Giuliano, and then gives it a try. "You know that story in the newspaper about the seniors..."

"Stefanino, fuck!" shouts Giuliano. "There you go starting from the wrong end! What the fuck do you think you're telling him? Why do you always beat around the bush? Let me tell."

"It was just to introduce..."

"Yes, but you suck at introductions, big-time. You have to start from the beginning." He turns toward me and begins. "You know that story in the newspaper about the seniors ... that patrol they set up. Come on, Fiorenzo, they're in the *Italian Chronicle*, on the front page."

"I heard about it."

"There's even a picture, a giant photo on the front page! They call themselves the Muglione Guardians, a lousy name if you ask me. First an article came out in *La Nazione* and now this. How long do you think it's going to be before they're on TV? Basically, there's a ton of publicity about them. And they say their number-one enemy is an anti-retirees gang. A group of young people, like skinheads, who are out to get them."

"Here in Muglione?"

"Exactly! Can you believe that bullshit? But in town everyone's taking them seriously. They're all afraid. My grandma is terrified, she's even stopped doing the grocery shopping."

"Sure, whatever," I say, "now tell me about this brilliant idea."

"The brilliant idea is simple. Simple and brilliant. Since this story is on everyone's lips, nationwide, I'd say that we should take advantage of the opportunity. And by we I mean Metal Devastation."

"What are you saying? Like, we should join the Guardians?"

"No way. They're a bunch of old geezers. But we can become the *enemies* of the Guardians, get it?"

"I'm not sure I do."

"Think about it. Those idiots are fighting against a gang that wants to exterminate the seniors, except the gang doesn't exist. In other words, there's a hole in the story, and we're going to fill that hole."

"You mean, we're going to exterminate the old folks?"

"No, no, we don't have to do shit. The important thing is not to raise any suspicions, any rumors about us...for example, we could write something on a wall, like 'Death to Old Folks,' and underneath we could sign it 'MD,' or 'Metal D,' which is clearer. In other words, we could build some suspicions around the band, so that people would talk."

"Like, talk about us hating old people?"

"Talk about the band, damn it. And *bam*, everyone will know who we are. Can you imagine it on TV? They'll talk about Muglione, a quiet little town but where there's a dangerous gang that beats up old people. And in the same town there's this fierce, mean musical group. Could they be the anti-retirees gang? Maybe yes, maybe no...they interview us and we're vague, we say we don't want to be disturbed, but always with this weird attitude, you know, suspicious, neo-Nazi...come on, it's perfect: we play heavy metal, have long hair, people already think we're monsters."

"But long hair isn't neo-Nazi," I say.

"Yes, it's true, Fiorenzo, I know, you know, but these people don't know jack, they don't know jack shit."

I look at Giuliano, I look at Stefanino. I have to admit that today they're not talking bullshit.

"So what do we have to do?"

"We have to get busy, right away. Tonight we need a nice anti-old-folks message on a wall."

"But I'm not free tonight."

"We're off to a good start. Where the fuck are you going?"

"I have to do a couple of errands, for the shop, errands that...for the..."

"Hold up! What I'm talking about is major, we've got to get on it right away!"

"But I won't be long. After dinner I should be free. As soon as I'm free I'll call you."

"Okay," says Giuliano. "In the meantime we'll buy the spray paint."

"Red or black?" Stefanino asks.

"Red. Black would be too neo-Nazi, but red is like blood," says Giuliano.

"Hey, wouldn't it be better to use real blood?" I say.

"I was thinking the same thing, but Stefano's family is super rich, if we slit his throat they'll have our asses in court."

But we don't need to sacrifice Stefano. This shop is dripping with blood.

COLD RICE

So, Tiziana, let me tell you what's going down.

What's going down is that the old guy came to the store and interrupted you with all that stuff about chum and blood, and he did you a huge favor. That's right, not because he gave you an excuse to run away. On the contrary, he gave the two of you a reason to get together tonight.

Because you were in that smelly shop together with a kid who's younger than the youngest of Raffaella's younger brothers and for some impossible reason your only hope was to see him again. And tonight you will. And this makes you happy. Whether or not you realize it.

But you do. In fact, the word *stupid* is bouncing around in your head more than usual tonight. And the sensation is worsened by the fact that you're waiting in front of an awful diner called Il Fagiano, and one after the other three meatheads came up to ask you if you needed something, if you were waiting for someone, if you were Italian.

It's like, whatever, men are idiots — and here there must be some kind of special competition for the biggest idiot of all — but the truth is, you can't expect to come dressed like this and be left alone. It's Raffaella's fault. She's the one who made you put on the skintight flower-print dress and sling-back sandals.

You saw yourself in the mirror and felt like a wide-hipped idiot and you hated yourself for having these arms.

But at the same time you realized you looked hot. Too hot for a parking lot full of guys who speak to each other from the lowered windows of their rally cars. Every now and then they tear off, tires squealing, pull a doughnut on the street, and then come back to a round of applause. Not to mention that your feet are hurting in these tight sandals. You go to the low wall that surrounds the parking lot. It's cement and on top it's rough and bumpy. You place a Kleenex over it and sit down. And wait.

I see her sitting on the wall by the parking lot and realize what an idiot I was to say we'd meet here, at Il Fagiano. I mean, I already realized it earlier, but now I do even more.

I go toward her past the rumbling of a Ford Focus that makes my stomach vibrate. The car has a giant spoiler in the back, flames painted on the sides, and the fascist slogan DEATH TO QUITTERS stenciled on the windshield. I look at it out of the corner of my eye, but I mostly look at Tiziana, who's straight ahead of me and doesn't fit into these surroundings at all.

I go to her and I realize that I'm keeping my right arm in my jeans pocket. But I've got a good reason. When I'm really nervous, or when it's humid, my hand hurts. I feel pain in my fingers, a stabbing sensation, and my palm itches. Yes, exactly. The palm of the hand that's not there.

It happens. It's called phantom limb syndrome. Once in the hospital I met an old lady who when she was a little girl was hit in the foot by shrapnel from a land mine. When she was old they amputated her whole leg because of circulatory problems, but some nights she still couldn't sleep because of the pain from that shrapnel. She told me, I swear. It really is weird how we're made.

"Hi," I say.

"Hi," she says.

Tiziana is wearing really nice perfume and a beautiful dress. The first will sound stupid if I tell her so I keep it to myself.

"That's a beautiful dress," I say.

"Thanks. Uh, it's not really so beautiful. I got it at the open-air market for fifteen euros, but it's not bad. I like your T-shirt, too."

I thank her. Before coming here I went home, or rather to my former home, to put on something decent. This time Dad was in the kitchen getting dinner ready, which I'd never seen in my life. In my room the friggin' Little Champ was on the bed, writing. He told me he had another composition ready and I told him who cares. He said I was right what I said about the races, I asked what he meant, he just shook his head and repeated that I was right. I put on my Social Distortion T-shirt and came here. To this lousy diner.

"Sorry about the place," I say. "I'm an idiot. I was fixated on the idea of eating at the diner tonight so when we said eight o'clock the first thing to come to mind was the diner."

"Are you a fan of diners?"

"No. I mean yes. At home I don't have a stove and I can't stand another sandwich."

"What do you mean, you don't have a stove? How does your mother cook, if you don't mind my asking?"

"No, I don't..."

"Oh, forgive me! But your mother...I mean, you...please, tell me that you live alone."

"In fact, I do. I live alone."

"Oh..." Tiziana laughs and starts to breathe. "Thank goodness, for a second I was worried your mother was dead and I sounded like a jerk..."

"Yes, well, she is dead. But apart from that I do live alone."

Tiziana turns to stone. "Oh my God, I'm such a jerk. I'm so sorry, I apologize, I..."

"Don't worry about it. And since I know how to cook fine on my own, I don't need—"

"Okay, all right, but I still have to apologize."

"What for? It's not your fault. Anyway, the problem is that at my house I don't have a stove, which is why I wanted to eat at the diner."

"I get it." Tiziana fixes a lock of hair that always falls in front of her face. She tries to stick it behind her ear and I want to tell her to let it go because she looks really, really nice with that lock of hair in front of her face. Except that it would sound stupid: if I see a movie and a guy says something like that to a girl, first I throw up and then I change channels. So like hell am I going to say it.

"So, do you have any dinner plans?" she says.

"Me...yes, maybe. And you?"

"I don't know, maybe at home."

"Yeah, I don't know either. I mean, I really couldn't tell whether we'd be having dinner together or not."

There, I said it. And what was I supposed to do? It was true, for crying out loud, it doesn't sound so ridiculous to me. If two people make a date for eight o'clock, one of them might have thought they might be meeting for dinner, right?

And in fact Tiziana says that she hadn't known either, and just in case she had the girl she lives with leave her a plate of cold rice.

I say, "Cold rice is good," because it's one of my favorite meals. And one of hers, too. And we bad-mouth the hipsters who would turn up their noses and say *How gross*, the ones who like food tastings and fine wine.

"They're just a bunch of losers," I say, "with their tastings and samplings and complicated stuff... Life is already complicated enough, at least eating should be simple, right? One day they're even going to teach us how to go to the bathroom."

Tiziana laughs. Every time I'm afraid I've said too much, she laughs.

"You're right. I used to go out with these men, you have no idea how boring they were with their truffles and special oil from a certain hill and wine aged in oak casks with an aftertaste of... my God, I couldn't take it anymore."

So Tiziana says that and I laugh on the outside and I say, "What idiots," but on the inside a giant bitter stain begins to spread: Tiziana went out *with men*? Men? How many men? Two, three, fifty? A busful of males who took her around to all the restaurants in the area? And maybe among those dozens was the usual show-off who took her to have fried fish in Santa Margherita or oysters in Monte Carlo, and come on, I'm sure Tiziana gave it up to him, or at least gave him a little taste at the end of the evening.

I know it's ridiculous. I mean, until the other day I didn't even know that Tiziana existed and she the same with me, but I feel this thing itching inside and repeating *with men, with men*, and it shows me these pampered men, super rich and super expert in gallantry, and it parades them in front of me, in my Social Distortion T-shirt in the parking lot of Il Fagiano.

"They're people who don't even consider cold rice to be a meal," she says.

"Then they don't understand a thing. For me it's one of the best dishes in the world, especially if you have pickled mushrooms. Does your girlfriend add pickled mushrooms?"

Tiziana looks at me, nods twice, then looks into the distance. Over my shoulders but way into the distance. Or maybe she's looking at nothing and it's just a pose of her eyes while her mind is working, like the little clock that appears on the computer screen when it takes time to load something so it tells you *Wait a second because I'm all tied up.*

Then she comes back to me, bites her lip, and places the lock of hair behind her ear.

"Fiorenzo, do you want to come to my house for some cold rice?"

I swear she says it just like that.

THE DEVIL'S NIGHTMARE

We enter Tiziana's house and she says the same thing I said when she came to the shop. "I'm sorry about this place. And I'm sorry about the smell."

"What's to be sorry about? It's the smell of the ditch. I like it, it reminds me of fishing."

I smile, take a look around, and manage to pretend that I'm interested in the furniture the curtains and the lighting in the room, but in reality the only thing that matters is that the girl who lives with Tiziana is out. We're alone, she and I, it's almost nine o'clock by now and in a little while it'll be dark, so we're a man and a woman alone at night in a house, and we're not friends we're not relatives we're not minimally colleagues. We're a man and a woman and we have only one reason for being here, in my opinion.

"So, the cold rice." Tiziana rushes to the refrigerator and bends down to the lower shelves, from behind I take in as much as I can and her shapes are as clear as day under the flower-print dress. I keep gazing at her until she stands up with the bowl in her hands. She sets it on the table and takes two plates from the sink.

"It's really cold," she says. "It's better if we wait a second before eating it."

"Okay, but cold rice is supposed to be eaten cold, right?"

"Yes, but now it's *too* cold. It's freezing-cold rice."

"You should apply for a patent on frozen rice pops," I say.

I'm such an idiot. Frozen rice pops. What the fuck is that supposed to mean? It's not even a joke, it's just words thrown together. And it'd be better not to talk about the cold, since the atmosphere in here is chilly enough as it is.

"What do you say, should I put it in the oven a second?"

"I don't know. I mean, I eat it like this."

But Tiziana has already turned the oven on, opened the door, and slipped the rice bowl inside.

To do it she has to bend over even more. Her back and ass are pressing against her dress and I'm one step away and if I extend my arm I can touch her. And the more I look at her the more her body parts are telling me *We're waiting for you, so what's it going to be, are you coming or not?*

I listen to them and want to answer *Yes, here I am, I'm coming,* close my eyes and plunge in and do everything. But I don't know how to do anything, I don't even know where to begin.

Because it's not exactly easy. How are you supposed to leap from normal life into sex? How do you go from being two people standing up and dressed and pressed with normal things to do (eat rice, converse) to ending up as two naked bodies sweating and rubbing and penetrating and saying dirty words and squirting all over each other? There has to be something in between, I don't know, a transitional phase.

In songs, for example, it's not like you go straight from the verse to the chorus. It wouldn't make sense, it takes a buildup that grabs you and lifts you and then lets the chorus go on as long as it wants. The buildup is called the *bridge* because it's a bridge from the normal world of the verse leading to the heaven of the chorus, where the music is louder and pulsating and will stay in your head for a long, long time.

And here, instead, with Tiziana bent over the oven trying to reheat the cold rice, where is my bridge? I don't see it or feel it, do I have to conclude that it doesn't exist? Maybe it's like with the smartest bands, such as Black Sabbath or Motörhead. They couldn't care less about doing things by degrees. They ignore the rules and make fierce songs that go straight down a path without bridges and without middle ways. So I'm going to go straight down my path, too, yes, I'm the lead singer of Metal Devastation and no one can stop me! Yes, yes, yes!

That's why I throw myself on the hunched-over Tiziana, and even if I do have only one hand I grab everything there is to grab, I squeeze her tits and press myself against her back and rub myself on her ass, I lift up her skirt and lower my jeans and bite her hard on the neck. She jumps up straight and rigid, tries to stop me and shouts, but after a second it's as if she were someone else. She catches fire and squeezes my hips and rubs against me and says, *Yes, oh yes, like that, like that,* she grabs my hand and passes it over her whole body and tits and thighs and then down there in the middle where it's hot and wet and Tiziana is thrashing and moaning and saying *Oh my God, who are you, you make me crazy, the losers my age are impotent femmes, oh my God yes, I can barely stand, oh yes, yes, yes . . .*

But I don't. I don't do a damn thing. We sit and eat the cold rice.

Because it's not exactly easy. And because I'm an imbecile.

"Unfortunately, there's not much rice," she says.

"Really? No, it's just right. And it's good."

"Yes, but there's too little. I'm sorry, maybe we can figure something else out for later, yeah?"

I don't look up, I don't feel like it, I only nod with my eyes staring at my plate. *We can figure something else out for later,* she says. Yes, why not, don't go looking to me for ideas.

Suddenly a text from Giuliano explodes in the silence of the room.

Ready to go. U? Excalibur first.
Still with the babe? (8:58pm)

I put the cell back in my pocket. Yes, I am with the babe, but the only thing I'm getting out of tonight is half a plate of cold rice.

I'm pathetic, the lead singer of Metal Devastation is a baby doll who wets his pants every time he's near a woman. I'm a disgrace to the whole tradition of hot and horny singers like Vince Neil and David Coverdale, guys who brought women into their dressing rooms three at a time, mixed it up with them left, right, and center, and then sent them packing with a kick in the ass and a T-shirt with the band's name on it.

But here I am in a perfect situation and I can't manage to do shit. And so of course everything goes cold, we chew surrounded by a block of silence mixed with forks scraping against plates, and in the end Tiziana starts talking about things that are about as sexy as wet socks.

"You see, it's like ... I mean, I wanted to say I'm sorry about that stuff with your hand."

"..."

"I mean, the other day in the office it was so sudden that at the moment I ... in other words, I was a little surprised. Then you ran away and ..."

"I didn't run away, I walked away."

"Yes, okay, but I wanted to tell you that it's not a problem. I mean, right then it seemed weird, but I got over it a second later. Except you didn't give me enough time to..."

"I know. The problem is that I've given a lot of time to a lot of people, and it hasn't made any difference."

"I can imagine, I can, I'm sorry. But listen, can I ask you how it happened? If you don't mind, otherwise forget I said anything, we can talk about something else."

"Why bother? It was a firecracker accident."

"Jesus. On New Year's Eve?"

"No, in July. I was fourteen."

"Oh my God, Fiorenzo, I'm so sorry. Does it make any sense to say I'm sorry?"

"I don't think so, but a lot of people say it anyway."

"You see, I'm sorry for that, too."

"No, get over it. Actually, thank you. It's much worse when they say *I feel your pain.* Now that gets me pissed off as all hell. *I feel your pain*... What the fuck do you feel? Once I even heard it from... a girl I know, and I told her that she didn't feel my pain for shit: she thought she did, but this is something that if you don't go through it yourself no way can you feel it. So you know what she did? She took some gauze and wrapped it around one hand and spent a whole day with just one hand."

"That's so wild! I like your friend. Did she understand you better afterward?"

"A little bit, yes. But a lot of people know zilch. Sometimes they even ask if I was born this way."

"Get out, what morons. But are there people who were born that way?"

"I don't know, I've never heard of any. I mean yes, once, but in a horror film. There was this kid born without a hand, because of a curse that—"

"I saw it! I saw it! It was on TV the other night! There was a castle, a kind of castle, and a half-crazy peasant who—"

"The title is *And Now the Screaming Starts*," I say, I sit up nice and straight in the chair and I speak in a professorial tone, because now we're getting on to a subject where I'm the expert and everyone else can sit down and listen. "It's an English movie from a producer called—"

"Amicus!" Tiziana gets there first. "Yes, you could tell from the lighting, the cinematography."

"I mean, like, you know Amicus's movies?" In real life I had never met anyone who knew them, apart from me and Giuliano.

"Yes, but their stuff is too gothic for me. I prefer horror set in the present, if possible in the countryside. Horror movies that take place in the city make no sense. You have to have trees and fog and owls going *hoo-hoo*, otherwise it doesn't work."

Tiziana speaks and I can't believe it, I swear it's like listening to myself. I agree one hundred percent, I nod to everything she says, stronger and stronger. If I don't stop I'll break a vertebra, but who cares?

"And the one the other night is called *And Now the Screaming Starts*?"

"Yes," I say. "With Peter Cushing. It's not highly rated, but I like it a lot. Maybe because I can identify with the story of the guy without a hand." And I swear without even thinking I raise my right arm, which I was keeping under the table, and I let it go free in the air.

Tiziana looks at it but just for a moment, like you would look at a normal arm that ends in a normal way. Then she comes back to my eyes and she is interested only in what we are saying.

"I agree with you," she says. "There are films that objectively speaking are amazing. *Night of the Living Dead, Halloween,* the first *Nightmare on Elm Street, Friday the 13th.* And then there are others that are important for our own reasons. I call them personal classics."

I continue to nod, I can't stop. Tomorrow my neck's going to be killing me, but I don't mind.

"So your personal classic is *And Now the Screaming Starts,*" she says. "Now guess what mine is."

I think but it isn't easy. What title would work for Tiziana? Something Italian or American? Those boring old films with Bela Lugosi or the golden days of the seventies? I need some help.

"Tell me at least the genre. Vampires, witches, zombies, mummies?"

"Well, it doesn't really fit it into a precise category."

"Okay, maybe a detail then, like a—"

"It's *The Devil's Nightmare.* There, I told you, you wouldn't have guessed, anyway."

"Says you!" I shout. But Tiziana's right. Goddamnit, I never even saw *The Devil's Nightmare.* I only know that it's got Erika Blanc, and shit, I can at least tell her that: "Erika Blanc is in it, right?"

"Exactly. The original title is *La plus longue nuit du diable,* directed by Jean Brismée, in Belgium, 1971, but in reality it's an Italian coproduction that came out in 1973."

"Jeez, you know everything."

"Well, it's my personal classic. And would you do me a huge favor, Fiorenzo?"

"Sure..."

"Could you please ask me why it's my personal classic?"

"Sure, I was just about to ask. Why is it your personal classic?"

"So, the first reason..." Tiziana smiles and turns her eyes to the ceiling, straightens her back, and gets comfortable in her chair. She ticks off a list of reasons and keeps count with her fingers like a child. "First thing: it starts with a Nazi flashback. Second thing: the sound track is fantastic. Third, Erika Blanc is wearing this *fabulous* black plastic dress that she made herself. Fourth, and there's Erika Blanc. Fifth..."

"You know I've never seen it," I say.

And Tiziana sits there with her fingers stuck on five. "What?" she looks at me as if I had said that I was never in a club or I had never kissed a girl, both of which are fairly accurate. "You never saw it? You must be crazy, that's not possible!"

I say that actually it is possible, but at this point I want to see it as soon as I can. And then she says that we have to watch it together. I swear, she says it, she says *together*. And she also says, "I've got it on DVD, come into my bedroom and I'll show it to you."

Into her bedroom.

These three words change everything. I mean, maybe not everything, but to hear her say *into my bedroom*, at night when we're alone and with that voice that was maybe deeper when she said it, it has a big effect on me. Because in bedrooms there is a lot of furniture and knickknacks and scattered accessories, but above all there is a bed. And if Tiziana brings me there I don't know what's going to happen.

I'm guessing that she doesn't know either. She said to go to her room and suddenly we've stopped talking, we've stopped looking at each other; I clear my throat just for the hell of it.

In the meantime another text arrives on my cell phone, and another: now there are three and all three are from Giuliano. Tiziana says to me, "Wow, there sure are a lot of people looking for you." I act nonchalant and follow her. Now we are in her bedroom.

There are stacks of books and magazines, on the shelves on the furniture on the floor, piles of newspapers and notebooks and loose sheets of paper and two black-and-white posters on the walls. One is a picture of a little boy lugging two big bottles of wine, the other is a building, I don't know which, in the middle of other buildings that look like skyscrapers.

But I obviously couldn't care less about this whole panorama. The only thing that grabs my attention is the bed, nice and comfortable, a double.

Tiziana gets the DVD and hands it to me. On the cover is Erika Blanc screaming and behind her a castle with a tower and the title of the film in red letters. And obviously I couldn't care less about the DVD either.

"Look inside," she says. "There's the original poster, it's wild."

I try to open the DVD case, but it's really hard. I hold it to my chest with my right arm and work at it with my hand; it usually only takes a second. But now it seems complicated even to breathe, so it takes me a little longer. And here's Tiziana in front of me looking at me and at one point she makes like she's going to help me but thankfully she restrains herself. I try to open the case with every ounce of energy in my body but the piece of shit won't budge, like an oyster or a safe (even if I've never seen either of the two in real life), so I put more strength into it, I stop breathing and pull, I pull and I squeeze, and in the end the damn thing slips and, goddamnit, falls to the floor. And naturally as soon as it hits the floor it opens, the DVD shoots away, and it disappears under the bed like an arrow.

"I'll buy you a new one," I exclaim.

"What are you talking about?"

"Maybe it got scratched, I'm an idiot."

"Get over it, shit happens."

"Yes, but it happens because I'm an idiot. Don't go thinking it's because of the hand, I open DVDs every day, I swear. It's that I'm a little agitated. I'm here with you and..."

Then I stop talking. I can't even look at her, I feel industrial-size embarrassment. I want to disappear, no, I'm going to disappear. I'm young and fit, if I run away she won't chase me down.

Tiziana checks to see where the DVD ended up, and of course it's stuck in the most distant corner of the universe. She gets up on the mattress, lies down, and stretches her arm between the end table and the wall to feel around for it. And in this position she's ridiculous. The lower part of her dress climbs up slowly and I can see her naked legs up to a point that is not far off from where the thighs end and the splendid rest of her begins... and everything about the scene is saying *Fuck me now, Fiorenzo, fuck me now or die a virgin*. But I just stand there and watch without moving, with my head down and the DVD case in my hand, who knows what Giuliano would say if he could see me. Maybe it's so outrageous that even Stefanino would tell me to get a life.

But what can I do? Tiziana is there stretched out on the bed and working her pelvis and extending herself as much as possible, but she's doing it to save her favorite movie that I've just shot into the most godforsaken hole in the world, since I'm unable to open a fucking DVD case. How am I supposed to find the nerve to throw myself on her and make her mine?

After an endless minute, Tiziana manages to recover the DVD and get back on her feet. She's all red and sweaty and she looks at me as if she's just finished a race. I extend the case to her with my outstretched arm like a spastic child. "I'm sorry," I say.

"What for?" She looks at me, looks at me a little strangely, then says, "You know what, Fiorenzo, I'm going to do that thing, too."

"What thing?"

"The thing with the hand. I'm going to wrap it up, like your friend."

"Why are you bringing that up now?"

"I don't know, but I'm going to do it."

"No, please, it's crazy stupid and..."

"Listen, if that girlfriend of yours did it, I'm going to do it, too."

"But look, with one hand there's not a whole lot you can do."

"Whatever, it means that for one day I won't open DVD cases. Big deal."

"But the DVD had nothing to do with my hand, I swear! I knew that's what you were thinking, I knew it." I say it, then I can't help but laugh, because Tiziana is pointing at me and laughing her head off. She's making fun of me. And I like it. I like the way she laughs, too.

"You know, maybe I have a roll of gauze in the house," she says. "I don't know where but I've got one."

"You're crazy, don't do it."

"Give me a break! I said I'll do it, end of story. Anyway, tomorrow is perfect, since it's Sunday. Sunday is the day of gauze."

"Suit yourself. But I would call it the day of the phantom hand, it has a better ring to it."

"All right, the day of the phantom hand. It sounds like it might even be fun." She looks at me and smiles again.

"If it makes you happy," I say. But I'm happy, too. Very happy.

So happy that it's not a problem when just then we hear the metallic creaking at the gate — the door of the house opens up, and in comes the girl who lives with Tiziana.

She's crying, she holds on to Tiziana and I don't know how she keeps from falling backward with all that blubber on top of her. Her friend is moaning and uttering curses and bits and pieces of words. Tiziana speaks to me from over her friend's chubby shoulder and her voice is like a whisper, she says sorry and she doesn't know what to do and...I smile and with my finger spinning in the air I indicate that we'll see each other soon.

I leave and close the door behind me, and at the click of the doorknob the wailing of her roommate gets louder and more desperate.

But I'm happy. Okay, I didn't manage to do anything besides look like a jerk, but this bit about Tiziana wanting to do the phantom hand test makes me feel full of energy and happy and I want to go down the stairs in leaps and bounds.

And as always happens when I feel really great, my brain starts spinning "The Boys Are Back in Town" by Thin Lizzy. I sing it the whole way down the stairs.

The jukebox in the corner blasting out my favorite song
The nights are getting warmer, it won't be long

Won't be long till summer comes
Now that the boys are here again.

I sing with my hand in my pocket and I walk at a good clip and I look around myself, smiling, even if no one comes by to receive that smile.

Then my cell phone rings again, no, it rings twice. The number of messages is up to four, all unread.

Yes, because the best part is behind me now, but the night is not yet over.

DEATH TO THE HEDGEHOG

I've been walking for twenty-five minutes now and my feet are hurting and I'm hungry and thirsty and the fucking post office is nowhere in sight.

I'm going there because of the messages. Three from Giuliano:

Annoying pool tournament at Excalibur. We're outta here. (9:16pm)

We're in the car. Where are U? With that babe? I can't believe it. (9:17pm)

Going to the post office. Stefanino says you're too gay to do her. (10:34pm)

And one from Stefanino.

I didn't say it. Giuliano did. I swear. (10:35pm)

I don't answer them till now. I go down the street past the Gym Center Club and I tap on the keys of the cell phone without looking. After a minute they write back.

We're at the post office. Hurry! (11:15pm)

I walk faster, I smile to myself. Tonight I'm cheerful and a walk at night seems like a nice idea. There's no beating it, if you look at a place at night you understand more, in the dark you can see things better. I look at the houses sleeping in uncomfortable positions on the ground, the streets with the temporary patches for underground work, the trash cans chained to the ground since that summer two years ago when it was fashionable to steal them, climb to the top of Boar's Head Hill, and roll them down for the trash-can race.

It's a sport that sounds stupid if you describe it that way, but I swear the real thing was exciting. There were the competitors but also a lot of spectators. Then came the tragic death of Mario Gavazzi, aka Thunderbolt, and now in Muglione the trash cans are chained to the ground.

And tonight I walk past them and they make me laugh, and I think that a town where you have to chain trash cans to the ground is still an interesting place to live. Basically, tonight Muglione is less disgusting than usual. Tonight is a beautiful night.

I'm happy about the evening, about all the things we said, but what's most awesome is this thing about the bandage, how Tiziana heard the story about my girlfriend so she wants to bandage her hand up, too.

And I continue to say *girlfriend* but it's not one bit true. In reality the bandage test is something my mom did. Except it made me sound like a loser, and given the age difference between me and Tiziana, *I want to be like your mother* didn't sound exactly ideal.

But there's no one at the post office. It's a boxy gray cinderblock building and if someone were outside I'd see him immediately. Instead there's no one in sight.

But wait, there in the corner near the entrance is a dark stain that starts from the wall and expands to the ground, across the sidewalk and all the way to the street. It's right under the street-light and it shimmers, it moves, it looks like a living thing that crawls along slowly.

I get close and I have to say it is pretty effective. Maybe because of the dark, maybe because the stain is a big red puddle and it smells like blood, and there in the middle is a round, spiky thing covered with blood and I can't figure out what it is, but it's definitely dead.

And I know that those two dickheads Giuliano and Stefano were here with the blood for the band's anti-old-folks project, but this nasty mess still scares me anyway. Maybe the Guardian patrol found them while they were writing on the wall and executed them. Or maybe the real anti-old-folks gang nabbed them and did them in, even though they're not old.

And what is that round and bloody thing in the middle? I get closer for a better look and kneel down, careful to avoid the blood, then I feel a huge shadow looming up from behind, moving over me and over the wall of the post office. Then darkness is upon me.

I freeze in position, down on my knees, covering my head with my arms without knowing why. I only know that I don't want to die, not now that I've got Tiziana. Give me at least one week, just one, I swear it'll be enough. But not now, not...

"Not now!" I shout.

"What the fuck are you screaming about?" says Giuliano. I look up, turn around, and there he and Stefanino are, on their feet looking down at me. "Were you scared?"

"No, not scared, but, you know, it's not like I heard you."

"You see, moron?" he says to Stefanino. "It scared the shit out of him, too. See how good it works?"

"Yes, well, it's like I told you before, I know that it works, it scared me, too."

"You don't count. You're scared of everything, for Christ's sake. But anyway it works, hallelujah. Is it easy to make out the writing?"

"What writing?" I ask as I stand up.

"What do you mean, what writing, the writing over there, goddamnit. Next to the blood. There."

I go up to the wall and see something written with a black magic marker, small and shaky. It says:

OLD MAN, PICK UP YOUR LAST PENSION
AND DIE.
NATIONAL REJUVENATION BRIGADE.
    METAL D.

"So, do you like it?"

"Umm, I don't know. I mean, it doesn't sound so neo-Nazi. It's more like something you hear at a stadium."

"What are you talking about, it's perfect. We're at the post office. At the post office they pick up their pension checks . . ."

"Okay, okay. Anyway, I can't see shit. Weren't you supposed to do it with blood?"

"Yes, master, and we tried, but it's not possible! It drips all over the place and you can't make anything out, you make a V and one second later it turns into a blot. Thank God we had a magic marker in the car, and we thought we'd pour the blood out on the ground, like a pool of blood. I think it looks pretty cool."

"I get it. And what's that round thing in the middle there?"

"What thing?"

"That round thing in the middle."

"Oh, it's a hedgehog."

"What? You guys killed a hedgehog?"

"No, you moron, it's roadkill. We left Excalibur and someone had run over it with a car. It was already dead, I thought it would be a shame not to use it."

I say nothing. I continue to study the pool of blood that's covering the wall and the sidewalk and the round thing in the middle that looks like the reason for all the red spattered around, like a really gory bloodbath. And you might feel bad for the hedgehog or think that it's sad to use it like that after it's been run over by some motor head, knowing that over time hedgehogs will disappear from the face of the planet because we're running them over at an exponential rate. But it's also true, no escaping it, that sometimes hedgehogs are complete idiots, they stand there by the side of the road and when they see you arrive they wait for the exact moment when you pass and *bam*, they cross.

So there's nothing strange about their ending up on the post office's sidewalk, in a pool of ox blood, threatening the old folks with death.

THE RIGHT TO A CANE

"Jesus, Mary, and Joseph," says Repetti, for what must have been the first time ever.

Usually he just says *Jesus* or *Holy Mother*, but this morning the scene is too overwhelming and in front of such horror he can feel his stomach coming up through his mouth.

"What is wrong with the people in this world?" Divo struggles to maintain a calm and collected tone, but this abomination on the wall of the post office has upset him, too.

Last night it was too humid and the Guardians decided to postpone their first real patrol. It wasn't a slacker excuse. It's just that otherwise they risked spending the rest of the week in bed with Voltaren. And they made up for it this morning with this nice walk at dawn, armed with cell phones and memo pads to mark down anything suspicious.

But last night all hell broke loose.

"How could they?" says Repetti, "Hedgehogs are so nice."

"THEY—ARE—SWEETHEARTS," says Mazinger.

"Listen, Repetti, it's time to cut the bullshit," says Baldato. "You're the one who came up with this story about the gang that hates old folks and now it's clear you weren't making it up. Is there something you want to tell us?"

"No, guys, I swear. I was making it up! The other night I was watching TV, it was late and I couldn't sleep. I had eaten roasted peppers, which I can't digest."

"ME—NEITHER."

"So on the television they were talking about this wild gang in Russia. They're young and they've got a big chip on their shoulder about immigrants and other people, and they're mean as hell. They kill people, cut off their heads, take pictures with them while they're butchering them. After that, thank God, I nodded off, but I slept badly, I was dreaming about those faces that were looking at me and laughing and coming at me. And the next day I couldn't stop thinking about them, and when the reporter asked what dangers there were in Muglione, well, that's the first thing that came to mind. That's the whole truth. I swear."

The Guardians think for a second. Repetti's story makes sense. Everyone knows the powerful effects of roasted peppers. And they thought they knew their town, too, but seeing this bloodbath, they no longer know where they are.

"Guys, I said it once and I'll say it again," says Baldato. "We have to arm ourselves in some way. Let's say that we did go out last night and found ourselves face-to-face with these guys. What were we supposed to do with a memo pad, write down how many times they stabbed us?"

"I'VE—GOT—A—DOUBLE-BARRELED—SHOTGUN—FOR—PIGEON—HUNTING."

"Behave, Mazinger!" says Divo. "You'd better forget about guns, men, otherwise we'll end up like the pigeons ourselves."

"Yes, Divo, fair enough," says Baldato. "We weren't expecting rifles and pistols, but come on, there has to be a middle ground between shooting a gun and writing things down on a memo pad, right? Me, for example, I'd feel a lot safer with a cane. You can hardly call it a weapon. You could just say you need it for walking. We're old, we use canes, what's wrong with that? We have a right to a cane."

Baldato says this and waves in the air an imaginary cane, jutting his jaw forward and laughing in a way that couldn't be more different from the sort of kindly grandpa who passes you ten euros. The most you can expect from this grandpa is a *thwack* from his cane, and then it's *sayonara*.

WHAT DO CHAMPIONS KNOW?

Sunday, 9:30 a.m. Rottofreno (Piacenza).

Today's race is really important. Roberto has taken Mirko to another region to see if he can handle the stress and to start circulating his name outside of Tuscany. And even though everything has already been checked and inspected, Roberto takes a last look at the bikes anyway. Either he doesn't trust the mechanic or it's just an excuse to hang out among bike frames, wheels, and the rubbery smell of tires.

Every now and then some middle-aged fan takes advantage of the situation and approaches with a postcard of Roberto when he used to race and asks for an autograph, puts it back in a transparent sleeve, shakes Roberto's hand, and leaves. Today it hasn't happened so far, but every now and then it does.

The meeting point was set for five o'clock in front of the clubhouse. Roberto was in the team car and Sirio was driving the minibus for the boys, and unfortunately one of the fathers demanded to come along. But Roberto's rules are clear: *No fathers allowed.* The guy protested a little but no more than a little. He turned around and that was the end of it.

Fathers are really the worst, and over the years Roberto has seen everything: fathers carrying megaphones to shout insults at their kids, whom they send to bed without dinner if they lose, and if they race poorly they don't speak for a week.

His father was like that, too. His father's name was Arturo and he drove a truck and stuttered, and everyone teased him and called him Machine Gun. A shy man who couldn't even look people in the eyes, and when they teased him he didn't answer because with his stuttering problem it would have taken him half an hour and they would have teased him even more. So he kept his head low and sucked down the bitterness all day, waiting for the moment when he could finally go home to his loved ones. And take everything out on them.

Once, when Roberto was eight, he was raring to go at the starting gate of a boys' race in Livorno. That day there was a photographer from *La Nazione* who was fixated on him and kept taking his picture. Roberto puffed up his chest and immediately grabbed a tight hold of his handlebars. He struck a pose and looked straight ahead, dead serious with a tough look on his face. The photographer squatted down to take a nice picture from below and Roberto turned ever so slightly to check whether he was still being photographed and yes, he was, and... suddenly he was struck by a blow upside the head, making him fall off his bicycle and hit the ground together with two other little kids who tumbled like dominoes right after him. He looked up and there against the sky was his father staring down at him. *Wha-wha-what the fu-fu-fuck y-you doing, st-st-stupid! Co-co-co-concentrate... act se-se-serious and you'll wi-wi-win the race!*

No, fathers are deadly, they expect to be in command, which is why they need to be kept far away from the race. At the race the kids have to obey Roberto and only Roberto.

Because if there's one thing in life that Roberto knows it's how to win a cycling race. During his own career he didn't have a fast start or pure power, but as *Bicisport* reported in a special issue on the domestiques of the eighties and nineties, *Roberto Marelli, nicknamed the Bartender, never won a race himself but enabled countless to be won.*

And after their careers are over, domestiques like him are the ones who become the best athletic directors. People think that the more races you win the better you'll be at making the kids win, but that's bullshit. Like getting painting lessons from Van Gogh. Do you really think Van Gogh is going to teach you? He'll put a paintbrush in your hand, set you in front of a canvas, and say *Come on, paint me a masterpiece.*

It's no accident that none of the great champions in the history of cycling has ever become a great coach. During a tough climb, Federico Bahamontes would advise you to simply stand up on the pedals and leave everyone else behind. For a hilly racecourse on a wet and windy day, Eddy Merckx's plan would be to grip the handlebars really tight, pump on the pedals, and cross the finish line all alone. The greats can't advise anyone because they don't know what a race is, they just stay at the front of the pack, all they see ahead of them is the finish line and victory, with no idea of the dusty hell they leave in their wake.

Roberto Marelli knows that really well. He knows what you feel when your legs turn to wood, he knows that hunger pangs can make you freeze to death under the August sun, he knows the satisfaction of the domestique who runs out of gas halfway through a stage with seven peaks left to climb and still makes it to the finish line: an hour after the front-runners, when the crowd has already gone, but still in the race and ready to help his captain one more day. Because every race is made up of many races, one next to the other, and every racer has his job to do. Everyone has his own way of being great.

His hometown never understood this. When he first turned pro, it was a big party in Muglione, but it didn't last long. They had a fellow citizen who raced, yes, but he never won a thing, not even the Camaiore City Grand Prix, not even a stage of the Giro di Sardegna. Rather than a source of pride, this story about the racer from Muglione started to sound like a joke.

But now there's Mirko, now there's a kid who knows how to win a race, and everyone knows that if Mirko is racing for the Muglione Cycling Union it's thanks to Roberto, who discovered him in some tiny godforsaken town and who always manages to lead him to triumph.

Okay, so it's not difficult, all you have to tell Mirko is *When the feeling strikes, go for it and win*, but only because he's still in Beginners, a level where to win all you have to do is be the strongest. But that's just the starting point, soon it'll be time for the Junior and Under-23 races, and then Roberto's coaching will be fundamental. And as the kid grows the regulations will allow him to have a radio connection with the team car, so Roberto can tell him what to do moment by moment and the two of them will win together. The legs of the Little Champ, the mind of the Bartender. Who can beat that combination? No one, not even when they make the great leap to the professional world, the big teams, the Giro, the Tour.

Not to mention today's seventeenth annual Rottofreno Town Trophy. Which starts soon, and there will be a lot of competitors but only a single winner. Roberto already knows his name, as does anyone who knows the least bit about cycling or has a little common sense on hand.

But instead...

WHO ARE YOU TO TALK?

Sunday, twelve noon. Actually, almost twelve-thirty. If there's one thing you detest it's waking up late in the morning. And today it's not even late, it's beyond late, it's practically afternoon.

Not to mention you're not even rested. You slept with Raffaella who didn't feel like being alone, and as soon as you started to nod off she would pull you out of it with a lament, a sob, a mumbled word.

Pavel told her he likes another girl, someone who works at the supermarket with him. Nothing's happened yet but it will, and soon.

Having to console a girlfriend all night is difficult, especially if you don't know what to tell her, because you have to keep to yourself everything that you really think.

What do you care about that moron, you should be happy that he's up and left. Actually, you should have been smart enough to send him packing yourself. Here you are crying and saying that you'll never get out of bed again when instead you should be jumping for joy and running all the way to the Montenero chapel to light a candle to the Blessed Virgin for the grace she has bestowed upon you.

But these are the exact things that you can't tell Raffaella. First, because Raffaella doesn't want to hear them, and second, because maybe you could have delivered these clear, sensible and severe opinions once upon a time, but who are you to talk now?

You're a girl who takes home a boy thirteen years younger than you, and the two of you even have a good time together, and since moving back to this shitty little town it's the first time you've had an interesting conversation. For a second you're almost tempted to... not tempted, no, you're way too hard on yourself. It's not that you were tempted, no way, but when you were in the bedroom lying flat on your stomach looking for the DVD under the bed, for a second your mind went to the fact that he was standing and you were on the bed and if he jumped your bones it would hardly have been the most unpredictable thing in the world.

Once after a party in Berlin you took the elevator with a girl-friend's brother, you told him you didn't mind the weather in Berlin and he jumped your bones. Well, let's just say that last night in your room the same move would have been a little less surprising, and maybe, when you think about it, it wouldn't have ended the way it did that time, with a swift kick in the balls.

But you're not sure, and you don't want to be. Besides, Raffaella arrived with her tragedy and blocked everything else out, so there's no sense even thinking about it.

It only makes sense if you focus on what you're doing right now, because for twenty minutes you've been trying and failing to wrap a bandage around your right hand.

And what is making you do it, Tiziana, what's the sense of it? Are you doing it for you or for him? And if you're doing it for him, is it because you feel sorry for him or because you like him? And at the end of this experiment, what's going to happen? Are you going to call him? Well, you don't even have his cell number, but if you did what would you do? And what would you have done last night if Raffaella hadn't come back?

Shut up and stop thinking about it. Get busy and wrap that hand. It's getting late. Wrap it tight.

SHIT THAT TRUCKERS DO

Tonight I could try my luck with a hooker.

On the county road there are lots, you leave town and run into so much activity by the side of the road you'd think there was road work ahead.

I've gone by many times and thought of trying it, with a hooker, especially after Giuliano did one night and told me *So much stuff, Fiorenzo, so much stuff.* But I still haven't, and tonight the moment could finally be here. This way at least if something happens with Tiziana it won't be my absolute first time.

Now it's four o'clock and it's still daylight, but I'm sure if I take my scooter and go there'll already be lots of them, a fact that truly amazes me. I mean, you picture hookers in the dark, under streetlights, but instead they hang out at all hours of the day all year long...so it means they've always got a circle of customers.

But who would go looking for a hooker at nine o'clock in the morning in January? Or at noon on a hot and muggy August day? A trucker might, because when it comes to anything nasty and raunchy people always say it's shit that truckers do. Like if you see a shower at a rest stop and wonder who the hell would take a shower there, the answer is always the same: truckers truckers truckers.

But me, I'm no trucker; can I do it with a hooker? I don't know, I don't think so. I mean, I get too embarrassed, and then I'm afraid it's one of those things that's habit-forming and if you do it once you can never stop and you're done for.

No, it's better if I stay here at the shop and practice my music: tonight at six we're getting together at Stefanino's. Metal Devastation is finally going to play for the first time since that damn festival.

Usually we rehearse at nine, but Antonio says he's busy but it's okay if we do it at six. The important thing is to play like men so we can exorcize that awful voice I've still got in my head yelling *OFF-THE-STAGE, OFF-THE-STAGE*, which is actually many voices all together, because that stuff was last Saturday and today is Sunday, which means that a week has gone by and we have to put it behind us and move on. Today we're playing again. Today I don't want to think about anything bad.

And I have to say it's not hard, because ever since I woke up the only thing I can think about is Tiziana.

Okay, I know this sentence is totally cheesy and even as I'm forming it I'm making myself puke, and I'm ashamed that with all the albums and all the songs that show me the way things really are, I'm still falling for it like a jerk. For years my idols have been telling me that we're "Too fast for love" and that "Love is for suckers," yet here I am thinking of her and the fact that today, unless she was talking bullshit, Tiziana is spending the day with just one hand.

I could call her to see how she's doing, only I don't have her number. Because I never asked for it. Because I'm a moron. And maybe this is why I'm sitting on the cot reading a new composition by the Little Champ: because it reminds me that there's someone who's even more of a moron than me.

I found the sheet of paper this morning, slipped under the gate. But how can I explain to the twerp that I'm not interested in his compositions? I tell him every time, and every time he gives me another one and every time I read it. The perfect circle.

Mirko Colonna
3-B (Ms. Tecla Pudda)
May 7, 2010

Assignment: *The splendid Petrarchan sonnet "Yon nightingale, whose strain so sweetly flows" is an incredibly modern masterpiece. What can it teach contemporary society, with its dearth of moral and civic values?*

That stuff you were saying about losing races, Mister, I wanted to tell you that I agree with you. I tried, and I know you told me that losing a race is the easiest thing in the world, but instead I have to say that for me it's not. Because if I lose there are a lot of people who lose with me, and I'm more sorry for them than I am for me. But I did try once.

It was March, my fifth official race. I'd won the other four, and my teammates were already saying that I was a show-off and that I'd ruined the team and that their parents had told them I was doping so I could race faster than everyone. And then I thought it would be better to do like I do at school and not always be number one, so on that day I didn't want to win.

So I hung back in the group the whole time, and five kilometers from the finish line there was a sharp and narrow curve and a guy from the Antico Borgo Cheeses team named Tenerani jumped ahead and earned a few-second lead over the others.

I immediately realized we needed to catch up right away or he'd be waiting for us at the finish line, but my whole point was to lose so I stayed in the pack. We were down to the 4th, 3rd, 2nd kilometer and I was already imagining Mr. Roberto getting pissed off and screaming that we were a bunch of imbeciles. At the last kilometer we stopped even pretending to put up a fight,

Tenerani had the race in his pocket and could get ready for his victory lap.

And I didn't see it at that moment but they told me how at a certain point he was overjoyed and pedaling and every now and then he'd take a look back and see no one so he'd cheer, but at the final curve his father had taken up position and was waiting for him with a bucket of water. His father thought a good bucketful of cold water would refresh him, Tenerani, so he was waiting for him on the side of the road and when his son passed by he shouted WATER! and emptied the bucket over him. Tenerani's eyeglasses went flying and he lost his balance and clearly hit the front brake too sharply and the wheel got stuck and the bike went flying against the wall of the house on the other side of the street and smashed into pieces.

After a while we passed and saw a ton of people on the path and Tenerani on the ground and then the race opened up again. We all kicked into high gear, every man for himself, even me, and I instinctively gave a couple of pumps to the pedals and found myself in the lead, two more pumps and I broke away from the pack, looked around, and won by a huge margin. But I swear I didn't raise my hands, because that time I wanted to lose and in fact I'd been about to lose, and if I did win it's the fault of that idiot father.

But you were right the other day, Mister, when you said losing is a great idea and it could solve my problems, in fact on Sunday in Piacenza I'm going to lose. It's the first time that I'll be racing outside of Tuscany. Last night Mr. Roberto couldn't sleep from the tension and he drew some game plans and made me study them every second, but on Sunday I'm going to lose. Thank you very much.

And if you don't mind, I'm dedicating the defeat to you.

THE LITTLE FRIENDS
OF THE PHILOSOPHERS

You turn the page, you're at 176, and you only started reading the novel after lunch.

You've never read so much in a single afternoon, if you continue at this pace you'll be done by dinner. If you really did have only one hand you'd be the greatest reader on the planet.

Of course you would. What else can you do? It took you an hour to make lunch, you burned two fingers and in the end could only manage a little rice with tomato sauce. Then you tried to wash the dishes but you gave up, you tried to make the bed but you gave up, so you lay down on the bed and read. And now you're on page 176.

Not to mention bathroom matters, almost all of which are impossible. Anyway you're staying home today and will stay like this, in shorts and the oversize T-shirt from the University of Heidelberg, and you don't have to worry about a thing.

Not even about Raffaella, who's in the other room in total crisis mode and it's practically as if she weren't there. You went to her room and it's really hot, the window is locked, she's there with her head stuck in the pillow saying weird stuff. You asked her if she wanted to eat and she said no, if she wanted a magazine and she said no, if she wanted you to turn the TV on and it was still no. She didn't even turn to answer you. She didn't see your bandaged hand and didn't ask you jack shit.

It's much better this way. You had thought about using a story about a wasp that bit you or a knife that slipped from your hand while you were slicing a tomato. Raffaella's studying to be a nurse and any story connected with a wound could be risky, but you couldn't come up with a better excuse: Why would someone bandage a hand without cuts or bruises?

Come to think of it, why would you? During this long afternoon you've had a lot of time to ask yourself this question. Why are you doing it? You're doing it for yourself, yes, only for yourself. You simply enjoy understanding things, knowing what you're talking about. You're curious by nature and see no reason why you should renounce any possibility to understand something better. You're trying to see what it's like to spend a day with only one hand, but it could have easily been a foot, an eye, it's sheer curiosity that tomorrow will make you appreciate all the more the ordinary good fortune of having two hands.

So why do you have this desire to call Fiorenzo and tell him everything, and have a couple of laughs about how you managed to boil rice? Maybe you could ask him how he handles bathroom matters. How the hell do you manage to shave, Fiorenzo?

That is, if he does actually shave, because maybe he doesn't need to yet. Maybe he's a beardless boy, like the ones who drove the Greek philosophers crazy, the ones they lusted after and tried to bed.

But you are not a Greek philosopher, you're an Italian woman in the year 2010, you're a thirty-two-year-old spending Sunday at home with a hand that's been wrapped for no reason thinking of phoning a child to ask him whether or not his beard is growing.

But above all you're stupid.

Stupid. Stupid.

And your only good fortune is that you don't have his telephone number.

You turn the page again, even though for the last few pages you've absorbed nothing. The book slips and falls from the bed, closes. You've lost your place.

Yes, you've lost your place.

THE CURSE OF ITALIAN ROCK

Antonio arrived late, but apart from Giuliano, who took the Lord's name in vain a couple of times, we didn't complain; at this point it's a big surprise that he came at all. While we were waiting for him we talked about the anti-old-folks writing on the post office wall and how there'd been no reaction. None whatsoever. Maybe for the newspapers you have to wait till the next day, or maybe we were too soft and need to go bigger, or maybe…then Antonio arrived and we stopped talking.

We didn't ask him why he had gone AWOL for a week, it didn't matter, the only thing that does matter is that there's a new song and we gave him the music and the harmonies a week ago, so today we can start to rehearse together.

But it's clear that he's seeing the piece for the first time here in front of us. Giuliano counts to four and we're off, we want to play the whole song with all the breaks and rhythm changes and maybe even a nice guitar lick, but Antonio doesn't have the least idea what's happening.

"Stop, stop, stop," he says. "Guys, I really don't like this song."

And for a second there's only silence in the garage. Silence and the humming of amplifiers waiting to play.

"How the hell can you say you don't like it? We haven't even played it yet."

"I know, but I can already tell from the harmonies."

"What the fuck are you talking about? It's totally ass-kicking," says Giuliano.

"It might kick your ass, but not mine. It's the same old stuff, full speed ahead and a lull after the second chorus. It's not working for me."

"Can't we practice it at least once?" I say. "Then maybe we can change it and—"

"You say change it, I say throw it away. I don't like it, am I allowed to say that I don't like it? No, I'm not, because here I get the impression that you two make all the decisions and Stefanino always says yes, and you don't give a shit about what I think."

"What are you talking about? If you've got ideas, shoot. But you never do."

"I don't? Really? My idea is to throw this song away, okay? And it's not just the music; the lyrics suck, too."

Antonio is nuts. I wrote the lyrics and they talk about a medieval town where one night the women all turn into nymphomaniac witches and jump into the men's beds and make them have sex till they die of heart attacks. The title is "Witches and Bitches."

"I've told you two thousand times, guys, you should never write lyrics about women and sex. You don't know shit about them and you just make everyone laugh. I don't want to make people laugh. You have to write about stuff that you know, get it?"

"Okay, I get it," says Giuliano. "So I'll write lyrics about a guitarist who's an asshole." He stands up from the drums. "Listen up. You're breaking my balls. When you do come you come late, and when you're here you don't like anything. *This song is too fast and that one is too heavy, I'm not going to wear studs and T-shirts are uncomfortable, I'd rather wear a jacket . . .* Are you sure we're still on the same wavelength? Are you sure you've got the guts to stay in Metal Devastation, or would you rather join another band?"

Giuliano asks the questions and looks at him. I look at him, too, and so does Stefanino. Antonio puts down the music for the piece we're supposed to practice, and he smiles, but it's a smile that no one believes, starting with him.

"Guys, I've already got another band."

Silence. The amplifiers humming, eyes seeking each other out in the void. What did he say? Did he really say that? No, it's not possible.

He continues to speak. "I thought I could play in both, but the genres are too different and I can't do it."

"And what genre do the other guys play?" I ask. But I'm not sure I want to know. Because I'm expecting something awful, I'm ready for the worst of the worst. And as always happens when you get yourself ready for the worst, reality, that fucking whore, amuses herself by showing you that she's always one step ahead.

"We do Italian rock," he says.

Italian rock. The most dreadful pairing of words in the universe. Because rock is truly great—it is the number-one reason I get up in the morning—and *Italian* is an adjective that doesn't add or subtract a thing. But put them together, *rock* and *Italian*, and they become something horrific, the mere thought of which makes me feel like I'm drowning in a vat of fertilizer.

Italian rock. The same stupid tunes that Gianni Morandi used to sing, the same structures and the usual lyrics, but with the guitars just a little louder, a leather jacket rather than a blazer, and presto chango, Italy is filled with these cheap rocker wannabes. And kids going nuts over these loser has-beens up onstage with nothing to say, whose only goal in life is to carry on that great scam known as Italian rock, helping to feed trashy new material, year after year, to a festering wound infecting the entire country, the Sanremo Music Festival.

"Italian rock, eh?" says Giuliano, as a slight paralysis descends on his face. "Way to go. What do you play? Italian covers of Rick Astley? Or do you prefer Milli Vanilli? Pray tell."

"Both, but not only them."

"You make me puke, now I really do have to puke."

"Who cares? At the same time we're doing a lot of our own stuff, too. And you know what we do most of all? We play for people. Yes, because we actually get invited to play and people come and hear us, a lot of really chill people, and you know what? I like it. But I get the impression that you guys would rather gross everyone out and get booed off the stage before you even start to play. Whatever rocks your boat."

He says this, and I have to admit that it hurts, somewhere between my chest and my gallbladder.

Luckily, Giuliano is a fighter and even if he doesn't know what to say he fires back with insults. Antonio fires back and I throw myself into the mix, too. The only one who doesn't say anything is Stefanino, but it's not as if we need an extra voice. The garage echoes with shouts and nasty words and profanity and *fuck-yous* you can never take back. There's no sense writing them all down because the same ones get repeated a lot and overlap each other.

And to make a long story short, Metal Devastation is now minus one guitarist.

A gun without bullets, a car without a wheel, a food fair without porchetta. There you have it, the way we live today: we're a band without a guitar.

Antonio walks out of the garage and the group, and we are stuck here like three idiots, looking at each other and trying to come up with justifications for the idea that we're much better off this way. Nothing sounds believable and we feel like the scum of the earth.

That's why Stefano's next move is a blessing.

He opens his bass guitar case and takes out an envelope. Inside the envelope is money, a lot of money, and he gives it to us. And I have to say that two thousand euros a person is the perfect medicine for warding off a bad case of the blues.

It helps to think of something else. For example, you feel like asking where he found all that manna from heaven. With those photo mashups of horny couples he makes good money, of course, but giving such a big gift to us all at the same time seems like something different. And it is different, but Stefano only tells me a while later, when Giulinao is gone and the two of us are alone.

"The other night I was at the computer, I had to work but I didn't want to." Stefano is talking and checking his e-mail. Today alone he got 176 messages in his in-box. "So I said to myself, okay, I'll work later, and I started surfing the news. And I read that the pope said something tremendous about homosexuals. He practically said that they're diseased. Can you believe it?"

"Yeah, but what disease?"

"I don't know. Homosexuality, I guess."

"Oh."

"I mean, he preaches goodness, equality, and then he goes and says something like that..."

"Yes, but I don't see what that's got to do with the money. Did you sue the pope?"

"No. But it made me want to do a photo mashup. I came up with this idea: I would take a picture of a saintly pope, with little birds flying around and a halo, and next to it put an evil pope, at night, like a vampire with Dracula's fangs. And underneath I would write 'Dr. Jekyll and Mr. Pope.' Do you like it?"

"Whatever."

"Don't you think it's funny?"

"Not really."

"I thought it was a riot."

"You thought wrong, Stefano."

"What a pity. Well, I did it anyway. And I swear: it was hard as hell. Because I couldn't find a saintly image of the pope. I searched for an hour and there was nothing anywhere. So I made my own. I downloaded a normal photo, where he had that smirk he always has, you know, and I Photoshopped it a little. In the end he came out all sweet and gentle, and I put it next to the vampire version of the photo and I sent it to a funny website that published it."

"Did the site give you the money?"

"No, but the next day a guy wrote to me from Rome. A photographer. He deals with pictures of the pope, souvenirs, stuff like that. He came across my work by accident and told me it was awesome. He says that for years they've been trying to take a picture of the pope where he looks good but no one has ever succeeded. Even with Photoshop it's impossible, the more you fool around with it the more evil he looks. And in fact ever since this latest guy became pope the sale of holy cards and religious souvenirs has gone way down. People look at them and don't buy, it's a market where a lot of workers risk winding up on the street. To make a long story short, the photographer saw my picture of the saintly pope and asked me how I did it, then he offered me fifty thousand euros if I'd send it to him in high resolution."

"God damn, fifty thousand euros for a picture?"

"Yes, and he asked if I could Photoshop some others. He sends them to me in the original and I make the pope look saintly."

"At fifty thousand a pop?"

"No, I take a percentage on the products they make."

"Are you crazy?"

"Holy cards of the pope, pens of the pope, wall clocks, coffee trays, plates, calendars, aprons, magnets, barometers..."

"Okay, okay, so you're not crazy. But you're definitely crazy to share the money with me and Giuliano. It makes no sense. Why are you doing this?"

Stefano looks at me and then he answers as if it were the most obvious thing in the world. "Well, we're friends." He shrugs his shoulders and smiles.

It's true, we are friends. Actually, we're more than friends: we're a band. And tonight I can also say that we're rich. And I want to tell everyone, tell this shitty little town and the whole world.

Actually, no. I really want to tell only one person. Will she be home? Would she mind if I stopped by now? Will she already be in bed? No, damn it, it's eight-thirty, maybe she is a little older than me but she's hardly one of those doddering idiots who go into a coma right after the evening news.

And who cares anyway. I want to see her so I'm going. Rich people don't hesitate, rich people don't ask if you mind. We rich people do whatever we feel like.

PANTY RIPPER

"Hi, it's me, Fiorenzo."

Silence. Then: "Hi, sure, hi Fiorenzo." It's Tiziana's voice, I think, but it sounds metallic coming out of the intercom and could easily be the voice of Mazinger or of a killer robot that's just left a bloodbath in the apartment and now wants me to come up so he can murder me, too. And it's not as if she exactly told me that I could come up.

"I just happened to be passing by and...if this is a bad time I can go."

"No, no, it's fine."

"Ah, okay, good. And...should I come up?"

She doesn't answer right away. At least an hour, an hour and a half goes by. The clock says it's ten seconds, but what does a clock know? Finally: "Sure, come up, I'll open the door," and the main door opens with a click.

I take the stairs by twos and even threes, I'm energized, I'm fit, I'm a rich young man who's coming by and picking up a nice girl and taking her out by surprise, ready to offer her the world, precisely because I'm rich and I can afford it.

But then I get to the landing and to Tiziana's door and I see another man coming out. He's a really big guy who must be her age. He looks at me and smiles, a smile I don't like one bit. I stand there with one foot on the last step and my heart beating hard, as if it wants to tear a hole through my ribs as an escape route. If I could move my legs right now, then maybe I would run away.

"You ze little friend of Tiziana?" he says with that broadening smile.

"Yeah, you got a problem?"

Out the door comes the fat girl who lives with Tiziana. Tonight she's not crying; actually, she's euphoric, jumping into the arms of the guy, who staggers but manages to stay upright, and this is how they start to descend the stairs. While they're passing me he winks an eye and gives me a little slap upside the head, but it's okay. I'm a man who was dead for a minute and has come back to life, now I'm immortal. Nothing can hurt me.

I go into the apartment and say hi even though Tiziana's not in the room. Her voice replies that she's coming, I nod and inhale. The stench of the ditch has never smelled so good.

"Is this a bad time?" I ask at the door to her room.

"No, it's just that I wasn't expecting you and..."

"If you're busy I can go, you know."

"I'm not busy. But to tell you the truth, I'm not crazy about surprises."

"Ah, okay. Look, if you want I'll go." I say it sincerely, but also with an angry edge: listen, kid, watch me disappear. It'll only take a second. I've got two thousand euros in my pocket and if I feel like it I can go straight down the road, pick me up a couple of hookers, ask for the deluxe treatment, and leave you to your precious little errands, get it?

But then the door opens and Tiziana comes out with a purple Talking Heads T-shirt that fits her so tight and rides up so high at her waist that I regret the stuff I was thinking and that I ever bad-mouthed the Talking Heads.

And she's put on the T-shirt in this weird way: on one side it's high up and shows some naked flesh, and on that side her hand is all bandaged up.

I point to it. "I can't believe it, you really did it!"

She smiles. "It's the day of the phantom hand, right?"

"Yeah, of course, but I didn't... how's it going?"

"Bad. I can't do anything. It took me ten minutes just to put on this T-shirt. Actually, would you mind giving me a hand?"

Tiziana raises her arm in the air and comes toward me with the side left naked by the T-shirt. I extend my hand, try to grip the cotton with two fingers and pull it down. But my index finger brushes against her skin, which is smooth and warm and has other qualities that have no name but filter into me through my fingertips and enter my brain incognito.

"This T-shirt is nice," I say.

"It is? Thanks. Do you like the Talking Heads?"

"No, but I like the T-shirt."

"That's good. Because after all that effort no way in hell am I going to change it. And when I think that now I have to get dinner ready, I feel sick."

The usual lock of hair tumbles over her eyes, Tiziana starts to get her right hand ready to shift it, stops halfway, then does it with her left.

"To be honest, I didn't just happen to be passing by," I say. "I'm sorry if I surprised you, but I'm here to solve your problem. Come to dinner with me."

"..."

"Come on, that way you don't have to cook."

"Yes, but I had already—"

"Relax, I won't take you to the diner. You choose, a good restaurant, someplace classy. Even outside of Muglione. I mean, if it's classy it obviously has to be outside Muglione."

"Thank you, Fiorenzo, but tonight I've already decided to stay home and—"

"Come on, my treat. Tonight I'm rich and you have to take advantage."

"Really?"

"Yes, I was rehearsing with the band, and I just withdrew two thousand euros."

"The metal band? They pay you?"

"Yes, sometimes, for the concerts," I say, and I look her straight in the eyes. Because in my opinion it's not really a lie, there are things that sound so good when you say them that it's a shame to keep them in your mouth. They're true, they're false, it doesn't matter. They sound so good you've got to let their music sing.

"I'm happy for you, Fiorenzo. But tonight I really—"

"Tiziana, I don't want to push it, but, well, in my opinion it would be really nice. We go out to eat and while we're out you can tell me all about the day of the phantom hand, okay?"

I know that I'm pushing it, and I can't stand pushy people. But each time I say *let's go* feels like the time Tiziana's finally going to say *okay*, and so I keep pushing. Even if she never does say *okay*.

Maybe she's one of those people who on Sundays likes to stay home and do nothing. They work all week with their heads down and to make it through they keep telling themselves that soon it will be Sunday, then Sunday arrives and they do nothing. Sad but true.

And if this thing between us keeps going, I risk getting sucked into that sad spiral. On Sunday we stay home and watch talent shows on TV and say things like: *Oh, what a talented host, he sings, he dances, he reads books*, then I put on NASCAR racing and fall asleep to the sound of cars circling around and around, I wake back up and it's evening and I go out to get a plain pizza and bring it back and we eat without speaking to each other.

Yes, that's the risk I'm running: the risk of horror. So I have to be really careful. And maybe it would even be better right now if Tiziana told me she isn't coming to dinner because—as I imagine—she's ashamed of me. I'll feel bad for a few days, but at least I'll be safe from the horror and continue to be a rocker, a guy who grabs life by the balls. Yeah, that's right, now I'll even tell her that I haven't got time to eat with her, I'll call my friends and we'll go to Excalibur and have a beer and burp our asses off and everything's going to be all right.

"Would you mind if we got a take-out pizza and ate it here?" is Tiziana's proposal.

In a heartbeat I say, "Great!" I'm almost shouting. "It's a deal. Fantastic!"

So now I'm clearly incapable of saving myself, and my only hope for warding off an unhappy ending is for Tiziana to tell me to go fuck myself. On my own I'm a dead duck, a babe in the woods. On my own I'm totally fucked.

And now here we are, after dinner, sprawled out at the table.

There's a ton of leftovers. I got two giant pizzas and two bottles of fresh white wine and enough ice cream for six. Tiziana kept saying it was a waste but I don't care, a rich man doesn't notice certain things.

And the wine, we almost finished. I feel like laughing, at anything she says or I say, or even if we say nothing. I look at the leftover ice cream and laugh, I look at the humongous pants of her friend Raffaella draped over a chair and I laugh, I look Tiziana in the eyes and I laugh, and she laughs, too. We laugh and laugh.

And we think back on the scene when we entered the ice cream shop, one of us minus a hand and the other with her hand wrapped up, and since she was already holding the pizzas and I had the bottles of wine, I had them put the ice cream in a plastic bag and I hung it around my neck. You should have seen the look on the ice cream man's face! And the bag was swinging on my chest like a bell. So then we start laughing even harder.

It might be the money that rained down from heaven, or the skintight T-shirt Tiziana is wearing, or the wine rumbling around in my stomach while I am laughing, but I, Fiorenzo Martelli, the lead singer of Metal Devastation, start to feel something.

That something. Something that till then I'd only found on TV and in the stories of my deadbeat friends or in the one slow song they play on every hard-rock CD, usually at track eight. The guitars turn acoustic and the voice warm and the lyrics talk about him looking at her while she's sleeping, or caressing her hair, or remembering the days when they were together and she had two eyes like a starry sky ready to shower a thousand emotions on you. You know, the super-romantic pieces that we call "panty rippers" and that are especially popular with women, because the only subject is that *thing*, that girly sentiment that, incredibly, I, too, am starting to feel.

And I don't want to say what it is because I'm scared. Scared shitless. Not like being scared by songs about zombies or about a nuclear holocaust destroying the earth and leaving behind only cockroaches and river rats. No, it's this *thing* that really scares me because it is a genuine danger. I've seen it bring a lot of friends to a nasty end. I would look at them being all lovey-dovey and think, *How much of an asshole do you have to be to wind up like that?* But now I'm looking at Tiziana, who's laughing, and I'm feeling just as fucked as them.

No, no, *NO!* I say. I'm the lead singer of Metal Devastation. We do heavy metal and kick ass and if one day we manage to cut a CD you've got another thing coming if you think we're going to put in a slow song. No, we're going to do a whole album of hard songs, and for the eighth track we can put in one that'll really burn the house down. So I'd better think about getting out of here, and fast, I have to save myself before it's too late.

Or is it already too late?

I feel desperation grabbing me by the throat, I look at Tiziana and Tiziana is fantastic, and I know I'll never be able to just get up and walk away. And suddenly the only thing I can possibly do is clear. My only salvation.

To jump her bones.

That's right, jump her bones. And if she happens to be down with it, hot damn! If instead she isn't, if instead she screams and tells me I'm disgusting and kicks me out of her house and doesn't want to see me anymore, so much the better: I'll be saved from the danger of turning into a wuss, go back to my friends and normal life and metal and so on. So for me it's a win-win situation.

I stand up and walk toward Tiziana, who looks at me with a question mark on her face. And in a little while it'll be an exclamation point and immediately afterward I don't know what it'll be because I'll be out of her house forever.

She's sitting down, I'm one step away. I suddenly bend down and throw myself into what I think is a kiss. I stick my tongue out even before arriving at her mouth. I feel the coolness of the air, the saltiness of her skin, then the softness of Tiziana's lips.

For a second she doesn't do anything. She's rigid and stiff and trying to say something, but her mouth is completely occupied. So I put my hand on her chest to push away and come up for air, but it's a really weak push and I say to myself, *Okay, soon I'm going to be on the street but let's at least make this kiss last as long as I can.* I move my tongue, randomly but I move it, and I put my hand on all the tits I can find. I'm like a guy on an airplane and the plane goes into free fall so he throws himself on the girl next to him because he thinks *I'm dying so I may as well take advantage of every second.* And until this plane crashes I'm going to keep kissing Tiziana.

Except the plane never crashes. A few air pockets, a little turbulence, but now it's regaining altitude. I keep feeling her up with my hand and she also places her left hand on my side, starts squeezing it and pulls me against her, she stands up, and glued together like this we grope our way across the living room. We almost fall down but somehow we remain standing, we brush against the wall and slip through the door of her room, and when in the end we really do fall we do it deliberately, we let ourselves go, we feel ourselves falling through thin air and then *boom*, we're in bed.

Jesus.

IT'S INSTANT FIREWORKS

So, let's try to figure out what's going on.

We're in bed with the lights off and coming in through the window is some illumination from the streetlamp, which is yellow and dim. In front of me I have Tiziana's face stuck to mine because the kiss has been going on since the kitchen and it's lasting forever, while my hand is traveling randomly over her body and every now and then it finds a lucky spot because our mouths break apart for a second and Tiziana breathes strangely and heavily, then her lips come back to mine.

My heart's beating so fast it's ruffling my hair, I'm sweating and shaking, with my right arm I squeeze Tiziana and with my left hand I continue to travel over her smooth skin and curves and the folds between one part and the other. And in the meantime there's nothing in my head, everything's been thrown into the dumpster to make room for the single, hotheaded thought that's spinning endlessly like a broken record: *I'm doing it I'm doing it I'm doing it* . . . It's not a very elaborate thought but it's still a hundred percent true.

Then at a certain point we stop kissing and I realize the goalpost has moved and I have to come up with something better. Just when I was starting to move so well. Tiziana says bits and pieces of words, I understand nothing and maybe there's nothing to understand. Every now and then from her lips comes an *I*...*I*...even if nothing follows. Only *I*...*I*...and kisses on my neck and my chest and on my belly button, and while she's kissing me Tiziana moves down, down there under my pants and my boxers, to the point of greatest agitation and everything is all ready to shoot fireworks. Which would be great but at the same time everyone knows that fireworks mean the party's over, so I want to postpone them for as long as possible.

Jeans and boxers disappear, I feel something light and warm under my belly button. I like it, I like it a lot, actually I like it too much, so to buy time I do what everyone else does and start to think about the most horrifying things in the universe.

I stare straight up at the ceiling, focusing on a thin crack in the plaster, and I imagine the disgusting insects that could come through there and fall right on my face. Gigantic centipedes, hairy spiders, and scorpions filled with poison that would crawl all over my body to find the best spot to kill me. And that moist warmth I feel down there, almost between my legs, isn't the soft mouth of Tiziana, no, it's the crawling of a drooling black slug that has just emerged from the rotten skull of some dead body under the bed and is getting ready to come back to life to eat my brain and...

Nothing doing, there's something awesome about the way that slug is crawling, it circles around at just the right spots and passes over the best parts, and if it passes over them again, even once, I swear I won't be able to resist. So I jump up like a spring and push Tiziana's head away.

"What's wrong?" she asks, with such a sultry voice and expression they could bring me to the point of no return.

"I'm going to put it inside you," I say. It's ridiculous, I know, but I feel as if the party is about to end, it's just begun but the finale is near, and before it's too late I want to sneak in some real sex.

"But...wait a second."

"No, no, now."

Tiziana keeps looking at me with those eyes and that expression. I don't know if that's good or not, but to try to understand anything now would be ridiculous, like ordering a coffee while napalm is dropping: people everywhere are screaming and running away with their skin peeling off and pieces of their bodies falling to the ground, and I'm sitting there at a table amid the flames saying *What's a guy got to do to get a cup of coffee around here?*

"Fiorenzo, would you have something by any chance?" Tiziana asks me.

"No, I'm good, thanks." Only a second later do I realize that what she means is do I have some condoms. How could she expect an idiot like me to take care of the condoms?

"But don't you have any here?" I ask, and I don't know if I should hope. Because if Tiziana says *No* it's a problem, but if she says *Of course I do*, opens a drawer, and pulls out a box of condoms ready for use, well, I don't know if I'd be so happy about it.

She gets up and stands there looking down at me, with her hands by her sides, and I swear that just to have her here like this, naked in the dim light, throws me into a panic. A fine woman is standing there, stark naked, right in front of me and maybe I'm about to have sex or at least have a go at it. Can this be happening? Does it make sense? Is it a sign that the world is coming to end, like Giuliano says?

In the meantime she realizes that I'm staring at her and bends forward and covers herself a little with her arms.

"Raffaella has some in the next room," she says. I say, "Okay." But she doesn't move. She looks at the door, she looks at me.

"Can you please come with me?"

"Where?"

"Over there. By myself I don't... I mean, I'd rather you came."

I don't understand, but okay, I jump to my feet and follow her into Raffaella's room, which smells strangely of bread and is filled with jars of... oh, who cares, we're naked and we find the condoms and we go back to Tiziana's room right away, and who cares about the rest.

She hands one to me in its nice shiny square wrapper. She was about to grab it with her right hand but she thought twice and went with her left. And it isn't till now that I realize that for all this time Tiziana has continued to use only one hand. During all the kissing and rubbing she kept her right hand still, without throwing away the commitment she had made to the phantom hand. What a woman.

And now she remains seated on the bed looking at me while I try to open the wrapper but I swear it's impossible. In her presence I couldn't open a DVD case, can you imagine what it's going to be like dealing with this shiny slippery thing that's hard to get a hold of?

I try with my teeth but that doesn't work and it slips away once, twice, three times. Then my blood starts to boil, I chomp down on it hard and finally the wrapping breaks. The taste of balloon and oil on my tongue: I bit too hard and the condom got torn.

"Shit, what an idiot," I say. But Tiziana has already fished out another one and she gives it to me. And I wonder what more it will take for this fantastic woman sitting next to me to say *What the hell are you doing, get lost, get out of here, you jerk-off.* How much sadder does it have to get before a woman realizes she's made the wrong choice?

I take the wrapper, I study it. Tiziana extends her left hand and we try to pull out the condom together, one hand each. I pull from one side, she from the other, the thing folds and makes noise but it doesn't break. I decide I can't take it anymore.

"Tiziana, please, use both of your hands to open this fucking thing!"

She looks at me for a second, I slip a finger between her wrist and the bandage and I pull, the bandage loosens up and she finally removes it. She studies her hand for a second, moves her fingers as if they were a newly unwrapped Christmas present, takes the condom and peels it in a split second. She hands it to me and smiles, and I smile, too, because all I want from life now is this little piece of rubber free and ready to do its job.

But now that I have it here in my palm, greasy and flat and rolled up, I look at it and it looks at me and smiles with a slippery rubber smile, as if to say *Now I want to see what you're going to come up with.*

I turn it between my fingers and examine one side and the other. Putting on a condom must be difficult in general, I think, but trying to put one on for the first time with only one hand, in the dark and with an amazing naked woman waiting for you, is the worst thing you could wish upon yourself.

I rest it on the tip, try to keep it balanced and pull it down. But it doesn't cooperate and it stays like that. All it does is squeeze me and even hurt a little. I try to unroll it but only one part budges, and it slips to one side. I try to put it back on the tip, and I sweat sweat sweat. And I think, *Come on, come on,*

Fiorenzo, you know how to spear a fishhook through an earthworm, and they're really slippery and wriggle away and if you're not careful they'll bite your flesh off, and now you're going to let a little piece of rolled rubber get the better of you? I persist but it won't budge. It bends to all my moves but it outsmarts me, it plays around, it teases me. It slides off and falls on the bed, I pick it up, it slides off again.

Then Tiziana extends her hands and takes it.

"May I?"

I don't look at her, I keep staring at the ceiling, I feel like I did when I was little when I couldn't tie my shoelaces and in the end Mom had to take care of it or I would miss the school bus. I nod. She bends down and rests her chin on my leg, I feel her breath on my skin. She takes the condom and places it on the tip, then she begins to work with two hands to slide it down, down, down. But the damn thing puts up a fight, grips the skin to keep from going down and gives in only a millimeter at a time. Tiziana's hands insist on making it unroll and accompany it with a regular rhythm from above to below, from above to below, from above to below . . .

And before I know it, the mayor of the town shouts *Go!*, the technicians set off the detonator, and all heads look up at the sky: the fireworks have begun.

From my throat comes a chewed up *Hmmmguaaar*, I feel a punch to my stomach, *boom boom boom* and the party is over. All that's left is wastepaper on the streets and broken bottles, and my sticky belly. And . . .

. . . And then my head, in the struggle to help me survive, skips two minutes without registering a single second. I swear I don't know what happened in those moments, but I have the impression that we just sat there, horribly quiet and still. Then I gathered my clothes, I know because now I have them in my hand, and the first thing I remember is that I asked Tiziana if I could go to the bathroom. For some scary reason I spoke to her as if she were my teacher: "Excuse me, Miss, may I please go to the bathroom?" Like that, I swear.

And now I'm there, in fact, in the bathroom in front of the mirror: if it were mine I would spit in my own face. I think of Tiziana in the next room, of how she's feeling, and I know that the worst is still not over. The most embarrassing moment will be when I return to her and we look at each other. What will I tell her, what will she tell me, what will we do?

I open the window to get some air, I look down and see a balcony that looks out over another balcony next to a drainpipe sticking out from the wall, easy to climb down. Put one and one together and it always makes two.

I slip on my pants and I'm already out the window. I hook my right arm around the pipe and use my left hand to grab hold of anything I can. The wall scratches the bottom of my feet but it's a perfect anti-sliding surface. At one point the pipe makes a cracking noise and pulls away from the wall: I stop breathing. Here we go, I'm going to fall and die, and really, it would be the most logical thing. I mean, I can't even unroll a piece of rubber on a bed, how could I think I would slip out of a house down a rusty drainpipe?

Obviously I can't. It's much more logical to die.

Yet against all odds I manage, I make it down to within half a yard of the ground and I jump. The gravel underneath my bare feet hurts like hell, but it seems only fair. Like those guys who walk on hot coals or whip themselves to be forgiven for their sins. Instead I walk over pebbles and pieces of glass and I don't complain because I know I deserve nothing better.

And in fact I start to walk quickly and deliberately pound my feet into the ground to feel more pain, every step is a pang that goes all the way to my brain, but it feels right this way, it feels more than right, and I almost feel like laughing.

I get on my scooter, take off, I'm bare-chested and now the air is cool, actually it's freezing, but this, too, is right: after his wicked deeds, he walks on glass and then endures the cold the whole way home, thus atoning for his sins.

But evidently I've got to atone a little longer, because it's midnight and I'm frozen and exhausted, I arrive at the shop and I want to jump into bed and flatline. But in front of the gate I find a swollen little yellow thing on the sidewalk, like a package or a tarp or a dust heap.

It's the Little Champ.

TIZIANA IN THE MIRROR

You stand there, with your hand leaning on the sink and your eyes staring at the window. Which is open, and the curtain is flapping in the breeze. Just like when someone escapes in a cartoon.

The truth is, the whole situation could be a cartoon, but you look at yourself in the mirror and think that no child should see a cartoon like this.

Hair a mess, face swollen, with the usual runaway lock of hair over your cheek.

Stupid.

If you called yourself stupid after that first kiss in the office, what are you going to call yourself now? You look at yourself in the mirror and you don't know. You're pale, you've got bags under your eyes. You're a hundred thousand years old. Your right hand is still red from the bandage, you had wrapped it too tight. Is there anything you can do right, Tiziana? If there is, you don't know. You don't know anything.

Not even what you were thinking when you took a beardless boy and threw him on the bed and started to undress him. And he wasn't a young man, not one of the guys who according to Raffaella *are doing orgies by the time they're sixteen nowadays and know more than you and me put together.*

No, what you had on your bed was a boy who didn't have the least idea what he was doing. You understood from his fingers and his mouth, he couldn't stop shaking, and it's not as if you had some excuse like the two of you just happened to be there and you lost your head. No, he gave you a million opportunities to call the whole thing off and stop. And instead you continued.

This is wrong, Fiorenzo, that's enough, I'm sorry, it's my fault, please, you'd better go. It would have been so easy to say, and instead you didn't. Not even when you saw that he didn't know how to put on a condom. No, at that point rather than stopping you gave it a try, and then that gesture you made, and the spurts...then you finally came back to reality. To the world of Tiziana Cosci, and to the world of the kid that Tiziana Cosci just did.

Maybe the news has spread and is on the lips of the whole town, they'll point to you on the street, kick you out of the Youth Center, and maybe a nasty article will even appear in the paper.

But the crazy thing is that in the middle of this whole mess what you're really worried about is where in the world Fiorenzo is, and why he escaped through the window rather than coming back to your room.

He ran away like children do when they do something wrong and are afraid of their mothers. A stupid, childish reaction. But he's justified. He *is* a child.

Are you?

VICTORY IN DEFEAT

"Hey, wake up!"

I shake him but the idiot keeps sleeping. He's got his chest over the doorstep to the shop and his legs on the sidewalk, God knows how he can sleep that way. He opens an eye and looks at me, then he closes it. I shake him.

"Come on, wake up!"

"Good morning, Mister."

"What do you mean, morning? It's midnight!"

"Oh, I'm sorry. Are you all right?"

"What the fuck are you doing here at this hour?"

"I did it, did you see, did I do the right thing?" Mirko pulls himself up: the marble doorstep is imprinted in his hair and now it looks like a curly, cube-shaped rug, making him even uglier than usual, as if that were possible. "In today's race, didn't you see?"

"No, I don't give a shit about races. So what did you do, win again? Breaking news...hooray for the Little Champ..."

"No, I did like you said, Mister. I lost."

"Really?"

"Yes, and by a lot. I must have been...I don't know, twenti-eth, twenty-fifth..."

"Holy shit, really?"

He stands up, smiles, nods yes harder and harder, and starts to jump for joy.

"Mister, the thing is, you were right. Losing isn't hard. I just stayed back in the pack, and then a little group pulled ahead, and it was clear that I had to squeeze in there, and then it was hard because I really felt like pumping the pedals a couple of times and then I'd catch up. But I told myself, *No, Mirko, concentrate, stop pedaling, you can do it*...and in the end I did it!"

He's totally psyched, telling me all about the best race in his life. I once felt an emotion like that when I was fourteen, at one of my last races before the afternoon at the ditch with the bomb and the hand and all the rest. I had come in third, I stood on the winners' stand, it was the best I'd ever placed and I felt like I was world champion. At the end Dad told me, *You see, Fiorenzo, what did I tell you? You don't have to worry if you don't win right away, you're a natural talent and you'll peak at the right time.* So then I asked him if that was the moment I was starting to peak. Dad looked at me for a second with a smile from ear to ear and said, *I think so, Fiorenzo, I really think so.*

Then what happened happened. But that day was a great day.

"Excuse me, Mister, can I ask why you're bare-chested?"

"No, you can't."

"Okay. I'm sorry. But I was asking because you usually have these really nice T-shirts and I would like to have one like them, too. One with skulls, if possible, I like skulls because they're always laughing."

"Sure, but listen up, what the fuck are you doing here at this hour?"

"I know, it's late, I'm sorry, Mister, I know this is your house and—"

"Well, actually, my house is supposed to be the place you're living in now, dickwad."

"Yes, you're right, I'm sorry. But tonight I couldn't stay there. Mr. Roberto is really angry and acting weird. He said some awful things and shouted and smashed up stuff."

"What did he say to you? He didn't lay a hand on you, did he?"

"No, no, and the awful things, he wasn't saying them to me. He was saying them to himself, to the world, and to people whose names I didn't know. And then to his wife."

Mom. Ever since she died I haven't heard Dad say a single word about her, and now I have to hear about it from this twerp the Little Champion.

"What did he say, did he insult her?"

"No, no, not her. He said a lot of bad words and was swearing at God and the Madonna and a lot of other people, but not at his wife. With her it was more like he was talking."

"He was talking to her?"

"Yes, Mister, he was saying, *What should I do now, what should I do?* And what I think, if you don't mind my saying, Mister ..." Before finishing his sentence the Little Champ looked around to be sure we were alone, even though we were surrounded by the usual nuclear wasteland of Muglione after dinnertime. He cupped his mouth anyway and whispered in my ear, "What I think, Mister, is that Mr. Roberto had also been drinking a little ..."

Madness. Dad doesn't drink. He won't even have English trifle because there's liqueur in it. Once at a baptism he threw down two Mon Chéris and got dizzy.

"Listen up. Was today an important race?"

The Little Champion's eyes pop out and he answers proudly, "Oh, yes, super important, I raced outside the region for the first time!"

"Ah, that's it. And you lost."

"Yes, Mister, it wasn't easy but I did it. Thanks to you, Mister."

I nod, but only a little. I look at his stupid smile that never goes away, then I see myself reflected in the shop window. It's dark but I can see myself a little, and the thought that pops into my head has nothing to do with what we're talking about. And believe it or not, one second later Mirko says the same thing I'm thinking.

"Mister, you know when you're bare-chested like that it's easier to tell that you have only one hand."

I swear, the same thought, the same words.

"I know without you telling me, jerk-off, why don't you mind your own fucking business? Just because you've lost a race, don't go turning into a wiseass."

I continue to study myself in the window and I think that this is how Tiziana saw me for the first time in her room. A monster, a drawing of a man that was done badly and never finished, and yet she gave me a chance. And what I did with that chance really sucked. Luckily there wasn't much light. Luckily the apartment was on the second floor.

And luckily a black Buick Terraza with a giant skull on the door is coming down the county road.

"Where the fuck were you?" says Giuliano while he's getting out. Stefanino says hi to me and to Mirko, who answers with a small bow.

Giuliano gives me a thumbs-up. "You're bare-chested, too? Great, it's the new look!"

I say yes, because it's the smoothest and fastest way to keep things moving along. And at this hour of the night I want everything to go nice and easy, without a glitch. Even if in the Terraza I see a motionless white face sitting in the backseat and something tells me that nice and easy is not part of tonight's program.

"Who the fuck's the kid?"

"How do you do, my name is Mirko."

"God, you're ugly. Wait a minute, are you that jerk-off who rides a bike? Is that you?"

"Yes, Mister, good evening."

"*Yes, Mister, good evening*...Who the hell are you, Little Lord Fauntleroy?" Giuliano laughs and hits Stefanino upside the head. "Whoa, Stefano, this guy's an even bigger twerp than you!"

I laugh and so does Stefanino. The Little Champ laughs, too, and nods his head.

"What are we supposed to do with the kid? We can't just let him tag along."

"Why not?" I ask. "Where are we going?"

"To do our number on the old folks, no? We can hardly stop—" Giuliano hesitates mid-sentence and looks at Mirko. "Come on, kid, go stick your nose someplace else for a few minutes while we talk adult stuff. Go over there, look, behind the corner. Quick!"

Mirko huddles in his jacket, looks at us for a second, then takes off toward the corner of the building. When he gets there he stands still, like a bright-yellow bowling pin.

"Over to the side, over to the side, behind the corner," Giuliano tells him.

And believe it or not Stefanino raises his hand and gestures that he's got to scram, and he shouts, "We said over to the side, shithead!" Then he goes back to looking at us with two schizoid eyes I've never seen on him.

Giuliano starts to explain. "So, guys, you thought I'd go blow away two thousand euros in one shot, didn't you? But you're wrong. I mean, not entirely—I also went to Bientina to the theater where my aunt works, and take a look at what I got."

He opens the door of the Terraza and starts to pull out the pale guy sitting in the back. But it's not a real person, it's a life-size dummy that slams into the car roof and the door and makes Giuliano swear up a storm. It's stuffed and made out of cloth, but the head is plastic. It has a white crew-cut wig, a fanny pack around its waist, and glasses.

How it went from then on I think is predictable. I opened the gate to the shop and the Little Champ entered through the hole in the door, I put on a sweatshirt, and then with Giuliano and Stefano got into the car and took the county road all the way to the foot of Boar's Head Hill. From there we took a small road that is paved at the beginning and then becomes all gravel and in the end we arrived at the municipal cemetery of Muglione.

Everywhere it was dark and there was a kind of low fog that had the stench of the ditches. The only lights around were on the gravesites, and in the fog they looked round and alive and trembled in midair like souls lost in the night.

We took the dummy and hung it from the gate with a noose around its neck. And I have to admit when we took a few steps back and looked at it like that, hanging in the mist with lights and gravestones in the background, I felt something strange moving in my bowels.

And then there was the fact that Mom's buried right there in that cemetery, in an area in the back, at the foot of a wall where

the mausoleums of the prestigious families begin. And I felt
a little bad because it seemed like I was disrespecting her. But
that was bullshit: all I had to do was think for a second about
what Mom was like to realize that she actually would have gotten a big kick out of this.

She's the one who got me into horror movies. She liked
them better than me and Tiziana put together. Horror movies
are always shown late at night, and I was little but I stayed on
the sofa and watched them with her while hearing the sound of
Dad snoring from the bedroom.

The movie would begin and we'd watch it from under a
blanket, huddling together, without saying a word. Some films,
especially the ones from the seventies, had these really over-the-
top scenes of horror and monsters but also extreme sex, orgies,
lesbians who decide to do it in a crypt before being killed by the
ghost of a werewolf baron.

And when these scenes came on, Mom had a technique to
keep me from seeing them: she would send me to the kitchen to
get her chocolates. Maybe on the screen there was a nun walking down the corridor of a convent and there were lamps and
the nun would open the door a crack and see another nun half
naked, aroused, and saying strange things in Latin, and...Mom
would send me to get a chocolate.

I'd grumble but she'd frown and say, *I'm so hungry I'm fainting*...and so I'd go, get the chocolate, run back, but by then
the scene had changed and it was daylight and everything was
peaceful. And the more heavy-duty scenes there were, the more
times I had to get up for chocolate. Once I told her, *I'll bring you
the whole box*, and she said, *No, no, just one or I'll get sick*. And
in effect I could measure the heaviness of the horror films we'd
seen together by the number of chocolates I brought her as we

were watching. *Frankenstein and the Monster from Hell*: no chocolates. *Tombs of the Blind Dead*: five chocolates. *The Shiver of the Vampires*: that night I must have worn a hole in the floor of the hall, and Mom risked becoming diabetic.

So, there you have it, in other words: I'm saying this just to show that, in my opinion, the idea of a dummy hanging in front of a cemetery, at night and with the fog, Mom would have liked it a lot, so I shouldn't worry about it too much. Actually, while I was finishing up the noose I even felt like laughing. I was laughing together with her, if it's true, this idea that the dead can see what we're doing. Under the dummy we placed a piece of cardboard with red writing on it, then we looked everything over, patted each other on the back, got back in the Terraza, and we were on our way back home.

And the next morning the first person to arrive at the cemetery would find this puppet of an old man hanging from the gate with red writing underneath that said:

NIGHT WILL FALL ON THIS NIGHT
AND THE CEMETERY WILL BE YOUR HOME.
THE NATIONAL REJUVENATION BRIGADE
    METAL D.

I return to the shop. I go in. Mirko is asleep in a chair with his head on the wooden part of the counter. I try to wake him up but he seems as fake as the dummy hanging in the cemetery.

And my father comes to mind. Who knows whether he's finished busting up everything in the house. I hope he didn't touch my room. That would have been too petty, but I look at this ugly little twerp and I think about Dad letting him come here to sleep on the sidewalk by himself at midnight, so nothing should amaze me anymore.

I take two carp air mattresses, inflate them with my breath, then stop for a second because I'm getting dizzy. I put them on the ground in the back room near my cot. It's not that I want him to be close, but the space is what it is. I add the towel that I keep in the bathroom, then I go back to the front, get the kid on his feet, accompany him to the back room, and have him lie down there, while he's still asleep in his head.

Lucky him. I don't even try to sleep. A lot of things have happened that are going to have a lot of consequences and I don't know what they'll be or what I'll be able to do. I only know that tonight I won't be able to sleep. I sit on my bed and start to leaf through the latest issue of *Popular Carp*.

"Mister, do you have something against old people?" Mirko's voice is mushy and trembling. It sounds like the voice of the ghost of a parakeet.

"Are you sleeping?" I say.

"I heard . . . you wanted to do something against the old people . . . did I hear wrong?"

"Yes. Go back to sleep."

"But, Mister, there's a strange smell, what—"

"It's the worms. Go back to sleep."

"And also a strange noise."

"It's the worms. Any question you ask, the answer's always going to be *the worms*, get it? Go back to sleep."

A few seconds of silence. Then:

"Um, excuse me, Mister, the woman from the Youth Center came by earlier. She was looking for you."

That's how he said it, I swear, and I stop breathing so I can hear the rest.

But the friggin' Little Champ has started to snore.

FISH WITHOUT BAIT

"Catch anything?" I ask.

Dad shakes his head without taking his eyes off the floater. To see him here fishing at the irrigation ditch seems so weird. He's the one who taught me, when I was five years old, but since then I've never seen him with a rod in his hand. Normally this is the last place I would have come looking for him, but a clue led me here.

This morning when I woke up (I managed to get in a couple of hours' sleep in the end), I found the Little Champ lying on the ground and he scared the crap out of me. A few seconds later I remembered more or less everything. I got up and prepared milk with cookies for him and me, cold milk because I still don't have a camp stove, then I sent him off to school. He didn't want to go and he told me, *Please, Mister, no, I don't feel like it today, I'm not feeling good, please don't send me.*

I explained to him that his grades suck and in June he's got finals, so he'd better at least show that he's applying himself and not skip class. Wise advice that I should follow, too, except in the end I took him and forced him out on the street and I can hardly do that to myself. Then, rather than go to high school, I went to see what had happened at home.

The door was wide open and so were the windows, even though Dad's car wasn't in the driveway. I called and no one was there, just my old house, quiet and empty but devastated by an angry demon: the kitchen table broken in half and thrown through the living room window, the TV set exploded on the rug, the sofa massacred and abandoned in the hall, just before the doorway to what used to be the bathroom.

My bedroom was perfect, though. Everything in order, just as I'd left it, except for the tackle cabinet, which was open, open and empty.

So I came up with this ridiculous idea that maybe Dad had gone fishing, for the first time in fifteen years. I took my scooter and went looking for him along the ditches. I checked out all the good spots, meaning the places where there's a curve in the ditches or they're wider, or where two bodies of water come together. But nothing.

Then, by sheer accident when I was trying to keep my scooter from slipping on the dirt patches that line the municipal dump, I saw Dad's car parked way back in the fields, in the middle of a flat gray and brown area without trees or shrubs: a yellow station wagon covered with giant letters is hard to miss.

So now here I am on the banks next to Dad, actually a little behind him, at one of the most useless and poor spots where anyone might choose to fish. The water is too shallow and covered with lime, while from the dump comes the steady smell of melted plastic and very dead things.

But Dad ignores it all. He's there hunched over with his chin leaning on one hand, the fishing rod resting on a wood fork, and his eyes staring at the floater.

"How long have you been here?"

"I don't know. Three hours?"

"Catch anything?" I'm speaking in snatches because the smell of garbage goes down my throat every time I breathe.

"No, nothing."

"Not even a nibble? *Nada de nada?*"

"Nope. It's better this way. Otherwise it'd be a real pain, reeling them in and getting my hands dirty."

"So what did you come here for?"

"For the heck of it. To breathe. My head's exploding. I drank too much."

"You drank?"

"Yes, I went to bed and the whole room was spinning, the ceiling, the walls, the furniture. I got up, I felt like I was in a cage, I needed some air so I came here."

He stops talking. He takes the rod in his hand, and with a minimal movement of the tip he shifts the floater a few inches, to move the bait down below it and arouse the curiosity of the fish, in case by any chance some perverse fish were to decide to pass by these parts. And when he starts to talk again his voice is different. It comes from his throat, from his stomach, maybe from that twisted mess known as the bowels.

"He lost, Fiorenzo. He was a washout. Pitiful."

"Who, what?" I ask, because it seems wrong that I already know everything. I don't know why, but it seems wrong.

"Yesterday I took him outside the region. To Piacenza. Easy race, favorable course, piece of cake. And he lost."

"Come on, it happens, no way can you expect him to win every time."

"Yes I can! Actually, he has to. He has to win every time we've got the chance. And he had the chance. That's the whole point...it's not that he lost, it's that *he didn't want* to win. That's the problem."

He suddenly leans forward and squints for a good look at the floater, which might have moved but I didn't notice. The gestures, the timing, the attention, everything tells you that Dad is a great fisherman: why he hasn't been fishing in fifteen years only he could tell you. On second thought, maybe not even him.

"You should have seen the papers this morning... *The Super Champion Is Not So Super, The Muglione Missile Runs out of Gas, Mr. Marelli Gets the Tactics Wrong and Goes Down with the Ship*...It's normal, those people never understood shit about cycling, but anyone who was really watching the race could see that Mirko wasn't pedaling, he didn't want to win. And that is a hundred times worse."

"Why is it worse? In my opinion it's better, like, it means there's nothing wrong with him physically."

"What the fuck do you know? It's worse, Fiorenzo, much worse, because if the legs aren't working all you have to do is train and you're all right. But if the head isn't working, the game is over. And what's not working is his head. I told him, *It's okay, this time you wanted to act crazy, but next week you have to kick ass*. And you know what he answered? He said no, he won't win next week either, he doesn't want to win anymore. So I let off a little steam, did some screaming and yelling, busted up a few things. There you have it. But what could I do? It's not like it's my fault."

"You also destroyed the house."

"Yeah, a little."

"Do you at least know where he is right now?"

"Where who is?"

"Your Little Champion."

"Of course I know. With you, right? It's clear."

"No, I don't think there's anything clear about it. In fact, it's just the opposite."

"What do you mean? It's clear as day."

"Clear as mud, you mean. It's the most ridiculous thing in the world that he'd be at my place, it's something that—"

"Listen. Is he or isn't he at your place?"

"He is."

"See? It's clear. End of story."

I grit my teeth to keep in the last words I wanted to say, and then neither of us talks for a while. Just the steady low noise of the dump, some unknown animal making its way between the dried grass and the brambles, and Dad reeling in a little line.

"What are you fishing for?" I ask.

"What?"

"I said, what are you fishing for, what bait are you using?"

"None."

"None? What do you mean, none?"

"Just the hook. Is that okay?"

"No, it's not okay." I feel like raising my voice. "It's not okay at all! What do you think you'll catch without bait?"

And then, for the first time since I arrived at the ditch, Dad stops staring at the floater and whips around. He sets his eyes on me and they're two red shiny balls that are spinning randomly in their sockets.

"And , if I use bait what the fuck do you think I'm going to catch, Einstein?"

"..."

"I'll catch shit! Do you think bait would make any difference? Do you really believe that? You're eighteen years old now, Fiorenzo, eighteen," he says. I'm actually nineteen, but no way am I going to correct him. "And you still believe that bullshit? Maybe bait is important in a place where there are possibilities and you want to make the most of them. But the problem here is that there's nothing, get it? Nothing, nada, zilch! You spend your whole life here and wait and hope and every now and then there's a strange move or a little glimmer and you pay attention and say *Here we go, this is the moment, my big chance*, but instead it's all bullshit and everything's the same as it was before, and you're still the same asshole you were when you were born in this fucking hole. There's nothing to catch here, Fiorenzo, and nothing to hope for. You're eighteen now, when are you going to get it?"

These are his exact words, and he looks at me with these crazy red eyes. Then he kind of shivers and looks back toward the floater, places a hand on the rod and gets ready for a nibble. But nothing has moved. The floater is still there, half asleep on the still water. I look at it, too, and I think of the hook underneath, naked and thin and golden, waiting for something from the muck on the bottom.

A PIGEON BY MISTAKE

I was stupid to send Mirko to school. Last night Tiziana came by the shop looking for me. She found him but she had come for me, and at that hour of the night it's not as if someone drops by for no reason or to make small talk. What did she want? Was she nervous, pissed, did she leave a message for me?

Who knows. The kid is at school and until two o'clock I can't ask him anything. But I can't wait, I want to know everything right away, I go to the source. And the Youth Center is on the way: on my way back from the irrigation ditch, it's right there. I mean, not exactly right there, but, well, I've decided I'm going to stop by there.

Outside on the sidewalk there's no one, not even the seniors. The door is open but I knock anyway. Silence. I go in and am enveloped in the usual darkness of the catacombs.

"Hi." It's Tiziana's voice. She's in the corner sitting in a vibrating armchair like they sell on TV. She jumps to her feet and in the dark I can't tell if she's smiling at me. I think so, or maybe not, I don't know.

"Hi, Tiziana. I . . . Hi."

The good thing about the dark is that it's hard to look each other in the eyes and everything seems a little less embarrassing. Almost like talking on the phone.

But embarrassment rears its ugly head with the question she shoots at me point-blank:

"Listen, why did you run away last night?"

"..."

"And don't go telling me that you didn't run away. For starters, you could have gotten hurt."

"I know, I know, but at that moment it seemed like the best option."

"The best option for who?"

"For me, maybe, but also for you, I think."

"Spare me the phony excuses, I think I know what's best for me."

"Yes, I didn't mean to say...I mean, now that I think about it, you're right. I wasn't really thinking. It was stupid."

"You can say that again," she says.

But she's not angry at me. At least not too angry. She goes to the desk, opens a drawer, takes something plastic from it, and hands it to me. It's the DVD of *The Devil's Nightmare*, the one I tried to break the other night.

"This way you can watch it and tell me what you think."

"Thanks. I'll check it out and give it back to you."

"Good. And don't forget: pay attention to the sound track, and to Erika Blanc's dress, and—"

"Excuse me, Tiziana, why don't we watch it together? That way you can point out all these things to me. Otherwise I might miss them."

I say it because it seems like the most obvious thing in the world. But maybe only in my world, seeing as how Tiziana frowns and looks at me strangely.

"Yes, but...well, you can also watch it alone, I don't..."

"Come on, are you busy tonight? I can come over and we can watch it."

"No, Fiorenzo, tonight I have to finish some things and I don't..."

"Okay, so let's make it tomorrow night, then. Come on, take the DVD back and we'll see it together."

"I don't know if I'm going to be home tomorrow night either, I'm probably—"

"So Wednesday, Wednesday would also work for me. Or Thursday, or Friday, or..."

"Look, Fiorenzo, apart from my being busy, I don't know if it's a good idea."

"You don't know if what's a good idea?"

"To see each other."

That's how she says it, delivering a big punch to my gut. I mean, she didn't really punch me, or maybe she did and it was so fast I didn't see it. But the pain I feel is just like that. It spreads to my whole chest, up to my throat, through my whole body, leaving damage everywhere it goes.

"I mean, Fiorenzo...I don't know, there are too many things I have to understand and I need time."

"What's to understand?"

"Many things, unfortunately, so many. Maybe for you it's easier, but I—"

"What's that supposed to mean, it's easier for me? For me not a fucking thing is easier, nothing is easy for me!"

"There, you see how we react differently, don't you get it? I see a lot of problems and I can't pretend they don't exist, and I have to solve them because otherwise the situation will become really—"

"The next time I'll last longer, I swear!" I say. I don't know why, I didn't mean to, but that's what's in the air right now so I take the plunge. "The next time we do it I'll last longer."

Tiziana looks at me as if I were a retarded pigeon that came in through the window by mistake, that tries to fly away and in the process breaks every vase in the living room.

"What's that got to do with it?" she says. "Fiorenzo. What the fuck does that have to—"

"Listen, this is how it works. The first time a man doesn't last very long, the second still not much but a little longer, the third is already better. It's a question of practice. All we need is for me to practice a little."

Tiziana doesn't answer and maybe that's almost better. She stops looking at me and shakes her head, sits down at her desk and turns on her computer. She's in her office and in theory she should be working, so this is a very kind way to remind me of that fact.

"Tiziana, I'm sorry, I swear I'll leave. But the thing is, I . . . I mean, last night you came by the shop, so I don't get it. I mean, what did you want? Did you come by at midnight to give me the DVD?"

She lowers her eyes to her desk, looks for something in a blue folder, pulls out a sheet of paper, and places it near the monitor.

"No, Fiorenzo. I came by because I wanted to talk to you, because you ran away through the window and I was left . . . you know? But I swear I don't know what I wanted to tell you, I didn't even know last night. And I don't know if I'll know in the next few days either. But I want to think about it, and think about it carefully. I'm not one of those airheads who likes to string a guy along, I'm not a tease, I really want you to know that, Fiorenzo. Do you?"

And she looks up from the monitor. But with her face still pointed toward the screen, that gaze from below through her hair has such a powerful effect that it makes no sense for her to ask me whether or not I believe her, because right now I could believe anything. Alien abductions, Aztec mummies, secret recordings of Led Zeppelin jamming with the Bee Gees. Right now I could fall for anything.

"Fiorenzo, if I tell you that I need to think, it's not an excuse to play for time; I don't even like keeping you waiting. I'm telling you that I need to think for a simple reason: because I need to think. Do you believe me?"

"I...uh, I think so, yes."

"Good. This is important to me. And while we're on the subject, this stuff about lasting...I mean, about how long you lasted. It has nothing to do with that. Nothing at all, understood?"

"..."

"Shit happens. I'm not stupid, that's not the problem."

"Okay, okay, so what is the problem?"

"I don't know, Fiorenzo. I don't know. There are many, many problems all tangled together. And the bigger the mess we make, the more tangled they get, and instead I want to try to untangle them. So it's better if you and I keep our distance for a little while," she says. And she stops looking at me.

She double-clicks on something. The computer starts to work and so does Tiziana. The noise of the hard drive is like a warm, enveloping wind that blows toward the door, stronger and stronger, pushing me away. Away from the Youth Center, away from everything good, with a DVD in my hand that I'm supposed to watch all by myself.

TYRANNOSAURUS

Sensational. Today Mirko Colonna discovered something amazing, something he would have never expected. Like someone who goes to a supermarket, digs through the frozen foods aisle looking for popsicles, and instead finds the lost city of Atlantis.

Mirko discovered something like that today. Actually, he's discovering it right now, while he's sweating and gripping the handlebars on this killer climb. He's discovered that he likes winning, he likes pedaling fast and leaving everything and everyone behind, and he's decided that from now on he's never going to lose again.

He gives himself the go-ahead, supercharged, lowers his eyes, and for the first time notices these awesome muscles that have grown in his legs. They're all gnarly and hard, they don't even look like his legs, and they push and they push but Mirko never feels tired. He shifts his focus back to the road, stands up on the pedals, and cuts another blind curve. And who cares if from up there maybe a car or a truck is bearing down full speed ahead: Mirko is a missile launched toward the top and nothing can stop him.

But this morning he still didn't know it, this morning he was just a kid who had lost a race and didn't want to go to school, in the end he only went because otherwise Fiorenzo would have given him a good kick in the ass to make him go.

As usual he arrived on his bike and as usual he chained it to the most forlorn corner of the schoolyard. But this morning something was different: he didn't have his backpack with his books, he hadn't brushed his teeth in forever, and he had spent the night surrounded by a billion worms scratching in the dark. But above all, this morning the whole school had gathered in the schoolyard to look at him.

They were quiet and they stared at him, a classmate started to laugh, another one clapped, and then a storm of *morons* and *you sucks* and *jerk-offs* erupted, and everyone ganged up on him, saying he was a loser and had run out of dope and he should get the fuck back to his own town.

Gladly, Mirko was about to answer, and right at that moment that's exactly what he thought. But he didn't want to answer anyone, and no one wanted to listen to him. They only wanted to scream the worst possible insults in his ear and give him a few slaps upside the head as he advanced, saying *excuse me* the whole way to the entrance of the school. Every now and then he even felt some drops on his face, but maybe it wasn't intentional spitting, maybe it was just spittle coming out by itself in the midst of all that hollering.

Then he finally made it to the steps, went through the main door, and the rubbery smell of the floor made him feel safe. Except the corridor in front of him was filled with smaller kids who were already inside but wanted to treat him as badly as the kids outside; meanwhile, the kids outside were coming in and had no desire to miss their turn. The insults and slaps doubled, the rumbling between the walls of the entrance got louder, and they were throwing everything at him from every direction like a meteor shower, and then Mirko couldn't take it anymore. He hadn't done anything wrong. Instead of shouting *moron* and *dope fiend* and pantomiming a syringe in the arm, why didn't they explain to him what he had done wrong? He suddenly turned back to the main door, lowered his head, throwing himself against the wall of bodies, and somehow managed to make his way through. He found himself outside again, and raced through the schoolyard all the way to the bike, to his bike, unchained it, and leapt up on the seat. And by the time the mob made it to the gate to see if they could throw something else at him, Mirko Colonna had already disappeared like a shot at the end of the county road.

He pedaled faster and faster, farther and farther away from the shouts the laughter the venomous saliva. What was wrong with what he had done? He lost, okay, but everyone loses all the time, couldn't he lose at least once? No, he couldn't, he's a champion and people massacre champions who lose. Because then it means that you're not some god, it means that you suck, it means that you're the same as them.

And Mirko isn't the same as anyone, he doesn't know whether that's good or bad but it's true.

He pounds on the pedals, leans over the frame to spin as fast as he can, makes it to the end of the road, and throws himself into the giant roundabout that comes before downtown. He wants to return to the bait-and-tackle shop, maybe go back to bed or tell Fiorenzo everything, but now Mirko can't stop pedaling: there's this wild rage in him that grows bigger and bigger and swells his muscles and his lungs, and if he doesn't let it out something's going to explode inside and he'll die. He thinks and he pedals, he looks at his thighs and he pedals, and in the meantime he's already circling the roundabout for the fifth time. Faster and faster, like a merry-go-round gone berserk, the tires start to slip on the asphalt and if he keeps it up in a little while he's going to skid and they'll find him in pieces on the roof of a nearby warehouse. So he aims for the first exit he sees, it's tight and there's not even a road sign saying where it leads, which seems like the right way to go. He leans to one side and goes for it, ignoring the traffic and the car horns beeping behind him.

Ten minutes later Mirko is in the middle of nowhere, the only thing he can see is the ditch along the road, scattered cows on the black soil, and far ahead the big, dark, rotten tooth of the San Cataldo Hill. There used to be some kind of caves on the hill, and there are still signs along the road, but whatever there was must be gone because now the only people who go up San Cataldo are poachers, lovebirds, and amateur cyclists who compete on Sundays and puke from the strain. And now they're all being joined by Mirko Colonna, who wants to hurl himself at the uphill road and tear it limb from limb.

He pushes on the pedals and puts one hand between his legs to shift into the hardest ratio possible. This bike must be six thousand years old, it's as heavy as an iron gate and has the gearshift below, attached to the frame. Mr. Roberto used to race on it when he was young, and he gave it to Mirko as a pleasure bike because he says that if he can get used to this one, then when he mounts a real carbon-steel bike he'll feel like he's flying. He says that Bartali did the same, he trained for climbs wearing a backpack filled with bricks, so that when the real race came—without the bricks on his back—he would feel as light as a feather.

Bartali was a man who raced a million years ago, then he stopped and in the end he died, but as far as the people in this area are concerned, Bartali never got off his bike. People called him the Man of Steel because he was never cold or hot, and he didn't know the meaning of hunger or thirst. Bartali's leads were so huge that often by the time the second-place finisher had crossed the line, he had already taken his shower and was watching the race in his bathrobe. Mirko had done races in the province of Florence where there were still fans with signs that said BARTALI WIN ONE FOR US, and sometimes, when he was ahead of the pack and on his way to an easy victory, he imagined that Bartali would come out of nowhere and pulverize him with a scorching sprint. And who knows, maybe this could even have happened. But not anymore. Mirko was sorry for Mr. Bartali, but from now on it was take no prisoners.

Finally the first hairpin turns of San Cataldo, which are instant leg killers. Mirko downshifts, passes a curve, and sees two amateurs in front struggling and staggering in the middle of the road. And then something strange and new happens that Mr. Roberto has been telling him about forever. *When you see your adversaries struggling, that's your moment, Mirko. You have to be like a shark who smells blood. You have to feel hungry, you have to be drooling, get it?*

No, so far Mirko hadn't gotten it, but now he does, damn it. He feels his legs sparking, a crooked smile on his face, he sets his eyes on his prey and suddenly bears down on them, stays next to them for a second to enjoy the moment, then stands up on his pedals and takes off like a jet that leaves them nailed to the asphalt.

Once Gianni and I were climbing San Cataldo and at a certain point who but Mirko Colonna himself passed us, dressed normally and on a normal bicycle, they'll tell each other one day to impress people. *I swear, he was a fast as a motorcycle.*

Exactly, like a motorcycle. Because people think the difference between a bike and a motorcycle is that a bike doesn't have an engine, but now Mirko realizes that's bullshit: a bike does have an engine, and that engine is you. Your heart is pumping blood through your veins, your legs are spinning quickly, the chain that dances between the cassette and crank, the breeze from the spokes spinning lightly through the air. Lots of full, round movements that meet and mix and in the end become a single thing, strong, fast, and silent. The most fantastic engine there is.

Mirko keeps pounding on the pedals with the same power as when he left the school, but he's no longer being propelled by the same fuel. First it was pure rage, every spin of the pedals was a kick in the heads of the assholes at school. Now instead it is a whole new force that doesn't give a shit about what happened. Now he isn't running away from anything, now he is racing toward something different.

He sweats, spits, dries his eyes with the back of his hand, sees the top of the hill approaching but can also feel his breath growing shorter, his lungs burning, his heart beating in his eardrums, knocking on the door to his brain to tell it *Hey, you idiot, stop everything now or this is going to end badly*... Yes, just like that, for the first time in his life Mirko Colonna feels like he is giving it his all: after all the hard training and important races, here by himself on a climb with no sponsored finish line or judges in cars, Mirko Colonna is finally winning.

Because up to now he had never won, up to now he had only come in first. Now instead he's triumphant and wants to carry on like this forever, he wants to tear up all the records and see his name painted on roads throughout the world. He also wants a nickname, something fierce like the big champions. Maybe the Cannibal, el Diablo, or the Pirate. But what he'd really like to be called is the Tyrannosaurus.

He stands up on the pedals again, spits and laughs, spits and laughs. His brain and his muscles and every part of his body are telling him *Enough, please, why are you treating us like this?* And then he pushes even harder to show them who's boss. He wants to make it to the top of San Cataldo and see if from up there Muglione is a little less ugly, but he'll only look at it for a second and without setting one foot on the ground, because as soon as he arrives at the summit the Tyrannosaurus will shift to the long ratio and throw himself into the descent, pressed against the bike frame, toward another plain and another mountain on the horizon and onward that way, without ever stopping.

Yes, fantastic, an endless race. Once Mirko read how in the beginning the cavemen used to be nomads, they traveled and traveled, and then they learned to till the soil and then they stopped in one place and never moved again. And he doesn't know whether it's true or if it's just more of the bullshit they write in books, but one thing is for certain: if instead of agriculture primitive man had invented the bicycle, he would have jumped right on with his club strapped around his back and raced through the whole history of the world without ever stopping.

A FINCH AT THE FAIR

For a while I stared at the ceiling in the company of the worms, who have started to become my friends. Well, not exactly friends, let's say acquaintances I'm stuck with whether I like it or not. So I suppose I can say that the worms are now my relatives.

I listen to them squishing and squirming against each other in their boxes, trying to crawl from the bottom to the top. The ones who do get there find there's no place else to go and they give up the fight. The others climb over them and before you know it the first ones are back at the bottom, where they forget there was nothing up there anyway, and start their upward struggle all over again.

I imagine them wriggling around me in the dark, and at the same time, my head is spinning with Tiziana's words, with thoughts connected to what she said, and with others that have nothing to do with her and are shorter and more ridiculous, like dreams along a river that captures my mind and carries it downstream all the way to sleep.

Afternoon naps are for old people. Usually they fill me with dejection, but today a one-hour rest after lunch sounds like a good idea. Also because I've only been getting an average of three hours' sleep a night lately, and I could almost blame some of the stupid shit that I've done on sleep. It's not that I'm an idiot, it's that I'm sleep deprived. That's what it is.

But at three o'clock, before opening the shop, I have to stop by the pharmacy to buy two boxes of condoms. If I want to know how to put one on, fast and easy, when the right time comes, I'm going to have to start practicing at home. The next time, Tiziana has to find me ready, willing, and able, with a much faster left hand and a much slower little friend between my legs.

That is, if there is a next time. Judging from what she said at the office, I'm not so sure. Actually, maybe she dumped me, so gently that I didn't even realize it was happening. Like my Grandma Ines, who used to give people injections and the whole town came to her because she was so smooth you never knew she had just stuck a needle in your ass. Then again, if Tiziana really doesn't want to see me anymore I'd feel pretty bad, so maybe she isn't like my grandma after all.

Which is good, for a number of reasons.

"Is...sore...pee..." are the first sounds I hear. The loudest bits are hammered into my head before whole words can finally make their way in. "Mister, I'm sorry, are you sleeping?" A hand is tapping my arm.

I open my eyes and no one is there; then I see something at the foot of my cot.

"What the fuck do you want?"

"Are you sleeping, Mister?"

"Not anymore, you dipshit, but I was."

"I'm really sorry, but I have to tell you something amazing."

"Can't you tell me later?"

"But it's super amazing."

"What a pain." I try to yawn myself back to consciousness. The Little Champ raises his curly-haired head and stares at me, filled with excitement. He's covered with mud stains and streaks of dried sweat around his neck.

"Mister, I discovered something today."

"Stop the presses, breaking news."

"Yes, maybe later, but I wanted you to be the first to know." He pulls himself up. "Well, this morning I went to school, remember?"

"Vaguely."

"Well, I didn't want to go, and I was right not to, because they were all waiting for me in the schoolyard to tease me. It looked like a party, Mister, the whole school was outside waiting for me, and when I got there they started yelling and making nasty gestures with their fingers, their arms, and even their—"

"Get to the point."

"Yes, I'm sorry, Mister, I don't like it either when people digress. Like with jokes, I mean maybe the joke is funny but when the person telling it takes forever it's not funny anymore because they never get to—"

"Get to the fucking point."

"Yes, I'm sorry. Like I was saying, my classmates were teasing me, screaming that I was a loser and I really sucked and that in my first real race I was pathetic, and stuff like *Couldn't get your hands on any dope this time?*"

"Assholes. And you?"

"I kept my head down to avoid looking at anyone and went in."

"You went in anyway?"

'Yes, Mister, but then I ran out."

"You did good."

"I think so, too, so I went to the top of San Cataldo."

"Holy shit, when you run away you really run away."

"Yes, but it's not like I planned it, I just went." The Little Champ stares at me with that lost look in his eyes, I can see them, small and dark in the dim light. "And while I was going I could hear all the shouting in my head, but at the same time a big chill ran through me, energizing my whole body, making me clench my fists and my jaw, and my legs were ready to explode. Then I realized something amazing, Mister...what I mean is, I don't like to lose, Mister. I like to win!" And he says this like someone who has just made an earth-shattering discovery.

"Welcome to the club, everyone likes to win."

"You knew? I didn't, I swear. My only excuse is that I never lost until yesterday, so I didn't know what it felt like. But you've lost so many times..."

"Fuck you, asswipe."

"I'm sorry, Mister, I wasn't trying to be mean, I thought I was saying something positive."

"What's so positive about it?"

"Nothing, I'm sorry, I was wrong. I'm not thinking straight today, I'm still really shocked by what I learned, you know?"

And he looks at me with those eyes that won't let you tell him to fuck off. The eyes of a little bird for sale at a fair, surrounded by the crowd and firecrackers going off and kids with cotton candy screaming and crying and carrying on and people sticking their noses through the cage and sneezing, and there the bird is, behind bars, hopping from one perch to the next with no way out, looking at you with these two little black dots above his beak that say *Please, buy me, put me in a bag and take me home with you. I may not live till tomorrow, I may even die on the way home, but please take me away from here.*

"All right, already," I say. "So you realize you don't like losing, and?"

"From now on that's it. From now on I'm not going to lose. I mean, it might happen sometimes, but not if I can help it, and if I do lose, I won't be happy. I can't wait till the next race, Mister. I want to know what it feels like to win."

"Cut the crap! You've already won a million times."

"No, Mister, I'm sorry, but you're wrong. Till now I've never won, don't ask me to explain, it's just the way it is."

I was about to ask, and I freeze. I don't know what else to say. It's ridiculous the way he changed his mind in half a day, but what's even more ridiculous is that until yesterday I would have done anything to sabotage him (and I actually did a couple of times), but now that he's telling me this stuff about wanting to win, I don't care one way or the other. Who am I fooling? I'm listening and I'm happy. Maybe for Dad, who'll otherwise turn into an alcoholic and die penniless by the smelliest spot on the irrigation ditch. Maybe for the glory of Muglione, which risked missing even this train to fame. Maybe I don't know why I'm happy and don't want to keep asking.

"Uh...Mister, now that you're awake, can I ask you something?"

"Fire away, but be quick."

"Why do you guys hate old people?"

I clam up, study him, he has the same stupid look on his face. "What?"

"Last night you were talking about an anti-seniors gang, you and your friends, and..."

"Come on, you misunderstood, I already told you we were just bullshitting."

"But there was that huge dummy in the car, what did you do with it?"

"What do you care?"

"I don't know, but I do, a lot."

"What a pain in the ass. It was a toy for Giuliano's nephew, he bought it for his birthday."

The Little Champ nods, says nothing for a second, looks down and lowers his voice. "Mister, I don't want to make you mad, but you guys were saying you were going to take it to the cemetery."

"..."

"I'm sorry, I didn't mean to listen, but your friend Giuliano has a really loud voice."

"All right, already, we put it in the cemetery. Near the cemetery. There's this thing...a kind of dumpster to put clothing for the poor...and toys, too...Actually, no, there's nothing there, we put it in the cemetery because we felt like it, okay? Are you happy now?"

Mirko puts together the pieces of his bed and lies on them. "No, Mister, not really."

"No? So what the fuck do you want? You got a problem?"

"No. Well, yes. You see, it's like when I told you there was no special reason why I used your Sylvester glass, and I think we were each telling a lie." Then he turns the other way. That bastard.

"I knew it! I knew it, damn it!" Now I'm the one who jumps up and sits on the cot. "You know everything about the glass, you know everything! Tell me what you know, you little shit!"

"I'm sorry, Mister, I'd rather not."

"Tell me what you know or I'll break your head open, asshole!"

"No, Mister, please, don't."

"Then tell me what you know."

"Let's make a deal. I'll tell you why I use your Sylvester glass and you tell me about the dummy and the anti-seniors gang."

I look at him, all I can see is his narrow back lying straight on the floor, with this head of thick curls on top that looks like a dust bunny gathering under the bed.

"Okay, deal. But you go first because I don't trust you."

"Okay, I'll go first, Mister, because I do trust you." He turns toward me, one second and he's already sitting. Now we're face-to-face, no more bullshit.

"Well, Mister, I'm going to tell you something, but I don't want to make you mad..."

"It depends on what you tell me, go ahead."

"First I want to say that I like your dad. Not as much as I like you, but I really like him. But I like you even more, Mister."

"Okay, I get it, now tell me about the glass and cut the crap."

"Yes, you're right. Well, there's this thing your dad does, not on purpose, but a lot of times when we're eating it gets to me. I'm not fussy, at home we're four boys and two are older than me and you can't believe the stuff they do at the table. But with Mr. Roberto what really bothers me is that when we're eating he talks and explains what I have to do in the races, or at practice the next day, but he's got his mouth full and you can see all the stuff he's chewing inside. And when he drinks it's the same, he guzzles down his water and talks, then he sets his glass down and there inside the water are these pieces of food floating, I see them and I feel like I'm going to be sick."

The whole time I'm nodding my head. I have no idea what any of this dad stuff has to do with my Sylvester glass, but let's see where it's going.

"Well, sometimes it even bothers me to drink from a clean glass because I think maybe Mr. Roberto used it with all those pieces of food floating in it. Then one day I looked in the cupboard and I saw the Sylvester glass way in the back. I was sure Mr. Roberto had never used it, so I took it and I decided to use only that glass, and when I go to bed at night I take it with me for safety. That's why it's in my room, Mister."

Which is actually *my* room, by the way, but I don't say that because I'm not sure the story is over, though I think it is.

"That's it? That's why you use it?"

"Yes, Mister, why?"

"Do you mean it or is this more of your bullshit?"

"No, I swear, see?" He crosses his index fingers over his mouth and kisses them. I used to do the same thing when I was little. With only one index finger it doesn't work so well anymore.

"So why didn't you tell me before?"

"I . . . was afraid you'd get offended if I told you how your dad drank."

"What the fuck do I care about my dad, how can I get it through your head that I don't give a shit about him?"

"Yes, I'm sorry, Mister, you already said that. It's just that it doesn't seem like that, so I don't know how to act."

"It doesn't seem like what, like I don't give a shit?"

"Yes, it doesn't seem like that to me."

"What the fuck do you know? You're just a kid from some shithole and you think you know more about me than me? I don't give a shit about my dad, I—"

"I believe you, Mister, I do. It's just that it doesn't seem like that to me, but if you say so it must be true. I'm sorry. And I'm sorry for interrupting you, but I really want to hear the story about the old people and that dummy. I'm sorry."

"Sorry, my ass! You're getting to be too much of a wiseass, so I'm not telling you anything."

Mirko lowers his head, looks at me from beneath his curls with those eyes of a little bird at the fair.

"What a shame, Mister, I'm sorry, because I really wanted to know," he says.

And now I remember exactly what kind of bird he reminds me of: a finch. The littlest bird of all, and they pack so many of them into tiny cages that at every fair one or two don't make it. There are always two or three on the lowest perch, with their little heads tucked into their breasts, trembling all over. Who knows where they throw them away when they die. Maybe they feed them to another animal. At any rate, I'm looking at one right now, and maybe he is just an incredible actor and a world-record-holding son of a bitch, but when I look at him I can't get angry, just the opposite, out of nowhere my tongue is untied and I can't get the words out fast enough.

So I end up telling him the whole story about the dummy at the cemetery and even about the hedgehog and the fake anti-seniors gang, and when I get to the end I don't stop, I'm on a roll and I look around and keep telling him things that have less to do with the story and then things that have nothing to do with it that I never tell anyone.

There are words that stay inside us, buried deep inside our guts, and they spend a lifetime down there without ever coming out. But they are connected by a kind of string, and if by chance one word gets loose and comes out of our mouths, the rest come tumbling after.

MOMMY DEAREST

Of the thousand ways you could come up with to punish yourself, going to your parents' is the most excruciating. Especially today, with your dad away, it's just you and your mom at the kitchen table.

The house is big—four bedrooms, two bathrooms, a den in the cellar and a spacious living room—but Mom is always in the kitchen. It's the only place where, even if she's not working, she *could* work. So she feels less guilty.

It's almost like what you used to do before finals in college. You would study from seven in the morning till one o'clock, take an hour-long lunch break, and go for another round till eight. After dinner you didn't study because you were tired, but if someone asked you to the movies you'd say no because even if it was okay not to study after dinner, going out would have made you feel too guilty.

It's more or less the same with your mom. And every time you find something in common with her, your heart stops cold.

"He's always running around," she says. "He goes to all the fairs, and if there's no fairs then it's a town festival or a bike race. As long as he's not home he's happy."

"I know, Mom, but it's his job, and he's good at it. I mean, look at this house..."

"True, but he should start to think about retiring. We've got a nice little nest egg, so anytime he's ready."

"You can tell he still wants to work."

"I'll tell you what he wants, don't get me started." She leaves it at that but makes a couple of noises that sound like a submarine coming up for air: *whoo, whoo.* She nods to herself, as if to agree with the discussion going on in her head.

Your mom is all wrinkles and bones and white hair on top of her head like a giant bag of popcorn. Her face is so leathery that if she ever cracked a smile it would tear a gash all the way up to her cheekbones. No need to worry about that, because the last time she smiled was on a Saturday night in September 1990.

You were about to turn thirteen and you remember it perfectly. The comedian Gigi Sabani was on TV and your mom must have been in a good mood, because at one point he put on quiz-show host Mike Bongiorno's oversize glasses, took out his clipboard, and everyone knew, even you, who were only thirteen, what he was about to shout with his arms in the air. All the same, when Sabani raised his arm and put the mic to his mouth and shouted *Allegriaaaaa!* your mom burst into a long, hearty laugh that you had never heard before. You and your dad looked at each other, shocked at this unrepeatable, cosmic event, which has, in fact, never been repeated since that Saturday night in 1990.

But now, out of nowhere, you gasp at a terrible thought: on that fateful day when your mom laughed, Fiorenzo hadn't yet been born. You were almost thirteen and had a nice collection of cassette tapes, your favorite book was *The Diary of Anne Frank,* and you felt stupid because you were almost the only girl in your class who still hadn't made out with a boy. And Fiorenzo wasn't even alive. Oh God, oh God...

"And do you know what your daddy wants to do now?" Your mom's nasal voice snaps you out of your thoughts. But she is doing you a favor this time. "He wants to start working at night, too. He says there are nightclubs in Montecatini where people go and when they come out they're hungry, so you can sell a ton of sandwiches. But I can tell you what's really going on around there."

"Why, what's going on?" you ask, although you already know what she's going to say.

"Figure it out for yourself, Tiziana. What's in Montecatini?"

"I don't know, spas?"

"No."

"The racetrack?"

"Stop acting stupid. Montecatini is where the hookers are. And your dad wants to work there at night, get it? Where you find those home-wrecking Russian hookers. Don't you remember what happened to Caterina's husband? And to Mrs. Balducci's husband? Now he's in Cuba because he went nuts for a girl who worked at a nightclub."

"Yes, but Dad doesn't go to nightclubs, he stays in his food truck."

"What difference does it make? The hookers throw themselves at anyone, what do they care where he sleeps? But there you are with your head in the clouds as usual, thinking everyone's sweet and kind. And when you get screwed, you feel hurt and come running home to cry."

You were about to reply, but you bite your tongue. Better to drop it. You already made the mistake of coming here, at least try to avoid the slippery slope of the usual tit for tat. It'll only take your mom a second to roll out thirty years of episodes and fragments of episodes that she always remembers in whatever way she feels like, and she spits them out at you in a dense, clear, and sharp shower that feels like hydrochloric acid.

Raffaella was right: *Why the fuck are you going to your mom's? Even your dad's always running around to avoid her, so why the fuck are you going there?*

Yes, as simple as that. Just as your mom finds everything difficult and wrong from the start, for Raffaella every situation is simple.

And in fact, when you told her about last night, about you and Fiorenzo in your room and the condom, Raffaella laughed. She called you a slut and laughed. And she asked you how he was hung. You laughed a little, too, and said he wasn't half bad. She asked you if next time you could make it last at least a minute, you answered that you didn't know if there would be a next time, she called you an idiot and laughed at all your doubts, then she was about to say something else but she stopped to look at you, tense and anxious, and started laughing again and that was that.

That's the way Raffaella is. The other day she wanted to die because Pavel had decided to hook up with a coworker, but then he came back to her with a bouquet of red roses, and it was so obvious that the coworker wanted nothing to do with him so he went running back to Raffaella to avoid being left high and dry. Raffaella hugged and kissed him and changed from sadness to jumping for joy. And you can't tell if she's stupid or simply prefers to turn a blind eye to things she doesn't like. But she certainly is happy, that's for sure.

And what about you, are you happy? No. Are you any less stupid? No. So...

"It's easy for him, very easy...," your mom says. For her the word *easy* has to be spit out like the seed of a sour lemon she bit into by mistake. "Always running around in that truck of his, one day here one day there. On Sunday I was supposed to go on a trip, too, you know, to Assisi with the parish, it was only twenty euros, and lunch was included."

"So what happened?"

"Nothing. I didn't go."

"Why not?"

"*Why not? Why not?*" She mimics your question with a tight mouth and an idiot's voice. You hate her when she does that, at times like this you really hate her.

You resist the temptation to take one of her very clean, very dry dishes and smash it into her teeth. You take a breath and say, "What I wanted to know, Mom, is why you didn't go to Assisi if you wanted to."

"Simple, Tiziana, because I couldn't. It was a Sunday and who would stay home to cook for your dad, you? You weren't around, you never are. And him, the few times he is home you should hear how he complains if he's not happy with his food. And do you want to know something? In the end he didn't even eat at home. He went to Pistoia because there was a race, and that was that."

Your mom finishes torturing the silverware and puts it away in the drawer, sorting out the forks, knives, and spoons. All facing upward, knife blades to the right. Sometimes she's such a stereotypical sixty-year-old mother with a bug up her ass that you wonder whether she's real. Unfortunately she is, she's here, and she's your mom.

"Well, if he wasn't here, you could have gone to Assisi."

"Of course, why not, at the last minute. They always save a free seat for you if your head's in the clouds, right, Tiziana?"

"Did you ask if there were any free seats?"

"No, I didn't, but I know there weren't. Anyway, how do you think it would look if I changed my mind at the last minute, when I had already said I wasn't going? What would they think?"

You don't answer, you say nothing. Your mom has her back to you, arranging the silverware in the drawer, and you get up, take your bag, and leave the kitchen. Maybe she thinks you're going to the living room or the bathroom, but no, you leave the house. Through the garden then into the street; you get in the car, turn the key, and leave. Without saying goodbye. Without saying anything.

The only upside to talking with a person who thinks you're stupid, a misfit, even abnormal, is that you don't have to worry about making a bad impression when you leave.

THE PHYSICALLY ATTRACTIVE
NEED NOT APPLY

Wahhhhhhhhhhhhhhhhhhhhhhhhhhhh!

A double drumbeat ending on a roll from hell, the bass pounding all around us and my high-pitched shriek getting higher and more satanic. Wow, what an ending—I'm scared of myself. We've become a sensational band practicing a song for the first time and bringing it home with terrifying power.

At first the song was called "Cannibal Apocalypse" but now it's "Killer of Old People." To make our name a little more suspicious, even if I don't think we're succeeding. We haven't heard a single word or comment about the hedgehog in front of the post office, or about the effigy of an old man hanging in the cemetery. Doesn't anybody care? Everyone's going on and on about this senior patrol watching out for the anti-seniors gang, but when the gang comes out in the open, they don't care.

Nobody except the Little Champion, he's almost too interested. He was asking so many questions I started to suspect he wanted to rat us out. So I told him if he squealed I'd split his head open and he asked who could he rat us out to, so I said to the *police*, and then he said it hadn't even crossed his mind. So I said, *Better keep it that way, better keep it that way.* And maybe right now I'm feeling a little weaker than usual, it must be that this Tiziana situation is messing with my head, but I actually do believe the Little Champion.

He's interested in this story about the anti-seniors gang because it really is interesting, and what's ridiculous is that neither *The Tyrrhenian* nor *La Nazione* seems to care. They're full of write-ups about festivals, columns on Tuscan food, and nasty articles about Mirko and about Dad, and how it was all very well to talk about a Little Champion, but when push came to shove, he made us all look like idiots in a neighboring region. And not a word about the gang.

Maybe we're in too much of a hurry. It was too soon for last night's dummy to be in the paper, maybe it'll make the front page tomorrow. All we have to do is wait. It's just a matter of time, and if there's one thing we've got in Muglione it's time.

Right now we're lying low in the garage and practicing, even if at the cemetery we wrote that tonight would be the night of the massacre. No sense putting too many irons on the fire. Let's wait and see.

And it's not as if we're doing nothing. Giuliano got Stefano to give him a big chunk of money, went to Florence to a store that sold period costumes, and picked out three amazing uniforms for Metal Devastation. They have shiny black satin capes with hoods and a red ax stenciled on the chest: from now on we're going to play in this getup. That's right, we'll be entering into the hard-core heavy metal category of masked bands — such a great idea I can't believe we didn't think of it sooner.

And there's more. Tomorrow night we're going to start walking around town in costume. I checked myself out in it in the store bathroom, and I swear I freaked myself out. Can you imagine what effect we're going to have at night, pitch black with the usual fog and the yellow streetlamps illuminating three black, hooded figures with axes on their chests ... The first person who sees us is going to drop dead, but if he survives, he'll tell the whole town about us, so the name Metal Devastation will be engraved on everyone's minds.

And if this stuff with the costumes doesn't raise some suspicions, I don't know what we're going to do. We might have to wait for the International Day of the Elderly to go to church and throw ourselves on the altar yelling *Death to seniors* in front of the whole town. But I'd rather avoid it. Not to mention that the Day of the Elderly won't be for a while yet.

And Tiziana would find out about it immediately, since she works at the Youth Center and spends so much time with the elderly. She doesn't want to be with a grungy kid who's minus one hand and lasts all of one second in bed, so I can imagine the fact that I belong to a secret sect aimed at eradicating retirees won't help my cause. Though she hates seniors even more than I do, so maybe ... ah, I don't know, I don't know anything. I don't even know when I'll be seeing Tiziana again, *if* I'll be seeing her again.

Well, actually, I'll be seeing her tomorrow, because I have a plan. Except I don't know if she'll be happy to see me. My plan is genius, because it's all well and good that we're Metal Devastation and we kick ass even without a guitar player, but tomorrow morning we still need to put up flyers around town to see if we can find one. At bars in stores at bus stops and even at high school, where they've taken us for a complete joke ever since the festival, but fuck them: we don't give a shit.

I could even put up a flyer at the Youth Center ... *Sorry, Tiziana, it's not that I wanted to see you, it's just that we urgently need a guitar player, we don't even have to talk if you prefer, just give me a second to hang this thing up and then I'll disappear, okay?*

Oh, and by the way, how are you, what did you do today, are you busy tonight?

Genius.

A genius ad, too:

ACCLAIMED HEAVY METAL BAND SEEKING GUITAR PLAYER
MINIMUM 18 YEARS MAXIMUM 21, WILLING TO TRAVEL
FOR CONCERTS ALSO ABROAD, MUST HAVE TECHNIQUE
AND MORE IMPORTANT BE FIERCE AND HARD CORE.
SERIOUS APPLICANTS ONLY. THE PHYSICALLY ATTRACTIVE
NEED NOT APPLY.

But for tonight we're fine, just the three of us. Kicking ass and sweating and getting bigger and bigger, and as for what's out there we could give two shits.

The seniors can sleep easy tonight.

THE DEVIL'S NIGHTMARE

Darkness. Actually, not just darkness; it's pitch black, a moon-less night with a few shabby stars, as dim as the flickering lights on the tombstones beyond the gate. The fog sweeps over the ground and the branches, spreading slowly, carrying the smell of dead flowers all the way behind the willow, the only tree in the area, and the only place to hide.

Being surrounded by the same fog that passed among the tombstones and the photos of the deceased makes them feel strange, they hang back a little to listen to the sounds rising up from the grass or from who knows where. After half an hour of silence and shivering, the wine kicked in, and now the four Guardians are pretty loose.

"What do you mean, it's the style, they're naked, for crying out loud, *naked*. And if tomorrow it becomes fashionable for men to walk around with their dicks out like in Africa, would you still go along with it?" Baldato speaks, the others shake their heads no. "No, it's slutty, and if it's fashionable to walk around with your ass hanging out, then that means it's fashionable to be a tart."

Physically the idea of the night watch might kill them, but morally it makes them feel like kids. Young partisans hiding, waiting to spring an ambush.

It all started this morning, when Repetti's son woke up and decided to go boar hunting. He's the caretaker of the Muglione cemetery, but some mornings he wakes up with shaky hands and has to go shoot, to keep himself under control. It doesn't matter if the season is over, or if the cemetery has to be opened. He calls his dad and goes. So Repetti Senior steps in to open the cemetery, as he did for forty years before handing down the job to his son.

He was already out this morning with the Guardians for the dawn patrol, at the end of which he asked the others for a ride, so they all came together to the cemetery. The vision of that dead man hanging motionless in the air, against the light at the end of the unpaved road, made their hearts stop for a moment.

And when they realized it was an effigy it scared them even more. An effigy of an old man with gray hair, hanging in front of the cemetery, hovering over a threatening sign written in red:

NIGHT WILL FALL ON THIS NIGHT
AND THE CEMETERY WILL BE YOUR HOME.
THE NATIONAL REJUVENATION BRIGADE
    METAL D.

"STINKIN'—NAZIS," Mazinger said while touching the dummy with a stick. "OH—HE—EVEN—HAS—A—FANNY—PACK—LIKE—US."

"Guys, I made the whole story up," said Repetti. "I swear on the Blessed Virgin Mary."

"YEAH—BUT—THESE—GUYS—EXIST—FOR—REAL."

"Yeah, they exist, Baldato said, "but not for long, 'cause we're gonna get 'em tonight."

"..."

"Guys, we've got one of two choices: either we make an early counterattack, or these assholes will get the better of us. The sign speaks clearly: tonight, here, so we'll come back after dinner and set up our grand ambush, what do you say?"

Divo thought for a second. They were supposed to meet a journalist yesterday for a special on the Guardians. The journalist needed a photo of each member, so Divo spent the night looking for one where he came out better. Then the journalist called and said he had to cover other news so everything was being postponed to who knows when. A nurse from Verona is pregnant with her own son's child, an abandoned dog in Biella finds its way down to the shrine of Padre Pio and falls asleep next to the museum. Every day tons of new, sensational things happen, so the Guardians will have to be put on the back burner. Unless they come up with something new, something big.

"Count me in." Divo shook Baldato's hand and Mazinger nodded his head. Repetti would have preferred to say no, but at that point he couldn't back down.

They spent the whole day studying the best place to hide, and now they're here in the dark behind the weeping willow, scanning the cemetery.

Because it's night. No, it's the night on which *night will fall*.

Holy shit.

"What if there are a lot of them?" Repetti asks.

"Then we'll hide, get it, we'll take their pictures and bring them to the police." Divo shows them his camera, an old contraption that still uses film. "If there are a lot of them, we take pictures. And if not, we clobber them."

Everyone nods in agreement, but Repetti gets the shakes. Shaking and sweating at the same time. He spent forty years of his life in that cemetery, more years than the number of corpses buried there. He ate there, watched TV there, and went to the bathroom there a million times. But at night the cemetery becomes another place. He knows this and is worried.

The others, however, are guzzling down the wine and talking as if they were at the bar.

"PASS — ME — THE — PECORINO," says Mazinger, who is immediately hushed because his metallic croak is too loud. It echoes in the dark and is really creepy.

The silence returns but is broken by a distant crunching of footsteps on the gravel. Steady footsteps, distant but getting closer and closer, slowly and surely.

"Jesus Christ. Who the hell is that?"

"Who do you think? Guess."

Repetti doesn't answer or try to guess. At night anything can happen at the cemetery, anything.

Divo and Baldato stare into the darkness and reach for their bats. Mazinger's breathing sounds like a pump inflating a punctured ball. They remain silent amid the constant chatter of the crickets and the steps marching in time, getting louder and louder and slower and slower, the footsteps of someone dragging his feet and in no hurry to reach his destination. Maybe because he has all the time in the world, maybe because nothing can stop him.

"What, only one guy? So the big brigade consists of a single idiot?"

"I dunno, maybe he's the leader." Divo struggles to sound confident, but it's hard because his heart is pounding.

"Or maybe it's not the brigade," Repetti says, barely able to get his words out.

"Then who is it at this hour of the night at the cemetery, a ghost?"

"It's nothing to laugh about, Divo."

"What, you believe in ghosts, Repetti?"

"Yes, I do. Very much."

"You? Who worked at the cemetery?"

"Yes, and that's why. Believe me, I know what I'm talking about, believe..."

He quiets down. Everyone does, listening only to the footsteps that make their skin crawl along with the dampness of the night and the smell of the soil. The hard soil of the fields and the softer, overturned soil down where the tombstones are. And just when the Guardians' hearts can pound no harder, the mysterious footsteps take shape. Down there in the dark the outline of a figure appears, moving closer, leaning forward, completely black and hooded.

And then the pounding of their hearts is joined by the churning of their stomachs.

"Holy shit!" says one, it doesn't matter who. They squat down even lower, their bones creaking.

"Oh, Jesus," says Repetti. "Jesus, Mary, and Joseph."

The figure is as black as night, with a hood covering its face. It comes closer, walking slowly, then it stops. It's carrying something white in its hand, but you can't see the hand, so it's maybe just bone, and under the cloak maybe a skeleton. Or the Devil. Or his evil assistant.

Whatever it is, it has ended its slow procession and is standing before the cemetery gate. It looks inside, its back to the Guardians, stands there motionless for a minute, and then slowly raises its arms.

"What's it doing?"

"It's calling the dead," Repetti gasps.

"What?"

"The writing was clear, *the cemetery will be your home*...now it's going to open the tombs and prepare them for us, oh my God!"

"What the fuck are you talking about?"

"Yes, it's like that night, I never told you this but one night I saw a tomb being...It was dark, I heard a thump and then scraping against wood and something inside scratching and...oh my God, oh my God..."

"Hey, save it for another time, right now we're gonna go see what the hell that thing is."

"Divo, are you crazy? You don't know what you're getting into!"

"Get a grip, it's the four of us and we have bats, you'll see how we're gonna fix your ghost."

Baldato grips the handle as tightly as he can. It's all metal and shaped like a lion's head, perfect for whopping a ghost.

In the meantime the dark figure puts its arms down, takes the white thing it was holding in its hand, and places it against the gate. And maybe it's the effect of that whiteness or maybe some other horrifying reason, but the lights on the tombstones are glowing brighter.

"Jesus, shine your light on me," says Repetti. Even Mazinger is saying things, but without putting the device to his throat, so he sounds like a gasping fish.

"So, me and Baldato are going that way," says Divo. "You go this way toward the figure, so when it sees you it runs in our direction. Got it?"

"But...what if it doesn't run?"

"So much the better, we'll surround it."

"And what if it charges into us?"

"Run and we'll get it."

"But I'm slow," says Repetti. Mazinger nods in agreement, points to himself and makes a sucking sound, as if to say he isn't too fast either.

"Don't worry, we're here and we've got the bats. First we whack him to subdue him, then we talk. Now let's cut the crap and get on with it, go go go..."

"Jesus, Mary, and Joseph," says Repetti, adding a sign of the cross and standing up at the same time as Mazinger. They turn one last time toward Divo and Baldato, who have already disappeared into the dark, and start off. They move to the right, like thieves in the night, trying to reach the corner of the cemetery farthest from the dark figure.

But in the silence of the night it's impossible not to be heard. The hooded phantom stops, leaves the white thing hanging from the gate, and turns toward them.

"Okay, now!" Divo and Baldato come running with their bats straight up in the air. The figure sees them, too, but holds its ground. It doesn't move. It doesn't do anything. It lets the two with the bats advance toward it, and when they're only one step away it raises its arms to the sky and lets out a terrifying howl.

"ROOOAAAAAAAAARRRRRRRRRRGH!"

The crickets stop singing, two dull thuds land in the silence of the clearing. A few empty seconds, then the crickets start up again with their love song, because it is in their nature and they could care less about what happens to humans. Nature goes on as it pleases, straight down its path, singing.

And it doesn't care if something might be lying there dead on the ground.

THE TALE OF VLADIMIR

The smaller the hospital or cemetery, the better: it means that the people in that town don't get so busted up or die too often. But the emergency room in Pisa is bigger than an Olympic stadium.

There's a glass door at the entrance that opens automatically when you arrive, then a wall of vending machines for coffee, soft drinks, and sandwiches and a blue door in the back that opens in only one direction, leading to the emergency room. The injured vanish on a stretcher behind that door, the anxious stay behind in this gigantic room walking in circles and shaking their heads.

It's night now and in addition to me there are five Chinese guys asleep in a corner, a sixtyish woman making call after call without speaking, and a guy with bags under his eyes who might be here only for the coffee. An emergency room this big is a bad sign for a city.

When I was a little boy my dad would tell me a story every night before I went to sleep, it's weird and seems impossible now that I think about it, my dad sitting next to the bed to tell me a story, but I swear that's exactly what happened. People change, for better or worse depending on the period, and during that period Dad would sit next to me and tell me this tale

episode by episode where there was once a guy named Vladimir who traveled the world on a donkey that sometimes had no
name and sometimes was called Panizza. Every night Vladimir
would stop somewhere and witness an injustice or a catastrophe that he always managed somehow to fix. Then, when the
townspeople praised him and asked him to stay and be their
local hero, he would look around and see the cemetery and ask:
Excuse me, but what's that? They would answer that it was the
town cemetery, then he would shake his head and wave goodbye
and head off on his donkey to another far-flung corner of the
world. Because Vladimir was looking for the place where you
never die.

And now it's three o'clock in the morning and I'm in this
gigantic waiting room in a hospital as big as a small city, I'm
thinking about that story and if I were Vladimir I would thank
everyone and make a beeline for the exit.

But I'm not Vladimir, and I don't even have a donkey. I'm
Fiorenzo and I came to Pisa on my moped, and I'm not leaving
until I know how Mirko is doing.

He was brought here by Divo, the old guy who used to fix televi-
sions. He said he was taking a walk near the cemetery, around
midnight, and out of nowhere a guy dressed in black appeared.
Divo had a walking stick and he was so scared that he struck the
guy but then realized it was Mirko.

His story doesn't add up, but who cares. I can already figure
out what really happened, probably even better than Divo and
the other Guardians waiting outside, hiding at the far end of the
parking lot in Mazinger's Panda. The only thing I don't know
is what the fuck Mirko was thinking. He put on the cape with

the red ax on the front and wrote death to seniors on a piece of cardboard and then walked all the way to the cemetery. Why did he go, what did he think he was doing? Maybe when they let me see him he'll explain, but I'm not holding out much hope.

I get up, I stretch, I walk in a circle. I'm uncomfortable sitting, I'm uncomfortable standing, I'm nervous and tense, and I feel like I'm suffocating. And with good reason.

I've been in this hospital a few times for the usual treatments and exams and stuff, but especially because this is where I found out that I had only one hand left, and where I later found out that Mom had died. So obviously in here I feel like the Christians being led into the Colosseum.

Maybe I should go out, yes, I'll wait outside in the parking lot in the open air. Maybe I can have a chat with the Guardians to kill time. I turn toward the exit and see a hand waving in the dark, waving hello. I try to figure out who it is, I squint, take aim, and fire: it's Tiziana.

I stop dead in my tracks in the middle of the waiting room, and my mind launches various missile-like thoughts, fired in such disparate directions that I can't follow them. All I can do is stand here and wonder how she found out about Mirko, even though it was me who sent her the text.

She walks quickly down the ramp. She's wearing a light-green dress and her hips are swaying from side to side. It's so beautiful to see, even in a situation like this, even in a place like this. Actually, the contrast with the surrounding ugliness highlights it to dangerous levels, at least for me.

But just before she enters, the blue door at the other end of the room bursts open with a loud screech. A man in a white coat appears and yells, "Mirko Colonna's brother, Mirko Colonna's brother." He looks at me and points to me, I look at him a second, yes, it's me. He tells me I can come in, but by myself, on the double. He's rude and it pisses me off, but I thank him anyway when I walk by. In hospitals there's no such thing as people having dignity and defending it with their teeth. In hospitals either you cave in or you die. Or both at the same time.

"Mister, I'm sorry, I'm so sorry." The batteries are dying in Mirko's voice and he ends each utterance with a sigh. "I'm so, so sorry."

"What the fuck were you thinking?"

"You see, Mister, it's that I really liked your plan a whole lot and I didn't understand why you didn't want to do anything last night. I thought it would be better to be there every night, Mister, to scare those friggin' old folks."

"You thought wrong."

"Yes, that's true. Now I know."

"Yeah, but you had to go and break your leg before you realized it."

"Yes, it sure looks like it, Mister, I'm sorry."

Because this is how it went down: a hard blow fractured his tibia. And now he's here on a hospital bed under a green and gray blanket, and his leg is sticking out from one side, wrapped in this white stuff that's holding the broken limb in place. They even put a plastic cap on his head, I don't know why. I guess the sight of his frizzy, curly hair was so nasty that the nurses decided to stuff it into the cap. Then he showed me a dark bruise on his shoulder, from the first blow, the one that knocked him to the ground. He says it felt like a lion jumping him in the savanna, and he says it with a lot of satisfaction. The possibility that the Little Champ isn't faking but really is a moron is getting more believable by the minute.

"Now I'm going to miss practice, and I feel bad. Even today I did so many kilometers. I stopped by the clubhouse and the others were ready to go, but Mr. Roberto wasn't there."

I know, boy do I know. As soon as they called me from the emergency room I called my dad: it must have been two o'clock in the morning and he said he was watching TV, as if I didn't know he had smashed it against the wall. And then all those frog voices in the background told me that in reality, at two in the morning, Dad was still by the ditch near the dump, fishing without bait.

"Oh, he went fishing today," I say.

"He did? Did he catch anything?"

"I don't know."

"I hope so, I would really like to go fishing, too... In the end he never showed up at the clubhouse so the other boys went home. But I did a hundred and fifty kilometers instead."

"Are you stupid? That's too much, you'll hurt yourself."

I know, Mister, except that I told myself, *When I'm tired I'll go home.* Then I saw the hours tick by and I still wasn't tired, so I said at a hundred fifty I'd stop. Except that now I'll be missing every practice, I'm really sorry."

I nod my head. I want to tell him that practice is called off but I don't want to bullshit him. It'd be more truthful to tell him not to worry because after a fracture like that he'll probably never race again, but I keep it to myself. It's not like you always have to tell the truth. Sometimes the truth sucks so bad it should be left alone in a corner to reflect on what it's done.

"Mister, I'm sorry, can I ask you a question? I was thinking, now that I broke my leg, like, when I go back to riding do you think I'll be a little weaker?" He asks me so cheerfully and hope-fully that I think I've misunderstood.

"Come again? I mean, in what sense?"

"I mean..." He sits straight up in the bed. He's totally ener-gized, I really don't get this kid. He's got a broken leg and we're at the hospital because he got beat up in front of the cemetery, but you'd think we were celebrating his birthday. "Do you think that when I get back on my bike maybe I'll be a little slower?"

"Ah... well, how would I know? Unfortunately that's pos-sible. Let's wait and see."

"I hope so, Mister, I really hope so."

"You hope what, that you're weaker than before?"

"Yes, I thought about it, and in my opinion it is possible. I mean, in my opinion it could really slow me down, it could make me weaker." His smile is too wide for his teeth and reveals his gums.

"But didn't you just say that you liked winning?"

Yes, I did, Mister, it's true. And I really hope I will become weaker, but not as weak as normal people."

I try to understand what the Little Champ is talking about, but I already know it's impossible. Then the door opens behind me, I turn around, and Tiziana appears with a smile. So I sit there staring at her and my mind goes blank.

A FAMILY OF SWEDES

Hello, good morning, it's a pleasure to meet you. Unfortunately Mr. Roberto Marelli was unable to reschedule a very important meeting he had in Milan with Italian sports directors who are fighting for clean competitions. He will be back tomorrow, and in the meantime he has asked me, his son and also a manager of the team, to take charge of Mirko and all of his needs at this critical time.

This is the story I told Mirko's parents, in the hallway in front of his room in the orthopedic ward, while they nodded in agreement with tired eyes staring into a space that reeked of hospital, with its smell of alcohol and boiled potatoes mixed together. I had also prepared some other statements to answer any questions, I even had written notes, but I didn't need them. They asked no questions, showed no curiosity, and in the end I could have probably even told them the truth about the situation. Namely, that it wasn't a very good idea to see my dad because they'd find themselves face-to-face with a dirty drunk who had spent the past day and a half living next to an irrigation ditch by the dump, leaving it up to me to take care of their little boy, me, who up until a day ago had been plotting for him to flunk out and lose races and who had hated him more than anyone else on earth.

So maybe I couldn't tell them exactly what the situation was. But they had no objections, they stood there listening to what I had to say without a sound and everyone was fine. A little bit too fine, if you ask me. I mean, it didn't look like they cared a whole lot. They went into the room, saw Mirko again, and said hello and hugged, but all in a stiff, standoffish way that wouldn't even suit a Swedish family visiting a second cousin twice removed.

I spied on them through the crack of the door and thought about what it would have been like at fifteen if I had been away for months and my mom had come to see me. Shouts, tears, hugs, more tears, more hugs. Even the doctor who came to see Mirko before lunch was more enthusiastic. He's a cycling buff who complimented him and asked if it was true that once, toward the end of a race, his front wheel came off but he still won by popping a wheelie for the last two hundred meters.

It's true.

But later the same doctor told me that Mirko's cycling days were over.

It's very, very unlikely he will ever be able to compete again. I'd say impossible, but I would also have said it was impossible to win a race with only one wheel. I'd settle for him keeping both feet on the ground and setting a reasonable target, i.e., not to remain crippled. You see, there's a risk he will remain crippled, and that he'll have to drag this disability around for the rest of his life, and you know how difficult a situation like that can be.

That's what he said, I swear, and he pointed at my right wrist even though I had it in my pocket the whole time. He took off his glasses, wiped them on his sleeve, smiled, and left. This is why I admire doctors, tough guys who have seen it all and don't beat around the bush.

After lunch, Tiziana was supposed to make an appearance. Last night she spent a long time with me in the waiting room while Mirko was sleeping in his room. We talked about a lot of stuff, nice and easy, no problem. As if nothing had ever happened between us and there was no unfinished business, just two friends who had a good reason for being where they were and chatting in the meantime. But then when she left she kissed me on the lips, and I swear my mind went blank.

Anyway, the plan was that at lunchtime Tiziana would come back to play the part of team comanager to put Mirko's parents even more at ease. Except there was no need, since they grabbed some lunch at the hospital snack bar, brought an ice cream to their boy, and spoke with him a little while longer before getting up to leave. They said the rehabilitation facilities here were better, and that according to the doctors a long trip would be too stressful for him, that they had to run home but would be back real soon.

I listened to them without saying a word, gritting my teeth with rage. A part of me wanted to grab the IV stand and use it to break every bone in their bodies. But another part of me was almost happy those two were shameless enough to leave like that. I don't know why. Actually, I do. I was happy they were leaving without Mirko.

"We're four brothers, Mister," he explains now that we're alone. There are six beds in the room, and his is closest to the door. Two are empty and the other three are occupied by a couple of old men with broken hips and a biker wrapped in bandages who keeps moaning. "There are four of us, I'm the third, I like them all a lot and I'm always thinking about home and what they're up to. But, Mister, I think they're better off without me."

"What are saying, are you stupid? Stop talking bullshit."

"I say it because it's true, Mister. When I was around they were worse off. I mean, when I was really little, I remember we were really happy. There was Mattia, the oldest, who was really good at volleyball. Giuseppe, on the other hand, was great at school. Then I started playing volleyball and going to school, and from the get-go I was a hundred times better than either of them. So they stopped practicing and studying and got dark and moody, and then they started to do a lot of really stupid things, especially Mattia. And then the fights at home started. Mattia and Mom would say mean things to each other. I would listen behind the door and sometimes Mom would catch me there and look at me in a way that made it clear she had it in for me. She said she didn't and would hug me, but she had it in for me."

"Stop talking bullshit, she's your mom, no way does she have it in for you. Why would she, because you're too good?"

"Well, yes, I mean, a little. Once I came straight out and asked if she resented me and she said, *No, Mirko, what are you saying, I love you so much, with all my heart and soul.* Then she looked at me, she had just finished fighting with Mattia because he had stolen a scooter and they wanted to expel him from school, and then Mom said, *It's just that sometimes... sometimes life isn't easy, Mirko. I mean for you it is, for you everything comes easy, but for the others...* And that's when I started to cry, and I hugged her and I said, *I'm sorry, I'm sorry, Mom,* and she said, *For what, what do you have to be sorry for? Nothing.* And so I stopped talking, but if I hadn't been crying so much, I would have told my mom, I would have told her that nothing is easy for me either, Mister, it's not easy at all."

Mirko stops talking, stops looking at me, turns his eyes toward the leg sticking out from under the blanket. Then he lies back and hides his face behind the sheet. While I listened to his story I told him a million times that he was being a jerk and talking bullshit, but in reality I did kind of understand him. And maybe now I kind of understand his parents, too, just enough to not find them as shameless as before.

That's why I don't like knowing too much about people who do bad things. Because when you do, you start to understand them a little and end up being angry and lost, with no one to hate.

THREE MONTHS LATER

Okay, so these things happened in May, and now it's the end of July. Almost three months have gone by and the things we saw on the horizon are now upon us.

Like finals, for instance. For Stefanino it was a stressful time, but not for me, since I wasn't even allowed to take them. No surprise there, no one had seen me at school for months, my grades were below zero, and I didn't even bother checking the bulletin board for them. The only thing I did do was ask Stefano to text me if there were any shocking developments. He never did.

In the meantime Stefanino had decided to stop Photoshopping pictures of the pope. Newspapers had started putting them on the front page, tons of souvenirs were being sold, according to the news the Holy Father's popularity had skyrocketed, and in Mexico there were sightings of him in water stains and on faded, old rags. So Stefanino, who didn't like being a part of this factory of lies, said enough is enough, I don't want to have anything to do with this anymore. And for a month here in Muglione we saw every rank of clergymen driving up in super-luxury cars on a mission to redeem him. Even the bishop of Pisa wanted to talk to him, and so did a foreign cardinal and other monsignors with really weird names. And in the end they

won him over, but it cost them a pretty penny and, more important, an awesome meeting that Stefanino demanded as an absolute prerequisite, so he's going to spend an entire day, on the
tenth of September, I believe, face to face with the pope. That's
what I said, Stefanino with the pope. I don't know what he plans
on saying to him, but whatever it is, this is his chance. Unbelievable, I know, but crazy shit like this happens and only God
knows why, if She exists. Not even the pope knows, otherwise
Stefanino could ask him in September.

And to stay within the realm of the ridiculous, I'm still seeing Tiziana. For two months now we've been together, if that's
what you call it. And I'm still in the back room and I'm looking
at myself in the mirror and I fix my hair because we're going
out in a little while. Tiziana says long hair is for meatheads,
which means that she likes meatheads, because I've got long
hair, and no way in hell am I going to cut it.

The day Mirko was discharged from the hospital, Tiziana
came to visit and then the two of us went out for ice cream. We
talked about lots of things, really vague and nothing personal,
but in the end we kissed. A French kiss, and when we broke
apart I asked her if she had thought about us since she said she
had to think about it.

Yes, I thought about it, but I'm so confused. So I thought that I
shouldn't think about it, at least not now.

I didn't quite get it, but we kissed again and so who cares.
And then I told her that I was practicing with the condoms, I
was getting really good at putting them on. Tiziana said that was
great but I still had time to practice: this time she wanted to take
things slowly, she said.

All right, I'll admit, slow is not my thing, but in the end it
was worth it because one very hot night at the end of June I

got some action. Again we were at her house, but this time it went better, much better. I must admit, it was mostly thanks to Tiziana. She did things to me that a second earlier I didn't even know existed, but once I got a taste I realized I'd been waiting for them all my life. Then it was my turn and she was great at letting me know when I was doing it right and had found a good spot, through the moves and groans coming out of her, and if I didn't get it just right she would tell me directly with words. *Yes, Fiorenzo, like that, yes, there, perfect, no, go back where you were, there, that's perfect, like that, don't stop, perfect like that, oh yes, perfect like that, oh yes.*

The long and short of it is that Tiziana taught me a lot, and I might not like school, but I have to say I really liked her lessons. It might be the subject, or my teacher, but I've made a lot of progress. I've even improved in endurance. The first time it was a whole minute, and the second was even better. The third time for some strange reason was a little worse, barely thirty seconds, but it was Tiziana's fault because she was wearing these bikini panties that looked like they were painted on her ass, and even before starting I knew I wasn't going to get very far.

Mirko ended up not getting very far either, but with his bad leg he's almost always in the back room of the bait-and-tackle shop or in the front with me. But he was promoted, the little asshole. I explained to him that if he ever wanted to race again (because I still didn't have the guts to tell him the whole truth), he couldn't afford to flunk out. He said *Okay, what grade do I have to get?* I thought a B-plus average would keep him safe and at the same time ward off the hatred of his classmates, so he went to school and did all of his work and took all of his quizzes, and every time he got the same exact grade: B-plus.

After his oral exam I went to pick him up on my scooter, we stopped to buy five pastries (two each, plus a bonus to share) and then came back here to celebrate.

He asked me if he could move into the back room with me, he says it's tight but okay, and I thought how ridiculous it was that before I had a beautiful and comfortable home, and he came and kicked me out, then I set myself up in this place and he ended up here with me, and now that he's messed up I've even given him my cot, and now I'm the one sleeping on the floor. But the most ridiculous thing of all is that I'm okay with it.

Anything's better than staying with Dad, who isn't living by the ditch but is back at home, or rather what's left of it: he stuck two pieces of furniture in the middle of the rubble and that was that. And every day he makes his rounds talking to all the doctors about the Little Champ's chances of recovery.

Because one afternoon Mirko asked him when the Golden Cup of Borgo Valsugana was starting, and if the finish line was a bit uphill. Dad asked him what the hell he cared and he answered, *I'd like to break away from the others a little early so I can raise my arms when I win.* Then Dad went crazy and yelled, *He's cured, he's cured*, and started to pester all the hospitals and clinics, he even made overseas phone calls for advice. He often makes me call because I speak English. They don't understand how I can expect them to diagnose a case they haven't even seen, and it's not that easy to understand each other because even though I speak English pretty well I learned it by listening to records, so I know words like *storm, hell, death, violence, murder, metal, sword, battle, rebellion*, and we've had a few communication breakdowns that could sometimes be almost dangerous. It's a good thing that after a while they hang up on me.

This face, this one that's looking at itself in the mirror and smiling. Yes, I put up a mirror because a good look at yourself every once in a while can really come in handy. I even bought a camp stove, so every night Mirko and I cook meat and for lunch we make pasta. To make things easier, I eat what he eats. He's on a strict diet even if everybody is saying *What do you care, take advantage of the situation and eat ice cream, cake, and lasagna.* But not him, he insists on keeping his nose to the grindstone, and every day Dad or Tiziana comes by in a car to take him to physical therapy. The doctors say he should be okay, by which they mean he won't be crippled.

But Mirko's got enough ambition for everybody. He reads cycling books and we watched the whole Tour de France together. I put a TV on the counter and even if it's a little cramped we can still watch the different stages here. Mazinger comes around, too. For a while he disappeared, and then one day he poked his head in the store. Mirko said hello and said he wanted to thank him very much because that night was really important to him. Mazinger said to him: *I—WASN'T—THE—ONE—WHO—HIT—YOU,* and Mirko replied, *Don't worry, Mister, I want to thank you anyway.*

But enough talk and staring at myself in the mirror. I put on my shorts and Carcass T-shirt and say goodbye to Mirko, who's reading the sports page and wearing the team jersey. Tiziana is meeting me in ten minutes in front of her office, and I think that while I dash down the road I just might start singing.

THIS TRAIN
ONLY STOPS TWICE

What do you say, Tiziana, interested? Should I find out for you?
An e-mail from Cheryl, from Birmingham. You answered yes.
Okay, it's worth a shot, should we sign up?
And again you said yes. Besides, signing up is free.
Guess what, Tiziana? It looks like they're going to take us.
And you replied, *Stop pulling my leg, I don't believe you.* And
you don't know whether to believe it or not, but today you got
another e-mail from Cheryl with ten exclamation points in the
subject line. And a whole lot more mixed in with the words,
which explained that her professor was very interested in the
project and that there were European funds just right for this
kind of research, and that by the end of August you would need
to be in Berlin so you could find an apartment together and be
ready to hit the ground running.

Because everything is taking off, Tiziana, everything is actually taking off again. You jumped off the train right before it
was about to arrive at the most important stations and found
yourself in this moldy little town in the middle of nowhere, like
an asshole who missed her connections and has to ask the first
passerby, *Excuse me, but what town is this?*

Yet for some inexplicable, miraculous, and completely unde-
served reason, the train has done a loop and decided to stop

by your station once again, and it's slowing down to let you hop on.

The crazy thing is that you're not even sure you want to take advantage.

After all, you're in a good place now, a pretty good place. Not at first, but now you're getting used to it. You go out with Fiorenzo, who has one hand less and is thirteen years younger than you, and every time you get together your relationship seems a little less ridiculous.

Between the two of you there are a lot of differences, really major differences, but while others might have a problem with it you certainly don't. Not like in the beginning, at least. Of course, the problems are still spinning in your head and you can't pretend they're not, but they're speaking to you in a more faint and wavering voice lately: for once in your life you realize that being in a good place is not impossible, especially when you stop playing against yourself.

But now this e-mail. And the game gets complicated.

Because it's true that *now* you're in a good place, but life isn't just *now*. Time will pass and things will be looking up for Fiorenzo and his world will be getting bigger and he'll be discovering lots of new things. But you, instead, even if the thought overwhelms you, are on a downward slope.

Especially if you remain stuck in this godforsaken hole.

Up to now you dealt with the problem by thinking, *All right, in the meantime let's try to be happy in the moment, let's try to enjoy the here and now.* Except now, in addition to the here and now, there is also a there and then: there's Berlin and a career opportunity in your field. You studied all your life for this, and your future could be the one you've dreamed of ever since the day you enrolled at the university.

In a situation like this how the hell can you think of the here and now?

You reread the e-mail with all the exclamation points. You reach the bottom and start over, reading it for the third time, the fourth, and over and over. Maybe you hope that in the end it'll tell you something different.

BUT IT'S FREEZING IN BERLIN

So I'm going to tell her this morning, because last night when it happened I couldn't even speak, I couldn't even find my way home, so I wandered around for two hours through the streets of this shithole of a town.

And if I told her that I woke up this morning and I felt better I'd be feeding her a double dose of bullshit: first, I didn't wake up because I didn't sleep; second, I feel worse now than last night because now the reality is starting to sink in.

"What do you mean, you're going to Berlin, when, for how long, why?"

"Fiorenzo, I don't know, no...listen, I didn't even want to tell you."

"Sweet. You were just going to run off and say *adios amigo*?"

"No, you idiot, of course I was going to tell you, but not right away. I wanted to wait, think things through, and..." Tiziana's face was red, her eyes puffy, there were no teardrops but she was crying. We met in front of the Youth Center but step by step we wound our way through the smaller streets. "I don't know, I still don't know anything, I have to think about it..."

"You always say you don't know anything and that you have to think about it, but I think you know exactly what you want."

"I do not. I need to look into this, this is a long-shot opportunity . . . but you came into my life and, I don't know, I had to tell you."

"Tell me what, Tiziana? Because I swear I don't understand a thing you're saying. I mean, I get that you want to go away and move to Berlin. Am I warm?"

No, I'm not. Just saying "Berlin" is crazy. I've never been but I'm sure it's cold there, freezing cold.

"I don't know, Fiorenzo, I don't know. I have to think about it."

"Okay. How long?"

"How long what?"

"How long do you need to think?"

"Not long, because I have to give a response by the end of the month."

"By the end of the month?" I said with a fit of laughter that was anything but laughter. And rather than my voice, out came this awful, high-pitched shriek. "Today's the twenty-ninth, the end of the month is now!"

"I know, Fiorenzo, I . . . don't know, I don't . . . I mean, think about if something like this happened to your band, a golden opportunity to go to Berlin."

"The heavy metal scene sucks in Berlin."

"Whatever, take another city where heavy metal is big. I don't know, London?"

"Let's say Kraków."

"Okay, Kraków. Suppose they invited you to cut a CD in Kraków, at a top recording studio, to launch you worldwide. What would you do, you wouldn't go?"

"Of course, I'd go, we'd cut the CD, and then come back. What's so difficult about that?"

Tiziana doesn't answer right away, but from the corner of her eye she looks between the building and the street, or maybe she's not looking at anything at all.

"No, Fiorenzo, it's not difficult. Except that I'm not cutting a CD," she says, and stops. There's nothing more to add.

And there we were, all out of words, each facing the other, just a step apart, standing next to the neon signs for the fanciest sales in town: one read GREAT DEAL ON ORTHOPEDIC DEVICES AND WHEELCHAIRS, another read LAWNMOWERS AND SEWAGE PIPE TOOLS: EVERYTHING MUST GO. Who would have the nerve to ask Tiziana to stay?

I would. And that's exactly what I did.

"Stay, Tiziana, don't go."

"I ... it's not that simple, Fiorenzo, you can understand, it's an important decision ..."

"Okay, whatever. But I honestly think you've already made your choice."

Tiziana looked at me. I don't know if she was deciding right then, or if she was waiting for me to decide for her.

"No," she said, but with a kind of question mark at the end: *No?*

"I think you have."

"You do?"

"Yes, Tiziana, I really do."

"I don't know, Fiorenzo, I really don't. But if I did, and I say *if*, you would understand, right?"

I didn't answer. Understand? At that moment I didn't even know where I was; what was there to understand? How could she have the nerve to ask me something like that?

Yet when I was able to form some words, they sounded something like: "I think I do, Tiziana. I mean, I'm pissed off, I'm mad at myself, you know, but I do kind of understand."

So Tiziana scrunched her eyes and twisted her mouth and officially began to cry. She took a step toward me and hugged me tight, there in the crooked alley that takes you to the post office, with so much strength that she hurt my ribs, but I was hurting in so many different places I didn't even notice it.

I just wish I'd had the strength to push her away and say *No, what the hell, I understand you but you can't expect me to hug you.* Instead I accepted the whole thing, the hug, I even closed my eyes and felt something fizzy under my eyelids, and then in my throat and my nose. And much to my surprise, in a second, in that dark alley, Fiorenzo Marelli, believe it or not, was crying.

So I held her tight, too, out of the sheer terror of losing control and her seeing me. I even tried to hold my breath, because the damn sobs could have given me away, too. Unbelievable, I was blubbering, too, me, the lead singer of Metal Devastation, with a kick-ass voice, blubbering as he hugs a girl who is about to say goodbye and leave.

Until recently—not so long ago, you know, just a couple of months—I would have gotten royally pissed off and yelled that the world is scared of me so it gets back at me by raining down every possible curse, and Tiziana is just a moron who wants to hurt me but can't because I'm a warrior and all evil bounces right off me and goes back to the hell it came from.

But last night I didn't have those thoughts. Last night Tiziana held me and I held her and we stayed like that for a while but I don't know how long, I wouldn't know how to measure it. It wasn't a time you could measure with a watch, a clock, a calendar. It didn't flow in a specific direction, and it wasn't a world where one plus one makes two or anything like that. No. It was something different.

At a certain point in this thing without direction, Tiziana started to say, "I swear, I really didn't want to, I swear, I don't want to. But years go by, Fiorenzo, unfortunately they do. You are nineteen now, then you'll be twenty, think about when you'll be...let's say, twenty-five. At twenty-five, do you think you'll still be here, do you see yourself here at twenty-five? I don't, I don't see you here for anything, but you can still say you don't know, you can afford to wait and see what happens, because you still have so much time and so many opportunities ahead of you: you can pass on a million of them because you have another hundred million lined up. With me, I can't pretend...and you, do you remember the day we met, and you told me that I was right to run away from this town, and that it was a mistake to come back, and that you, yourself, as soon as you had a chance, you'd—"

"Tiziana," I said, trying to fit my words into the sobless intervals.

"Yes?"

"Could you please shut up for a while?"

So Tiziana said nothing. Just one laugh came out, just one, mixed in with her crying. And we went on hugging each other for a long time, because that was the only thing we could do. In fact, after that, there was nothing left.

TWO GIRLS:
ONE BLONDE, ONE BRUNETTE

BUTLER	Do you see that footprint on the floor?
SEMINARIAN	What is it?
BUTLER	There is an ancient legend.
SEMINARIAN	Please tell it to me.
BUTLER	It dates back to 1569. They say that this is the spot where Enrica von Rumberg stabbed a monk who had come to perform an exorcism on her.
SEMINARIAN	An exorcism? But why?
BUTLER	Because of the curse, naturally.

The Devil's Nightmare. Tiziana lent me the DVD three months ago and I haven't watched it till tonight, the night after we broke up. Maybe a good movie will take my mind off things. Seeing a story on the TV screen might keep me from thinking about my own story. But if the idea was to not think about Tiziana, then I chose the wrong movie.

Actually, it wasn't me who chose it. Mirko saw it and kept begging me. *I'd really like to see it, Mister, I get so bored and this movie looks exciting. And I've never seen a horror film. Is it really scary? Is it terrifying?*

I told him I didn't know because I hadn't seen it, so he went nuts: *If you haven't seen it then we have to watch it together, absolutely, for the first time the two of us, for the first time the two of us together!* And since tonight I'm in no mood for an argument or for any problems or for doing anything, actually, I said okay and slipped the DVD into the player.

I have to admit that Tiziana was right, the sound track is phenomenal. Except I can't tell her anymore. And I get a lump in my throat. Now I'm going to pick up and go to her house, because I have to make her understand she's making a huge mistake...

No, it's over, I have to go it alone and bite the bullet and run someplace so far away that when I turn around and see a forlorn little dot I'll wonder *What's that dot down there? Oh, it's Tiziana, or rather, it was Tiziana.* And I laugh at the thought.

After what she said last night we had two choices: to see each other as much as possible till she leaves, or to stop seeing each other completely. Only a gutless wonder would choose the first, but after my crying and sobbing yesterday I guess I lost my guts and don't know where to find them, so my vote was for us to see each other as much as possible till Berlin. Tiziana cast her ballot for the same solution, saying she really liked the idea, as long as the goal was just to have fun, not *to have fun so she'll change her mind.*

But that's exactly what my goal was, and I told her, so she said, *No, Fiorenzo, that would only make us feel bad.* And I said, *Any worse than we already do?* And she insisted it would be even worse. So I got up my pride and shouted *goodbye forever*, and threw in a *fuck you* for good measure, and I left thinking it would be the last time I'd ever see her in my life.

Then Tiziana called three times and sent me two texts. I didn't answer the phone calls, and I texted back only once, but real blunt and curt. So I felt like a tough guy, the kind of man who can suck it up and swallow it down without making a face, clear his throat, and then get on with the business of the rest of his life.

But it ain't easy. Where am I going to find another woman like Tiziana?

Where am I going to find another woman?

"Mister, I'm sorry, but why are those people spending the night in the castle?" Mirko watches the movie with a mixture of fear and confusion. He put his blanket over his mouth and when the scary scenes come he covers his face.

"The road was blocked and the barge doesn't leave till tomorrow. Jesus, can't you follow?"

"Yes, I was just saying, they know all these people have died there and the owners are crazy. Wouldn't it be better to sleep in the van?"

I don't answer. He's got a point: his questions are sensible and reasonable in everyday life, but if you start asking them during a horror movie you may as well forget about it. Why doesn't the girl run away when she sees two eyes glowing in the dark, rather than go and inspect them? Why all the thunder and lightning? Why do the cars always stall? If you're going to ask about that you may as well turn the TV off and go out for a walk, smarty-pants.

In the meantime the movie goes on and even though it is real low-budget and the actors are all amateurs and the dubbing is atrocious, I have to say that *The Devil's Nightmare* really works. In that mysterious and incomprehensible way that Tiziana says. I mean, that Tiziana *used to* say. I have to learn to use the past tense. I have to bury her in the past, under tons of past perfects, past progressives, and past absolutes.

But it hurts.

BRUNETTE   (*wearing a bra and panties*)
            Hurry up, your bath is getting cold.
BLONDE   (*lying down wearing bra and panties*)
            I need another five minutes, I'm so tired.

Then the brunette joins the blonde on the bed.

I knew it: here comes the lesbo scene. I knew it as soon as the camera framed the brunette and the blonde, and when they assigned them to the same bedroom. I knew it because I'm watching a European horror flick from the 1970s, and back then I don't think they even released them if they didn't have a lesbo scene.

Normally I'd be happy, but with Mirko sitting next to me I don't know what to do. He's a child, a baby, who the hell is this curly-top twerp sitting next to me?

BRUNETTE   Don't you like my touch? Let me help you.
            (*She removes the blonde's bra.*) You know, it's
            such a rare pleasure to meet an attractive girl
            like you. Here, let me help you, otherwise
            we'll be late for dinner. Your skin is so soft...

Mirko is sitting on the cot with his leg propped up on a chair. He's leaning closer and closer to the screen, his eyes popping out and his mouth clenched with excitement.

I suddenly realize how my mom must have felt all those times she let me watch horror movies with her. It's a weird situation: on the one hand, she wanted the hard-core scenes;

on the other, I was there and maybe I didn't understand them, maybe they would upset me, whatever. Except she had that trick of sending me to get chocolates, and I can't use that with this crippled twerp. So what should I do, turn off the movie, fast forward? I don't know.

I'd better act fast, because now the brunette's on top of the blonde and they're fondling each other and I think the good part is about to begin. And they're both really hot, the brunette has this body and this face that...well, I look at them and feel better, because in my opinion these two are much prettier than Tiziana. But the world is obviously full of girls prettier than her, and she's getting a little long in the tooth and if they picked her for this film they wouldn't have her playing the part of one of the two girls. No, in my opinion she'd be the playboy's wife, a mature woman who's a little less hot, not to mention a little greedy, like Tiziana, who might be going to Berlin because she hopes she'll make more money there than at the Muglione Youth Center, and...

And while I'm trying to convince myself of this bullshit, the two girls keep at it with the fondling and the kissing and at one point the brunette looks the blonde in the eye, gives her a hint of a smile, and then moves down to her tits, sliding down toward her belly button, and then gets lower and lower...

And then I look at Mirko, whose eyes are popping out and whose lips are trembling, and I think, *Who the fuck cares, they're two naked pussies rubbing against each other on the bed in a room in a cursed castle, it's nature, and since when does nature hurt anyone?*

"Mister," he says to me with a croak, "those two girls are really pretty."

"Big discovery, Einstein."

"Are they what you would call two pieces of ass?"

"You've got that right."

In the meantime the brunette has gone back to kissing the blonde on the tits and fondling her everywhere. It feels a little weird to be watching this scene with Mirko, but it's even stranger to think that Tiziana saw it a ton of times, and this might even be one of the moments that make it her favorite movie, who knows. I want to ask her, I really do, I'd be curious to find out. But I can't think about it because the time is over when Tiziana and I could talk and ask each other things and laugh and tease each other and go to bed together. Over and done with, I have to accept it. Enough, no more, I have to take the list of people in my life and cross off her name.

But it really sucks.

"What are they doing now, Mister?"

"They're hugging each other, can't you see?"

"Yes, but . . . they're two women."

"Exactly. They're lesbians. Never heard the word?"

"Yes, at school. Lesbians are women who sometimes don't have a man to go with so they do it with each other. Right?"

That's not the way I'd put it, but I don't answer. Anyway, the kid's all caught up in what's happening on the screen and next to him I could be like drywall. And I want to enjoy this scene, too, for crying out loud, a little sugar after so much bitter medicine might do me some good.

And who am I to contradict what he learns at school, anyway?

NO COFFEE, JUST SEX

It's me, Mirko, and Dad here at the irrigation ditch, fishing, and maybe from the outside it makes a nice picture. But don't widen the angle too much, otherwise you'll see the dump back there with walls oozing poison. And don't zoom in either, because then you'll see my face and realize how lousy I feel.

But Mirko insisted, in that tremendous way he has of insisting by practically asking for nothing, just repeating like a broken record how much he'd like to do something and how nice it would be to do it, and how if he could do it he'd be the happiest person in the world and...and to make a long story short, I loaded him on the scooter and we came here to where Dad is to watch him fish.

The doctors warned me that it was dangerous to ride with him on the scooter, because of the shaking and the risks and all that, but doctors say a lot of stuff that in my opinion not even they believe, like don't smoke or don't eat fried food. Stuff that they have to say but in reality they're thinking, *Do whatever you feel like, buddy, it's all just a lottery anyway, and when your turn comes, it comes.*

Even Dad would get really pissed off to know that I'm riding on the scooter with him, his Little Champion, but when he saw us coming he waved and asked (only Mirko, of course) whether he was feeling in shape, he didn't stop to think about how we got all the way there. The four empty beer cans and the carton of wine next to him at five in the afternoon say that he isn't very lucid, and for the moment I find that convenient.

I only hope that he doesn't degenerate, you know, that Dad doesn't become an alcoholic. He can drink as much as he wants, like all the men (and many women) here in Muglione. Wine at lunch and dinner, a couple of glasses of sparkling wine for a snack, then in the evening all the grappa and amaro he wants. As long as he doesn't wind up in the hospital, otherwise he'll become officially an alcoholic.

Here in town everyone drinks a lot, there are men you can't talk to after three in the afternoon because they don't know where they are, and they stagger toward a bench or a dry ditch where they sack out till sunset. But that's not a problem, that's normal, that's how Muglione operates. The problems start when they hospitalize you, even for a day, even for a minute: taking you to the hospital means that you have a problem, which means that you're an alcoholic. And in town everyone looks at you differently, even the ones who drink more than you.

We in our family also have a precedent. Marino, a cousin of my dad's with red hair, I don't remember what happened to him anymore. And so alcoholism could be in our DNA. As a matter of fact, do you think I could wind up having it, too?

Yes, maybe I could, and maybe during these crazy days when I'm thinking only about Tiziana and remembering her voice and the smell of her T-shirts and the lock of hair that always fell over her face, maybe the only way to feel better would be for me to start drinking.

I've already made a plan with Giuliano and Stefano to go to Excalibur tonight and we're going to drink a lot of beer and say that women are all sluts and that we're better off without them. It's nice to have friends who like you and keep you company when you're down.

And I told them, my friends, that now they see me all wimpy and wounded but they can relax, because this pain is like fuel, an accumulation of fuel inside that later when I'm full and can get back on my feet will become an awesome fire of rage, and my howl will be back to devastate the world.

In the meantime, however, my days of being wimpy are still not over.

Of course not, how can I get over them if Tiziana keeps coming and looking for me? This morning she sent me a text asking if we could have lunch, even at the diner. I wrote back a loud *NO* right away and I felt like a real man. A man with muscles dressed in animal pelts, tough and powerful with two gigantic balls, and I was on top of the world looking down at everything for at least ten minutes of total domination.

Then I came down from the mountain of power, took my cell out, and sent her another text:

K for diner, but not till 1. K? (11:36am)

We met in front of Il Fagiano, which at that time of day is still doable. At that hour the rally and video poker fans are either at work or in bed, before five you can still breathe a little. But today it would have been better to have them there, the meat-heads, even just two or three walking around the parking lot. At least that way we would know what to talk about.

Instead there were these long silences. I didn't want to say anything bad, and nothing good came to mind, and when something did it sounded so lame that I kept it to myself. Because basically, for crying out loud, she's leaving me and she's going to Berlin, and was I supposed to sit there and entertain her and pretend that everything was all right? Even that meeting, after I told her fair and square that I didn't want to see her again, what was the sense of it? She doesn't care what I prefer and she doesn't respect my wishes. She knows perfectly well that if she asks to see me, in the end I'll say yes, so she shouldn't ask me anything. If Tiziana won't help out I've got no chance of acting on my intentions. But she doesn't help out and I don't put up a fight, and so I feel sad, abandoned, and also idiotic. Are you happy, Tiziana?

But then, since we're seeing each other, we could at least do dinner. A serious date, like with a friend or a colleague or a next-door neighbor, of the kind she must have hundreds of in Berlin. And I know perfectly that maybe not at the beginning, but slowly but surely, one of those colleagues or neighbors will be better than the others and will say something right and then Tiziana will end up in bed with him and they'll have sex and she'll squeeze him and make those sounds she made with me. Maybe this guy will be better in bed and more mature and more expert. It wouldn't take much.

Those were the thoughts in my head there at the diner, they shook and they blended and I swear that at one point I was about to say *Okay, Tiziana, this is messed up and makes no sense, if you want to go then go, fuck it, but at least stop torturing me.*

But at that moment the Romanian at the cash register informed us that the coffee maker was broken, and then Tiziana said we could have coffee at her place, if I liked the idea.

"Will we have sex?" I asked, out of nowhere. At this point it doesn't make sense to say anything we don't mean.

"..."

"Will we or won't we have sex?"

"To tell you the truth, I was just thinking about coffee."

"No coffee. Sex. Tell me now."

And Tiziana looked at me, in a more and more crooked and weird and impossible to understand way, and I swear if another second went by I'd run away and never see her again. But one second before the limit she said, "Well, okay, let's go." And then we went.

And I was incredible. *In-cred-i-ble* in the true sense of the word: I could hardly believe it myself. I must have lasted for at least three minutes, maybe four, an eternity. And I thought it was really unfair that Tiziana was leaving now, of all times, since I had become a stallion. She doesn't know what she'll be missing, what I'll be missing, it's nuts.

Even if maybe it was all because of that huge sadness that I have inside. A normal man in this state of distress could never get it up, my equivalent is a three-minute duration before coming.

Whatever the case, Tiziana appreciated it a lot and the noises she made were new, louder, and longer than ever, she squeezed my back and made a face that was really awesome and without even thinking I asked her if she liked it.

From the sounds she made it was clear, but I still wanted to hear her say it. And she said, "Yes, oh yes, I like it, Fiorenzo, I like it."

And that would have been enough. It should have been enough. But I continued on. "Stay here, Tiziana, stay here and it'll be like this every day."

And all of a sudden, nothing, everything stopped, every-thing quiet. No more sounds, no more hands squeezing me, just me sweating and carrying on and trying to pretend that I didn't understand, with Tiziana below me staring at me without moving.

"Fiorenzo, stop, this is bullshit."

"What? But no, why do you say that? It's not true."

"We're a couple of morons. Actually, I'll admit it, I'm the moron."

She folded her legs into her chest, her arms wrapped around them, and stayed that way, staring at the wall and biting her lip. She tucked herself in a ball, apologized, and even took away my right to be as stupid as her.

And then silence: How much silence can fit inside a room? Here we were, at the risk of exceeding the limit. So I spoke.

"Listen, do I have to escape through the window again?"

"..."

"Would you mind if I used the door?"

Tiziana didn't answer, she just shook her head, said something with her nose blocked and I couldn't understand anything, but I didn't think it was for me. And when I understood that if I left she wouldn't mind, I again felt that thing fizzing in my eyes.

But no, fuck, not this time, no. I was naked, my dick was still hard, crying in that condition is the most horrifying thing in the universe.

So I threw myself on the floor to recover my clothes, I picked them up like a ball, and I started putting them on every which way. Shorts, T-shirt, flip-flops, how long can it take? I'm nineteen years old and I do it every morning, how could it be taking so long?

"Fiorenzo, really, I didn't want to. I mean, I did, but everything's so complicated. I don't want to hurt your feelings. I feel bad, so do you, and what we just did was idiotic. I don't know why I did it, maybe because I don't...I don't know...maybe I wanted to understand whether..."

But at that point I was dressed, more or less, and I was already out the door and down the stairs and on the road. And if Tiziana had something else to say, I wasn't there.

And all of this happened three hours ago. So now, at the ditch with Mirko and Dad, it doesn't take a lot of imagination to know how I feel.

"Here, have a seat." Dad takes the stool out from under his ass and passes it to Mirko.

"No thank you, I prefer to stand, I never get to."

"And you never do because you're not supposed to. Sit here."

"Thank you, but I would rather—"

"Sit down and quit pissing me off."

Dad throws him the stool and sits down on the ground with a frown. Mirko sits.

I remain on my feet instead. Which isn't the right thing to do when you're fishing, because the fish see you and get suspicious. Fish are afraid of vertical shadows, which cut across the ditch from one bank to the other. But I get the impression Dad is still fishing without bait, so what the fuck do I care.

"Did you catch anything, Mr. Roberto?"

"No, it's better this way."

"I'm sorry."

"I said it's better this way. Much better this way."

The Little Champ nods in agreement and stretches out his bad leg. He rests his chin on one hand and starts watching the floater.

"How are the kids doing?"

"What kids?"

"The others on the team, my teammates."

"*Bleh*, they're not worth shit. No style no class no nothing. Better hurry up and get that leg better or we're fucked."

A pigeon goes by. A dragonfly goes by. And I wonder how come these animals, who can fly wherever they want, have decided to stay here in Muglione. I can understand the reeds, the water lilies, who have to stay where they're born, but not them.

"I'm done. Enough of this shit." Dad stands up, clumps of soil and dirt are sticking to the seat of his tracksuit. "I'm going."

Mirko sits there and looks at him, then he turns around toward me, all worried. I don't want to go anywhere. If I go downtown I'm afraid I'll run into Tiziana, who might be making the rounds of the stores to buy some last-minute things she needs before her trip. Warm clothing, sweaters, maybe even new lingerie to make a good impression when she finds a guy who wants to go to bed with her . . . no, I don't want to run into her, I don't want to see her ever again, I'm feeling bad enough as it is.

"Dad," I say, "if you leave your rod the two of us can fish a little."

Mirko shouts for joy and leaps to his feet and starts jumping. So high that each time it looks like he won't come down.

"Yippee! Yippee!"

"What the fuck are you doing?" shouts Dad. "You're going to hurt yourself, you're not supposed to put pressure on it!" Then he looks past the kid, toward me. "Can you believe how high he's jumping? He could even be a champion at basketball."

"Basketball? Fantastic!" says Mirko. "I'd really like to try it!"

"No fucking way! Basketball is bullshit. Like soccer, tennis, all bullshit. You can tell from the name, a basketball *game*, a soccer *game*. But not cycling. Cycling is a sport, cycling is suffering, and you, Mirko, are born to suffer, get it?"

He huffs and puffs, nods his head, and sits back down with his chin leaning on his hand, his eyes staring at the water.

The last doctor willing to talk to us said that Mirko shouldn't stay crippled, but the most he could do on a bike was a few short spins. But Dad keeps on insisting, without a thread of doubt.

He finishes his speech and turns one way, the other, he's groping around looking for something, maybe the money to buy more stuff to drink. Then he goes, leaving by the ditch the empty cans and the carton of wine, and us.

I WISH I WAS A FROG

"Thanks, Mister, I'm so happy, I was really hoping we would stay to fish, what a great gift."

I didn't do it for him, but I say, "You're welcome."

"Do you think a fish will bite now? Will it be big? Are there big fish in this river, Mister?"

"It's not a river, it's a ditch."

"Are there big fish in this ditch?"

"Uhhh, pretty big."

"What's the biggest one you ever caught in the history of your life, Mister?"

"A carp, it must have weighed twenty-six pounds."

"Twenty-six pounds!"

"Maybe twenty-eight, I didn't weigh it, I didn't have the scale with me."

"Couldn't you weigh it at home?"

"No, I freed it right away."

"You freed it?"

"Yes, I unhooked it and put it back in the water."

The kid stops talking. With him silence is a rare thing, so I turn around to check that he's okay and I see him staring at me in a way that no one has ever looked at me.

They're the eyes of an admirer, of someone who came to a

concert and traveled thousands of miles to be there and now is in the front row looking his idol in the face. And I can't say I mind. I wish I knew someone I could look at like that. Someone older I could ask a lot of things and drink in his words like Mirko is doing with me. But I don't and I never have. But the Little Champ does, it would seem. Even though in his case that someone is me. Incredible.

I stop looking at him and check the floater, but I realize it makes no sense: there's no bait, how can you expect to get a bite?

I reel in the line, Mirko stands up and comes next to me quickly. "Did you catch something, Mister? Did you catch something?"

I shake my head and rest the hook on my hand. Like I thought, no bait, just the shiny, wet hook.

"Isn't there supposed to be a worm on the hook, Mister?"

"Yes, or a kernel of corn, or corn bread. Something, it doesn't matter."

"So why isn't there?"

"Well, you can tell some fish must have eaten it without getting caught. They're smart."

"So there are fish, then! Let's put the bait right back on, Mister, let's catch them!"

Easy for him to say. I look around, on this muddy soil I might be able to find an earthworm or two. I bet there are some big juicy ones growing by the dump. But it hasn't rained for a while and the ground is dry and hard and I'd need a shovel to dig deep. So I tear off a piece of a weed and roll it into a ball with two fingers, it becomes a kind of mash and I stick it on the hook like a little green ball. I throw it back in the water delicately so it won't fall off, the floater lies on its side for a second then straightens out to do its job.

"Grass, Mister? You used grass?"

"Yes. There's lots of fish that eat grass. Tench, amur..."

"Amur?"

"It's a kind of carp, but it also looks like a chub. And it gets real big..."

I've never seen an amur around here, but who knows, people throw all kinds of stuff in the ditches.

Now there's also the killer crab, a dark and terrifying thing that comes from Louisiana. And how did it get from Louisiana all the way to the irrigation ditches of Muglione? Easy, they were imported, hush-hush, by a guy who had a restaurant near Viareggio, he kept them in a big dug-in vat and he served them at the restaurant, passing them off as lobster. Then, I don't know how, I think it was either an overflow or the fact that those beasts can crawl easily on land, the killer crabs ended up in the Massaciuccoli Lake, and since they're terrifying and they devastate all the local species, from there they spread wherever they wanted. So in Muglione, too, you just might happen to find a killer crab attached to your ankle.

"Mister, can I ask you something?"

"Huh?"

"But it's personal, I don't want to make you angry."

"So don't ask."

"But I really want to know."

"Yes, but right now I really don't feel like getting angry, so don't ask."

"Okay," he says. He looks at the floater and keeps his mouth shut. One minute goes by, then two, three...

"Okay, you win, what was the question?"

"But, Mister, I wouldn't want—"

"Just ask and get it over with."

"All right, okay. I wanted to ask you ... is this where you lost your hand?"

He says it just like that, I swear, and sits there staring at me.

How does he know that I lost it at the ditch? Did he ask Dad, hear something about it, read my mind? In fact, this isn't the spot, but it's not far away. Down there is a big curve and the ditch meets up with another branch, no more than a mile from here. Never lower your guard with the Little Champ, never.

"How the fuck did you know?"

"I don't know anything, I swear. Is this where it happened?"

"No, it was somewhere else, a spot in another area that's got nothing to do with here. Are you happy now?"

"No, I mean, not no not yes. I was just curious." He keeps studying the floater. But he doesn't fool me, the evil child. Or rather, he fools me every time, but every time I say *You don't fool me* and try not to let him fool me again.

"Listen up, you, how the fuck do you know about my business?"

"I don't, Mister, I was just asking."

"You're not fooling me. Who told you, Dad? And do you mind telling me what the fuck you care?"

"It's nothing, Mister. I mean, I care about you, so I care about your business."

There you have it. That's the kind of talk that he uses to fool me, and the bad part is, he succeeds. But I can't always be such a sucker, today I've already burned through my dose of stupidity with Tiziana, now I have to be tough.

"I've got your number, kid, you don't fool me. You pretend to know nothing but actually you know a little too much. Even that story about the Sylvester the Cat glass, I know that you know ..."

And this is the thing that burns me the most. If this evil child has some way of knowing every fuckup in my life, well, that would drive me absolutely insane.

Without that I'd be a better person, I think, or at least someone who manages to visit the grave of his mother every now and then, which I haven't done in the past sixteen months. Not once, because I'm terrified of going there and bowing my head and hearing something, a breath, the distant voice of my mother saying *What did you do, Fiorenzo, I could still be alive, my son, I could still be alive...*

I get a chill that shifts the T-shirt on my back. I give myself a shake but it doesn't go away. I try to get pissed off at the kid and take it out on him.

"Don't be a wiseass, dickwad, you know everything about Sylvester the Cat, too!"

"What am I supposed to know, Mister? I swear I don't, I swear it."

"You know everything, and don't swear or you'll go to hell."

The kid looks at me, he's serious, but with that air of a forlorn finch that leaves me helpless.

"Mister, let's do this: Why don't you tell me the story?"

"Tell you what?"

"The Sylvester the Cat story."

"Huh? What the fuck do you want from me? It's my business."

"Yes, but if I'm supposed to know anyway, what's the harm in telling it to me again?"

Bastard. He says this and then he turns back to studying the floater, which is sitting there without moving, as useless as us. Do you really expect something to nibble on a little grass stuck to a hook?

I look at it, too, and I think about the bottom of the ditch and the muck and the shiny steel of the hook in all that darkness.

And almost without thinking, believe it or not, I start unraveling the story of the damned glass. Which I've never told anyone. I've been keeping it inside for a long, long time and with the passing months it's been swelling bigger and bigger and I'm afraid if I don't get it out it'll explode in my heart and I'll die.

And Mirko already knows, anyway, what difference does it make if I tell him again?

"It was last year, and . . . oh, Champ, this story's got some jerking off in it, you won't get upset, will you? You jerk off, I hope?"

The kid doesn't reply, he stares at the floater and makes a weird face.

"I said, do you jerk off or don't you?"

"..."

"Come on, you do, right?"

"A little bit," which sets off a series of ridiculous twitchings around his mouth and eyes.

"Hey, relax, there's nothing wrong with it. We all do. Now I don't so much anymore because I've got a girl, a nice piece of ass that I go to bed with, but I'm an exception."

Or rather, I *was* an exception, but I've gone right back to the ways of the hapless. In my mind's eye I see Tiziana naked below me and the face she made in those moments. She was splendid, but I'm already thinking back as if it were a distant memory, and I'm afraid that it won't be long till that memory is just a dream, something imaginary and impossible. Did it really happen? I remember the sensations, the smells, but everything is confused and distorted. Now the only real thing is pain.

"To make a long story short," I say, "it was last spring, and I couldn't sleep. I would go to bed, give myself a goodnight jerk-off, but even then I was awake. You know what a goodnight jerk-off is, don't you?"

Mirko doesn't take his eyes off the floater, those ridiculous twitches continue, and he doesn't answer. But I'm sure he knows what I'm talking about. The goodnight jerk-off is a classic, it's like a magic bridge that takes you from the real world to the world of dreams. It's a place where your female friends realize they don't want to be just friends, and the new substitute teacher wants to speak to you in private in the faculty lounge, or maybe you go to see a friend but you get the door wrong and you open it and find her older sister standing there half naked and you apologize and she says, *It's no biggie, I'm so bored, will you help me unfasten my bra?* In other words, you go on with these fantasies until you get to that point, then when you go past that point you find yourself light and empty in a land of dreams and sleep is the most natural thing in the world.

"But after the goodnight jerk-off I still couldn't sleep. And do you want to know why? Because at that point I had to get out of bed and go wash myself, so of course I woke back up. Outside of the covers it was cold, the water was freezing and the bathroom light was really strong, and when I went back to bed I was more awake than ever. So to solve the problem I started using a Kleenex, but it's really uncomfortable. And then, having only one hand, I had to be careful to hit the mark and not get the sheets dirty and in other words it was becoming a kind of job. And you, Little Champ, did you ever try doing it with a Kleenex?"

Mirko doesn't reply, doesn't look at me, doesn't breathe.

"Oh, out with it, do you or don't you use a Kleenex?"

"Mister, I'm sorry, but how is this story connected with the Sylvester the Cat glass?"

"Don't be a wiseass, you know perfectly well that it's connected. It's connected, and how! In fact, right after the Kleenex I had this brilliant idea about the glass," I say, breathing heavily. "I mean, it seemed brilliant at the time, but you know what happened so now we can see that it wasn't brilliant one bit."

I quiet down for a moment. I think of Mom, of the way she smiled when I would tell her something and then at a certain point I would stop because maybe I was embarrassed or I wanted to drag out the wait for the news. Even for nice things, like when I would come back from school and tell her that I had had a quiz that day and she asked me what grade I got and I didn't answer her right away, but Mom was already preparing a nice big smile because she knew that at a minimum it was a B-plus, and she would shout, *What is going on with you, come on, don't stop, tell me already, you're killing me.*

I miss Mom, damn, do I miss her. And now that I miss Tiziana, too, it's not that I miss Mom any less. Actually, I miss her even more. It's not like missing one replaces missing the other. There's room for both here inside, there's no limit to sadness.

And when I think that Mom could still be alive if it weren't for that Sylvester the Cat glass . . . could she? No, yes, maybe, I swear I don't know.

"Mister, if I understood you correctly, you used the Sylvester the Cat glass to . . ."

"Yes, you understood correctly, good boy, go to the head of the class. I used it instead of the Kleenex and it worked fantastically. A clean and perfect job. Except that afterward, you see, if I had to get up and go to the bathroom to empty it, the problem didn't go away. So do you know what I did? Of course you know, you know everything, tell me what it is I did."

"But I don't—"

"Come on, otherwise I won't tell you the rest of the story."

"You left the glass the way it was and fell asleep?"

"Exactly. I knew you knew. I placed it under the bed, I thought I'd empty it the next morning, and I slept like a rock."

I freeze. I see a slight circle of water around the floater. It's the sign of a nibble, but it could be anything, even a stupid tadpole who bumped into the cork while it was swimming. Or else it's my impression, I'm nervous and I don't know what I'm seeing. This thing about the glass I've never told anyone, this tremendous thing that I think about every day but the only one who knows is me. Me, and my mom.

"But the next morning I forgot it, I went to school and I left the glass under the bed. I came back after lunch and no one answered the door. It was Wednesday and Dad was out with the team, I climbed the stairs and didn't hear a sound, I got to my room and I found Mom flat on the floor. With one arm extended, like that, and next to her the broom she was using to sweep, and near her hand was the Sylvester the Cat glass turned upside down."

"Um, excuse me, Mister." For the first time Mirko takes his eyes off the floater and looks at me. "Is that the way your mom died?"

"No, you dimwit, she fainted. She revived right away. She said she had felt really tired for a second and went to the bathroom to put some cold water on her face. In the meantime I went downstairs and washed the glass. And we didn't say another word about it."

"Oh, I see, I had thought that was how she died."

"No, she fainted, I told you." I look at the water again, two more ripples around the floater. "Mom died at the bank. *The next day.*"

Silence. Only the frogs. The frogs and my heartbeat.

There, I said it. I didn't think I would ever tell anyone and instead I just told it to a stupid and really ugly kid. Maybe I should have told Tiziana, she would have understood why this story knocks the wind out of me. Instead the kid stares at me, motionless, and from the eyes he's making it's clear he didn't understand shit.

"Mister, begging your pardon. I had thought that the story about the glass had some connection with the thing about your mother dying. I'm sorry, it must be the horror movie the other night that put strange ideas in my head."

"Don't blame the movie, it's just that you're a moron," I say, and I'd like to end it like that. Except I can't, I really can't, I keep talking. "Well, yes but, it's somewhat connected, right? I mean, it could be. Don't you think?"

"No, Mister, in my opinion there's no connection, but I believe you."

"Of course there is, you moron. I mean, Mom died at the bank, the lady who was in line behind her saw her go down and that was that. And a few days later the doctor gave me this speech how the human body is made that way, sometimes there's a little switch that clicks and it's funeral bells, without any warning signs, there's nothing you can do about it. And I asked him if with some sign we could have done something. And he told me yes, maybe yes, and then I asked him if a fainting spell could be considered a sign, and he said yes, certainly yes... Do you get it, dickwad, now do you get it? The sign was right there, the day before, Mom fainted right in front of me, shit, and what did I do? I went to the kitchen and rinsed out the glass and pretended that nothing had happened." I'm stuck for a second, I try to breathe and I can't, but

I can shout, "Do you get it, dimwit? I pretended that nothing had happened!"

My voice echoes between the banks of the ditch, and for a little while even the frogs quiet down. Then they start up again, even happier than before.

God I wish I was a frog, too. I wouldn't be missing out on much, anyway: I spend all my time at the ditch and have the same senseless life. Except that they have no thoughts and carry on without a care, watching out for killer crabs and rats, and they can sleep peacefully, they don't dream of their mom on her feet staring at them, as white as a corpse with her hair stuck to her forehead and a Sylvester the Cat glass in her hand.

Why oh why didn't I break that damn glass, why didn't I disintegrate it that same day, why did I hide it in the back of a cupboard where this ball-busting kid plucked it out in an instant?

And why is this kid looking at me right now, struggling not to laugh?

"You son of a bitch, what the fuck are you laughing at?"

He shakes his head, eyes popping out, jaw clenched shut.

"What the fuck is there to laugh about, asshole? I'll throw you in the ditch, then we'll see who's laughing."

"No, Mister, I'm sorry, I'm not laughing."

"You are, too. You're laughing."

"No, I swear I'm not, I swear on my family."

"That's a stretch, your family doesn't give a shit about you!"

"Yes, but I do care about them, so the oath is still good. I admit that I felt like laughing, but I didn't."

"Why the fuck would you feel like laughing at a moment like this? I told you my mom died, that maybe it's my fault, and you laugh?"

"Yes, Mister, I'm sorry, but at first I thought it would be something serious. I mean, I thought that your mom bent down to pick up the glass and hit her head and died like that. Or that she mistook it for a glass of milk and drank it and was poisoned to death. Or that you came home and killed her because she had discovered the trick you did with the glass..."

"What? Are you nuts? You're sick, kid, what the fuck goes on in your head? Do you realize the bullshit you're talking?"

The kid looks at me strangely. He's not a forlorn finch anymore. He's serious, he looks me straight in the eyes, he almost scares me.

"Yes, Mister," he says, and even his voice is different. He's not trembling anymore. We trade places and now I'm the one who's trembling. "Let's make a deal, Mister. I'll admit that I'm talking bullshit if you admit that you're talking bullshit."

"Me? I don't talk bullshit."

"Have it your way. But then I'll laugh."

"No, you can't—"

"Yes, I can laugh, Mister. I'm sick of never being able to do anything. I can't run, I can't pedal, I can't even walk well with this leg here. Unlike you, who can do anything you feel like, you can even say that it's your fault your mom died because she found a glass that you jerked off into. Well, if I can't even laugh at that bullshit, then you tell me what I can do..."

Nothing, he's allowed to do nothing, this evil child. Even if in a certain sense he's doing lots of things. For example, he makes me feel stupid, really stupid, more stupid than I've ever felt in my life. And yes, lately I've had the opportunity to be stupid at remarkable levels.

But now it's different. Now I'm almost happy to feel this way. And so I think that Mirko could also laugh, laugh really hard and point his finger at me while he's laughing his ass off. And laugh so hard he cries, like Mom used to do whenever she heard something really ridiculous. Like she might do now if she could hear me tell this story.

I feel stupid, retarded, confused, and maybe even a little lighter. A little lighter, that's what it is. I look at Mirko and I want to almost say thank you, even if I would never do it. Never.

But suddenly his face changes again. He doesn't feel like laughing anymore, he twists his mouth and starts to cough and spit on the ground.

"What the fuck are you doing?"

"I'm sorry, Mister, I know that I shouldn't, but how gross can you get?" And he spits again.

"What do you mean, gross?"

"Oh my God, to think that I drank out of that glass so many times, *bleh*!"

Now I'm the one who's laughing. It's incredible, but I'm laughing. "And you complain? You should be proud you can drink where I came! You should tell everyone, it's an honor that—"

But suddenly we both jump up with our eyes on the ditch, and there's no room for words anymore. The floater has disappeared underwater so powerfully that it sounds like a stone hit the surface. I barely make it in time to see it jet away like an arrow, the frogs escape toward one bank or the other, trying to save themselves.

I grab the rod, reel in the drag, and jerk the rod hard to sink in the hook: it's like trying to hook a running train. A wild force, a tremendous weight, the rod curls all the way downward and is carrying me away.

"Come here, quick, help me!"

Mirko grabs a hold of the rod, too, and the two of us pull together. I keep the tip high and release the drag for a little slack to avoid breaking the line. But the usual precautions for a big fish make no sense with this thing on the hook, it's like wearing your helmet on the day of the apocalypse. This thing here is a train, it's a truck, there are no techniques except to grit your teeth and pull.

"What do I have to do, Mister, what do I have to do?"

"Pull, Mirko, pull as hard as you can."

The water opens in two but we don't see anything. Only a gigantic shadow and two waves beating against the banks, the water sizzling, foam, and a huge whirlpool that spins and pulls, spins and pulls.

And *crack*, the rod splits in half like a toothpick, the line breaks and so do a few of our bones, perhaps, when we fall backward onto the dry land.

The two of us are left gasping for air, a piece of broken rod in our hands. We look at each other for a second, look at the water down there, look at each other again.

This time not even the frogs have the courage to start up again.

AND THEN IT DISAPPEARS
FROM SIGHT

The taxi arrives at the gate and beeps the horn twice, but you already saw it from the window, picked up your suitcases, and went downstairs. You had promised Raffaella that she would take you to the airport, but you called a taxi instead.

It wasn't to be mean, it's that you wanted to have a last look at the town while you were leaving. You wanted to look at it and focus and listen to the thoughts that came into your head without Raffaella's sobbing.

Two suitcases in the trunk, a small bag on your lap along with *Corriere della Sera* and *The Tyrrhenian*, which you bought for some reason not even you understand.

"You like to keep informed, eh?" the lady cab driver says, pointing to the newspapers. You would have preferred a man, a guy pushing sixty who has been doing this job for a lifetime and can't stand it anymore, a guy who stays quiet and wants only to make it to the end of his shift.

Instead the driver asks where you're going and if in Germany it's also cold this time of year. She has never been to Berlin but she has been to Munich because she has relatives there who sell bathroom tiles. She recommends it to you because it's a nice city and you eat well there though of course not as well as here, no one can beat us Italians with our spaghetti and pizza, no way, our food is famous all over the world and there will definitely be an Italian restaurant in Berlin so when you're up there you'll be able to go, right? And how long will you stay? And why are you going?

"I'm going to a funeral," you say. A stroke of genius.

"Oh, I'm sorry, I'm really so sorry."

"Think nothing of it, thank you, unfortunately these things happen," you say with a sad face, shaking your head, relieved because you know there won't be another word out of her until Pisa. Excellent. This way you can look out the window at Muglione, passing by slowly in the mist, rubbing against your eyes as it goes.

The county road, the irrigation ditch, the Youth Center that is closed for the holidays, and when it reopens someone else will be inside in the dark and the solitude. For a second you think of the vibrating armchair, of the salesman who is supposed to come back to pick it up. He'll come by sooner or later, or has he already forgotten about his miraculous product and the forlorn place in the middle of nowhere where he left it one day by mistake? Maybe yes, maybe no, the only thing for certain is that you will hear nothing more about it.

Like that mysterious message on your blog: *Tiziana, how nice to wead you.* In the end, who sent it to you? Luca? Pavel's friend Nick? An illiterate who was there by mistake? You don't know and you never will, but it doesn't matter because now you're leaving and all this will cease to exist, probably.

The county road is almost empty. It's August and anyone who can has gone to the seaside or the mountains or anyplace without the putrid smell of the irrigation ditch. But you had the taxi come early because you never know, something unexpected can always happen and in this type of situation you prefer to give yourself plenty of time. That way you're safe and sound, and end up spending half the afternoon in the waiting rooms of airports and train stations, like your mother when she goes to the doctor's and appears two hours before the appointment. You and your mom, two peas in a pod, the only difference is the place where you wait with your hands in your lap. You feel yourself drowning.

Then from behind comes the infernal racket of a scooter going at full speed. It reaches the taxi, comes up on your side, and slows down. But you don't look right away, first you try to catch your breath, comb your hair, understand what Fiorenzo is doing on the other side of the window. Does he want to say goodbye one last time, insult you, convince you not to go? You turn with a mix of six thousand different expressions on your face, and finally you look him in the eyes.

It's not Fiorenzo. It's a meathead like so many others who like to show off how fast their scooter can go, it passes the taxi, pops a wheelie, then disappears down the road on only one wheel. And you start to breathe again, the trip quiets down, the road before you is straight and empty.

But how does it sit with you, Tiziana, what do you have to say now? *Thank God* it wasn't Fiorenzo, or *what a shame* it wasn't? You can't have it both ways, you do know that, Tiziana. Well, do you?

No. Right now you know nothing about nothing. And for some reason you think back to the Sunday in June when the two of you went to Viareggio. A customer from the bait-and-tackle shop runs a restaurant on the dock and he was always saying, *Come anytime, Fiorenzo, I'll give you the royal treatment.* You arrived at nine, it was still light out, but the restaurant was closed that day. In summer, on a Sunday, in Viareggio. And it started to rain. One of those cloudbursts you get on the shore, a wall of water that pelts you for ten minutes and smashes everything to the ground.

There was a stand on the dock with a Chinese guy frying fish, you got two bags of shrimp and squid as hard as rubber and you ran to chew them under the awning of a shop that sold outboard motors. Fiorenzo said it was his dream to buy a boat and sail the seas; you reminded him that his dream was to become famous with his band and he said it was true, but in life it's better to have lots of dreams because it works like bingo cards: the more you have, the better your chances of winning.

And it's a sentence that seems really important right now, but back then it was quickly forgotten. Then Fiorenzo started listing the things that he wanted to do on the boat, he already had a name for it even if you've forgotten it. On board he would put in a stove so you could cook fish right away, and then a keg of white wine that would fit in perfectly, and he would spend all his vacations sailing on the Mediterranean, every day someplace different. And while he was talking and talking all you could think of was the fact that you didn't fit into any of Fiorenzo's future plans, no matter how pointless or silly. He kept saying, *I'll get, I'll go, I'll look for*, and you regretted a little that he was the only one on that boat.

And meanwhile he went on with the list of fish he wanted to catch—tuna and hake and mackerel and pandora and sea bass and bluefish and striped bass and gurnard and...

"And here's a squid coming right at you!" you said, and you hit him right in the nose with a piece of fried seafood. It came to you spontaneously, so you were the first to be surprised. Then you burst into laughter.

"Are you nuts, Tiziana? My Destruction T-shirt? Oil doesn't wash away!" It was a black T-shirt, obviously, with a drawing of a butcher staring at you with crazy eyes and a meat cleaver in one hand. "Now it's ruined forever!"

"Not that it was much to look at in the first place."

Fiorenzo stared at you without answering, and with his right arm he pressed the bag to his chest, dug around inside, and shot a shrimp straight in your face.

So began the fried food fight, and in the wild battle that ensued the two of you came out from under the awning. The rain was coming down in sheets and in a second you were both drenched in water and nasty oil, you had gone through all your ammunition and finally even the empty bags. And then you stood there like that, looking at each other, gasping for air and wearing crooked smiles, under rain that was already dying down and lightning that had moved on toward Pisa.

People started to come out from their shelter and the road that leads to the dock filled up again, and the passersby looked at you like you were crazy. Especially you, Tiziana, who are no longer a girl.

"Tiziana, can I tell you something?"

"Go ahead."

"You're really ugly like that. I mean it, really ugly." Fiorenzo pointed at you and started laughing, and you laughed, too, while trying to brush away the hair that was stuck to your face, but your hands were oily and only made the situation worse.

And you smile now that you think about it, in the backseat of a taxi. You see yourself in the rearview mirror and feel stupid, you press the newspapers in your lap and try to stop.

Another scooter passes you on the other side, but this time you don't even look. Fiorenzo doesn't know that you're leaving today. And even if he knew he wouldn't come anyway. He's definitely out fishing or playing or trying to feel good however he can, and it's right that he does. And you have no right to hope differently.

And then, the airport. There are a lot of people looking at the signs with their heads craned, not knowing where to go: for a second you feel at home.

You think of Muglione and get a bitter feeling in your throat, you're half an hour away by car but it seems like another continent. You get out your phone and send a text to Raffaella, you write that she has to come see you as soon as she can, that it doesn't matter if she's afraid of flying, she can come on the train, in a car, however she wants, you'll be waiting for her and you really care.

You reread it, send it, in front of the Ryanair counter you start to put your phone back in your pocket but you immediately get a text. The girl at the counter tells you in a severe tone that on the plane you will have to turn off your phone. You say yes, you're well aware of it, you're not the usual Italian. You hand over your luggage, take your phone, and read Raffaella's reply.

But it's not Raffaella: the display says FIORENZO. That bitter thing from before turns into a lump, it expands so much you can no longer swallow.

> According to my calculations you'll already be in Krautland when you read this. I wanted to tell you (and it's just the opposite of what I wanted to say) that if by chance you realize that you don't feel good there and that things weren't so bad here, I'm here and I'll take you back. I won't let my pride get in the way, nope, if you return I'll take you back. I'm an idiot, I know, but that's the way it is. Bye. F (7:01pm)

But how did he know that today was today? Even the time is almost exact... It's telepathy, computer espionage, or simply Raffaella, who doesn't know when to mind her own business...

You don't know, but you reread the message two, three times...

The fourth time is interrupted by a finger tapping you from behind.

"Excuse me, but I'm in a rush," she says. It's a girl with a shaved head, she's twenty years old with a giant backpack on her shoulders. She's practically you fifteen years ago, the first time you left. And she's in a rush? *She's* in a rush? You torch her with a glance, little slut in military pants and combat boots, you'd think she was going on a mushroom hunt. You move slightly and let her pass.

You make it through a thousand more checkpoints, make it to the glass corridor where the airplanes are, the air is more and more filled with disinfectant. More and more international.

You had asked for an aisle seat, instead you're by the window. Next to you is a priest. The twenty-year-old student is a few rows back. The sound of the engines gets louder and everything is ready for takeoff.

You take out the newspapers, pick *Corriere* but then opt for *The Tyrrhenian*. You see the place names and they already have an exotic flavor, distant and unreachable. And the lump in your throat is more and more insistent, it climbs from your throat to your temples and all the way to your eyes. Maybe it has something to do with anxiety before flying. Maybe.

Then your eye is caught by a short article in the corner that mentions Muglione.

Startling discovery last night at the house of an elderly woman, Noemi Irma Palazzesi, 87-year-old resident of Muglione. The ambulance service volunteers had been called for an emergency, but in the kitchen in addition to the elderly woman they found numerous dead cats, some long dead, others less so, and another one thawing out in the sink. The police found quite a few bones in the trash of Mrs. Palazzesi, while other poor kitties were stored away in the freezer for future consumption. The woman confessed to having gathered them with the excuse that she wanted company and then storing them, but she defended herself by claiming that cat is no different from rabbit, and with her 400-euro-a-month pension she could hardly afford...

You stop reading, fold the newspaper, and put it back in your bag as deep as you can. Poor kitties. Poor things. You were right not to trust that old witch; at least you were right that once. You can't always be wrong.

The engines are at maximum power, the runway outside starts to move, the plane start to move, accelerate, take off. You close your eyes as tight as you can, and like every time you leave, your mind seizes on the things you've left at home.

Books, notebooks, clothes, bracelets, your bed, the nightstand you've had since you were little, with the Smurf stickers attached. What will those things do now that you're not around anymore? Will they stay still and quiet and stupid waiting for you to return? And your toothbrush, you forgot your toothbrush! It was practically new and now it's there in the bathroom in a glass, as lonely as a dog on the highway. And what does it think, what does it feel, you almost want to have the airplane turned around and run on foot all the way to Muglione, go into the bathroom and take it and brush your teeth to make it understand that it still has a meaning, that you haven't forgotten it, that you will never forget it.

And while you're on the subject of Muglione, Fiorenzo is there waiting for you. Fishing, at the shop, or wherever he wants, he's there and if you return he'll take you back, he said so, actually he wrote it. And you don't know exactly what you want out of life, but this is certainly one of the things you would like.

A job that fulfills you, a city where you enjoy living, a boy with whom you're happy to spend the evening together ... that's a lot of cards for one round of bingo, but the more you have, the better your chances of winning something in the end.

But how can you keep all these cards together, how do you do it, Fiorenzo, how do you manage?

By now the plane is in the air, you look down and the land below is flat, the houses and streets look like toys lost in a random corner of the world.

Who knows if someone down there is watching you, someone who for some reason at this moment in his tiny life feels like looking up toward the sky. A passerby reading the name of a street, a woman looking for her cat in a tree, a boy with only one hand fishing by an irrigation ditch and checking the end of his rod.

He looks up in the sky and sees a little white speck that shines and advances straight and slow and soundless, smaller and smaller in the blue, smaller and smaller.

And then he can't see it anymore.

THIRTY YEARS OLD, AMAZING

Ten years have gone by. Ten, goddamnit, and it feels like one second.

I close my eyes for one second and *boom*, I'm thirty years old. Thirty, me, amazing.

Until I turned twenty the years seemed to last an eternity, I could have told you the best thing that happened to me in the summer when I was sixteen, or what my favorite group was in the fall when I was seventeen, then I finished high school and everything went by in a flash. When I turned twenty-seven, for a second I wondered whether I wasn't really twenty-eight. I might be, what difference did it make? I had to count the years. I swear.

But this time it was easier because I made it to thirty, a round number. I'm a thirty-year-old, I say it and I feel strange, but that's the way it is. I'm a thirty-year-old man.

Am I happy? I don't know. There are happy people and there are sad people, and then there are real people, who sometimes are happy and sometimes are sad. But now I'm happy, because tonight here in Muglione there's going to be a big party and we're all ready to welcome Mirko, who yesterday became world champion.

In Stuttgart, after a 270-kilometer race. Ten kilometers from the finish line a small pack had formed with the best inside, except that among these best racers was *the* best, him, and as soon as the road started to climb Mirko stood up on the pedals and started off in his way, with that burning escalation, without ever looking back (so as not to humiliate the others, he told me). With every spin of the pedals his advantage grew and the crowd went wild and I destroyed my sofa with my kicking. Now my foot is killing me, but it's all right. World champion.

They interviewed him right after the race, he was out of breath and the helmet on his head was crooked. He greeted his wife, who is Spanish, his son, Ignacio, and then me, too. And when they asked him how he managed to be so strong, Mirko answered, *I learned to win when they taught me to lose.* In a second this sentence echoed around the globe, but I think I'm the only one who understood it.

And who knows if Tiziana was watching it, the race. She was in Germany, after all, where she lives. We saw each other again two years ago, or was it three? Christmas. She had come back to see her folks and she had a German husband, blond but less tall than I would expect from a German, and a baby girl, all blonde, who in my opinion will become taller than her dad.

We greeted each other and kissed each other two times on the cheek, and for the whole time I kept my arm in my pocket. But only because sometimes little kids get scared when they see that I'm missing a hand. We said that before she went back to Germany we had to have a coffee together, maybe at Il Fagiano. We laughed and wished each other a Merry Christmas and didn't see each other again.

At the time I was going out with Marta, a girl from Parma who studied archaeology and worked at the University of Pisa. She had come to Muglione thanks to continued requests from the mayor, after the work on the sewage system in the new residential neighborhood, located next to the former industrial area now known as Muglione 2, had unearthed wooden structures that could have been Roman or Phoenician ships that sank who knows how in the hinterlands of Pisa.

In reality they were scraps from some construction site that had been illegally disposed of: it didn't take Marta and her colleagues long to figure it out. But it took even less time to figure out that between the two of us it couldn't last, and in fact two weeks later we broke up. I could say that seeing Tiziana again had shown me that she was still in my heart, that she had wrinkles and looked like my aunt but deep down her eyes still cast a spell over me. Except it wouldn't really be true. It's more true that Marta was married to a colleague, who was in Turkey and about to return, and our story ended at the same time as the Roman or Phoenician dream of Muglione.

But it's okay that way, it ended with Marta and the year after that it ended with another girl, who by the way was also named Marta and worked at the optician's store downtown. It's strange, but the first time a story ends you feel like the world is ending at the same time: nothing matters anymore, you could die in a fire and be sitting there surrounded by flames and think that it's right that way. Then a second story ends and you suffer the same way, but a few days less. Then a third, a fourth, and eventually you get used to it. I mean, it's not that you don't suffer anymore, but that you get used to suffering.

And maybe Mazinger was right the last time I saw him. I went to visit him, they had released him from the hospital so he could die in his own bed. He was wearing his pajamas, he looked at me and smiled, and I thought it was the first time I had seen him dressed like a person his own age. Maybe that's why he looked so old to me. He didn't speak because he didn't have much breath anymore, and just for the sake of talking I asked him whether it wasn't annoying to have to put that little device to his neck every time he wanted to speak. He picked it up, pressed it against his throat, and said, *IN—LIFE—YOU—GET—USED—TO— EVERYTHING—FIORENZO—TO—GOOD—AND—BAD— AND—IT—SUCKS—IN—BOTH—CASES.*

I understood, I didn't understand, who knows. But that stuff about getting used to everything is true.

I also got used to the idea that Metal Devastation wasn't going to devastate the world or even Italy or even this friggin' town. But we still play, fuck yeah, and we're still really fierce. Once a week we play and we kick ass. We even found a guitarist, Federico, who's Stefanino's partner. At first they kept their relationship secret because Stefano has now become the manager of the pope's image and spends a lot of time at the Vatican. But one day he got fed up and said, *When I come back here I want to come with my boyfriend, if you don't like it fire me, in no time I'll find another dictator in Asia who'll pay me twice what you do.* And so it came out in the town, too, but it didn't make a splash because everyone had understood, like, forever that Stefanino preferred men. Everyone had understood except Giuliano and me.

At first Giuliano made some jokes and some faces, but once he heard Federico play there wasn't another word out of him. At least until the day that Federico proposed adding a keyboard to lend atmosphere. Giuliano tore into him with a string of obscenities and that was the last we heard about keyboards.

And tonight, yes, Metal Devastation is playing at the party for Mirko, world champion. The mayor had said absolutely not, the commissioner for culture and tourism (or also the commissioner for sports) had said absolutely not. Then Mirko called to say if we weren't there he wouldn't be there either, and so we're playing.

And Mirko also said that he wants to stay for a few days. Maybe not right away, because he's got a ton of interviews and invitations to appear on TV, but he wants to do a week in Muglione soon. He lives in Seville now, but he bought a house here. I told him he's an idiot, what the fuck does he want a house in Muglione for? He explained to me that the real estate value is so low that a house in Muglione costs less than a trailer home. And he can at least come to see me.

Even if Dad says he's coming to see him. Dad, who trained him and led him to cycling success all the way to the Under-23 category, and who now is a kind of guru for junior cycling. The professional teams call him to learn the new names to follow and he even writes a column for *CycleSports* that's called "You guys understand nothing about cycling," in which every month he attacks someone.

He stopped drinking, or at least he's doing a good job of hiding the bottles when I go see him. Because I never did move back home. I stayed in the back room and slowly but surely fixed it up nicer and nicer, until I was levied a mega-fine and I made a real apartment right above the shop; that way in the morning I wake up and in two minutes I'm at work. And I often already find people outside waiting for me.

Because maybe I didn't make much headway with heavy metal, but I sure did with fishing. A new DVD is about to come out in my series dedicated to the least prestigious fishing holes in the world. I already did ones on the irrigation ditches of Muglione, the swamps of southern Tuscany, and the Arno floodway, and people buy them.

I wanted to call them *Rediscovering Your Waters*, but they chose *Fiorenzo Lends a Hand*, which as a title is in bad taste, I know, but what can I do? In them I explain how to make simple and effective setups, how to experience great emotion at the pond right behind your house, how to survive mice and tick bites, and other stuff like that.

Even right now I'm fishing, at the irrigation ditch, of all places, and I feel like I wouldn't want to be anywhere else.

Also because Silvia is arriving in a little while. It's not like we have a date, but in a certain sense we do. It's been almost a month since she came back to Muglione, and every day at the same time she comes here together with Diletta.

Diletta is four years old, speaks Milanese dialect, and calls me Fioretto, like her mother when we were kids. Until the summer of eighth grade, until the afternoon that we were here at the ditch and played one-two-three shoot to decide who got to toss the bomb and I won and right after that I lost my hand.

And I figure that life is this thing here, a river of stuff that hits you all at once, some you catch, some you miss, and some you don't even realize passed you by, and maybe that was the very thing that was right for you. But you can't know or waste too much time thinking about it, because you're still in the middle of the river and the stuff comes and passes and leaves.

Or maybe life isn't a river, maybe life is an irrigation ditch, which changes matters significantly. Because a river runs and in the end arrives at the sea, but a ditch goes nowhere. It goes straight without a goal and the most it can hope for is to run into other ditches and mix with them a little. And if there's a meaning to all of this water moving around, I don't know what it is. I know only that I'm more than happy to be here, especially if I can throw some bait in and fish.

And for a month now I've been feeling even better. When I catch a fish Diletta jumps and comes close, she pats it on the head, wipes her finger on her T-shirt, and says, *You're lucky, little fishy, but next time be more careful,* then she gestures to me and I let it return to the dark water, the fish gives a flap of the tail and immediately disappears underneath.

But yesterday the little girl wasn't here, Silvia came by herself, she stayed for at least an hour, and we talked about a lot of things. She has jet-black hair like she used to, but now it's smoother and all the way down to her shoulders. And she smokes. For the first time in a month she didn't stay standing the whole time; at a certain point she sat here close to me, very close, and spoke with her eyes half closed because of the sun.

She said that at the beginning she kept the windows at home open day and night to get rid of an awful smell of mildew, then she realized it wasn't the house's fault, it's actually Muglione itself that smells that way.

I took a deep breath and told her this was too ugly a place for such a pretty girl. It took her a little while to answer, and she told me, *Here the silence is too beautiful for such unadulterated bullshit.* We laughed, then we were quiet, and my arm holding the rod was ready to yank in case of a bite, but also ready to feel her hand resting on top of it. There are things that are just right, things that simply *have to* happen because they're so beautiful, even if then they don't happen. But no problem, because maybe they'll happen tomorrow, or the day after tomorrow, or whenever they feel like it.

In the meantime you smile and keep your eye on the floater that's motionless in the water, which is flat and firm, but I can feel that it won't stay this way for long. I reel in the line, check the bait, it's a big fat juicy worm that in my opinion is almost happy to be speared on a hook in the muck at the bottom of the ditch. So I throw it back in at precisely the spot that I want.

Because when you decide to fish, the bait is important. You can't be sitting there waiting with nothing on the hook, you have to stake something on it, otherwise there's no sense playing.

And it's not true that nothing ever happens anyway.

I look at this place: it's a hole, I agree, yet here is where one day a beautiful woman arrived from Germany who at first wanted to bawl me out over a bad explanation of a poem by D'Annunzio, and instead in the end we had sex.

Here is where Mirko Colonna flourished, the new world champion and the three-time Giro d'Italia winner and two-time Tour de France winner.

Here is where a fierce band plays that only ridiculous fate and a musically illiterate nation have kept on ice.

Yet here is where a species of incredible aquatic monster lives, a quiet black beast that can stay hidden for years and years but once, every now and then, when it feels like it, suddenly rises from the bottom and passes right in front of your eyes.

And at that moment you have to be ready by the ditch with the right bait, so that he'll bite it and mess you up and leave you on the bank gasping for air. And he teaches you that you might know all the theories and techniques in the world, but every now and then in life something enormous arrives that comes right at you and all the things that you know make no sense anymore, all you can do is sit there with your ass on the ground watching the water go crazy and the frogs escaping and the chaos and the splashing and the waves.

Then the water slowly calms down, the frogs resume their singing, and all of us here come floating back to the surface.

Acknowledgments

Well then.

I care more than a lot about thanking Giulia Ichino, who came all by herself to fish me out of a muddy irrigation ditch without fear of getting her shoes dirty. In a better world we would have grown up together.

Antonio Franchini, his eyes see far, his mind thinks deep, his fists hit hard.

Marilena Rossi, the most precious qualities of a hundred fantastic people rolled into one, I didn't think it was possible, I was wrong.

Thanks to Francesca, I don't know who gave you to me but I am grateful to him or her.

To my parents, who let me stay home from school when the sun was shining.

To Michele and Matteo, for now the pine cones are still on the branches.

To all the fish that bit, I hope I didn't hurt you too much.

Thanks to the many, many others who helped me through this stage of the Dolomites. Some are no longer with us, but their presence is strong. Corky and Karen, Andreino, Emanuele and Barbara, Andrea and Francesco, Stefano, Michele, Stefano, Debora, Andrea and the refined friends, Violetta, Edoardo, and Daniela, Edoardo, Gian Paolo, Carlo, Fabio, Clara, Giulio at Transeuropa, Giulia, Alessandra and Nicolò, Cinzia and Franco, Jacopo and Sabrina, Alex and Milena, Filippo and Ester, Alberto and Nada, Ettore and Lea, Giuseppina and Arolando, Mariuccia and Dino, my cousin Luca, Mariella, Alberto, Emanuela and Leonard, Giada, Matilde, Serena, Cisco, Cosimo and Sofia, Pier-Paolo, Claudio, Filippo, Giacomo, Luigi and Daniela, Irene, Duccio, Dania, Claudia and Sabrina, Alessandra and Federico, Gianluca and Matteo, Chiara, Alessia and Marco, Alessandro, Paolo, Annalisa and Massimiliano, my fishermen friends on the bridge (including the guys with the scales), Ugo and the patrons of the bait-and-tackle shop, Mario and Laura, Ruggero and Camilla, Katia and Manuela, David, Elisabetta and Matteo the Count, Marco Pantani, and Fiorenzo Magni (from whom Fiorenzo got his name).

And thanks to all of you for casting your eyes over these pages. You don't live forever, now we are done, so everyone please go outside to see what's happening.